I0761216

WEAVINGSHAW

WEAVINGSHAW

HEBA AL-WASITY

NEW YORK

Del Rey
An imprint of Random House
A division of Penguin Random House LLC
1745 Broadway, New York, NY 10019
randomhousebooks.com
penguinrandomhouse.com

Hardcover ISBN 978-0-593-98257-0
Ebook ISBN 978-0-593-98258-7

Printed in the United States of America on acid-free paper

1st Printing

First Edition

BOOK TEAM: Production editor: Loren Noveck • Managing editor: Paul Gilbert • Production manager: Erin Korenko • Proofreaders: Alice Dalrymple, Megha Jain, and Bridget Sweet

Book design by Caroline Cunningham

Title and part title background image: stuart/Adobe Stock

The authorized representative in the EU for product safety and compliance is Penguin Random House Ireland, Morrison Chambers, 32 Nassau Street, Dublin D02 YH68, Ireland. https://eu-contact.penguin.ie

To Mays Al-Wasity Abbas

Before anyone, you were

The first reader.
The first editor.

And the first to be haunted by Weavingshaw.

PART ONE

THE RECKONING

1

The Saint of Silence

"Tell me how to seek the Saint."

The old woman stared at the girl for a long moment, eyes narrowed, shriveled lips pursed. Without lowering her gaze, she inhaled a slow drag from her pipe. "Got a confession, Leena?"

Leena shrank back, although the emaciated form of the old woman posed no threat to her.

"Margery . . ." Leena began, then paused, her conviction dimming. "I only mean to seek him out."

Faster than she thought the old woman could move, Margery dug her yellowed nails into the soft flesh of Leena's forearm. "No one—and I mean *no one*—goes to see the Saint without a reason," Margery snarled. "Are you looking for a bit of coin, girlie? Some pretty baubles?" Her grip bruised. "Do *not* seek him."

Leena didn't respond as, not for the first time, something else had caught her attention. Her gaze flickered to a point past Margery's shoulder, and she stared at it for a second too long. When Margery turned to look, there was nothing there but peeling papered walls.

"What are you staring at, girlie?" Margery demanded.

Leena startled before shaking her head.

Leena's eyes roved the interior of Margery's home, directly abutting her own. Each house was an exact replica of the other—squat and terraced with sparse windows and a barely functioning fireplace, their only source of water an outside pump.

The old woman had lived here for as long as Leena could remember, the only resident in these clustered spaces of cramped houses who was not an Algaraan refugee. Unlike Leena, whose own parents had fled the Algaraan civil war more than twenty years ago before settling uneasily into Morland, Margery was salt-of-the-earth and Morish through and through.

Leena did not think the old woman had ventured once out of Golborne, Morland's capital city, or even farther than the limit of her own house these days, her fluid-swollen legs barely carrying her past her front step.

Despite Margery's lack of mobility, Leena never dared question how she seemed to procure a steady stream of Tar.

Whenever Leena knocked on the old woman's door, it was always the same picture: Margery hunched over a hookah, her eyes red from the cloying Tar smoke, her blue-veined hands shaking for the next addictive puff.

"Rami is unwell. He is going to . . ." Leena trailed off. "I *need* to see the Saint."

"Your brother?"

It took all of Leena's strength to force her voice to remain steady, even as terror slithered down her body at the mere utterance of the illness. "He has Sweeper's Cough."

Margery withdrew, leaving half-moon welts on Leena's skin. "I had it once and barely survived it."

Leena knew this, or else she would never have dared enter Margery's house and invite the sickness into her home. Sweeper's Cough could only be had once and never again—as long as one survived it. Baba had once said Leena had caught it as a young girl in the refugee camps, and she had been so unwell that the camp overseer had told her mother to start sewing a white burial shroud.

"So, you see, my worry is justified." Leena pulled at a stray thread unraveling from the hemline of her skirt. "I must go see the Saint of Silence."

"No—even *that* is not enough." Margery swallowed harshly. "What secrets can a green girl like you have? The Saint of Silence does not accept schoolroom scandals."

Once again, Leena's eyes flickered to the nothingness behind Margery's shoulder.

"Have you not heard the stories that swirl around the Saint?" Margery demanded again, and Leena stiffened.

Of course she had heard the rumors; everyone had. He was the first of his kind to pay for secrets; the more shameful the divulgence, the higher the price. But even the most trivial of confessions, seemingly useless to anyone, received some coin. So at first, the rest of the cityfolk—Leena included—thought it was an act of charity: another so-called philanthropist who had made his wealth in the factories, or abroad in the wars, and decided to *give back.* A do-gooder who had arrived suddenly in this soot-ridden city eight years ago and would disappear just as abruptly.

Although his name was St. Silas, he was often referred to as the *Saint of Silence* instead—a play on his surname, after the country's oldest Saint, whose crumbled statues still littered the outside of cathedrals and cemeteries. A Saint who had once granted blessings in exchange for sins back when Golborne was a mere settlement, not a thriving metropolis built of smoke and greed.

No one prayed to any of the Saints anymore.

People wanted bread, not sacraments.

But if this new Saint of Silence, like his former namesake, was willing to offer coins for a few measly secrets—*the fool*—why stop him?

It soon became apparent that it was not charity.

And that he was no fool.

Rumors began to spring up. Those who confessed to him came back *changed,* as if despair and terror had carved a home between their eyes. Others—those St. Silas claimed had lied in their confessions—had their tongues cut out. Ribs cracked. A bloodied X sliced through their mouth, the vermilion border of the lips gouged and carved: the scar of the Saint.

Some never came back at all.

Leena knew all this, but her heart was already so engulfed with death and loss she could not bear burying a brother. She knew this—and she chose to seek the Saint of Silence anyway.

Margery saw the change in her face: the subtle lift of her chin, the determination that drew her dark brows in. The old woman lowered her voice. "Do you remember what he did to Mr. Jamil?"

Leena's thoughts recoiled at the memory of the man who had once lived a couple of doors down from them. He had also been a refugee, escaping Algaraa at the same time as Leena's parents did.

She remembered Baba's distrust of Mr. Jamil; it was widely known in their small district that Mr. Jamil had been an informant for the Malik's police back home. Gossip swirled that he'd been the one to turn in his own nephew for hiding illegal pamphlets belonging to the Liberation Party.

The nephew had been taken, then found a few weeks later, tortured into madness.

Leena had heard that the Malik had sent Mr. Jamil a slaughtered sheep for his acts of loyalty—a rarity as hunger swept through the country.

When the war broke out in Algaraa and the Liberation Party rose, Mr. Jamil had fled to Morland in fear of being captured and punished by the rebels for his terrible acts of service to the Malik.

Baba, ever the revolutionist, had warned Leena and Rami to stay away from Mr. Jamil, stating that those who turned on their countrymen on their own soil would not think twice of doing so in a foreign land.

Baba was not wrong.

Leena never forgot the way Mr. Jamil had looked after visiting the Saint of Silence nearly four years ago. They had found him in the morning, a crumpled mess on the stoop. The intersecting X on his mouth shone with blood, his broken body racked with shudders. *I didn't lie,* he sobbed as Baba and a few other men carried him into his house. *I swear I didn't lie to the Saint.*

He took to the bottle not long afterward. Hard drink. In one of his drunken stupors, he admitted to Baba that he'd thought no harm would come from telling the Saint of Silence small falsehoods about the neighbors to fill his gnawing hunger.

By that point, the alcohol had made Mr. Jamil's belly protrude and the whites of his eyes turn a deep yellow.

He was dead by the spring.

"I do," Leena said steadily, but her head throbbed. "Have you ever sought the Saint of Silence?"

Margery toyed with the pipe between her fingers. Finally, she nodded. "It wasn't an act of release for me, though; it was reckoning. It felt like death . . ." She trailed off, a vague look in her rheumy eyes. "The nightmares that came afterward—*he never even touched me*—but the very act of confession . . . like being gutted . . . left to rot . . ."

The old woman took a long, desperate drag on the pipe, her eyelids fluttering from the effect of the drug. "Some say his mother's a demon."

"*Demon?*" Leena lifted her brows. Spirituality had faded in Morland with the first cropping of factories, leaving sparsely filled church pews in its staid and ghostly cathedrals, but some still clung firmly to their belief in Saints, demons, and curses.

Algaraans feared evil under a different name. Leena had grown up with stories of jinns, and even now her bedroom was filled with old charms shaped like eyes to ward them away.

There was not a lot of time in Leena's life to debate the existence of jinns, demons, or even Saints, but all she knew was that none of them had helped her survive.

A faint humorous glint crossed Leena's eyes. "Is he a Saint or a demon? He cannot be both."

Margery's lips thinned. "Do not make a mockery of things you do not understand." With shaky hands, she pulled an idol necklace from her bodice, her lips muttering a whispered prayer to cast off wickedness. Leena peeked at the small wooden figurine of a woman holding an olive branch. She could not remember which Saint the imagery corresponded with, but the way Margery gripped the effigy made it clear that it brought her some measure of comfort.

Leena never assumed Margery was religious; fewer people nowadays believed in the old relics. Still, she bowed her head, apologizing for causing the old woman offense.

"Do. Not. Seek. Him," Margery rasped again, interrupting her apologies.

"I don't have a choice—"

"You always have a choice. Do not choose wrong."

This time it was Leena who grabbed the old woman's arm, the papery skin fragile in her grip. "I *will* find him, with or without your help. So spare me and give me some guidance. I cannot waste any more time."

Margery regarded Leena for a long moment: the brown Algaraan features, the firm eyebrows, the gaunt cheeks, the dark eyes that could not conceal a single emotion.

"Your face reveals too much," Margery whispered, almost to herself. "A lie would look foreign on you. Do not attempt it."

"I won't."

The old woman brought a trembling hand to her forehead. "He's in the Northern Quarters . . ." Her thin chest rattled with emotion as she detailed the exact directions. She huffed another puff of smoke, a tinge of pink appearing on her wrinkled cheeks, before she continued in a hazy voice. "*What isn't learned in the cradle . . .*"

"*. . . will be learned too late.* Thank you." Leena rose to leave, but the old woman's voice stopped her.

"Do not lie to him, Leena," Margery warned again.

Once more, Leena's gaze focused on the corner of the room.

Once more, Margery turned to look. *Nothing.*

"Mrs. Khalid next door tells me that you're mad, girlie," Margery said, peering closely at her. "You have already lost one promising employment due to your . . . *eccentricities.* How much further will you allow yourself to fall?"

Leena had been a lady's companion, back when her future still had promise. She had fled that life when her circumstances changed and she realized she could not swallow her new oddities. If the aristos had noticed her strange behavior, they might lock her in the asylum. Now, rather than an esteemed lady's companion, she was the gossip of old crones, the shame of their street, a warning to all immigrant parents about the dangers of overeducating a girl.

Leena's eyes blazed. "Until there is no distance left to fall."

Leena knew the city like the back of her hand, even in twilight.

After Baba was taken, she'd roamed these streets either looking for a job or searching for Rami. She'd often found her brother in the shadowy corners frequented by the Black Coats. She passed three of them now on the steps of a well-known brothel, slinking around a tired-eyed woman with painted lips, each smoking cigarettes imported from Algaraa.

The Black Coats stopped their chattering once they saw her, watching Leena as she attempted to move past them as quickly as possible. Rami had once told her that each Black Coat hid a knife in their sleeves, and she kept her head low to avoid attention.

One recognized her anyway, likely from all the times she'd dragged Rami back home, usually by the collar, while they both hollered at each other.

"Your brother all right?" the Black Coat farthest to the left shouted, a tall, freckled boy with a cap pulled low over his ears. "Not seen him in a while."

Leena didn't answer, quickening her stride although it caused a stitch in her side.

The boy continued, his voice now taking a jeering edge. "He's missed one fight. Mr. Orley won't be pleased if he misses another." She felt his gaze burn into her. "Perhaps the boss will take you as payment instead. Lucky man."

Leena swallowed, breaking out in a near-run, leaving the Black Coats' mocking laughter behind. She didn't stop until she'd reached the small abandoned church that straddled the edge of New Algaraa District. She heaved in lungfuls of air beneath the shattered remains of a stained-glass window, surrounded by the statues of the five Saints, their stone bodies defaced with paint-splattered words: *The Saints don't see us.*

The Black Coats' threat sat heavily on her. She had begged Rami not to fight for the gang, knowing that whatever coins he earned in the process would never guarantee their safety, but as always her brother never listened.

Although her joints ached, she forced herself to keep walking, now more desperate to trade for his medication than ever.

As she continued to weave her way through the claustrophobic district, with its tilting tiled roofs and cobbled streets, she had to stop twice more to rest, frustrated with her own body's needs. She was glad for the darkness of the night, which hid the ugliness that was Newtorn Prison—the ominous building that stood staring at her no matter the direction she went. She did not have money to hail a hackney, and not for the first time Leena silently loathed that her townhouse was situated where it was. Nearest to the docks and the Old Market, New Algaraa District was not only a constant cacophony of noises and drunken singing, it was also farthest away from the middle-class wealth of the Northern Quarters where Mr. St. Silas's shop was located.

It took her hours to reach her destination.

Within the Northern Quarters, the townhouses were far more respectable, surrounded by black-painted gates and thick rose bushes. Raised three stories high, each house held a vestige of glamour. Leena knew that although the aristos did not reside here, instead situating themselves within the far more exclusive Maybury District, a lot of the middle-class tradesmen built their homes here to mimic the architecture of the nobility. To Leena, it felt disorienting to see such old styles replicated in such modern ways.

The district might have been charming in the daytime, but at night the lamplight threw tall shadows on the clean streets, distorting shapes and creating faces where there weren't any. More than once, Leena halted suddenly, a cold sweat beading her brow, only to find herself staring at a tree or a postbox.

Her heart was galloping in her chest by the time she reached the Saint's shop.

It was a surprisingly discreet building—too immaculate for such a sordid business. On either side, the houses were vacant, a "to let" sign creaking and swaying in the wind. The shop was bereft of any vulgar advertising, the steps swept clean, the door freshly painted. A single neat sign had been hung, which read: *Mr. St. Silas, an inquisitor.*

Leena swallowed, her throat dry.

An inquisitor.

He can taste lies.

She pounded at the door.

No answer.

She tried until her knuckles throbbed. Then she rattled the lock.

The shop was closed.

Of course it would be at this time of night. How could she have been so foolish? She had come too late. Fear had stalled her. Now fear would sign her brother's death certificate.

No. Her eyes jolted to the empty street. Then she cried out, "You have taken everything from me. Give me something back. Lead me to the Saint of Silence."

Nothing stirred.

"Please," Leena whispered. Then she tilted her head as if she'd seen a flutter of movement, although anyone peeking through the window at that moment would have seen only a girl standing by herself.

She began walking again, now to the back of the shop. There was a house attached to the rear, complete with a stableyard and a small stone courtyard enclosed with elegantly trimmed trees. Leena knocked once more at the back door, flinching from the ache in her knuckles.

After another minute of tense waiting, the door *did* swing open.

A woman stood at the threshold, wearing a spotlessly ironed apron over a plain black dress. The candle in her hand flickered, bathing her harshly angled face in light. Leena stepped back—*those eyes.* For a moment she swore that the woman's black irises swallowed the whites entirely.

Leena quelled her panicking thoughts, telling herself that she was not mad. The woman's eyes were now perfectly normal, merely a trick of the shadows.

"I've come to see the Saint," Leena said, more confident than she felt.

The woman's voice carried no emotion. "What business do you have with him?"

"A secret to share," she responded, even louder this time.

"The master is unavailable." The woman moved to shut the door. "Come back during business hours."

Leena jammed her shoulder into the narrow opening. "He will not forgive you if you let me leave."

Leena knew it was an odd statement—especially coming from a slip of a girl like her. Her shawl was too ragged for the cool autumn, and there was a burn hole in her cambric skirt from where she'd stood close to the fire that morning. Still, the woman seemed to consider her—Leena's face openly full of hungry hope—and, after a moment of deliberation, bade her to follow.

Leena tried to quiet her rasping breaths as she trailed the woman down a long hallway, the wooden floors gleaming, all the sconces lit as if a party was expected. St. Silas must have money to burn.

The woman stopped in front of a closed door. "Your name, madam?"

"Leena Al-Sayer."

The woman slipped inside to announce her. Leena only heard muffled words, followed by a harsh reprimand. Without having to be told, Leena knew that she would be thrown back out onto the street.

Desperation built in her throat. Without stopping to think, she burst through the door, pushed past the woman, and tumbled onto the floor. A hand jerked her backward and Leena twisted her torso to see the servant woman grasping her shoulders. They both struggled; Leena was not above throwing her entire weight to knock this foreboding lady down and free herself.

Words streamed from her mouth. "You will regret not receiving me, sir. My secret is . . . is—*unhand me!*—one you will never hear again—"

A curt word interrupted her ramblings and the woman's hands released her.

Leena darted toward the back of the room, behind an armchair, clinging to one of the many shelves that lined the walls, but there was no need. The woman had already left.

She was alone with the Saint of Silence.

Black waves receded from her vision, and it took her a moment to compose herself. Her teeth chattered. *Why was it so cold in this room?* The fireplace roared, but it did nothing to dispel the chill.

Steeling herself, Leena finally turned to face him—Mr. St. Silas.

She was surprised to see that he was young, perhaps only three or four years older than herself. From the gossip swirling about him for the last eight years, she had expected a sharp-toothed beast. A monster in an impeccable suit. Distantly, she was aware that he was handsome—another surprise. But it was not the sort of handsomeness that was comforting. Everything about him evoked a brutal sense of disquiet; he was intimidation at a single glance. Even his heavy-lidded eyes, at once both aloof and callous, concealed a sharp alertness.

He sat idly behind an oak desk, an impressive figure with dark hair and a grim mouth, a ledger in his gloved hand. The only sign of disorder about him was the loosened cravat at his throat; otherwise he was immaculately dressed.

"What matter disturbs me in the dead of the night?" His tone was light, almost conversational—and it had the desired effect of chilling Leena to her bones.

He hadn't stood when she'd entered the room, as per the custom among the Mors, nor did he offer her a seat. Instead, he stared at her in contemplation, his thumb tapping a beat on a timepiece attached to his chest. The silence stretched; he didn't seem to mind.

"I have a secret," Leena repeated, unable to bear the silence any longer.

"We all do."

Frustrated, she said, "I have a secret for purchase."

"Ah," he said, raising his brows slightly.

Horror dawned on her when he didn't continue.

"You are Mr. St. Silas who trades in secrets?" she asked.

"I am *that* St. Silas, but I am at a loss as to why you would think your secret would hold any interest for me—especially at this hour," he said, his voice smooth, his accent cultured. She wondered if he had hired elocution tutors, for how else could a mere merchant of secrets speak in such well-educated tones? All the tradesmen she'd come into contact with spoke in her accent, often growing up in similar streets to hers before they'd crawled their way into new wealth.

"I could not wait until morning. My brother is unwell. He has Sweeper's Cough, and I have heard of your ability to grant impossible wishes for the price of secrets. I cannot afford the medication—"

"There *are* cheaper alternatives."

"I have tried those, but he is still dying," Leena replied flatly, her gaze not wavering from his. "My father banned me from seeing you a few years ago—"

"Good man."

"—but I would never have sold my secret for anything less," she asserted with more firmness than she felt. "My secret holds power."

Once more, dots swirled in her vision and she shut her eyes to ward away the sudden lightheadedness. When she opened them again, she saw that St. Silas had paused his rhythmic tapping to watch her intently.

"One life is a hefty price," he said after a lengthy pause. Then he withdrew a blank parchment and began to write. He slid it toward her once he was done, and Leena, despite the awful dizziness, walked steadily to face it.

Mr. Bram St. Silas will provide one course of medication to Miss Leena Al-Sayer upon acquisition of her secret, if Mr. St. Silas deems it worthy, pending investigation of the secret's accuracy. Miss Al-Sayer confesses of her own volition, bearing in mind any emotional distress that may arise from making such a confession. Any falsehoods told in her confession shall result in punishment.

Leena thought of tongues ripped out of mouths, of a permanent scar carved into her lips declaring to the world that she was a liar. Of the still-frosted ground as they'd lowered Mr. Jamil into it.

No. She would not allow fear to distract her.

"Kindly be more specific," she said. "Mr. St. Silas will provide Miss Al-Sayer with one course of *Trimexicillin.*"

He gave her a single measuring glance before moving to change it.

"Trimexicillin *is* costly," he said, then turned the page toward her. The woman—the very same who had tried to drag Leena from the room—was called in to witness the signing. She was introduced as the housekeeper, and once more Leena had the uncomfortable feeling that there was something very *wrong* about her.

All three of them wrote their names on the dotted lines, and the housekeeper departed once that task was done, her steps drifting farther down the maze of halls.

Leena stared down at her own name on the contract, an intense foreboding building in her bones. St. Silas waited, his silence like a heavy burden.

The time had come—a revelation, a *reckoning.*

The secret burned Leena's throat. She'd held it so tightly within her chest for so long, every day the shame of it expanding and widening, until it felt like she was turning herself inside out to reveal it.

What would the Saint of Silence do with her confession?

Would he believe her? This secret was all Leena had in this world, her one currency. Once gone, her hands would be empty.

If she kept her voice even, perhaps the Saint wouldn't notice her distress. But he watched. He watched her so steadily.

"Mr. St. Silas, I am . . . I can . . ." She registered once more the dots floating in and out of her vision. She cleared her throat, her mind racing frantically.

Perhaps he would think that she was mad. Everyone else did. She looked at him in mute agony. His returning gaze was a cold indifference to her turmoil.

There was nothing for it now but to open the chamber, to reveal the unthinkable. She squared her shoulders and met his gaze with defiance. "Some who die—usually the restless ones, or the angry ones—linger in our world as ghosts: unseen beings that walk the earth after death. I can see them."

2

Newtorn Prison

LEENA WAITED FOR a reaction, an exclamation, a shudder of revulsion, but was only met with stark silence. Her nerves on fire, she rushed to fill the vacancy.

"I wasn't born like this. I began seeing the dead three years ago, days after I turned seventeen. I wish I knew why they suddenly became visible to me, but they did, and I cannot stop them, nor can I control them."

He continued to watch her from behind his heavy-lidded eyes. "Ah."

It was the lack of response that fanned her already strained temper. "Bless you, sir. Was that not a sneeze?"

"Hardly a sneeze, madam, but a proclamation of doubt."

"Doubt . . ." she responded slowly. She had expected this, but she could not stop the sudden fear that roared through her chest.

"The dead do not go on living after death."

"Then you have a very limited viewpoint, indeed."

His eyes widened and he let out a surprised half-laugh.

She had meant it not as a jest but as an entreaty for him to broaden his mind, but her tongue had slipped before she could curtail it.

He continued after a moment, the laughter dropping from his mouth. "You must understand, Miss Al-Sayer, that in my line of work I am often met with lies. A lie for a noble reason is still a lie—and it is not in my nature to look kindly upon liars."

Her heart sank. "I can assure you that I am not lying."

"But how can this be proved?" he asked, with a flash of teeth. "I am all eagerness to help your situation—and I wish a rapid recovery to your loved one—" He said this as an afterthought, before his voice dropped dangerously. "But I will not be made a fool."

"What must I do?"

He leaned forward. An odd hunger transformed his features, chasing away any vestiges of false sympathy. "Can you see any apparitions now?"

Leena scanned every crevice of the small room, across the multiple ledgers stacked in high shelves, toward the hearth that housed a healthy fire—*Why was it still so cold in this room?*—even behind the armchair.

Only the living remained. The ghost that had led her here—a boy dressed in white, his temple shattered by a rock—had been flickering in and out on the steps of St. Silas's shop when she'd begged him to take her to the Saint. But he'd disappeared the moment she'd crossed the Saint's threshold. She sensed that the dead were not pleased with the Saint of Silence. Could she lie? But Margery's warning came back to her and she banished the temptation.

Finally, she whispered, "No."

"How convenient. Your secret happens to be one that cannot be proven." There was now a trace of anger hidden behind his easy tone.

She brought a hand to her forehead, and St. Silas followed the motion. His eyebrows lifted as if he noticed something in that movement, and a strange chilling expression momentarily crossed his features.

She should run now—before he held her down, before his knife slid through her skin, splitting the tissue and tearing the vessels, marking her forever.

Still, Leena did not leave.

"I don't know why you collect secrets, Mr. St. Silas, or what you seek. But would you let this one go if it had only the smallest chance of proving true?"

A pause. He met her eyes. She didn't lower her own.

"You *are* clever." He weighed his next words carefully. "I'll give you an opportunity to prove the validity of your statement. Do you agree with this?"

"I'll agree to anything."

"Follow me." He stood up, leaving the room in long strides while commanding that his carriage be readied immediately.

She was led from the study, down the same bright hall, and back to the stone courtyard outside. There, a well-sprung vehicle, expertly crafted but inconspicuous, was waiting for them, two large grays already in the harness. St. Silas issued an order to the driver, too low for her ears to pick up, before he climbed into the seat across from her. Leena tucked herself as far into the corner as possible to avoid accidentally brushing against him, but this was difficult. His lithe form spread across the aisle with ease, his long legs taking up half the room.

Their moods were in direct contrast. If Leena's muscles were tightly wound, St. Silas was at his leisure. She wondered if he enjoyed eliciting such strong reactions in others, if he enjoyed grasping such power.

She heard the rattle of reins and the carriage picked up speed, navigating the bend toward the main thoroughfare.

"Tell me about who you're saving," St. Silas murmured.

The carriage lamp lit Leena's face but kept St. Silas's in shadow. Perhaps that was why he had chosen his seat, so that he might have a chance to study her while remaining in darkness. She could only hear his voice, so simultaneously smooth and sharp she wouldn't have known she'd been cut until the blood stained her dress.

"My brother, Rami. I'm older than him by two years," Leena replied slowly. She didn't want to continue. Having always been furtive with love, she feared revealing herself too much now.

"Rami Al-Sayer?" St. Silas leaned forward. "The Black Coats' sword fighter?"

"Rami's not a Black Coat," Leena replied curtly. She didn't like people thinking her brother was part of a gang. "He merely competes in their duels."

St. Silas raised his eyebrows. "I've seen him fight. He's talented. How did he lose the arm?"

Leena also hated that question, which reduced Rami to a single painful experience, a moment of tragedy that had birthed him. "A riding accident when he was fourteen. But he fights better now than he ever did back then."

Perhaps sensing her offense, he didn't press further. Instead he settled back, head leaning on the rest. A passing streetlight reflected a sudden harsh glare on his face, and she saw that his eyes were coldly observant, almost catlike, before he was plunged once more into the shadows. In contrast, his words were honeyed. "You're trying to save him—even going so far as to seek me. I am used to requests for cruelty, but your reason has honor." She squinted at him in the darkness but still she could not see his face. "At the very least, I admire that. Very few come to me with kindness."

A man like St. Silas didn't admire kindness; he manipulated kindness.

"Thank you, sir," she said, almost primly, "but I'm not susceptible to flattery."

He laughed, his teeth flashing white. "A dissimilarity we share. I am *only* susceptible to flattery."

Although it was only the beginning of the colder season, a thick mist clung to the cobbled streets, hiding the downtrodden, the shabbiness of the shops, the crumbling buildings, as if attempting to cover the city's shame.

They passed an eerie cathedral. A single burning candle shone through the stained glass, illuminating the stony faces of the five main Saints and a few of the lesser ones carved into the exterior. From the eaves, gargoyles and banished demons snarled down upon the street. Even though Leena was not Morish and rarely set foot in a church, she still recognized a few.

The Saint of Healing, depicted as a statuesque woman holding a blackened heart. The Saint of Fools, a lesser Saint that Leena always remembered since the grotesque grin stretched wide on his lips used to frighten her as a child. The largest idol, chiseled in the center of the cathedral, was the Saint of Silence. Leena's eyes lingered on the sculpture—at the face that was neither old nor young, the mouth covered with a thin gauze, symbolism for his devotion to silence. If that face was kind, then his namesake—the man sitting in front of her—was colder than stone.

The turn of the carriage led them farther into the interweaving alleyways of Golborne, the steady *clop-clop* of the horses' hooves breaking the odd stillness of the night. The Northern Quarters gradually gave way to cramped, thin houses in which curtains were permanently drawn for a semblance of privacy. But Leena knew from her own experience that privacy was a luxury not meant for these parts of the city. Not when paper-thin walls revealed every whispered fight, not when cheaply made floors echoed every footstep, every raucous laugh, every slamming door. Only heartbreak went unnoticed in this city—except by those who profited from it. She glanced sideways once more at the Saint of Silence, merchant of misery, but his own attention was fastened outside the window.

"We've arrived," he said easily.

Leena looked out the window as well, and her breath hitched.

Ahead of them loomed Newtorn Prison.

It was a hideous building, disfigured, its many towers like crooked fingers. So often she'd found herself outside the iron gates begging the guards to deliver a package to her father. So often she'd been turned away. The prison lay in the center of the city. Every road, every byway, every path led toward it. It was the heart around which Golborne was built, from which it nourished itself, from which it profited. It was the largest prison in the living world, even housing political criminals from other countries for a fee—a behemoth that seemed to eat the youth of this city whole. Half of the boys Leena had grown up with—*the motherless boys, the refugees, the eternally hungry*—now lay on the other side of that divide. As well as Leena's own father.

"They're adding another tower," St. Silas observed mildly, indicating the stacks of bricks and scaffolding left abandoned until the morning.

"Did you know that Newtorn Prison has never finished being built?" Leena whispered. Her heart quaked in her chest, the sight of the towers sending shock waves through her body. "It's larger than even King Edmund's palace. They keep adding more cells, more blocks, more padlocked gates."

He raised his brows, the deeper ache beneath her words seemingly not lost on him.

The carriage slowed by the broad iron barrier, a dappled moon lighting the walkway. The driver descended first and, after a brief exchange with the guard, the gate swung open and the carriage rattled on. She observed in stony silence the utter lack of green in the courtyard. Everything was gray: gray bricks, gray towers, gray pillars. She wondered if Baba missed the plants he had left thriving on the windowsill in their home.

By the time they arrived, a man stood waiting for them near the great steel entrance. Lanky, with hollowed cheeks and an ashen complexion, he rubbed his hands with nervous energy as they approached. He came to the window at once, holding up a lamp to peer in.

"Mr. St. Silas, what an honor," the man wheezed, eyes jolting from St. Silas to Leena. "If I had known earlier you'd be visiting, I would've made preparations . . ."

St. Silas held up a lazy hand to interrupt the man's hurried speech. "No need, Warden. I've come to call on Colson."

The Warden's mouth fell open. "Wha— Why?"

St. Silas lifted his brows. "Because I choose to."

The lamp in the Warden's hand jerked, and he hastily interjected, "It is merely protocol, sir. A-and who is your companion?"

"Someone you will endeavor to forget."

Leena stared at St. Silas, at this man who had the very Warden of Newtorn Prison in the palm of his hand. Who relished the hold he had over others. That was why only the desperate sought the Saint of Silence. Her stomach tightened; she had delivered her own weakness to him. If she survived the night, how would he use her secrets against her?

The Warden bowed, deep and low, before bidding them to follow.

Leena's chill had worsened, and her teeth chattered as she and St. Silas followed the Warden past the guarded gate and down a long corridor. She'd never been this far in, although she had dreamed many times of running down the length of the prison, finding the exact cell that housed her father, throwing off his manacles, and freeing him. Now, as she was led farther inside, the sheer volume of this place stunned her, lines and lines of prison cells stacked on top of one another like cages. She caught flickers of movement from within, feet pacing stone floors—disturbed, frenzied pacing—like animals circling bars.

She staggered, then gagged. The reek of the prison had reached her all at once—an overwhelming mixture of excrement and soiled, decaying flesh. Breathing through her mouth, Leena straightened, not wanting to appear afraid.

She searched hungrily for the faces behind the bars, but she doubted she could recognize even her beloved baba in this darkness. How could he survive this place? The image of her father here in threadbare clothes, eyes staring unseeing at the wall, unnerved her so much that she struggled to keep walking.

Ahead of her, the Warden spoke as if he was giving them a tour, his eyes continuously jerking toward and away from St. Silas uneasily. He gestured at one of the cells, inside which Leena could see only a shadowy silhouette. "A *special* visitor, sent from the Algaraan Malik himself," the Warden continued, despite St. Silas's lack of response. "One of Commander Yosif's best captains, captured moments before a planned invasion of Algaraa's capital."

Leena's head whipped up. "Which captain?"

Everyone knew of Commander Yosif, the charismatic leader of the anti-Malik movement—a university student who had led the first marches nearly twenty years ago, and had paid for it when the Malik's soldiers responded with violence. He was one of the few who had survived the ensuing onslaught. His comrades had been butchered on the streets, the gutters clogged with their blood.

Leena's own uncle, Baba's younger brother, had been studying to be a lawyer when he'd joined that first march; Baba had once told her in a choked voice that there had not been enough of him left to bury. All the corpses were set on fire by the soldiers. Unmarked. Desecrated. Ashes.

The Warden threw her a disdainful glance. "It is confidential."

She had grown obsessive about the Algaraan war ever since Baba had been taken. It tied her to him and to a homeland she had never seen. She combed through the newspapers, driven to anger when most of the Morish articles were skewed in favor of the Algaraan monarch, painting the Liberation Party as savages and the Algaraans who supported them as equally barbaric.

Leena screwed up her mouth but said nothing, even though she wanted to turn spitefully to the Warden and tell him that the capture of one captain would not save the Malik. That there would be many who would take his place.

None of the Morish papers had ever mentioned that the Liberation Party had gained so much power that they were now at the steps of the capital. This meant they were closer to taking the Malik's palace than she'd ever thought possible.

Leena wished she could tell Baba this. She wished she could scream it so loud that every cell in Newtorn Prison could absorb her words, and maybe Baba could hear her and gain hope from her voice.

Of course, she could not.

Instead, as she passed the captain's cell, she whispered to him in Algaraan—an old phrase that was said to loved ones when they left home, to remind them to be resolute in foreign lands.

May your spirit endure.

At first, she was not sure he had heard her from deep within his cell, but the responding tap on the metal bars confirmed he had. Spiteful gladness almost made her smile. She did not care that the Saint of Silence turned to her sharply, his eyes boring into her. He did not comment, though.

As they roamed deeper into the prison, a strange whirring sound sent vibrations through the walls, rattling the bars and raising dust from the ground. For an odd moment, disoriented and faint, Leena swore that it was Newtorn Prison's own stomach that rumbled, salivating for a feast.

"What is that?" Leena asked, goosebumps trailing across her neck.

The Warden turned around, the lamplight bouncing across the gritty walls, momentarily shedding light into the cell closest to her. This time she did manage to catch a glimpse of another inmate. His face was pressed flush against the bars, his hollowed eyes gaping, mouth slack, so close that he could have reached out to grab hold of Leena's dress. But she didn't shrink back. For a moment, she was unable to tell if he was another of her ghosts.

Evidently, he was not, for she felt a firm touch on her shoulder leading her to the center of the corridor. It was St. Silas, withdrawing once more behind her, collecting shadows in his wake.

"Mind your step," he said silkily, as if he was a gentleman escorting her down a promenade.

Leena nodded. She'd been purposely walking near the cells in hopes of finding her baba, but she now saw the hopelessness of that endeavor. Ahead of them, the hall stretched and stretched and . . .

"What is causing that vibration?" Leena repeated, her voice raised this time.

The Warden appeared pleased by this question. "I view Newtorn as less of a prison and more of a factory, and the inmates as workers. We give them earnings to stoke the fires, to manage the kitchens, to work the assembly lines packaging flour and other goods to feed the nation. They can choose to send those earnings to their family once they've reached a certain amount. It gives them a sense of purpose, essential in the rehabilitation process."

That was what the Algaraan Malik did as well—allowed his people to work their fingers stiff while he lived a life of decadence. The Warden, Leena thought, could not in his arrogance draw the parallels between the two countries. Hunger was hunger, and it always incited violent change, no matter if it was felt by an Algaraan or a Mor.

Leena had never seen a penny from Newtorn Prison. She knew Baba—knew how he'd worked his entire life for his children, knew that he must be breaking his back for the mere promise of providing for them. She wondered bitterly which guard's pocket the money must be disappearing into. Anger built behind her eyes like a headache.

"It is nearly three in the morning," Leena said through gritted teeth. "What benefit is to be had from working the assembly line during these dead hours? That is not rehabilitation, sir, that is profit."

"Any profit to Morland is profit to our great King Edmund. Long live the King." The Warden turned to her again, the heat from the lamp approaching too close to her face. "Would you not agree, madam?" When she did not respond, he laughed—a thin, weedy sound that grated on her ears. "An Algaraan, aren't you? Surely you should have more sympathy for the country that offered you shelter than your own kin who have been nothing but criminals?"

"*Warden,*" St. Silas interrupted. "Have I ordered you to stop?"

The Warden stared at her for a moment longer. His blue eyes bulged in his thin face, reminding Leena of a bug, and she stared back at him with the same amount of ugly vehemence. Finally, he wrenched himself away to lead them farther on. Leena, the headache now throbbing in her temples, dragged her feet after him. St. Silas took up the rear.

They walked for a spell before the Warden halted in front of cell number 342. Ahead of them, the corridor stretched even farther on into stark blackness.

"Colson," the Warden spat.

Behind the bars were only a single bed, an empty pewter plate scraped clean, and a steel bowl meant for refuse. A sleepy groan was emitted by a lump on the mattress, and what Leena had mistaken for a pile of blankets was actually a man. He was starved to the bone, so thin that his clothes enveloped his body.

"What did he do?" Leena whispered. Ghosts came to her in every state—bruised, beaten, bloodied—so she'd grown used to seeing the dead in misery. But seeing the living in this state was jarring.

The Warden looked at St. Silas, who gave a short nod, before continuing, "Murdered his business partner."

Another groan spewed from the bundle of bones on the mattress.

"Leave us, pray," St. Silas said, handing the Warden a coin.

The Warden didn't move. "You wouldn't hurt him?"

"Am I not a gentleman?"

The Warden's panicked eyes met Leena's. Even *she* didn't know how to answer that question. Finally, he gave a jerky nod.

"Then leave us," St. Silas repeated.

Just as the Warden turned away, Leena grasped his arm. "Please, sir, could you tell me if an Ali Al-Sayer is alive in this prison? He was sentenced for life nearly three years ago for attempting to start a union."

The Warden's mouth formed a thin stubborn line.

"Answer her," St. Silas commanded.

"The prison houses many immigrants. We are not given proper papers for most of them," the Warden replied grudgingly, shrugging away from her grip. "We only hold them. We do not seek to differentiate them."

Her cheeks burning, she kept direct eye contact with the Warden and wiped her hands on her dress as if she'd touched something rotten. The Warden's frown deepened before he turned back the way they had come, his footsteps drifting farther and farther away.

She turned to look at the prisoner again, blinking away the wetness from her eyes.

"How do you know the prisoner?" Leena asked, trying to speak through the burning in her throat.

"He is a former secretary of mine," was St. Silas's easy response.

She looked sharply at him.

St. Silas rapped his knuckles against the steel bars, eliciting another grumble from the prisoner. An eye poked out, then a tuft of matted hair. Then Colson caught sight of St. Silas and lurched forward, stretching his arm through the bars toward the Saint, who positioned himself just out of reach.

Through the litany of the prisoner's curses, St. Silas said quietly to her, "I could not have given you a better opportunity."

Sweat slid down her back. Her eyes searched the cell, her heart pounding, desperation collecting like a scream in her sternum. Nothing, nothing, nothing . . .

There!

She almost cried out in relief.

A figure—so still; they were always so still—stood over the prisoner.

She reeled off a description of the spirit. "A young man, russet-colored hair, a crooked nose, and . . . and . . . and a hole through his left temple."

"Very good," the Saint murmured. "Now ask who killed him."

Leena shook her head. "Somewhere between the living world and the dead one, ghosts lose their ability to speak. I can only see them."

"Ask him to point to his murderer, then."

She swallowed thickly and turned to face the phantom. "Sir, is the man who killed you in this room?"

The phantom watched her. She felt his anger like birds pecking her skin. He stepped toward the prisoner, partially blocking him, as if to shield Colson from their gaze. Leena thought it was an oddly protective gesture. Finally, the ghost gave a nod.

"Point to him."

A hard gesture, firm and sure—not toward the prostrate prisoner, but toward Mr. St. Silas. She stared up at the Saint as a dawning horror mounted, transforming her features and draining the color from her cheeks. He saw the change and a slow smile spread across his face.

"Congratulations are in order, Miss Leena Al-Sayer." The Saint bowed his head—not a remorseful action, but one of vicious triumph. "*Champion* of the dead."

3

A New Contract

LEENA SAT ALONE in St. Silas's study as she waited for the medicine to be procured. Outside, a hesitant dawn broke over the city. She'd not spoken since she'd left the prison—not in the carriage, and not when she was escorted back into the house. She was drained, so depleted that her tired body couldn't even find joy in proving her secret true. All she could remember was the prisoner staring at her from behind steel bars while the real murderer stood beside her—the accusing eyes, the face that had somehow morphed into that of her father.

She was sure that the ghost that haunted Colson would never allow himself to depart this world until his cellmate was liberated, if ever.

"You show an astounding lack of curiosity, madam," St. Silas said, striding back into his study, a small parcel in his hand. Oddly enough, he carried a thick book in the other.

She knew what he was referring to. Still, she played the fool, her eyes on the items he carried, but he placed them on a shelf away from her sight. "Curiosity regarding what matter?"

His eyes glittered. "The matter of me . . . er . . . *laying to rest* one of my employees and condemning the other."

"I'm an oddly incurious being, Mr. St. Silas," she said through pursed lips. They both knew that it didn't matter what information Leena had on St. Silas. Even if she did choose to go to the constable, anyone in New Algaraa District could attest to Leena's eccentricities. There was that incident that had occurred a handful of weeks after she'd begun to see the dead: Leena had run into the street dressed only in a white nightgown, the fabric billowing in the winter wind so that her bare feet and ankles showed, screaming that a tall man with sallow skin was trying to kill her. Of course, when the neighbors investigated, there was no sallow-skinned man. He was a phantom.

A few similar scenes after that had cemented her reputation. No matter how hard she tried to appear within the bounds of conventionality now—no matter that she had managed to secure employment as a laundress, that she always appeared kempt, that she spent her nights studying to be an Algaraan translator—her neighbors looked at her with faintly pitying, if not at times fearful, glances. She didn't have friends anymore, only a sick brother and the dead to keep her company these days.

"If I've learned anything from communing with the dead," she said bitterly, "it is to keep the business of the living quiet."

"Clever girl," he remarked again. He sat down behind the desk and withdrew the contract they'd signed earlier. "Let us read our agreement once more to ensure both parties are satisfied."

Leena resisted the urge to lean over and snatch the medication herself. This house, the Saint's very presence, seemed to suffocate the breath from her lungs. She shivered, longing to be back home, to tuck herself under a knitted blanket.

"Hmm." St. Silas's brows furrowed in confusion.

Leena shifted, uneasy. "What seems to be the problem?"

"Hardly a problem on my part," he said. "It is just that the contract specifies that only one course of medication is to be delivered."

"Of course," Leena said, with a nervous laugh. "I only need it for one person."

"But how could that be when it is two people that are sick?" St. Silas leaned forward, eyes laced with false concern. "Or did you not know, Miss Al-Sayer, that you too are dying?"

Silence.

She swallowed, her throat suddenly dry. "You are mistaken—"

"Sweeper's Cough is highly contagious. Were you not aware?" He waved his hand as if he was sharing a minor, uninteresting fact.

Leena rose to her feet, her face flushed. "Do not jest with me, sir. I had the infection when I was only a babe."

"Did you?" His look of incredulity was so drawn out that it was nothing short of mocking. It made Leena doubt herself. She was *sure* her father had said she'd had it when she was little, but had he specifically said Sweeper's Cough, or had he only said a cough? Leena could not bring forth a clear memory, but she thought—she assumed—*surely*—

"It seems you have reevaluated your earlier certainty," St. Silas noted with dry humor.

Leena shook her head firmly. "I do not even have a cough."

He lazily reached for the book he had earlier placed on the shelf, the firelight glittering on the embossed title: *Rayner's Guide to Medical Maladies.* A section was already dog-eared, and the pages slammed open with a thud. "Ah, right here. Sweeper's Cough. The first sign: blue-tinged nails. Peripheral cyanosis." He swerved the textbook toward her, watching her steadily all the while.

Leena's gaze snapped to the list of signs and symptoms labeled Sweeper's Cough, then to her own nail beds; she staggered toward the fire to observe them over the glow.

Blue.

She pressed down on her index finger hard enough to sting, but the color didn't diminish. She suddenly recalled that just the previous morning she had worried about the lack of blood flow to Rami's hand, his fingers cold, the outermost joints stiff and blue. She'd put a mitten on him to warm them, although his body raged with a temperature.

"Even now you look fever-touched to me," St. Silas said, seemingly amused at her agitation. "How long have you been caring for your brother? Sharing cups and linen?"

Leena slapped a hand against her own forehead. Was she running a temperature? She could not tell, but her teeth chattered from the cold. "Then why aren't you afraid of catching it?"

He shrugged. "While you may have . . . unfortunate doubts, *I*, however, am certain I had the illness as a child."

Her mind reeling, Leena sat back down slowly.

Now she understood. The study suddenly felt like a cage.

"What. Do. You. Want?" she rasped.

All manner of false concern dropped from his voice. He leaned even farther forward, eyes edged in hunger, eager for the slaughter.

"Hardly anything that is not worth your life. *What is your life worth, Miss Al-Sayer?*"

She was all fire now, lifting herself from the chair, her palms slamming on the desk, face slanting closer to his. "Do not toy with me, *Mr. St. Silas.* My life wasn't worth a farthing before you knew of my curse. The question is: What is my life worth to *you*?"

They stared at each other in silence, both breathing heavily—one in anticipation and the other in turmoil.

"Consider it a trade," he said, breaking their moment of stillness. "Come into my employment and I will give you medication that will save your life."

She seethed. "I cannot imagine the morally depraved task you will assign to me as your employee."

He gave a slow grin. "I tend to leave the depravity to myself."

"To work under such a man—"

His brows rose faintly. "No one said anything about you working *under* me."

Her face flushed at the obvious implication, but he continued smoothly, "And I am not asking you for anything that should repulse your morals. I need you to find someone. A ghost."

Leena sat back down in the armchair. Then rose to stand by the fire. *If only she wasn't so cold, perhaps she could think straight.*

"You did this on purpose," Leena ground out. She remembered the odd expression that had crossed his face when he'd first seen her hands prior to visiting the prison; he must've known since then. "You ascertained I was unwell, so you manufactured a situation to use me."

His glance was remorseless. "Of course I did."

Her fist felt heavy with the desire to redden his cheek.

"I will not work with you, sir." She turned her back to him, gripping the mantel to steady herself. St. Silas's voice stopped her, starving tone underlying careful words.

"How honorable and *uninspired.* You will expose your secret for your brother's sake, but to work with the likes of me is less preferable than death?"

She twisted to face him once more. "Not moral, but wise. Do you know that ghosts tremble when I speak your name?"

He looked oddly pleased by this revelation.

"We will set a new contract," he said.

"You've tricked me once," Leena countered. Her head felt foggy, her hold on the mantel tightening. "I do not want to be shackled to anyone."

His answer was careful. "I will not shackle you."

"You will, when my only other choice is death."

His voice lowered, and there seemed to be something close to anger in it. "Some get even less of a choice."

She thought of Mr. Jamil, his face bloated with drink, the scars on his lips a furious red. She thought of Margery, whose nightmares from her confession lingered on. She thought of terrified Wardens, of swirling rumors, of condemned prisoners.

She stared at him for a long moment. "Tell me why you killed your last employee."

St. Silas looked momentarily taken aback by this new line of questioning. "I could've sworn that you alleged yourself to be an *incurious being*."

"Curiosity tends to be piqued when one's life is in question."

"Loyalty," he said after a pause of deliberation. "Or the lack thereof. My former secretaries were plotting to kill me and take possession of the business. In truth, it was their lack of subtlety that offended me."

"And not their plan to murder you?"

He flashed another grin. "I find vulgarity to be a worse crime."

"And will you hurt me if I ever displease you?" She hated that her words were slightly unsteady, the black dots floating in and out of her vision like dark moons.

The remnants of a grin lingered on his lips, but he watched her with narrowed eyes. "Do you plan on wrapping your pretty hands around my throat?"

She shook her head mutely.

"Then you have nothing to fear from me."

Her fevered mind trailed back to Newtorn Prison, but this time, instead of Colson morphing into her father, it was herself sitting behind the bars. The Saint stood on the other side, whispering to the prison walls that they would make a feast of her yet.

"What are you thinking?" St. Silas asked.

She startled, and grasped the first answer to give him. "I was wondering if you tear hearts for a living."

His response was quick and fierce. "Make no mistake, madam, that is *exactly* what I do."

She tried to make sense of his words, but she felt oddly deflated, as if she was sinking, sinking, sinking . . .

No—*no!*

Panic welled in her body. She remembered the language books she had left on her windowsill, the ones she had spent nights poring over in hopes of one day finding employment as a translator. How she had learned to conjugate all the verbs in Morish and

Algaraan, memorized all the rules of grammar, practiced and practiced and practiced until her tongue ran ragged. She knew how the Mors viewed the Algaraans—uncivilized people who knew only how to wage wars between themselves, a country that exported only refugees. She dreamed of one day translating her mother's Algaraan poetry books, to show the world that her people knew more about beauty because they had seen so much destruction.

Leena would not allow herself to die now—not when she had just learned to dream again amid the chaos left by the dead.

"A new contract," Leena said, sitting back down in the armchair, sinking her nails into the plush fabric. She watched as St. Silas took out a fresh leaf, but interrupted him before he set ink to paper. "You will release me from your employment the moment I find the ghost that you seek."

The pen paused and he stole a glance at her. A tic in his jaw.

"As you wish, madam," he said after a long moment. "But you will work as my secretary until you have finished this task."

She nodded; she'd been expecting that. "You will provide me with all the necessities for life—including food, clothing, and medicine."

"You will take lodging here," he added, then raised a hand when she opened her mouth to protest. "Not for my benefit, madam. I am a feared man, not a loved one. Enemies I have by the handful. They will not hesitate to harm you as retaliation to me."

She knew this. Still, the confirmation made her heart sink. "Then you will provide an allowance to ensure that the rent of my house is paid, so that I have somewhere to go back to once all this is over."

She watched him copy this down.

"You will also make all adjustments to ensure my safety . . ." She momentarily lost her train of thought, the fever roaring in her ears. ". . . remains intact."

He nodded, writing that part verbatim. As they wrote a few more lines to perfect the details of the contract, it reminded her of the endless afternoons she'd spent haggling in the Old Market, both customer and merchant wanting to get the upper hand without losing the trade altogether.

Then, the tip of his pen hovering over the contract, he asked her abruptly, "Are there others like you?"

Leena had tried to find out in the early days. She'd spoken to Algaraan clerics; she'd sat on the wooden benches of the grand and empty cathedrals; she'd gone to see so-called mystics and shamans. She'd learned very quickly that those claiming to have such powers were mostly con men, bleeding the grieving of their purses. She'd been so afraid of being lumped in with these swindlers that she'd kept her ability quiet. "None that I know of."

"Does that make you feel unique?" There was only mild curiosity in his tone, an indifferent scientist dissecting a cadaver.

Leena's lips thinned. She would not allow him to see how much his question unsettled her, though she was sure that was exactly why he'd asked it.

"Please add the name of the ghost that you require me to find," she replied instead.

Another look was leveled at her before he finally wrote a name.

Percival Avon, 16th Marquess of Avon, Master of Weavingshaw.

Lord Avon, Leena thought. *An aristocrat.*

"Why do you seek him?" she asked, but she was met with only stony silence.

She kept a close eye as St. Silas continued to draft the contract, working herself past the point of exhaustion until the letters began to blur. Several times she forced him to change the wording of a few sentences. Each time he did so without complaint, and Leena swore that he seemed amused when she caught any of his escape clauses. That frightened her. If St. Silas was so adept at drafting contracts and planting loopholes, then there were bound to be a few more she missed. *Especially* in her current state.

"One last thing I'd like to add," she said in a rush. She attempted to keep her tone brusque, but relics of long-held pain bled through. "If you die before me, don't become a restless spirit. *Please—*" St. Silas looked sharply at her. "Please, don't come back to haunt me."

He considered her statement detachedly, his mouth a firm line, then moved to add it to the contract.

The housekeeper was called in once more to witness the signing. She didn't question this new contract, her face perfectly neutral—a well-trained servant—but Leena sensed her disapproval. She didn't linger afterward, the door shutting firmly behind her.

Leena couldn't tear her gaze away from the loop of her own signature, the second one signed that night—the first written in hope, this one in despair.

St. Silas looked victorious.

She *hated* him.

"I will send for you in a week. The Trimexicillin should have worked by then." He dismissed her easily, as if granting her the next week was an act of benevolence. "Mrs. Van, my housekeeper, will provide you with the second medication upon your exit. You will go home in my carriage. A copy of the contract will be delivered to you."

"Another course of the medication has already been prepared," Leena said, almost dully. She could barely lift her head. "You knew I'd agree to your terms from the very beginning, didn't you?"

"Aye, madam. In my line of work, it is dangerous practice to allow your customers to take you by surprise."

"Was it a lie?" she asked, staring down at her hands. They were red and chapped from her current work as a laundress—the only employment she could find—and she resisted the urge to tuck them away. "When you told me that I was one of the few to come to you with a request for kindness?"

Her cheeks flushed. She thought she was impervious to flattery, but a part of her *had* believed it and been proud of it.

He didn't pause. "I'm afraid it was. We all help and hurt others in equal measure. It is not special to want to save someone else." He moved around his desk and toward the door as if already thinking ahead to more important matters. But before reaching the threshold he turned. "If it's any consolation, you were the first one to *surprise* me, though."

That was no consolation. "And if the medication does not work? If Rami's too far gone?"

The Saint waved this away as if it were a minor nuisance. "Then I'll pay his life's worth in gold."

"His life cannot be measured in gold. No life can."

"Why, of course it can, madam." His eyes fell briefly to the timepiece attached to his chest, then to the contract on his desk. "You've just set the price."

4

The Salt Circle

Leena spent the days following her confession in a tangle of fevers and nightmares.

Rami fared no better. She could hear his coughing through the walls—a continuous rattle that never ceased even with the medication she forced past his clenched teeth. He was delirious, his eyes hazy, and more than once he pleaded with her to send away the landlord, even though the rent was not due for another three weeks.

On the first night after taking the Trimexicillin, it made no difference to either Leena or Rami. The fever still scraped across her skin like raw metal; she was sure she was hemorrhaging heat and could not stop it.

Rami was further gone than she was, and she worried that he no longer had the reserves to sweat through the soaring temperature. Every few hours, she would stumble to his room, praying that the fever had finally broken and cursing when she placed a hand on his forehead.

And there was the thirst—the ever-present thirst. No running water existed within their house. On the second day she staggered toward the pump situated at the bend of the road, filled a bucket only halfway, as she could not manage a heavier weight, then dragged it back along the cobbled street. No one stopped to help her; her neighbors saw the fever in her eyes and turned their collars up. She made Rami drink first, triumphant when even the smallest droplet of water breached his dry mouth, before guzzling the water herself afterward. All the while, she dreaded the next morning when she would have to refill the bucket once again.

But every day after that she opened her door to find that someone had left a pail brimming with water on her step. Living in Golborne was like being fed spoonfuls of cruelty or kindness, never quite becoming accustomed to the taste of either.

And throughout her illness, Leena kept vigil.

It had been three years since Leena had gained her abilities to see past the curtain of death, and she'd learned in that interim that ghosts had the awful habit of trying to possess her body when she was weak. There had come times—terrifying times—when she'd awoken in a random field or on a strange street with no recollection of having got there. What had she done in those moments of blankness? Had she hurt someone? Had *she* been hurt without knowing it?

In those first few months after Leena had first begun seeing phantoms, she'd rarely slept. She had been a lady's companion at the time, under the employment of the esteemed Lord Hargreaves and his mother. It was a coveted position that would've saved Leena from the horrors of the factories—that would've freed her lungs from cotton filaments, her eyes from flying shrapnel, her wrists from the lashes of the angry overseers. It was the reason her baba had pushed her and Rami to go to school; he'd worked his fingers stiff over the spinning mules in the cotton factory to do so.

Still, despite her father's sacrifices, she had quit nearly three weeks after she'd seen her first ghost. Leena's odd behavior had begun to arouse the suspicions of the watchful housekeeper and butler; they'd begun to comment on the numerous times Leena had been seen whispering to walls or striking back at nothing. Leena knew that it wouldn't be long before one of them would express their concerns to Lord Hargreaves, suggesting demurely that it might be safer for everyone if Leena was sent to the state sanatorium.

She ran before that could happen.

Baba hadn't yet been imprisoned by the time she returned home, although he'd already begun planning the walkouts with other union leaders. While her father's Morish was broken and stuttering, he was eloquent in Algaraan. He used to lecture in history at the University of Algaraa back home before the civil war broke out, and Baba's fluency could reach the migrant workers better than any Mor in a blue collar could.

Rather than be disappointed at Leena's abrupt termination, Baba had wrapped her in a fierce hug. He smelled familiar—like a factory chimney.

"You're home, *hayati.*" He spoke in Algaraan, calling her *hayati—my life*—before leading her inside their cramped home. He didn't scold her for quitting, as Leena had feared he would the entire journey from the south, but merely ordered her to go to sleep. They would sort it all out in the morning.

They never had a chance. For that very night, the soldiers had come for Baba.

The Al-Sayer siblings were left alone to face the bitter stings of their grief and Leena's horrifying new curse.

For their grief, they could only live through it.

For the ghosts, Leena and Rami tried everything to ward them away. They hung garlic cloves and dried thyme over the door, burned incense. Leena lost weight. Dark circles marked the area beneath their eyes. Any knowledge they stumbled on was accidental, through trial and error. Charms did nothing. But ghosts were repelled by the strike of two copper coins hitting each other, and the sound of humming disturbed them.

She'd learned that phantoms were at their strongest at noon and midnight, their forms taking clearer shape, their lost eyes at once alert, as if being pulled back into the world of the living. Leena learned to dread the hollow chime of twelve church bells.

It was Rami's idea to encircle her bed with salt; he had read it in an old book from the lending library. By that point, Leena was past the point of exhaustion, her skin so gray that she looked phantom-like herself. When she realized that ghosts could not cross the unbroken circle of salt, she burst into sobs. Every night, the phantoms lingered on the other side, various faces of the departed—some wrinkled, some starved with protruding eyes and bloated bellies, others with manacles and chains around their wrists. They watched her, still as scarecrows. They didn't pace, they didn't stir, they merely waited.

It was the first relief she had had in months. She wouldn't leave the salt circle except for her toilette. She kept the curtains drawn and the windows shut, muffling the sounds of life happening outside that she could not join. Rami silently brought her food, then took away the unfinished plates without a word. One day, he left an Algaraan book on the bed.

He cleared his throat. "If you study hard enough, you can find employment in the Algaraan consulate or you can translate in the refugee camps. You could even translate Mama's poetry books. You cannot hide behind your salt forever."

When she looked up at him, she noticed that her brother also looked haggard. Guilt bloomed in her chest.

Before this, she had grown up speaking Algaraan like a foreigner, in the same way many of the immigrant children born in Morland did, stumbling in and out of both languages, not being able to find a home in either. While her Algaraan had been heavily accented, she had learned to read Morish in the schoolroom with ease, and spoke it eloquently as if Morish—and not Algaraan—was the language of her heart.

She began studying linguistics, burying her pain in her books, then took her first tentative steps out her front door. Eventually, she found work in a laundry factory—a far cry from when she was employed as a lady's companion. For a while, things were better.

Until the night she woke up to a phantom hovering inches from her face, wild-eyed, skin mottled, as he tried to bludgeon his soul into her body. She fought him, humming frantically, reaching for the coins she kept under her pillow. She yanked and writhed, finally gripping the copper pieces and striking them together. The ghost lurched away, and Leena scrambled out of bed to find that a mouse had run through the salt, breaking the circle.

She never slept easy again.

Whether it was the effects of her weakened body or not, the nightmares that plagued Leena's fevered sleep were disturbing. She didn't think they were possessions. Several times throughout the night she'd stumble out of bed to ensure the salt circle remained unbroken, but it was as if her fever allowed remnants of the spirits to claw into her subconscious.

More than once, Leena had nightmares of running out of her house and into Margery's, petrified she had given the old lady Sweeper's Cough, only to find her on the floor, long dead from the illness. She'd awaken with a silent scream curling in her chest, only calming herself once she remembered that Margery had told her that she'd already had the disease and could not catch it again.

Leena also dreamed of the dead, their memories sinking teeth into her.

She was a little boy on the beach running from a foaming, rabid dog that snapped its jaws at her shoulder. She felt the agony of the bite as if she had experienced it herself, and she jerked herself awake with a cry. The flickering candlelight threw shadows across her small chamber, and beyond the salt circle was the little boy, his shoulder a mangled wound, his eyes unfocused from the effect of the virus. Leena reached for her copper coins, feeling comforted by the metal cooling her skin.

Afterward, Leena was an old woman on her deathbed. Her joints ached, and she felt the cancer eating her abdomen. Her husband was not beside her, the sheets crumpled but empty. She heard muffled movement from another room.

"John?" Leena called out in the old woman's croaky voice.

She heard a muffled response, then a sudden crash, the sound of a heavy body falling to the floor.

"John?" The old woman tried to stumble out of bed, but her bones were too weak. She crumpled onto the rug, her cheek pressed against the rough fibers. *"John? John?"*

She continued to beg weakly, each time her voice growing fainter and fainter as no response came. Leena, in the old woman's body, inched toward the door, but by the time she reached the threshold her consciousness had begun dimming. All she hungered for was to see John one last time, but she could not reach the knob.

When Leena awoke, it was to see the gaunt, jaundiced face of the old woman outside the salt circle, still on the floor, still reaching.

Finally, Leena dreamed of her mother.

Leena remained herself this time, except she was no more than five years old, growing wild in the refugee camps that bordered the shores of Morland.

Her parents had fled Algaraa when she was still in her mother's belly, months before civil war had broken out. Another professor at Baba's university had threatened to report her father for lecturing anti-monarch sentiment to his students. The punishment for that would've been swift—death not only to him, but to his entire clan.

Mama had been nearly seven months pregnant when they were smuggled out of the country, then onto a rickety boat to weather the tumultuous Westin Ocean to reach Morland. She knew some Algaraans had chosen to endure the deserts that surrounded the country, in the slim hope they would reach the lands beyond, but most had died of thirst and sunstroke on that journey.

There in the camps, in a state of transience, Leena was born. Rami would follow in two years.

Leena's recollections of the camps were brief. She remembered the salty sea air bringing cold gusting winds to rattle their tents, the constant gnawing hunger, the watered-down stews, her parents forcing her to practice her Morish letters while the other children played.

This time, in her dream, she was back in her tent.

She was a child again, sitting barefoot as she practiced reading from a book, *A Guide to Botany.* She remembered Baba's excitement when he managed to procure it for her from one of the camp overseers, and the hours she and Rami had spent marveling at the detailed pictures of trailing vines and thinly veined petals drawn in ink.

Grimvines for inflammation, Marigolds for cuts, Dew Roses for heartsickness.

Her mother sat beside her cross-legged on the floor, her dark-brown curls so much like Leena's own. She was darning a sock.

Leena sounded out the letters as she read aloud to her mother. "Deathgrip, also known as Death C-comes to Wolves, in large q-q-quantities can para-para-er . . . paralyze, but in small am-amounts can be used to treat . . . wo-wounds? . . . It has been historically used to hu-hunt wolves . . ." She trailed off, staring longingly at the rare sunshine, wishing to play with the other children, and frowning when she saw Rami toddling after the bigger kids. *Why was he allowed outside when she was forced to study?*

"*Continue,* Leena," Mama warned, catching that wistful look.

Reluctantly, Leena looked back at the book, but the words had disappeared and the page was now blank. Only the ink drawing of the Deathgrip remained, and beside it the detailed illustration of a dead wolf struck down with an arrow dipped in the nectar of the flower.

"Continue reading," Mama repeated.

"I'm trying to." Leena's voice was high and childlike; she was unable to tear her gaze from the dead wolf. She jerked upright, a sudden panic clawing her throat. "Is Rami still sick, Mama? Where is Baba? Is he alive in Newtorn Prison?"

Her mother's tone was exasperated. "Leena, *hayati,* you can go play after you finish your lesson." Suddenly, there was a flickering in Mama's expression, an odd change that transformed her pretty face into something subtly inhuman. She lurched toward Leena, grabbing her in a tight grip. "Leena, my love, you must listen to me. The Wake will take Baba. You must save him, my brave girl. I know you have suffered so much, but you must save him, *hayati*."

Leena cried, and when she looked down she saw that the book had disappeared from her hands. She looked around, unable to find it anywhere in the tent. She began bawling now—great hiccupping cries that tore through her small frame, afraid that her mother would scold her.

Mama cradled her to her body, as if desiring to return her child back into herself. "Beware the promise of Weavingshaw. All Avons are demon-kissed, my love—"

Leena jolted awake, panting as she lay alone in her bed. Her neck whipped back and forth as she searched for her mother, but the room was empty of all ghosts tonight.

Mama had died when sickness spread through the camps—perhaps a punishment on the displaced for daring to leave their homeland. This was the first time since Mama's death that Leena had seen her in any form; even her dreams had shied away from resurrecting that dear face. Leena held a hand to her aching heart, willing the tears to stop, willing those brown eyes to look upon her once more.

Leena remembered that she *had* lost the book, and had been so distraught about it that Mama had had to go fetch Baba to calm her down. They had later found it by the foot of an old tree near where the children usually climbed, and Leena had kept it close ever since. She withdrew it now from beneath her mattress to trace over the etched letters on the cover. But it was such a minuscule memory, it felt unfair that her brain had decided to take her there rather than the thousand times Mama had hugged her to sleep, holding her like a precious bird, or Mama nuzzling her forehead when she came in from playing.

Was this merely a murky dream left by her fevered state, entwined with a long-forgotten memory? But how could it be? Leena had never heard of the Wake before.

She was sure that Weavingshaw and Lord Avon had laced themselves into the alcoves of her mind, rising to the surface when the fever broke in, and yet—

The urgency of her mother's voice as she whispered *The Wake* . . . It didn't feel like the stab of a memory, but the infliction of a living fear.

Leena felt the constant throb in her head turn into a more blinding headache. She could not coherently think past it, or the need to close her eyes again and sleep deeply.

All she knew, Leena thought groggily as she laid her head down upon the drenched pillow once more, still gripping the botany book in her hand, was that the phantoms that existed in her mind were far worse than the ones that haunted her just beyond the salt circle.

5

The Old Market

On the third day of her illness, Leena cursed St. Silas to every imaginable hell.

He'd lied. He'd given them the wrong medication. It was not working. They were dying.

On the fourth day, Leena's fever broke completely. The rash that was spreading across her body changed to a faint pink color and the first signs of hunger began to assault her. She stood without fainting. And she cursed St. Silas once more, for now she was certain he'd fulfilled his end of the bargain.

Leena took no joy in her own recovery, however, when Rami's was much slower. He stayed in bed, asleep most of the time, although his temperature had finally broken as well and color had returned to his cheeks.

It was on this day that Leena made her first venture to the Old Market.

Leena had never once stopped to consider the varying smells of the bazaar, but the odor of frying fish mixed with the pungent smell of human flesh pressed close together was like a fist to her stomach.

Leena had seen the market grow ostentatiously since its foundation nearly twenty years ago by the first Algaraan immigrants; now it was even frequented by the most reluctant of Mors. She remembered that when she was a child, the market had consisted of only a few tents and wares placed on dusty sheets on the ground. Now it snaked along the coast, starting at the harbor and moving inward, with multicolored tents, caravans, shop fronts, and people of varying wealth and class thronging together. Over the years, Leena had seen every form of merchandise being traded and haggled over—herbs and medicines that were said to be able to bring about children, handmade clothes with intricate stitching that would far outlast any factory garment made in Morland, and even imported artifacts from across the world that held prestige and grandeur.

The crowd today was far thinner than usual, most people barricading themselves at home until the current wave of Sweeper's Cough had settled. Of those who were out, most wore scarves on their nose and mouth to ward off the infection. Leena had also covered half her face to avoid spreading the contagion further.

She was not surprised to find a growing line by the medicinal tents. Leena herself had stood there not long ago, spending precious coins on *Mr. Martin's Medical Cure for Contagious Diseases and Sweeper's Cough.* Yet, in spite of its popularity, it had not worked for Rami, forcing her to seek the Saint of Silence instead.

Leena weaved through the familiar caravans, dodging both the overzealous shopkeepers waving her in and the insistent ghosts that always trawled the market calling for her attention. She kept a steady pace, avoiding eye contact with mostly anything that moved.

Yet she could not avoid the pamphlet that was forcefully shoved into her hands.

Since the rapid boom of the printing press, flyers had become commonplace in Leena's life. Every other day was an advertisement for the unreal and fantastical. It was the same ruddy-faced man she'd seen all the times before, who often stood at the corner between the tents that sold rugs and the chai stall.

Leena glanced at the paper, taking a moment to decipher the smudged black ink.

The Saint of Hunger Spotted on Mount Syke!
Expedition to Explore Such Sighting to
Take Place on the Morrow.
Join Us at Daybreak at Ankler's Inn.

"The demons are stirring again," the man whispered to her, his eyes wide and twitching in his face. "And the Saints have returned to banish them back to their hellish world."

Leena thanked him with a polite nod while pocketing the pamphlet carefully, wanting to preserve the paper as intact as possible. Later on, she could write in the margins rather than spend a precious farthing to purchase new paper to practice her translations.

Her thoughts shifted when she passed a girl no older than her, with short blond hair hidden by an overworn bonnet and a scarf over her nose, handing out flyers. She wore a red twine of rope pinned to her lapel—a sign of the Morish rebels.

This pamphlet Leena did not take, for she had already kept one concealed at home, reading it at night when the candle was at its dimmest. She had the words memorized by now:

King Edmund is powerless.

The country is ruled by the aristos sitting in Parliament who do not represent our interests, but only seek to advance theirs.

More than ever: The poor are poorer, and the rich are richer.

Look across the sea: The Algaraans have paved our way.

The Algaraan Malik will fall.

So will our King.

So will our Parliament.

Take arms. Struggle. Resist.

Keep a lookout.

Further instructions will follow.

Long live the People.

Long live the People.

Leena remembered how desperately she had wanted to fling those words at the Warden when he had cornered her, hissing in her face: *Long live the King.*

What he had really meant to say was: Long live the corruption that lined his pockets with bribes and coins from desperate families begging for a word from an imprisoned loved one. All made possible by an infirm King who did not, ironically, have long to live.

Leena was startled out of her dark reverie by the ghost of a Morish boy that she recognized. Last she'd seen him, he was alive, handing out pamphlets in the same determined manner as the girl. Even now, he still wore the twine of rope on his chest.

Yet the ghost bore the marks of his death.

The sinuous muscles of his back lay in tatters; it was clear he had been flogged without reprieve until the bloody whites of his ribs showed—each slash of skin a punishment for his supposed treason. Leena muffled an exclamation, averting her eyes, the hunger disappearing suddenly from her stomach.

It was a jarring reality to see the ghost standing beside the girl. To Leena, it looked as if she was watching an inevitable future play out—that one day she would return to this street and it would be someone else handing out the flyers, and the girl nothing more than a whispered echo of a call to rise.

No. Leena's chest was already filled with all the things she could not change. She would not allow this feeling of helplessness to settle inside her, taking root and breeding complacency.

Leena, who had seen the blue-uniformed soldiers enter the market at the same time she had, slowed her steps before passing the girl, warning her in a low voice, "There are soldiers coming your way."

The girl gave a curt nod and discreetly tucked the papers into her cloak before blending back into the market, lost within moments. The ghost of the flogged boy followed closely at her heels. Leena knew that she would be back tomorrow.

Leena wished she could come every day to warn the girl when trouble followed, just as she wished someone had warned her father, but she knew that it would be impossible, especially now that she was contracted to the Saint of Silence.

It took a few more minutes before Leena arrived at the small stall she was used to visiting whenever her pockets could spare it. She bought herself and Rami two rolls of bread each, freshly baked, with butter and jam. The small jug of milk was a luxury she was willing to indulge in; Leena could not remember when they had last had fresh milk.

When she returned home, it was to find Rami taking slow steps from his bed. Seeing his growing energy, Leena tried to suppress her excitement, especially when he allowed her to feed him a few morsels of bread and butter.

Rami never liked to be fussed over.

On the next day, which marked the fifth day since starting the medication, Rami all but growled at her to leave him alone so that he might *recover in peace.* This led Leena to leave the house with a sense of relief that he was, albeit slowly, on the mend. She found her way to the lending library, a much-frequented address.

The lending library held a sense of tranquility that was hard to come by in the endless bustle of the New Algaara District. A once heavily frequented church, the abandoned building had been transformed into a book room sometime in the last decade. Its dome still arched proudly over the texts, the pews turned into a sitting area for the readers. Windows, large and magnanimous, shone colored light onto the columns of books, creating a world that, to Leena, looked like a painting belonging to another century.

Even the ghosts that frequented the library were different from the ones in the market. Leena did not venture to find out their stories and avoided them whenever possible, but a few she guessed to be scholars—though one or two phantoms still confused the place for a church from a time gone by, moving in an unhurried manner, as if in endless prayer.

Today, Leena wasted no time in beginning her search for any information about this *Wake* that her mother had spoken of in her dream. Perhaps it was a mad notion, but she could not shake off the heavy feeling that her mother's appearance was more than just the manifestation of her fever and anxiety.

That it held a meaning.

Leena began her search by rifling through old newspapers, journals, and any stored archives from the last decade. But there was nothing to be found there, and after hours of fruitless searching, she left depleted and hungry.

Perhaps, Leena thought with some trepidation as she made her way to the district's most disreputable pub, her answers were not to be found in old texts. Here was a place that was frequently visited by guards finishing their shifts at Newtorn Prison, where information was traded for a price and criminals held more knowledge than judges.

She released her hair, pinched her cheeks, and smiled sweetly at some of the more seasoned-looking guards. There was little doubt that they were, indeed, entranced by her and would have happily talked to her about anything once the cheap ale started flowing, but their expressions shuttered the moment she began inquiring about the Wake, subtle though she thought she was.

That in itself was suspicious.

Hard as she tried, all roads were barred.

It was in those dejected moments as she made her way back home that she questioned whether she was, in fact, slowly slipping into madness. Had she taken the misgivings of a fevered dream and spent precious hours searching for an answer to a question that never existed?

All Avons are demon-kissed.

Lord Avon, on the other hand, was not so difficult to find information on. Back at the lending library she had learned, among decades-old copies of *Peerage Review,* some useful intelligence which she transcribed carefully into the few empty pages at the back of her *Guide to Botany.*

She learned that Lord Avon had inherited the marquessdom at twenty and then died from an undisclosed illness at six-and-thirty, little more than sixteen years after becoming the 16th Marquess and inheriting Weavingshaw. There was little information about his wife other than to say she had died within a few years of their marriage. He had left no living heirs.

All throughout Leena's research, she could find nothing that could account for St. Silas's desire to locate this particular ghost. There seemed little to distinguish Lord Avon from any other blue-blooded aristocrat who had lived and died in the last century. Granted, Leena thought in annoyance, firmly shutting the extraordinarily outdated copy of *Peerage Review* in disgust, this library's newest copy was above two decades old, so any amount of useful information could have been printed since then that she had no way to access.

Then there was Weavingshaw.

While the tattered page in *Peerage Review* held no picture of Lord Avon, a book on *Landed Estates* carried a black-and-white ink drawing of the grand house.

Leena peered closely at it, the depiction of the place juxtaposing with her mother's voice as she begged Leena to be wary of the manor.

Here, in this single printed image, Weavingshaw did not look like any estate she'd ever seen in drawings before. It was not a house but a fortress, built to withstand the salt-laden grit of the northern sea, enclosed by ancient stone walls, resisting and enduring.

Leena scanned the accompanying text. Weavingshaw had been the last defense of the north nine hundred years ago, against both the wildness of the ocean and the invading marauders from Casland, the isles east of Morland. In the ensuing raids, the estate had been burned seven times and rebuilt anew.

Leena knew from her school lessons that the wars between Morland and Casland had ended in a treaty three hundred years ago, meaning that Weavingshaw no longer had a need to defend itself. And yet, Leena thought as she stared hard at the picture, Weavingshaw looked as if it had not forgotten its war-torn past, and behind its show of aristocratic gentility and remote beauty it looked ready to survive a siege even now.

Leena was disappointed when the book shifted to discuss the scandalous past of the House of Marlborough, thanks to the 5th Duke and his not-so-discreet nightly activities. Just as her attention wavered, she noticed she'd missed a section pertaining to the Avons. Half the page was dedicated to their familial crest, drawn in painstaking detail in the darkest of ink: a snarling wolf battling a Deathgrip—a predator and its poison. Between the flower and the wolf lay a vacant circle, quartered diagonally by a cross. Etched at the foot of the crest were the words *I complete what is mine.*

Beneath was a rare footnote by the author himself describing the unknown origins of the Avon crest and its unusual defiance of traditional heraldic rules. The author did not go into any further details as to why this might be—likely, Leena thought, because he did not know.

Leena was surprised to see a Deathgrip on the Avon crest. Something about the dream of her mother wavered behind her eyes, something familiar, but it was too distant for Leena to grasp. She shook her head, battling a headache that struck sharp pains through her temples.

There was also a short newspaper clipping she found that was more up-to-date than the *Peerage Review,* stating that the Avon ancestral home had been lost to the family line as there was no Avon to inherit it. It had instead been purchased by a Mr. Martin—no title.

Leena knew the name at once. Mr. Martin was the most well-known tradesman in all of Golborne. He had lifted himself up from the same poverty Leena had grown up in, and was now a man whose name was emblazoned on half the factories in Ridgeways. He produced both the medications Leena had used to treat the Sweeper's Cough: the expensive one she'd traded her secret for, as well as the cheaper alternative she'd purchased at the market. It felt almost wrong; Mr. Martin's reputation seemed too modern to own the ancient lands of Weavingshaw.

No—Leena thought to herself, staring back at the ink-drawn picture of the estate—Weavingshaw seemed much too wild a thing to be owned by anyone.

On the day before her contract was set to begin, Leena had one final task, which she tackled with determination if not apprehension. Yet again she left Rami to a more restful sleep as she made her way through the bazaar, this time not in search of food but a dagger.

It was a rainy day at the market. The tents, their cloth made thick to withstand the change of seasons, had a dusty, oppressive scent, filtering what little light slitted through. Leena was not a novice when it came to haggling. Teeth clamped in stubbornness, nose wrinkled in tenacity, most of the time she managed to bring down the asking price by half. Yet all her efforts were in vain this morning. Several vendors even laughed outright at the price she was willing to offer just for a small blade.

Leena, who was accustomed to having a safety plan for most problems, hated the knowledge that she was going to work and live with Mr. St. Silas without so much as a knife to keep her protected. The only one they had at home was a large butcher's knife that had grown rust on the metal—hardly something that could be easily concealed.

The *pittance* she offered, as the vendors had mockingly called it, did not even stretch to cover new fabric to make a modest dress. She could not bear the disgrace of being looked at askance by his customers or, worse, by *him,* should her own garments be deemed wanting. If she had nothing else of value going into this contract, she at least had her pride—although that rarely proved to be a comfort on cold nights.

Indeed, it would have been cheaper had she bought fabric to sew herself a dress in the Algaraan fashion—flowing skirts, cinched waistline, embroidered sleeves. But she knew, all too well, that to climb her way up the ladder in Morland society she had to speak like a Mor, dress like a Mor, and, above all else, think like a Mor. Still, her meager wardrobe held more Algaraan dresses than Morish—the only sentiment in her life she still clung on to with great affection.

Leena tried to fight the dejection she felt as she walked back home. Even with a knife, she comforted herself, there was very little chance of fighting off the Saint of Silence should he choose to attack her. It would serve her well to find other means to protect herself, but *what* those other means were, she had no idea.

Leena wore her best, and therefore least comfortable, Morish dress as she stood on the steps of the Saint's house. She tried not to think about Rami, of how she had purposely concealed from him her indenture. He would find out about Leena's contract to the Saint of Silence soon enough, but she wanted to delay that moment for as long as possible, until his health improved.

She told him instead that she had managed to secure employment as a nanny and would temporarily take other accommodations on the outskirts of the city. If Rami had been fully back to his usual self, he would've caught her lie, but he merely gave a drowsy nod in acknowledgment.

She was apprehensive about leaving him alone, but he'd improved to the extent that he could now walk to the cupboards—which she'd used nearly all her hard-earned savings on stocking to a fullness they had not seen in months, even years—for sustenance.

On the other hand, Leena's farewell to Margery had bruised her heart.

She'd gone to see the old woman to say goodbye, her eyes flickering to the ghost that always trailed at Margery's elbow—a man who had been stabbed in the abdomen with a dagger. The phantom was likely Margery's infamous husband, whom the old woman only ever mentioned in tandem with a curse. Leena had never known who killed Margery's husband, though a part of her wondered if it was the old woman herself who had done it. But Leena didn't want to confirm it, afraid that it might change the way she saw her friend.

The old woman, tears dotting her rheumy eyes, had insisted that Leena take a token to remember her by. Despite Leena's pleas that she didn't need a gift to remember Margery, the old woman had thrust a timepiece into her hand. Surprisingly, it was of exquisite make, molded in gold, with the name *Fray* etched on the lid in elegant strokes.

Fray. That was likely the name of Margery's husband.

Inside, the clock mechanism was broken, and there was a mistake on the clockface as well. Rather than counting up to twelve hours, it counted to eighteen, with only one hand, stuck at the starting position. Perhaps this mistake had made the timepiece harder to barter—Margery had sold nearly everything else in her life to pay for her Tar habit—although the gold alone should have brought a pretty penny.

Leena wore the timepiece now, tucked beneath her bodice—as if she carried a bit of home with her.

She smoothed a damp palm across her stiff skirts, holding her tattered suitcase with the other, aware that she was twenty minutes late for the agreed time at which she was to present herself.

Something worse than dread weighed down her spine—a stab of forewarning that told her crossing the threshold into the Saint's house would irrevocably change her.

Leena had migration in her blood, inherited in the womb, but this last migration would be the worst. She would be running toward bloodshed rather than fleeing from it.

A few rain droplets spattered her cheeks, the chilly autumn wind twisting mist and smog through the city. The brown bricks of the Saint's residence seemed to be siphoning the air from Leena's lungs.

Although Mr. St. Silas lived in a genteel area, there was nothing genteel about this building nor the residents inside it. She wondered briefly if the neighbors saw this house as their district's greatest shame.

She lifted her fist, but halted before her knuckles hit the door, a quake in her chest.

Suddenly, as if the weather sensed Leena's unease, the sky unhinged its jaw to release a torrent of rainwater just as the door swung open—before Leena had the chance to knock.

Mr. St. Silas was on the other side with gloves in his hands as if preparing to leave.

He checked his step. His brows drew together upon seeing her and his lips tightened; it was clear to her he was in a menacing mood. He met her gaze with cool civility, then bowed—an insolent incline of his head.

"Your health has improved." He took in her thin shawl, the worn boots, the drenched hemline with a contemptuous lift of his lips. "All radiance; you should thank me."

It was the first time she'd seen him since signing the contract. Leena's gaze quickened to details about him that she'd missed that night: the shaved bristles on his jaw, the faint scar on his throat in the shape of a knife wound, the freshly bruised knuckles.

He stood still under her scrutiny, but his mouth quivered upward as if daring her to share her assessment.

She didn't.

Instead she said, "This is a business transaction, Mr. St. Silas. I do not owe you my gratitude."

His brows rose faintly. "No, you owe me your time."

He stepped aside, opening the passageway for her.

Still, Leena didn't move. "Were you on your way out to come fetch me? Did you think I would go back on my word?"

"I had no doubt, Miss Al-Sayer, that you *would* fulfill your end of the contract." His voice was mild. "Even if I had to drag you here myself to do so."

She met his eyes with a hard stare of her own. She could easily visualize the methods which he would have deployed to *drag* her.

Then—deliberately—she took a step over the threshold as if to prove to him that she did so of her own volition. Her dress dripped on his gleaming hardwood floors, but if he noticed, he didn't comment.

He walked briskly ahead of her. "Come. I'll give you a tour."

6

The Interrogation

The house was wider than it was tall, and seemed to have all the comforts in the world—except warmth. Despite the fires blazing in most rooms, a chill still pervaded Leena's bones. There was something eerily empty about this house—a house that was as discreet and shut in as its master.

With Mr. St. Silas leading her, she noticed that the dining parlor looked untouched and the drawing room seemed unused. Even the bedroom that Leena was soon to inhabit, much more luxurious than the lumpy bed she was used to sleeping on, was desolate. This house felt like a stopping place—solely practical and utterly detached, like a posting inn that had been forced to become a home. She kept pace with Mr. St. Silas, his tour short and perfunctory, his hair even darker within the pools of light from the sconces. He didn't look in the least bothered by the presence of a stranger in his home—especially one who could see the dead—as if he knew that the house would keep all his secrets.

How could he leave the blistering world outside—a world designed to cut and bruise—only to hang his coat and wipe his shoes in a house made of sterility and stone? Did he seek the cold? Shy away from softness? Leena thought of the house she'd just left behind, small as it was, cluttered with childhood drawings and familiar smells. Another place that had burrowed into her heart.

At the very least, she thought, *the Saint's house will never haunt me in the same way.*

Their last stop was Mr. St. Silas's study, and the only room within the house that seemed inhabited. It was unchanged from Leena's last visit. Multiple ledgers encircled the room, some tattered and worn, others unopened and unused. The only new addition was a medium-sized canvas wrapped in oilcloth leaning against a shelf. It stood out in a place that shunned sentimentality.

Mr. St. Silas ordered tea to be brought in before taking a seat behind his desk. His hair was cut shorter than previously. His eyes—black as ink, a drowning well—seemed to swallow the light rather than reflect it: quick to assess, slow to reveal.

It occurred to Leena that she was in a room alone with him. That she would be alone with him day in and day out. Not for the first time did she worry about her safety, or how she would protect herself if all the rumors that swirled around the Saint of Silence were true.

The silence stretched between them. Neither was willing to break it, both locked in a battle in which the victor was the last to speak.

A tap on the door. The smell of tea wafted into the room, brought in by the same woman who had admitted Leena to the house all those nights ago. Leena remembered the way the woman had tried to drag her from Mr. St. Silas's office, and the interaction soured her still.

"Mrs. Van, my housekeeper." Mr. St. Silas again made the brief introduction as he arranged papers into a drawer in his desk.

The housekeeper's sharp gaze landed on her, distrust lining her harsh eyes. She was a severe-looking woman with skin stretched so tight across her face that it looked ready to split down the middle and reveal the white skull underneath.

As Mrs. Van poured from the teapot, Leena could not avert her gaze from the woman's hands. The palms were the same size as her own, but the fingers were so elongated that they curled over the teacup edge like the legs of a spider.

"Madam," Mrs. Van said, as if reading her thoughts.

Leena startled and flushed for the obvious lapse in manners.

Once the housekeeper had left, Leena took a long sip of tea to settle her nerves. Her throat burned full of questions; she wouldn't let anything curtail her now. "You told me previously that you'd like me to find a ghost for you," she began.

"Among other things."

She had been expecting this. Dread swelled in her chest. "What other things?" she asked slowly, fearing she already knew the answer.

"Nothing too odious, I assure you." He waved a hand. "You have a gift, a curse, an *ability*—whatever you'd like to call it—and I'd be a fool not to take full advantage." At the look on her face, his mouth twisted upward. "As part of your duties, you will sit in on my consultations and alert me to any spirits hovering around my customers. You will not question me on why I seek those spirits."

Leena pursed her lips at his autocratic manner. He'd been purposely vague about her "duties" when she'd first signed the contract. She had been too fever-touched at the time to ask him to list them. She'd caught that slip earlier on when poring over the copy he'd sent her, and she'd been berating herself for it ever since.

She wouldn't allow him to have the upper hand again.

Mr. St. Silas's smooth voice cut through her thoughts. "When did you see your first ghost?"

The question startled her and pulled out memories from the recesses of her mind: hazy summers, grand estates, dizzying excitement, dashed hopes.

She remembered that time with a certain perplexity, as if she'd suddenly woken up in a new country and must now learn to speak the language.

"Three years ago," Leena replied, weighing her answers carefully, "when I was employed as a lady's companion in Hythe House."

They watched each other, alert to every minuscule change in the other's posture. Mr. St. Silas's shoulders subtly stiffened at the mention of Hythe House.

Interesting.

"You worked for Lord Hargreaves, I presume?" he asked.

"I did, though I met him but a handful of times. I mainly worked for his mother, Her Ladyship. She is Algaraan, and Lord Hargreaves wanted a well-educated girl who could converse with her in her language." She kept her tone matter-of-fact; she would make sure that pulling answers from her would be like pulling teeth.

Mr. St. Silas drummed his fingers on the desk. "You didn't finish, Miss Al-Sayer. What triggered your ability to see the dead?"

She took another long sip of her tea, noticing that he didn't touch his. She remembered the fever that had started it all—collapsing in the estate gardens, then waking to ghosts.

Finally she shrugged, hoping the gesture would annoy him. "I don't know."

They both continued to level a look at each other, she over her teacup, he in obvious skepticism.

"It's the truth. One day I woke up like this and it has never left me since."

"Out of curiosity"—Mr. St. Silas toyed with the pen in his hand idly—"was there a ghost stalking Hargreaves?"

Leena stirred her tea and added a lump of sugar to it, then grimaced at the taste. She hadn't had sweetened tea in years, and she'd become accustomed to the bitterness. She busied herself stirring, trying to buy herself time to think. She didn't trust herself to lie.

"*Ah*," Mr. St. Silas said, and for a moment she saw through the nonchalance to the suppressed interest underneath. The pen stilled in his hand even if his posture remained relaxed. "You saw the ghost of his wife, didn't you?"

Leena's hand twitched, and she hated that he must've noticed the nervous action.

"Did she really die of a wasting illness?" he pressed. "Shocking, isn't it? She'd been seen in perfect health only days before."

A faint smile crossed Leena's lips. She leaned forward eagerly, the teacup tinkling on her knee. "No information comes for free."

A pause.

"She learns quickly." His tone was dry.

Mr. St. Silas stood up abruptly from his chair and walked toward the mantel. For a moment there was no sound except the crackling of the burning logs.

"What question do you have?" he finally said into the fire, his tone carefully indifferent.

"I beg your pardon?"

He kept his back turned. "I want to know about Lady Hargreaves. Ask me something in return."

Leena had a dawning sense that this request was wrestled out of him, that he was not used to making concessions, and she felt a surge of triumph.

Leena tried carefully not to show her hand. She took another sip of her cooling tea. "Tell me about the Wake."

It was a stab in the dark. She was still unsure if the Wake was a product of fevers or a real, tangible thing, but she would know for certain one way or the other—if not for her mother's sake, then her father's.

"Your secret first, madam." Mr. St. Silas turned, and she felt once more triumphant. That he didn't look perplexed by her question could only mean that this Wake was *not* a figment of her imagination.

She cleared her throat. Talking to his back was much easier than when he fully faced her; then she had to contend with the sharp intelligence of his eyes, and there was no hiding behind semi-truths and half-lies.

She weighed her words carefully. "The ghost that haunted Lord Hargreaves was indeed that of his wife. She didn't die of a wasting illness. She . . ." Leena hesitated, feeling a creep of shame for revealing His Lordship's grief.

When she fled His Lordship's employment and began working instead as a laundress, all the Wardens were cruel and quick to punish her for the smallest infractions. Working for His Lordship had been a completely different experience. He was a steady employer, not quick to rail against his servants, and she had never forgotten the unwavering way the phantom had followed him. As if his longing for his dead wife kept a part of her trapped on this soil. It was *unnatural.* Unholy.

It was the first phantom she'd ever seen.

She'd initially noticed the murky figure when she rose from a night of illness after fainting in the estate gardens.

It was a woman in a soaking dress, hair dripping, lips tinged blue, and bare feet that left no wet prints on the floor. No one else had noticed this woman trailing behind Lord Hargreaves, and Leena had learned very quickly not to ask.

"*Continue,*" Mr. St. Silas demanded, no longer hiding his impatience.

She didn't immediately answer, a part of her still missing in the past.

"Drowned," Leena finally replied into the still room, that single word echoing like water droplets in a cave. "Her pockets were filled with rocks."

He absorbed the information hungrily. "That's why they lied about the cause of her death." Mr. St. Silas's brows furrowed as if rapidly working through a puzzle. Watching him carefully once more, Leena wondered why a tragic family affair would interest him to this extent. Surely he had a *thousand* better secrets.

"I believe it is your turn now, sir," Leena challenged after a long interim.

Mr. St. Silas sat down again, folding his arms over the hard planes of his chest. "The Wake is a group of aristocrats that tends to work in the shadows, dealing in all manner of . . . *business.*"

"What do they have to do with prisoners?" Leena asked, her own hunger now showing. She thought of her baba. Why else, as her mother had warned, would this *Wake* take him?

Mr. St. Silas played this game too well. Now it was his turn to drag out the silence to torture. Finally, his response came, slow and calculated. "There is a booming business involved in trading prisoners, both across Morland and . . . to other continents. Most aristo families have not safeguarded their wealth sufficiently, so they must find other ways to restore their family coffers. Smuggling prisoners out of Newtorn Prison and . . . selling them . . . is extraordinarily profitable these days."

Leena's mouth went dry, and a wave of nausea rolled through her stomach.

"Who do they sell the prisoners to?" Leena edged forward in her seat in agitation.

"I believe I have met my end of the bargain, Miss Al-Sayer—surely you must agree?" Mr. St. Silas glanced away from her and toward the timepiece attached to his waistcoat, a habit Leena noticed he regularly displayed. "If you would like more information, then you must be willing to trade another secret in turn."

Fury burned Leena's face like a kiss.

"What do you want to know?" she spat through gritted teeth.

There was devilry in his eyes. "From you? More and more. *Everything.*"

"So that you can find other ways to use me for your own gain?"

His answering smirk was lazy. "Was there a doubt?"

Leena seethed silently. Just as he was siphoning her for precious information, she would do the same to him, until she bled him dry of every single fact about the Wake. Then she would find his ghost and be rid of him.

Whether fate or chance had intertwined their paths, one certainty was growing with every passing minute: Mr. St. Silas would be the answer to finding her father—to *saving him,* as her mother had begged Leena to do—just as Leena was the answer to the Saint's missing ghost.

Mr. St. Silas stood and walked toward the canvas situated in the corner of the large study, deftly removing the oilcloth that had been covering it. "I had Lord Avon's portrait sent for."

Leena swallowed her anger, turning her attention toward the ghost she was indentured to find.

"Is the depiction accurate?" She rose to view the painting better.

"True enough, but he was significantly less holy," Mr. St. Silas replied dryly.

Leena understood what he meant.

Lord Avon was divine—a fatal mix of power, vitality, and consequence. His aristocratic features, finely molded over sharp bones, were both remote and compelling. He sat in a wingback chair by a window, a hound by his feet, an easy athleticism to the set of his shoulders. He was unadorned with finery except for a wedding band on one hand and a silver ring on the other, carrying a red leather book in a relaxed hold. The scenery behind him was muted in the face of his glory; his fair hair muffled the sun; his blue eyes deadened the sky. All at once, he seemed to be both cradled by the world and superior to it.

Only death could claim such a man.

"What illness killed him?" Leena whispered, remembering his obituary in one of the old newspapers she'd found.

"None," Mr. St. Silas responded, his voice carrying no deference to the departed. "He was murdered—a sword through the heart."

Leena's mouth dropped open in disbelief. "He was *murdered*? By whom?"

"Unknown."

"Any guesses?"

Mr. St. Silas leaned back on the edge of his desk, his expression undisturbed. "It does not concern me."

"I've done my own research." Leena attempted to rearrange the tenuous image she'd built of Lord Avon with this new piece of unsettling information. "The cause of death in his obituary didn't mention *murder*. It was far more tame than that: *undisclosed illness.*"

He didn't answer her. Instead, he raised a brow. "What do you know about the aristos, Miss Al-Sayer?"

She shrugged. "I briefly interacted with a few of them while I worked in Hythe House."

"Then you will know that Avon is an old name, with a line that can be traced back to the first families in the country." A deliberate pause. "What is the one thing that the aristos value above everything else?"

"Power? Wealth?"

"*Legacy.*" Mr. St. Silas's voice held an odd note. "If Percival Avon died in mysterious circumstances, then it's not worth the scandal to investigate any further."

Leena could only stare at him in astonishment. That sort of ideology—a loyalty to an intangible concept—was far beyond her world of drudgery.

Seeing the incomprehension on her face, Mr. St. Silas smiled grimly. "For the aristos, the endurance of their legacy must be protected above all else. Very likely, Lord Avon would rather his death certificate be written with lies than have his family name tarnished with the truth."

Leena's face reflected a sharp bitterness. There was a certain privilege to having the resources to seek justice, but *choosing* not to, while the Al-Sayers—unmoored in this country, a fragmented family without influence and without power—would never have the chance to find justice for their father . . .

Mr. St. Silas didn't miss her disgust.

"And he left no heirs," Leena said after a long moment.

Mr. St. Silas regarded the portrait impassively. "By that point, there was no one left in this world to inquire after him."

"What about Weavingshaw?" Leena demanded, not allowing him a chance to take control of the subject once more.

She was surprised to see a subtle flexion of his jaw.

"What about Weavingshaw?" he replied in measured tones.

"If Lord Avon left no relations, who inherited the estate?"

"It was *purchased* by a tradesman named Mr. Martin following Lord Avon's death." He relayed the information without much pause, and Leena felt relieved that at least *some* parts of her research were confirmed.

Yet the chime of her mother's warning sounded once more in her ears: *Beware the promise of Weavingshaw.* Still, there was an ancient stirring in Leena's bones, a deep understanding that Weavingshaw held the key to the Avons—and, therefore, a key to her own freedom.

"We must go to Weavingshaw." Although her tone was decisive, she felt an odd ache in her words, that of a disobedient daughter. "The ghost of Lord Avon may haunt those halls."

"I don't doubt we will eventually have to step foot in Weavingshaw." Mr. St. Silas's words were stretched, grim. Leena could tell that the estate evoked some deep emotion in him, but whether it was hatred or love she could not say.

She wanted to question him further, to ask him why the grand house provoked such a reaction from him when everything else seemed not to bother him in the slightest. But she sensed that she would receive only harsh silence in exchange.

"One thing I've learned about the dead is that certain objects can anchor them to the living," Leena began again, watching him from underneath her lashes to see if another subtle expression could be provoked by her words. "Do you know of any trinkets, or even a person, that might've been important to His Lordship?"

He shook his head, hooded eyes returning to the portrait.

Her heart sank. She'd hoped that she might be able to find Lord Avon waiting beside a loved one. Now she didn't even know where to start.

"Why do you seek him?" Leena asked, no longer able to mask her impatience. She felt exasperation at his reticent answers. In theory, they were both on the *same side.* Surely more information would only help achieve their common end faster?

When he finally did give her an answer, Leena had to hide her surprise, trying to keep her face neutral so as not to show her ricocheting emotions.

"He owes me something, and I intend to take it back."

Mr. St. Silas didn't strike Leena as someone who accepted theft with grace. His words—and the memory of his previous secretaries—sat uneasily with her. Yet his answer was not enough, not really even a start, for Leena to use in any way. She opened her mouth to voice this, but he cut her off.

"Miss Al-Sayer, you'll be shown to your room. Ready yourself for tomorrow." It was clear from his voice that their conversation was over. With a flick of his hand, he rang the servants' bell that sat on his desk, the single clatter echoing a finality.

Leena had never worked for an employer who held such a menacing quality without once raising his fist to her. There was her most recent laundry Warden, who had slapped Leena for the slightest provocation, even though it was never her fault. The desperation for money in a time of gnawing hunger across the country had kept Leena's throbbing jaw locked and raging eyes lowered.

But it was not just the laundry Warden. There were also the ones before who strutted through the factories, who either growled and spat between missing teeth or leered from their seats at the women passing by.

Sometimes, they more than leered.

Those Leena had fought—tooth and nail and sometimes with broken shoe heels. All she had to show for those fights were days without bread, her starvation a bitter trophy for her dignity.

But Mr. St. Silas, Leena thought, looking at him now, was the opposite of dumb, brutish force. He instead had that sort of vicious presence that made one feel like exposed prey—uncertain where to step next, uncertain where the attack will come from and when.

Even if his body stood still, his eyes stalked—watchful, impatient, *prowling*.

He had that effect now as he looked at her with his hands in his pockets. Tall, powerful frame leaning back against the desk lazily, his posture deceptively relaxed while his eyes shone with sharpness—someone who always got what he wanted in the end.

It was far more lethal.

Leena would be a fool to underestimate the Saint or even to think that, underneath all that civilized attire and cultured accent, he was less of a threat to her than all her previous employers combined.

Here was a man who was not afraid to cause her real pain, and they both knew it. Already he had deceived her, indentured her, and separated her without a care from the only life she knew, throwing her into a perilous task from which she could not be certain she would emerge unharmed—or even alive.

A knock on the door thrust Leena from her bitter musings. It was Mrs. Van, summoned to lead her back to her new bedroom.

In truth, she was ready to leave the presence of Mr. St. Silas. Her day had been long and taxing before she even stood on his doorstep.

Leena was especially ready to leave the portrait of the last Avon, the golden lord who seemed to reject the very idea of death.

In her new chamber, everything was built for comfort. The bedframe was made of rich mahogany, and a fireplace—a luxury she couldn't even begin to fathom—was swept clean of soot. Even the thick walls allowed *privacy*. No whispered fights bled through, no drunken shouts, no loud snores. It was utterly soulless. Anyone could inhabit this room, sleep on the soft mattress beneath the thick covers, and leave in the morning without having made any dent in it. It was a bedroom designed for transience.

Her suitcase waited for her in the wardrobe. Not bothering to unpack, she found her nightgown and shimmied into it. She drew out her *Guide to Botany,* rifling to the few remaining blank pages at the back. She took her time now, writing down everything she'd learned today in the smallest possible handwriting: about the Wake, Weavingshaw, and Lord Avon, as well as her mother's warnings.

Demon-kissed.

It was very little to go on—almost nothing. But it was a start.

7

Bleeding Confessions

Leena's first day attending the Saint's consultations was wretched. So was her second. And her third. She knew she'd eventually succumb to the misery of this job, that it would become routine, but her heart was not hardening quickly enough.

Mr. St. Silas's shop was organized with an impersonal hand, perhaps seeking to separate itself from the very personal stories told within those walls. Or perhaps he simply did not care.

The confessors were usually led through the entrance, which opened up to a single eerie hallway, by one of the Saint's many bruisers. The hallway was long and straight, and contained several locked doors. Leena had no idea what lay behind those doors. *Likely torture chambers.*

In the early morning, the Saint unlocked the confession room—a claustrophobic space with red-bricked walls and a single shuttered window. Inside was a fireplace, a large writing desk that curved between her and Mr. St. Silas's chairs, and one last chair in the center of the room meant for the confessor. Mr. St. Silas's and Leena's seats were made of pliant leather, while the confessor's was wooden—the very same kind Leena imagined prisoners sat on while awaiting trial in the dock. Either an allusion to the courtroom or a mockery of it.

The consultations always ended exactly at half past noon, with lines of people forming at dawn for a chance to trade their secrets. At these consultations, the Saint was unyielding and exacting—a timepiece in one hand, a pen in the other. All the secrets he heard—all the terror they brought, all the heartache—seemed to affect him not at all.

On that first day, it was the *sterility* of the entire process that drove Leena nearly mad.

She watched as Mr. St. Silas tugged on a pair of leather gloves before withdrawing one of the black ledgers that she had seen lining the shelves of his study, and opening it to a fresh page. He glanced at Leena disinterestedly, his first acknowledgment of her that morning. "Never touch the ledgers."

"Why not?" Leena asked, already feeling stiff and uncomfortable in her chair.

Mr. St. Silas raised a brow at her question. "Because I command it, Miss Al-Sayer."

Leena swallowed a grimace at his order, said in tones that not only expected her total obedience but took it for granted. He handed her parchment and a dip pen, instructing her in a low voice to watch well and report exactly to him.

That first morning was a blur.

Leena's body tensed each time the door swung open, unsure what would meet her on that threshold and what secrets would be released from the darkness and into the light, stirring phantoms in their wake.

Yet the confessions she heard in those first few hours were . . . *nothing.*

Little more than gossip. A young man who admitted to stealing his mother's clothes to sell at the market for Tar, leaving his mama with only her underthings to wear.

A middle-aged woman who told them that her youngest child was not actually her child at all but birthed by her unmarried daughter.

A musician who had broken the fingers of his rival during a drunken brawl confessed he had not been drunk but had known exactly what he was doing.

Margery had been wrong—the Saint of Silence not only accepted schoolroom scandals, he also paid for them.

Leena sat there in the stifling room, the morning coffee Mrs. Van had brought during the break steaming in her hands, and it was all she could do not to look at her employer. Finally, she could not help it, and she gazed at him askance. Absentmindedly, he was stirring two teaspoons of sugar into his coffee while his eyes remained on his ledger, before swallowing it down with a twist of his mouth.

Putting down the cup, he met her look with one of his own. "A problem, Miss Al-Sayer?"

Even now, within the small confines of the room, he had a way of disconcerting her with a single look, just as she'd seen him do with all his confessors. There was a tempered menace about him that forced itself to be felt, that naturally overtook and bludgeoned any space to bend to his will. Perhaps that was why all the confessors had left the room looking as if they'd been battered although they'd never once been touched by him; they must have been absorbing the teeth of the Saint of Silence's presence.

Leena straightened, not wanting to begin her employment with a show of fear. Mr. St. Silas caught her movement wordlessly, and a slow, derisive smile spread across his lips. Nothing seemed to escape him.

She said carefully, "Only that I am surprised that you would pay precious coins for such trivial secrets."

"All secrets have value. What may seem trivial to you could be someone else's ruin."

"But *why*?" She tried not to sound demanding, already knowing the Saint did not take kindly to being questioned. "What can you possibly gain from it?"

What she really wanted to ask, but dared not, was: *Where do you get the money for such a grim exploit?*

"It is not for you to question, Miss Al-Sayer." His response was reticent, just as she should've known it would be. "Not when you still have not informed me of any ghosts following the confessors throughout the entirety of this morning. *Try* to be of some use to me."

Leena swallowed down her own bitter coffee just to have something to dampen her frustration. There had been no ghosts to report, and she sensed her employer knew it. Still, Mr. St. Silas seemed to clock her sullen temper and derive pleasure from it. "Anger is a very useless emotion and does not become you, madam."

"On the contrary, sir, I am not angry."

"You are," Mr. St. Silas returned easily. "It is clear that everyone and every*thing* affects you."

Leena could not deny that he was right.

Even in this they were ill matched. While anything could move her, almost nothing seemed to touch him at all.

She ignored his observation, and it took all her best efforts to keep her voice steady, but the toll of the morning had had its impact on her already. Her blood surged with the need to be free of this wretched house and its equally wretched master. "Sir, would my time not be better spent searching for Lord Avon's ghost? I am sure my presence here is not adding that much to the profit of *this* business."

Any delay to finding Lord Avon gnawed at her insides.

Mr. St. Silas had lost interest in the conversation, turning back to his ledger. "I regret if I have not made myself clear, Miss Al-Sayer. Your time was given to me the moment you signed that contract. Whether you feel it is better served elsewhere is no longer your concern."

Leena had expected this answer and, with a final withering look at his bent head, she turned stoically toward the door, waiting for the next confessor to walk in.

At least this customer was the last of a very long morning. It was an elderly Morish man, with liver-spotted skin and eyes a clear blue. He sat on the chair, his weathered hands skimming across his trouser legs with nervous energy. If he noticed Leena, he did not comment, only glanced at her warily once before turning away.

Disinterestedly, Mr. St. Silas introduced her as his secretary before sliding a waiver across the desk toward the confessor, with Leena ironically now acting as the witness to its signing.

Then . . . the silence.

Mr. St. Silas leaned back in his chair, idly watching the confessor, without once speaking. Leena had begun to notice the way the Saint manipulated silence as a tool, discomforting those who faced him into revealing more than they intended. Still, knowing his tactics didn't stop her from shifting again in her own chair, so quiet she could hear her pulse pounding in her ears. She could see the effect this had on the old man, the way he opened his mouth several times, before finally managing to croak out a whispered, "I have a secret."

"Clearly," an unimpressed Mr. St. Silas drawled.

The silence dragged on longer than it had with the others. Leena would've gladly revealed another confession just to have something to fill the stark emptiness.

It was the man who spoke first, stilted and low. She could see the hesitation play across his face, the way his fingers twisted a wedding band round and round the knuckle. "I . . . I used to own a factory that specializes in converting cotton fibers into fabric."

A tradesman. Leena should've noticed the superior quality of his clothes, although worn and a little shabby, the fashion dated from a decade ago. His accent, however, still resembled Leena's, his words lilting, the *R*s overemphasized—hallmarks of her own poorer district.

Still, no response from Mr. St. Silas.

Now the utter stillness was unbearable. She saw the way the old man leaned forward to fill it of his own accord. "Ten years ago, the factory went up in flames."

Baba used to work in a cotton factory. Leena knew the dangers of even the smallest match catching near the filaments. Her nightmares were filled with images of her father trapped in an inferno. With a sinking heart, she knew exactly what this man's revelation was going to be.

"I lost everything in the fire; the entire factory was burned to nothing. I could not return on my investments." The man continued when he saw Mr. St. Silas still did not speak. The rest of it came out in a rush—a sudden expulsion of truth. "I know ten years ago is a long time, but my wife is . . . She is now very sick, and I can no longer afford the medication to keep her well, therefore I have come to call upon you."

It was only when he uttered the word *fire* that Leena saw the flicker of movement from behind him, emerging from thin air.

Leena closed her eyes briefly in hopes the image was not real. But no, it remained. A phantom now hovered by the man, the first ghost she had seen in Mr. St. Silas's confession chamber, and she could not tell how young the woman was beneath the blackened and ashy skin. The smell of burned flesh filled her nose, even though Leena was sure it was only her imagination creating such an acrid scent.

In some odd way, this was one of the few times Leena was glad she could see these beings and bear testament to a suffering that would otherwise go unnoticed. Never once had the old tradesman mentioned the dead factory workers. Only the fire and how it had affected his investments.

The question spilled from Leena's own now-parched throat before she could stop it, her eyes never leaving the charred phantom. "Were there any casualties from the fire?"

She did not know why it mattered that she asked that question, for she knew that the tradesman's confirmation that the fire *had* resulted in death would not be enough to save this woman from her ensnarement to this world. Yet Leena had never shaken off that part of herself that desperately wanted to release these phantoms from whatever kept them here, although she had learned not to give in to it. Very rarely was she successful in freeing these ghosts, and the bitter sting of her failures always made her feel useless.

Rami was right, Leena thought to herself; she was now far more submerged in the emotions of the dead than the living.

She saw Mr. St. Silas half tilt his head toward her, his dark eyes shuttered, his mouth a thin line of irritation at her interruption.

Jerkily, the man nodded.

With one final warning look toward her, Mr. St. Silas shifted his focus back to the man. No longer did he use silence as a weapon. Now the interrogation was callous. "How many dead?"

A staggered breath from the older man. "In the hundreds."

Leena's eyes flickered to the burned woman once more, wanting to see if *this* would finally release her, but it did not.

"Do not waste my time. A factory fire that occurred ten years ago is not uncommon knowledge," St. Silas said, every word a strike. "What is *your* secret?"

The old man released a breath. "Back then, thieves used to run rampant in my factory. To prevent the pilfering of precious merchandise, I-I . . ." He stuttered, swallowing the words, before continuing in a whisper. "I locked them all in."

It took Leena a moment to understand.

There was no curiosity in Mr. St. Silas's face. It was clear that while Leena's disbelieving mind could not grasp the reality of the tradesman's words, Mr. St. Silas understood perfectly and was not surprised by it.

"Locked you in?" Leena demanded, appalled, staring once more at the phantom behind his shoulder. Then she realized her slip. "I-I meant . . . *who* is it that you locked in?"

She knew, even without directly looking at him, that Mr. St. Silas had pounced on her slip of the tongue, his eyes narrowing again.

With trepidation, knowing she would answer for it momentarily, Leena instead focused on the man's shuddering voice. "My workers, as I did not know who among them was responsible. When their shift began in the morning, I'd lock the doors until they were released home in the evening, with every person searched before their release. This ensured"—his voice broke—"that they could not steal material from under the nose of the foreman."

The images roared through her mind—the fire licking at the cotton wheels, the workers pounding at the locked doors. This was why her father had wanted a union. She could not tear her eyes from the phantom, hovering with half her face unrecognizable from the fire.

In Leena's peripheral vision, she saw Mr. St. Silas document the secret in his ledger, and in that moment she hated him more than she'd thought possible. She hated that he made her sit here and listen to such heartbreak, and she hated that he remained so unaffected by it.

"You may leave." Mr. St. Silas dismissed the man, handing him a slip of paper with the amount he was to be paid. "Knock on the second room on the right, and Jeremy will settle your account."

Vaguely, Leena noted that the number written upon the slip of paper had a higher value than any of the day's previous confessions. It would make sense, she supposed. The more fatal the secret, the higher the recompense.

Leena was jarred back to the present by the sound of the tradesman staggering from the room.

A change had suddenly overtaken the old man.

He looked ten years aged, his steps hobbling, his back now bent, the weathered face contorting beneath some invisible pain. She was unable to look away from this horrifying transformation, her eyes staring unbelievingly at the man. She had never known remorse to have such physical manifestations. Her head swiveled once about the room in search of something that could cause this kind of instantaneous alteration, but she found nothing.

The door shut behind him, the ghost of the burned woman silently trailing after the tradesman as she, too, vanished.

The silence that followed was deadly.

For a few moments, Leena stared fixedly at her white-knuckled hands folded in her lap, her mind still swirling from all she had witnessed.

Finally, when she could bear the stillness no longer, she raised half-weary, half-defiant eyes toward Mr. St. Silas. "I did not mean to—"

"Tomorrow, before the start of your shift, you will drop off your botanical book at my study. For every interruption, every missed opportunity to inform me of vital information, every inattentive moment you pass, I shall rip out a page and feed it to the fire." His smile was sardonic. "Three pages are already owed."

A Guide to Botany?

She stood up, chair scraping against the floor. He did not rise at her standing, as was customary, but continued to take off his black gloves, folding them into his waistcoat pocket.

"You . . . How did . . ." Never had Leena stuttered so painfully in her life. How on earth did he know about her book, her most prized possession above all else, tethering her to her mother and a childhood long gone?

She thought wildly. Had she been carrying it in her hands in front of him? And even so, how could he possibly know its value to her? Was it that wretched housekeeper rifling through her things who had informed him? Did he have some darker means of acquiring information about the people around him?

Finally, he stood up, giving her a slow bow.

"This concludes our day. I bid you good afternoon, madam."

"Mr. St. Silas—" He only turned slightly at her address, for which she was glad; her face revealed her near-panic. "Sir . . . I . . . I beg your pardon." She swallowed hard. "I lost my concentration, but it will not happen again. If you could only spare my book." She could not, even against her better judgment, pretend indifference to the immeasurable worth of that book—especially when it was threatened with being ripped from her and slowly destroyed.

"Sparing it, Miss Al-Sayer," he said, opening the door and barely glancing back at her, "is entirely at your disposal. Do your work well, and you will have nothing but peace from me."

His disdainful voice remained echoing through her mind long after he was gone, stinging her like a slap. For such a man to offer *peace* to her would be the equivalent of a burning flame offering condolences to a forest—a harbinger of devastation.

After the cotton-mill owner, it was as if a floodgate had opened.

Either her mind did not pay any further attention to the *nothing* secrets that passed or she did not care, for her entire horrified concentration was focused on the ones that came after. Those gruesome secrets ricocheted in her mind endlessly, building an empire from which she could not escape. *Bleeding confessions*—as she learned to call them in her head—sometimes appeared only once daily, sometimes not at all, and sometimes one after the other, each tearing across her skin and wounding her without salve or gauze.

Throughout it all, she watched Mr. St. Silas carefully.

Leena had been right. There existed no blade powerful enough to rip through the Saint of Silence, but *knowledge* was not a knife; it was far more lethal. And, if Mr. St. Silas had taught her anything, it was that even the most trivial of secrets can lead to ruin.

Leena's daily routine became fixed very quickly even within those first few days, revolving entirely around Mr. St. Silas's own schedule.

Everything he did, he did with vicious proficiency. If he slept, he slept but little. He drank his coffee searingly hot, always with two spoonfuls of sugar. He took his meals alone. His servants moved silently through the house; his bruisers bowed their heads to him.

He frequently took private meetings in his study—bankers, aristos, tradesmen—the entire city within his palm. All his commands were met with swift compliance. There were no half measures with Mr. St. Silas—not in his cunning, not in his ambition, and not even in the way he had his coffee.

Each morning began the exact same way.

The secrets documented in those black ledgers. The gloves.

The ripping of serrated emotion.

Then, the payment.

She supposed the only difference in his own routine was her entrance into it. Some days she would only see a single ghost swirling by a customer; other days the dead were ceaseless, continuously blowing in like the drafts of cold autumn air. Whatever information she quietly provided to Mr. St. Silas about the hauntings of his customers was used to expertly change the direction of his questioning, enabling him to reach the source of his confessor's pain and shame more quickly and ruthlessly, extracting lies like the splitting of flesh.

At first Leena, who knew the rumors around the Saint of Silence, believed he himself was the cause of the agony that the confessors experienced at leaving his confession room. But the more she observed him, the more she realized with dread that these changes occurred each time a confession was written on the sheets of those carefully handled ledgers.

Something unnatural occurred on those pages. Something horrible.

Leena's attention kept coming back to the ledgers obsessively. He'd never written her own confession in those books, she now realized, and she was fixated on the reason why. She noticed that Mr. St. Silas handled them as if they were a mix of something both hallowed and poisonous, for his bare skin never grazed the pliant leather covers.

The answers she sought must *surely* lie within them, and Leena was eager to claw the pages open and devour their contents. But he never left them unguarded, and Leena never found an opportunity to try.

Obsession, Leena thought wryly, must be a new bad habit she had developed, for if it was not the ledgers she was brooding over, it was Lord Avon's ghost and her absolute lack of any advancement in that regard. How could she ever find any time to start her search when Mr. St. Silas had her in his confession room for half of every day? Nor was she permitted to leave the premises and comb through the city without him. He had claimed contemptuously that it was for her own safety, when all Leena longed to do was to check up on Rami and Margery, and she felt like a prisoner within the limits of her own life.

And Mr. St. Silas, for all his initial urgency to find his phantom, seemed now to grind to a standstill in the matter of the ghost hunting, as if it no longer mattered to him at all.

Still she continued to observe him—every gesture, big or small, filed away to be carefully analyzed in the privacy of her chamber.

Even now, as he drank his coffee and focused on writing in his ledger, she watched him covertly.

Searching for any sign that might lead to his ruin.

8

Little Distractions

Leena's botany book had been gone for three weeks.

And every moment in between she had worried about Rami, and how he was faring. Every day she longed to steal out and visit both him and Margery, to assure herself that they were both safe and well.

Instead she was perpetually confined to the confession room.

Leena had learned to curb her tongue around the ghosts that swirled in with the confessors, manacled to the living. The worst phantoms were the ones that followed the customers who came to confess at noon; it was that *damned* hour. It breathed life into the dead. Those ghosts looked more solid; their misery carried weight.

Leena kept her head lowered, mutinous eyes on the paper as she wrote Mr. St. Silas notes about all the ghosts that followed his customers.

Whenever Mrs. Van brought in the refreshments, Leena tried to keep her wrathful gaze to herself.

She cursed Mrs. Van for informing her master about *A Guide to Botany*. She cursed the new clothes that had been commissioned for her and hand-delivered by the housekeeper to her room—each of the six boxes filled with corsets made of whalebone, silk stockings, soft cotton chemises, dresses of the finest material in colors of dark gray, light blue, and forest green. They even included gloves and a smart hat for when she needed to present herself outside the shop. No longer did she dress in her own worn but loved clothes; now she felt as sterile and cold as the rest of the establishment.

When she initially stepped into the confession room attired in her expensive new garments, Mr. St. Silas looked her up and down with a barely concealed smirk, causing her to gnash her teeth together forcefully to stop herself from replying in kind.

It was in these new clothes that she now sat and watched as the confessors yet again fell prey to Mr. St. Silas's damning silence.

She had begun to clear her throat during those moments of unforgiving quiet. Sometimes she would shift in her chair, causing the legs to creak. Other times, she would sneeze. Or tap her fingers. Anything to fill the silence that Mr. St. Silas was enforcing.

During the short break that morning, Leena kept her gaze on the dark liquid sloshing in her cup. She never took milk in her coffee, preferring it the way Algaraans made it, thick and slightly caramelized.

"Have you been counting?" Mr. St. Silas asked mildly, forcing her gaze to meet his. The smile he wore erased the callous lines of his face, forcing his handsomeness to be acknowledged—even by Leena, who often felt herself in the presence of a being more monster than human.

His fingers tapped on his timepiece, mimicking the way hers had done on her knee during the last consultation.

She knew instinctively that his smile was a prelude to some sort of savagery. Mr. St. Silas always hid his worst forms of barbarity beneath a veneer of civility.

Wearily, she asked him, "Counting what?"

He looked surprised by her question. "Why, counting the number of pages you've burned from your botany book?"

Leena's heart sank. "Only three." She barely mouthed the words.

"Come, Miss Al-Sayer, there is no denying your cleverness. I think with your most recent dedication to interrupting my sessions, you must have known it would be a little more than that."

"You are mistaken. I've not been interrupt—"

"Your face," he cut in, "is terribly honest. It reveals even the smallest emotion." Regarding her measured look, his tone was derisive. "I fear that I have not worked you *hard* enough if you have the time to pine over a book about weeds."

"Well, it is a pity *you* think so, for it would mean that I have successfully cheated the Saint of Silence."

His brows rose slightly. His hard frame leaned back against the chair, his long legs outstretched before him in a careless gesture. "Oh, how so?"

"If I am indeed not meeting your standards, as you say, and still had six new silk and velvet dresses commissioned for me, three full meals daily, lodgings fully paid, my house rent in New Algaraa District also fully paid for, and"—her smile widened to mirror his—"a smart new hat with ribbon *and* feather trimmings, then I am surprised, sir, that you have allowed my negligence to go on for so long and have not taken me to task much sooner."

They both stared at each other hard, each with a smile on their face that was more a snarl than any sentiment of enjoyment.

"How many pages," he murmured, "do you think your reply has cost you?"

"I should think"—she spoke between her teeth—"that it was worth my entire book."

He barked out a laugh. "That is a relief. I was growing weary of spending my evenings feeding the flames."

Leena tried not to jerk, crossing her fingers behind her back, praying that his threat was not in earnest. "I am glad to be of service."

"And how long will you be in my service, I wonder?" Guardedly, she waited for him to continue. His dark eyes had turned coldly watchful. "I confess to being disappointed by your *abilities* thus far—especially as you have not yet found a single trace of Lord Avon."

Mr. St. Silas might as well have been a carousel lamp. One minute he was all but disinterested in the search for the elusive Avon ghost, and the next he was all churlish impatience, suddenly filling her schedule with post-confession visits to just about any location Lord Avon might have owned, lived in, or visited. Already they had been to several places that Lord Avon had been known to frequent: the gentlemen's club, the House of Lords, even His Lordship's old tailor. It had stirred up nothing but dust and Mr. St. Silas's displeasure.

Yet he spoke now as if Leena had been purposely remiss, or lying about her ability to bring forth phantoms, although she desperately searched for the ghost everywhere they went. Even now, to her own mind, she shied away from a real and growing fear. What if Lord Avon had long left this world, never to be found? What then? She could not possibly recall ghosts, nor could she stay imprisoned like this forever.

"I have been looking tirelessly," Leena gritted out.

"Yet without any results to show for it."

"You have given me startlingly little to go on."

"I have given you *enough.*" He held out his gloved hands in a faintly contemptuous manner. "Have you been enjoying my company so much that you are loath to break the contract? Perhaps you require some motivation?"

Leena stiffened. "I am motivated well enough, thank you."

"Clearly, it has had little effect on you." He reached for the bell on his desk to alert whichever bruiser was outside to bring in the next confessor, but paused before ringing it. "By the by," he said in the same moderate tone, "your brother. Does he know you work for me?"

Leena stilled.

Suddenly, all her subtle acts of defiance felt at best fruitless, and at worst sinister. Mr. St. Silas knew exactly what Rami meant to her, how she would turn the earth upside down to protect him; she herself had delivered that information to him.

Any trivial secret can lead to someone's ruin.

Rami would find out soon enough that the excuse she'd given him for her absence was a lie. But what would he do when he learned about her contract?

Horror flashed through her mind as she thought of the real possibilities of Rami either coming here seeking retribution against the Saint of Silence, or joining the Black Coats to gain a semblance of power in an attempt to free her. Both possibilities ended in agony.

Leena *should've* told Rami the truth rather than lying to him; it would have been better coming cushioned from her own lips than if he found out on his own.

Leena tightened her hands into fists. She would need to see Rami very soon, even if it meant she crept out of this dreadful prison at night to do so.

She saw that Mr. St. Silas was watching her, a speculative look in his eyes. "Do not try it," he warned softly.

Leena tilted her head in forceful submission before he could see her deliberation. "Yes, sir," she whispered. Even though she did not look at him, she knew he had heard.

A man walked in, Morish, with a low-slung cap over his tawny hair. He bowed deeply to Mr. St. Silas, and the sentiment was returned with only a slight incline of the Saint's head. The coat the man wore was of the darkest fabric—a Black Coat. A twine of rope was attached to his lapel, reminding Leena of the girl handing out pamphlets in the market. Four phantoms followed him: three boys and a girl, each carrying bullet holes in their skin.

The influence of the Rebels had begun to swell. Leena, along with just about every person in the country, was well aware of the brewing discontent with the ruling class and its indifferent king.

The latest information Leena had managed to learn through one of the Saint's scullery maids was that the rural villages outside the capital, which were most affected by the heavy taxes and food shortages, were beginning to organize tentative riots against their wealthy landlords.

Even the most violent of the Black Coats had started to show real interest in joining the rebellion, or so claimed more than a few constables who had come in, not to confess but to report news to Mr. St. Silas. Often Mr. St. Silas dismissed her for these reports, but Leena had still managed to catch snippets of their conversations.

"It's cold in here," the Black Coat now said, his breath coming out foggy. It made sense that he felt the chill when four phantoms flanked him so closely. Leena could sense their wrath toward the living man like ice forming on her skin.

Leena kept her head low this time and wordlessly wrote a note detailing the odd array of ghosts that followed the Black Coat. She slid it over, and Mr. St. Silas barely glanced at it before turning to the man.

As always, the Saint breezed through the waiver he gave to all customers before falling into bored silence.

Leena did not interrupt this time.

But that morning she had doused her hair with droplets of lavender water in an attempt to chase away the claustrophobia of the Saint's confession room. To Leena, it felt like the equivalent of attempting to grow flowers in the cracks between stones.

The Black Coat rubbed his hands together for warmth, his bristled cheeks red with the chill. After a long, tense moment, the confession came like thread unwinding from a spool. "A few nights ago, there was a secret meeting held for the Rebels in an old warehouse in Ridgeways. It was discovered by free-patrolling soldiers, who did not hesitate to take aim. A few died, but most were taken to Newtorn Prison for treason." The chair groaned as he shifted in his seat. "I was supposed to be standing guard, but I took a few puffs of Tar that night to settle my nerves." He rubbed his red-rimmed eyes with the pads of his thumbs. "I fell asleep at my post."

There was something very wrong.

Leena watched as the ghosts that surrounded him became frenzied, the decayed tendons of their hands outstretched toward the Black Coat to hurt him, but their touch was like water. Leena feared that they might turn and direct their anger at her—the only one whose body seemed to respond to ghostly attacks—and she hunched lower. Her hand snaked to her pocket to hold her copper coins, feeling only marginally comforted by the metal in her damp palm.

Mr. St. Silas did not miss her shrinking movement and raised his brows coolly at her. His expression shifted slightly when he realized that she was not deliberately trying to interrupt his session, but rather had reacted involuntarily. His lips curved upward, and she remembered what he'd said once: *Everything affects you.* Leena detested that her own unchecked response had proved, once again, that his sharp analysis of her was correct.

Shakily, she wrote the new information of the ghosts' actions and handed it to Mr. St. Silas, who read it quickly.

He turned back to the Black Coat, now with a new acidic interest.

"Indeed?" he asked softly. Leena had seen the way the Saint rooted out liars. His technique was as precise as a surgeon palpating for tender spots, but instead of repairing the weakness, he only pressed more firmly. "Now, did you lead the soldiers to the meeting house yourself when you betrayed your rebel comrades, or did you merely pretend to be asleep somewhere and let the soldiers wander in by themselves?"

Leena whipped her head round to look at him.

The ghosts likewise reacted to Mr. St. Silas's statement, halting their movements as if they had been called. Leena felt the room's temperature drop a degree, but it went unnoticed by the two men.

The Black Coat's eyes widened. Shock had rendered his words nearly unintelligible. "How could . . . You couldn't have . . . but—"

He rose up suddenly, his face now markedly paler.

“Sit down,” the Saint ordered idly. “I have not finished.”

Slowly, the Black Coat sat.

The ensuing silence now carried its own claws, and Leena saw the way it ripped into the man, leaving him in tatters. He shuddered beneath its battery, slumping with his head in his hands. “The King’s soldiers paid well.”

Leena’s eyes flickered to the phantoms. By the Saints, they were young. One still carried the gangliness of childhood. She couldn’t look away, staring unblinkingly at those smooth faces that would never fold and wrinkle with age, the tragedy of it all a sudden burden.

She heard Mr. St. Silas’s fingers tapping loudly on the oak desk, wrenching her out of her near trance.

Mr. St. Silas looked as if he were about to say something to her, but he refrained at the last second. Instead, he turned to write the Black Coat’s secret in the ledger.

Instantaneously, the transformation was visible. Leena watched as it drained the Black Coat entirely of his color, his broad face contorting into a pain that was both coarse and devastating. Once more, he looked as if he’d been struck repeatedly, although no one had touched him. As he stumbled forward toward the Saint, taking the payment slip with trembling fingers, he looked as though he had one foot in the grave already.

Once the door shut behind the Black Coat and his phantoms, Leena turned to Mr. St. Silas, no longer able to contain her searing need to know. “What are you doing to cause such agony to these confessors?”

Mr. St. Silas barely lifted his head from his accounts. “Nothing they have not agreed to.”

Leena remembered how desperate she had been when she’d knocked on the Saint’s door, how she would have agreed to nearly anything if it had meant safeguarding her brother’s life. Although Mr. St. Silas had never written her secret in those cursed ledgers, Leena knew she would’ve had no choice but to bear it if he had.

Not only was the Saint taking advantage of the most desperate of souls, Leena was now *aiding* him.

Sometimes during the few weeks she had been in his employ, to make herself feel better, she had told herself that it was charity—that the Saint was giving money to those who needed it in exchange for a single secret. Except, it wasn't, not really—not when the price to be paid was the confessor's humiliation, their total degradation.

"How do you profit from this?" Leena whispered again, unable to think past all the terror she had witnessed him evoke, over and over. It all felt pointless. All these phantoms, the young and the old, did not gain any justice leaving the confession room. She hated to admit to herself that a small part of her had hoped that she could at least find *that* for them. "I have never seen even a single coin pass into your hands."

Finally, Mr. St. Silas put down his pen and turned toward her with irritation. "I wonder, Miss Al-Sayer, what must I do to gain some silence? Should I, do you think, wear gauze over my mouth?"

"No, sir." This time it was Leena who stood first, giving a stiff curtsey, barely restraining the mumbled, "For that would indeed deprive me of your charm."

She heard his chair scraping behind her.

"Prepare yourself; this afternoon we are visiting the boarding school that Lord Avon attended."

Leena could not dismiss the perpetual fear that Lord Avon had long since passed on with no way to call him back, thus entrapping her in this contract forever. She shook her head, as if that would be enough to dispel her anxious thoughts. There was still Weavingshaw, she told herself. Surely more visceral clues as to Lord Avon's whereabouts would make themselves known there.

Yet, after this, Leena began to have a recurring dream that it was she, and not the Saint of Silence, who had gauze wrapped chokingly over her mouth.

9

The Return of the Confessor

Leena lay on her bed fully dressed, the visit to Hardwick's Boarding School yet another useless and tiring endeavor. She'd developed a throbbing headache from how hard she'd squinted at every phantom (and the old school was riddled with them!), and also studying every portrait, every room, every scholarly statue, desperate for *any* sign of Lord Avon's ghost.

When that had proved to be fruitless, Leena had returned to her own chamber and tried to call forth Lord Avon's phantom the moment she heard the clang of cathedral bells chime midnight. Perhaps within the hours of noon or midnight—bewitching hours, where the cloak between the living and the dead was at its thinnest—Lord Avon might come. She had never tried this before, but perhaps . . .

But nothing stirred at Leena's summons. A disappointing, frustrating *nothing.*

Leena tried to cast these feelings aside, as she needed to focus on her next task of this never-ending night—to find a way to see Rami.

As the clock struck one, Leena stood up, brushing down her maroon skirts. She opened her bedroom door and stood listening for a moment, her heartbeat thumping, before taking her first steps out into the hall once she was sure that it was empty.

She crept down the stairs slowly, her blood freezing every time a floorboard creaked, the sound echoing tellingly throughout the still house.

As she descended, she could see light slitting from below the closed door of one of the rooms that usually remained locked during daylight hours. Just before her foot reached the landing, a sudden harsh thump from behind the door sent her jumping. Her new heeled boots lost contact with the step and she fell back with a loud *humph.*

The door suddenly opened then closed firmly again, and when Leena dared to look up, Mr. St. Silas was leaning against the frame, silently watching her attempts to scramble up.

"Miss Al-Sayer." Mr. St. Silas gave her one of his short, graceful bows. Although his voice held no anger, his sharp eyes bored into her like a hook. "I see that you, too, are in the habit of enjoying midnight . . . *activities.*"

Another shattering crash from behind the door caused Leena to startle again in spite of her best efforts. Worse, the thumping was followed by a choked male scream.

He noticed her alarmed eyes pivot toward the room, and a slow, caustic smile spread across his face.

"May I inquire as to what caught your interest at this time of night?" Although his tone remained conversational, there was no mistaking the hint of menace.

"It is my own time; I am free to come and go as I please," Leena replied, sounding more steady than she felt—especially as the guttural sounds continued. "Guest of yours?" she asked, trying to match his tone, but the clenched hand on the banister gave her away.

"A confessor," he corrected mildly. "A confessor who lied to me."

The door swung open again. Leena instinctively took a step back into the safety of the darkness as Mr. St. Silas moved aside to allow whoever was in the room to exit.

Two men emerged, one battered, gouged, and butchered, with an X slicing his salmon-pink lips and blood dripping from his mangled mouth. The other was dragging the battered man. Leena gasped silently when she saw that the unharmed man wore the uniform of a high-ranking King's soldier.

"Aye, these confessors never learn, do they, Mr. St. Silas? Thought he could run," the soldier said, a chuckle in his voice. "He won't make the same mistake next time."

"My deepest gratitude," the Saint murmured. "If you can so kindly deposit him away from the shop, I'll have Arthur bring you a token of my appreciation in the morning."

The soldier laughed again over the battered man's moans. "Always generous, sir."

Leena remained still even after the soldier had pulled the man out the front door, leaving blood splatters on the hardwood.

After they left, a deep silence hovered over them. Leena's voice finally came thready in the dark. "If you hold power over the men of the law, then—" Her mouth dried.

Mr. St. Silas's expression didn't change. She knew that he had informants within the constabulary, the judges, and even the House of Commons, but the mere fact that some of the most powerful men in Golborne were *answering* to him in the middle of the night seemed beneath his notice.

"Where were you going?" His tone remained pleasant.

Leena descended the last steps slowly. Several scenarios played out in her mind. She could tell him the truth, but she was desperate to try to keep Rami's name out of her plans as much as she could.

She decided to tread the line between the truth and a lie. "I won't be gone long, sir. A mere hour or two, certainly back in time for tomorrow's appointments."

As she'd expected, his brows rose.

She pretended to look down, lashes covering her eyes in an expression she hoped looked bashful, even if her shaking hands remained tightly folded behind her. The house still swallowed the echoes of the man's screams, and she was half worried he had died along the way and stood somewhere waiting for her. She longed to reach for the copper coins nestled in her pocket.

Mr. St. Silas didn't prompt her, merely waited.

"There is a . . . a special friend of mine who lives near this district. I do not often get a chance to see him, although he made an effort to visit when I lived back home. Unfortunately, we haven't seen each other since my . . . employment with you began." She kept her gaze pinned steadily on the banister, her cheeks burning, a trace of defiance in her voice. She knew her eyes would reveal her—and her painful lack of experience in *that* regard.

A moment's stilted pause.

"Look at me." The command was a knife's edge, lingering on the borders of something cutting.

She didn't obey.

She heard his swift step, followed by a firm hand under her chin. He tilted her gaze up. The glint in his eyes was unmistakable, as was the not-smile touching his lips. "If you ever lie to me again, Leena, I will personally see to it that your tongue will remember the value of truth."

Her spine stiffened.

She pushed his hand aside in a hard swipe before she could curtail herself.

"I did not give you leave to call me by my given name," she seethed. "And how are you so certain that I am lying, sir?"

"All right, *Miss Al-Sayer.*" His tone didn't change. "It is late for games, but I'll play. Nothing is more apparent than the fact that you obviously live a hermetic and isolated life. I am left in no doubt that your *special friend* is none other than your tedious brother. Which is"—he waved a dismissive hand—"quite sad, even for you."

He was right.

Leena's former school friends were all engaged—most were even now happily married—but her own life had stalled instantaneously when ghosts began to seek her out. For how could she find any romance when women with gouged eyes or men with slit necks trailed her day and night? Once or twice, the neighborhood boys had tried to court her, and it had ended in nothing short of disaster.

Still, she had never supposed that her lack of any romantic experience was so evident.

Mr. St. Silas did not give her a moment to regain her bearings before continuing. "You may visit your . . . er . . . *special friend* in a fortnight's time, in the *morning*, when there is less chance your throat will be slit a hundred different ways just for venturing out. With Lord Avon yet to be found, I cannot yet risk your inconvenient demise." The dismissal as he turned to go was accompanied by a prolonged bow, a deliberate play at formality. "I will expect you back by noon on that day. I bid you goodnight, Miss Al-Sayer."

Leena did as she was told, taking the steps back into her chamber with growing desperation.

His *permission* tasted like ashes in her mouth.

A knock sounded on the door of the confession room.

It was Arthur, the bruiser who stood over the crowds most mornings. He grinned at Leena, bowing low to her as if she were a lady. "Boss, there's a man who was asking for you. Says he has a score to settle over something that happened last week with a friend of his."

Last week? Leena thought. Was that the man whom Mr. St. Silas had marked with the X past midnight?

Displeasure curled Mr. St. Silas's lips. "Then go deal with it."

Arthur rolled his shoulders. "I did, boss—*too well.* He is on the steps of the shop, and it has got some of the ladies agitated and wailing. Don't know if he's still breathing."

St. Silas stood up, taking his coat and leading the way out of the room, his steps firm on the wooden floor. "This whole situation has become a headache . . ." She could hear his voice drifting farther and farther away as he barked out instructions.

Leena dropped her paper, wasting no time in jumping from her chair, knowing that this might be her only chance to discover how St. Silas was eliciting so much pain from his customers. She was certain that it was those black ledgers that caused such dreadful changes in his confessors.

She *had* to know why, with certain customers, Mr. St. Silas didn't document anything at all—like the young mother, a wisp of a girl, barely older than Leena, who'd come in that morning to confess that she could not bond with her baby. Her sobs of shame had broken Leena's heart. The ledger had stayed closed, and the young mother looked relieved as she left the room, as if this was an act of release rather than reckoning, holding a slip in her hand with the Saint's compensation. Although Leena had tried to glance at the paper, she did not catch the number he had written.

Leena reached for the black book.

The moment her finger grazed the pliant leather, she understood why he guarded it so obsessively.

It was a shockwave. Worse—it was like the hacking of an ax, cleaving skin from bone. Every bad thought she'd ever had, every shred of shame, every morsel of grief concentrated in her sternum and burned her from the inside out. She reared back, and her breath came out in gasps. Tears sprang to her eyes.

She stumbled as far into the corner of the room as she could, upturning her chair in the process, sliding onto the floor. She scratched her own skin trying to rip that feeling *out* of her body. It was a *death.* And she'd only touched the cover momentarily.

She couldn't even bear to open the book.

Slowly, the feeling dissipated, leaving behind only its essence like a festering rot. Tears continued to stream down her face, and she could not stop them. What *was* that? Those ledgers were as preternatural as her ghosts. Rapid, paranoid thoughts filtered through her mind, and she wondered if the Saint was cursing his customers.

What is he gaining from this?

She looked up suddenly to see Mr. St. Silas standing in the doorway, watching her. Wordlessly, he strolled toward his chair. Ignoring her quivering form, he took off his coat and sat behind his desk once more.

"I wondered how long it would take until your curiosity got the better of you." His tone was light, and his gaze fell on the ledger that was now out of place and tilting precariously on the edge of the desk. "Try as you may, these ledgers will never give away their secrets."

What Leena had previously eschewed as superstition now seemed very real.

"These are no ordinary books. Have you cursed them somehow to inflict such evil?" She knew she had severely overstepped her place, but it was too late to go back now. She had to know.

The look he gave her was chilling. "Needless to say, Miss Al-Sayer, you have failed my test."

"*Test*?"

He leaned back on his chair, regarding her detachedly. "I wanted to see what you would do if I left you alone with the ledgers after I explicitly forbade you from touching them."

Leena reared up; feelings of rage and powerlessness spat and crackled across her skin. At this moment, she hated him more than words could say. "Is it not enough that you have trapped me here? You are compelled to experiment on me as well?"

"It would have been an unsuccessful experiment, madam, if you hadn't participated so readily," he pointed out mildly. "Do not deny you have spent weeks watching me in the hopes you will find some sort of weakness that you can exploit."

Leena's cheeks flushed, but she met his eyes steadily. "I do not deny it."

Her honesty seemed to catch his attention. He leaned forward on the chair. "And what have you learned?"

Nothing.

Nothing of use. She'd learned he somehow cursed his customers, but she knew that even this knowledge would not sway his confessors. People would still line up to reveal their secrets for the promise of coin—and he did pay well.

Leena still had not found any explanation for why he extracted the most hideous of emotions, or what he gained from it. Every new tidbit of knowledge she gained about the Saint of Silence only served to reveal the magnitude of his power—and her ignorance.

He read the expression on her face. "Disappointing," he said, drumming his fingers on the desk. "Shall I tell you what I've learned about *you*?"

"I do not care to know."

He continued despite her objection. "Think of it as an employment review." This was one of the few times she'd seen Mr. St. Silas reveal more than he intended. "You have been a great disappointment." His eyes were heavy-lidded with displeasure, and his fingers continued to tap with obvious impatience. "Within this period I've spent with you, you have proven yourself to be insubordinate, without discipline, obstinate, an immeasurable nuisance—"

Leena's teeth gritted.

"—and full of temper." Without waiting for a response, he continued, "I have given you *multiple* chances, Miss Al-Sayer—more than I have given anyone else in recent memory. My patience wears exceedingly thin."

"*Your* patience wears thin?" she cried incredulously. Every day, Leena battled feelings of panic and dread while sitting in those consultations, while searching for Lord Avon, while returning to her chamber alone and more desperate to free herself by the minute. All these emotions rose to the surface now, and she could not stop the words tearing from her tongue. "Oh, how I *loathe* you."

There was a moment of loaded silence, his eyes glacial as they bored into her, before he continued silkily, "How unoriginal, Miss Al-Sayer, even coming from your pretty mouth. If you insist on remaining useless, at the very least be more interesting."

The door slammed open just as Leena was about to reply.

A man entered.

In her fury, it took her a moment to recognize him as the same Black Coat who had confessed to betraying the rebels. He had changed drastically within the fortnight since she'd seen him last, his cheeks scratched raw by his own nails, eyes hollowed, mouth flaky and jagged like a scar. He did not sit in the wooden chair again. The same ghosts followed him—a silent death march.

She instinctively crouched lower upon seeing him again.

Mr. St. Silas, his attention drawn away from her, rose slowly to a standing position.

The man swallowed. "I-I keep seeing things after my confession—"

"I warned you, did I not?" Mr. St. Silas interrupted cuttingly. "Must I be blamed for your decision to seek me?"

The man trembled, his movements jerky and untethered, as he pointed a pistol at the Saint.

Leena's heart slammed against her rib cage.

"Demons visit me in my mind. You've cursed me." He held a necklace depicting the Saint of Healing—the idol of a woman holding a heart—in a fierce grip, while his other hand jabbed the pistol right at Mr. St. Silas's own chest. "You're the demon, *Saint.* You lure us in, you feed on us." Then, as if he noticed Leena's presence for the first time, he swerved the gun to point at her, his eyes wide. *"Don't look at me!"*

Leena was suspended, unable to move or drop her gaze. The barrel of the pistol seemed to be pinning her in place as the man took a step toward her. She was so focused on the weapon that she did not notice Mr. St. Silas's quick, lethal movements as he reached the man in a single step. The knife in his hands was a flash as it angled toward the Black Coat's neck, slitting his throat without a moment's hesitation.

Leena was still staring at the pistol as hot liquid from the man's severed artery splashed across the room, a few droplets hitting her cheek.

It all happened within seconds.

St. Silas allowed the man's body to crumple. The glittering red knife was still between his fingers. The blade had also caught the Saint of Healing necklace, and it swung back and forth on its string. She wondered if that was the same knife St. Silas used to slice the mouths of confessors who lied to him.

"Unfortunate business," St. Silas said evenly, eyes flickering toward his coat which was left hanging on the arm of his chair. Distantly, she could see the gleam of a pistol poking out of the pocket.

Standing there, a dead man by his bloodied boots, the ruined icon necklace hanging from the tip of his weapon, a cursed ledger lying on the desk, St. Silas looked every inch the demon he'd been accused of being. Leena could not avert her gaze, her breath coming hard and uneven.

He caught her stare and lowered the knife by inches. "What is that expression in your eyes?"

It was the shock that loosened her tongue. "For a moment, you looked like one of those demons depicted on the stained-glass windows of old cathedrals."

Leena had seen them in the churches, too. The Morish demons did not look like the monsters or jinns depicted in Algaraan tales, with powerful arms and unblinking eyes. Rather, they looked human—or a form of human, allowing them to walk the earth undetected, leaving behind minds putrefied with nightmares. She knew why the Black Coat had carried the idol of the Saint meant to ward away these unholy beings.

Why St. Silas should find that amusing, she did not know. "Can you stand on your own?"

Leena didn't hear his question. Her shaking fingers touched her own cheeks, pulling back to see the man's blood on her fingertips. "Is he . . . Is he dead?"

It was an utterly foolish question, and she knew it.

The man did not stir. His corpse was being drained of blood even as they spoke, the acrid smell pooling in the room and overpowering the lavender she'd put into her hair that morning.

St. Silas did not bother answering. He strode toward her, holding out his hand.

Leena did not take it.

10

The Festival of Demons

The cooling, longer nights and the subtle hint of frost in the air always welcomed the Festival of Demons.

On the proceeding days, Leena watched as lights lit up the winding streets, stretching from here to New Algaraa District, then all the way to the bricked factories in Ridgeways. She could smell the hints of kerosene mixed with the oils from frying food that permeated the streets, and the resulting smoke caused a thin mist to weave between the roads. Every block would already be teeming with caravans selling services and wares: doughnuts fried to golden perfection, fortune-tellers decked in scarves, palm-readers, fire-eaters and jugglers, perfumers who swore to be able to bottle desire.

Night had not yet fallen, but she could see the revelers making their way down to the festival through her bedroom window. They dressed in masks to hide their identities, ranging from grotesque depictions of demons with snarling faces to coquettish ones with exaggerated red lips and crimson cheeks. She saw a man wearing the long flowing garb of the Saints as he tried to hail a hackney, an idol swinging from a chain on his chest, reminding her with a shudder of the Black Coat whose throat had been slit by St. Silas. She knew that this man, unlike the rest of the revelers, would not join the festivities, instead spending the night in prayer in one of the cathedrals.

Every year Leena wondered how this once-holy festival—a way for the Mors to celebrate the Saints' triumphant massacre of the demons—had turned into an excuse to get roaring drunk and pursue every form of debauchery known to man. She knew the history—back when Golborne was a tiny settlement that herded sheep, any misfortune that had befallen it was blamed on the demons. *A child dying young from pox? A mind turned with madness? Lustful thoughts?* All demon-cursed.

Then the Saints cropped up, offering blessings, curing the ill, and—most important—banishing the demons. Nowadays, Leena thought wryly, instead of blaming demons for their misfortunes, people often looked toward the aristos.

A note delivered by Mrs. Van told Leena that the Saint required her presence for the festivities. It had been a week since the Black Coat's death, and Leena would be seeing Rami tomorrow. She could bear a night with the Saint for that.

The housekeeper had laid out her garments—a stiff high-collared dress in a shade of emerald green with a simple half mask, in the form of a skull, that revealed her mouth.

One of Leena's earliest childhood memories was attending the festival with Baba and Rami. Algaraans often wore their traditional dress—the only time it was not frowned upon by Morish society—and Leena usually wore a long, loose kaftan with a delicately embroidered belt. When Mrs. Van left, rather than reach for the petticoats, garters, and whalebone corset, Leena found the white kaftan her father had bought for her birthday years ago.

Wearing the dress felt like home—a return to another life, to another Leena with far less worries. She tied the golden-flossed belt around her waist, then loosened her long curls until they fell down her back. She observed the effects in the mirror, unsure whether Sweeper's Cough had left any lasting traces on her face.

Her eyes, she thought, would always remain the same: brown like her mother's, large like her father's, speaking of other lands, like her blood. The rest of her—the cheekbones that rose high above her lips, the mouth that had a tendency to quicken into a smile as much as a frown—hadn't altered much. She wanted—Leena could not suppress the thought quickly enough—to look more carefree. And yet, even in the mirror, she looked burdened.

She pinched her cheeks before setting the mask carefully over her face.

Leena and St. Silas stepped out of the carriage in New Algaraa District.

Night had descended and the revelers were in full swing. Leena stood for a moment taking in the scene before her. Children weaved through the throng holding ribbons with cutouts of paper demons. A young man started playing a fiddle, the music filling the crowd with an excited buzz. The juxtaposition of bright colors coupled with the demonic disguises gave the festival an enchanted aura.

Ahead of her, a woman wearing a bone-white mask began dancing to the music, and a man in a smiling demon disguise joined her. Leena paused to watch for a moment, until the dance became wild and sensuous. Then she turned away quickly, feeling embarrassed without knowing why.

She focused on following her employer, his decisive gait cutting through the crowded street with ease. Like her, he didn't wear a demon disguise but a mask with lupine eyes that left the contours of his sharp jaw exposed. He hadn't shared his purpose in attending the festival with Leena, despite her questions in the carriage. Nor had he chided her for her change of outfit.

He led her away from the revelers, toward a cathedral that stood frowning over the festivities. It had been left abandoned for years, the structure weak, the roof caving in. In the quiet courtyard, the noise had dimmed to a low hum, the stone walls and the sullen statues of the Saints guarding them from view.

A man stood beside a bronze sculpture of the Saint of Silence.

Another Black Coat.

He didn't wear a mask. His watchful eyes were pinched over his bulbous nose; his frame was large, the muscles stretching the fabric of his jacket. He hadn't noticed them yet, although he kept turning to peer over his shoulder uneasily.

St. Silas's hand on her elbow stopped her by the iron gates just before they entered the courtyard. "That is Basil Richards. Do you see a ghost by him?"

By now, she knew there was no point questioning St. Silas's motives.

Leena trained her eyes on the courtyard. Yes, there was a flickering of movement directly behind the Black Coat: a gaunt man dressed in the striped uniform of the incarcerated.

Leena nodded at the Saint and reached for her copper coins as the phantom prisoner eased away from the Black Coat and drifted toward her, but she didn't strike them together yet.

As the phantom approached, she could see he was clearly Algaraan, his brown skin no fainter after death. When he turned around, she noticed a knife buried deep in his spine. Leena tried as best she could to describe him to St. Silas. "There are initials on the knife inserted into his back—*B.R*?"

"Basil Richards keeps busy, I see," St. Silas murmured, his smile thin, eyes alert on the nothingness beside her. "Good." He turned back to Leena. "Anything else?"

"There's also inking on the prisoner's wrist." Leena paused, assessing the phantom slowly. The ghost watched her with searching eyes. "No, not inking. A brand—" Her breath hitched when she saw the seven brutal letters burned into his skin. "*The Wake,*" she whispered.

St. Silas's head tilted toward her as if in confirmation. "Ah."

He stepped toward the entrance, but Leena moved to stand in his way. Her pulse thrummed in her neck. Waves of images flashed through her mind—of Mama pleading with Leena to save her father from the Wake.

St. Silas took in her defiant eyes, the harsh tilt to her chin. "You want to question Basil about the Wake?"

Leena gave a firm nod.

He seemed to consider this, then shrugged as if it didn't matter to him one way or the other. "You may do whatever you please *after* my business is concluded."

Leena stepped out of the way.

They walked into the courtyard, leaving the phantom behind them, the echo of their steps lost in the distant noise of the festival.

"Basil." St. Silas nodded at the man. His tone was pleasant, but it drew a shiver out of Leena. "You said it was urgent. What do you have to report?"

Basil bowed jerkily, his eyes flickering to Leena briefly. Then he took out a match, busying himself with lighting a cigarette. Leena noticed that his bulky fingers trembled.

"You've not been followed, sir?" There was a trace of apprehension in the large man's voice.

"I got rid of my shadow a fortnight ago," was St. Silas's laconic reply. Leena could not forget the beaten man in the Saint's study, and she wondered if that was the *shadow* he was referring to. "The only news I care to hear from you is whether your boss received my message."

Basil heaved a sigh. "Two Black Coats dead within the span of a few weeks. That's a lot even for you, sir."

"In which case"—St. Silas smiled—"Orley should not have sent his man to spy on me, posing as a confessor. I will not ask again. What do you have to report?"

Basil's cigarette drew shadows on his face. "Mr. Orley does not want a war. The two men you, er, disposed of . . . had also been taking bribes from an Algaraan gang in exchange for Black Coat information about Tar shipments. Overall, Mr. Orley's pleased by the outcome and sees no need for retaliation."

A dangerous frown twisted St. Silas's face. "It matters little to me what Orley's motives were for ridding himself of his two spies. If your boss decides to send anyone else to attempt to collect information on me, I would not hesitate to bury a hundred Black Coats, and retaliation be damned."

Basil nodded wearily. "Aye, sir. I think the boss has received your message very clearly."

St. Silas didn't immediately respond, watching Basil with a wolfish intensity, light glinting off his mask. "As matters stand, Orley should be more worried about spies in his *own* circle."

Basil tensed, and the hand holding the cigarette shook. "Mr. St. Silas, you know Mr. Orley would slit my throat in an instant if he knew I was sending reports to you—"

"Not *just* me, though, is it, Basil?" St. Silas's laugh was cutting. "Certainly being an agent for *three* organizations simultaneously must have vast rewards for you—and in truth," he continued, as smooth as the pistol that appeared suddenly between his fingers, "I cannot fault you for trying to sell information about *both* myself and your boss to a higher bidder."

Basil dropped his cigarette.

"Come, Basil, confess. You have also been spying for the Wake. The question I have for you is what it was you chose to divulge about *me*."

Basil eyed the gun fearfully. "I would never—"

The pistol clicked. "I do not take kindly to liars, Basil. Tread carefully."

Basil took a wary step back. "I have not—"

"I know many things about you," St. Silas interrupted easily. "For instance, in addition to spying, you also trade prisoners for the Wake—and when you are ordered, you execute them."

Basil opened his mouth several times before managing to croak out, "H-how did . . . did you . . . You couldn't have known . . . How . . . ?" He continued pleadingly, "Only a few Algaraans—criminals who would've got the rope anyway."

Leena's heart raged. To Basil, these prisoners—*a few Algaraans*—were not human enough to deserve a proper trial or a fair outcome, but a currency to line his pockets with. Who knew why the Wake wanted these poor men dead or why they traded the living ones, but it was a certainty that people like Basil Richards profited hugely from this business.

"Who runs the Wake?" Leena cut in, her breaths heaving painfully from her chest.

Basil eyed her once more with distaste, and for a moment she was sure he was not going to respond. She wanted to throttle the information out of him.

"Answer her," St. Silas commanded.

Basil's attention focused once more on St. Silas's gun. The words were twisted as he spoke. "Ten years ago, it was run by an aristo. But he's dead now—long may he rot."

"What was the aristo's name?" Though Leena had a sinking feeling she already knew.

"Lord Avon. I don't know who runs it now. I am not privy to that information."

Leena felt suddenly lightheaded. What was the connection between Lord Avon, St. Silas, the Wake, and her father? Why had Mama delivered her a warning without any explanation about how Leena should act on it?

She swiveled to look at St. Silas, but she could not read his expression behind the mask.

"Who do they trade the prisoners to?" Leena asked, afraid of the answer already.

"I have also not been privy to that information. I merely follow instructions."

There was a moment of tense silence.

"Any further questions?" St. Silas asked Leena, his exposed mouth upturned at her with a glimmer of interest.

She addressed Basil Richards again. "Do you know if an Ali Al-Sayer is a prisoner who has been traded by the Wake? He is Algaraan, less than middling height with black hair. He cannot speak Morish very well, but he has been sentenced to life imprisonment for attempting to start a union."

"I don't know an Ali Al-Sayer," Basil muttered. "But then, I don't bother to learn their names." An echo of the words of the Warden of Newtorn Prison.

Leena felt an anger so potent it drew stars behind her eyelids. She had just that morning learned an Algaraan word for this sort of anger—the kind that dragged ships of despair behind it: *thalam.*

"Have you now finished?" St. Silas asked her. "Basil and I still have to discuss what he chose to divulge about me to his new friends. Will this be a lengthy conversation, do you think, Basil?" St. Silas didn't acknowledge her stiff nod, nor the shudder that went through Basil's large frame. "Wait for me outside the cathedral. The rest won't be a fit sight for you."

She leveled one last look of disgust at Basil before weaving through the statues and back to the exit. Her palms dampened. She knew exactly what would happen behind her back, and she didn't flinch even when the gunshot sounded after a few long minutes, the noise ringing like another drumbeat of the festival.

11

The Pistol

LEENA RIPPED THE mask from her face the moment she reached the street outside the cathedral, leaning on a tree to catch her breath. Revelers passed her, their laughter and joy a discordant sound in her ears. She felt like a phantom caught in the world of the living.

A tug on her shoulder drew her attention. She looked up to find herself staring into brown eyes the exact same shade as her own.

"Rami!" she cried.

He didn't wear a mask, and it was clear that his health had improved since she'd seen him last. Tall, wiry, with a dimple appearing on his cheek, he had returned to the boy she'd always known. She wasn't supposed to see him until tomorrow and had been counting the days, so this felt like an unexpected blessing.

Except he glowered at her, his brows like slashes on his face.

"Come with me," he growled, tugging her into an empty alleyway. His right sleeve was pinned to his shoulder, and Leena had sudden images of the night Rami lost the arm. Her brother swaying on the threshold—*I lost control of the horse, Leena*—then flashes of the grizzled doctor tutting under his breath as he examined the mangled limb. *Gotta come off.*

Rami had been only fourteen.

Baba had forced Leena outside during the procedure, but she'd hidden beneath Rami's window, unable to bear the thought of her younger brother alone with the surgeon's steel. She must've soaked in all Rami's screams that day, for somewhere in the empty chambers of her body they still reverberated.

Leena shrugged away from Rami's grip, glancing over her shoulder for St. Silas. He had still not returned.

"What—" she began, but Rami interrupted her with a quick wave of his hand.

"You lied to me," he ground out. Rami had been running with the Black Coats ever since Baba had been taken away, and he'd adopted their quick, sarcastic speech. He even wore his hair like them, slightly long at the back, tied with a leather string. "You said you had found employment as a nanny. I had to learn from a damned Black Coat that my sister is now working for the most notorious man in Golborne."

Leena urgently glanced over her shoulder again. "I understand your anger, but I'll see you tomorrow and explain everything."

Rami jammed his hand into his hair. "I have a fight for the Black Coats tomorrow. You will explain everything *now.*"

"No, Rami, I can't. I will try to come find you the day after tomorrow, in the morning." Leena wasn't sure if St. Silas would accept the change in date, but pushed on despite her worries. "Wait for me until then."

"I won't go anywhere without you," he growled. "Whatever the Saint is blackmailing you with doesn't matter. We can outrun him."

Leena laughed mirthlessly, memories of all the men St. Silas had butchered roaring in her mind. "I am indentured to him, Rami. We *cannot* outrun him, and we cannot fight him. This is my life now."

St. Silas's smooth voice cut through the alleyway. "Ah, this must be your *special friend.*"

Leena whipped back to look at St. Silas; he was no longer wearing his mask. She noticed the flecks of Basil's blood staining his shoes.

Rami—always impulsive—stepped in front of her and unsheathed the sword he carried by his hip in one fluid motion. Leena silently cursed his stupidity. Of course he would reach for his sword as his first line of action.

Leena's gaze swung back to St. Silas, remembering the pistol in his pocket. Her heart thundered. A blinding image flashed through her mind of Rami's torn body bleeding life onto the cobbled street.

Before she could rethink her actions, she stepped between them.

"Leena," Rami warned angrily, "get out of the way. St. Silas must answer for what he has done to you."

"*I* went to *him,*" Leena snapped, barely turning to face her brother. "For the medication that saved *both* our lives."

Rami's eyes narrowed, his grip on the hilt white-knuckled. "It doesn't matter."

St. Silas's voice was a leveled taunt. "The infamous Rami Al-Sayer. I must thank you for almost dying. Otherwise, your sister would not have made her way to me."

Rami swore at St. Silas, profound and low. The Saint's expression didn't change. "Make no mistake, I will run you through, Saint."

Leena's senses were jarred by how quickly the pistol appeared in St. Silas's hand, aimed at her brother's heart.

"No! Mr. St. Silas—" She whipped her head around to face her brother furiously. "Rami! Do not be a fool. Go home—"

"*No,*" Rami grated out, eyes blazing with hatred.

"If you do not leave now, it will be *me* who is punished," Leena hissed through her teeth, searching for anything to make Rami understand and *go.* She saw hesitation flicker across her brother's face, then he let loose another low curse. His eyes darted between Leena and St. Silas in suspicious hostility.

Finally, Rami took a step back, sword still in hand but not held at the ready. "I'll be expecting you the day after tomorrow, Leena."

He finally sheathed his sword and Leena let out a long breath. "Or I'll come back for you myself and damn the consequences."

"Fine. Just go," she urged again.

St. Silas didn't lower his gun until her brother was no longer visible among the crowd. Leena stood alone with him in the alleyway, breathing as if she'd finished a race.

Still, St. Silas's gaze didn't waver from her brother's now departed back, a cold promise in his eyes. "If he attempts to break our contract again, mark my words, Miss Al-Sayer—brother or not, you will be left as the last of your line."

Leena, who felt more helpless than ever—trapped within St. Silas's palms, forced to act as his ghost-seer when all she wanted to do was to get rid of this bloody curse—bit her tongue to keep silent. She tasted blood from how forcefully she wanted to scream at him.

St. Silas didn't wait for her response. He slid his gun back into the pocket of his coat, hand already reaching for his timepiece . . . and in that moment, Leena saw the gun gleam, its gray edges reflecting bluntly in the flickering lights.

Without thinking—without even daring to *breathe*—she lurched toward him in one swift motion and pulled the gun out of his pocket, forcing it into his abdomen.

Neither moved.

Leena's harsh breathing sounded wild in her ears.

She felt St. Silas's muscles stiffen beneath her touch even as his face remained impassive.

"Have I *now* found your weakness?" Leena's hand spasmed over the cool metal, but her voice still held the echoes of anger that she had carried since touching the ledger.

His laugh was quiet. "I'm afraid not, but a good try." Then his voice dropped to a whisper, as if meant for the two of them alone. "Will you shoot me?"

He continued to stare down at her, his pupils dilating.

"Mark my words, I can and I will." Leena sounded far more steady than her racing heart, a part of her aghast that his reaction was so staid. Her finger twitched on the trigger. *Could she do it?* She'd never held a gun nor threatened anyone in her entire life. Could she live with the consequences of such violent action? "If I shoot you, think of how many confessors I can save from so much pain and misery."

"No doubt hundreds. *Countless.*" His reply was quick and sure, his gaze not leaving hers.

"As long as you live, you will use me as an object to inflict misery. I will be weaponized."

"You speak facts, madam."

Leena's mouth twisted. Every reason she listed was an unshakable truth, and yet the actions she would have to take to rid the world of such a beast would very likely shatter her.

The avid interest grew in St. Silas's gaze, until it seemed to swallow his eyes whole. He watched the warring expressions play across her face with barely concealed fascination. "You don't have it in you," he challenged softly.

A bead of sweat trailed across Leena's temple despite the chill autumn air.

St. Silas's voice dropped to a seductive burr. His head leaned toward her even as his body remained still. "I admire your bravery, Miss Al-Sayer, and thus far I have been lenient with you, but this has gone far enough. Give me back my pistol. I give you my word I will not punish you for this fruitless act of defiance."

"Does the Saint of Silence ever forgive any threat against him?" Leena's eyes blazed into his, daring him to contradict.

"Then shoot me." His response was low and gravelly.

When he saw that Leena remained still, St. Silas's mouth pulled upward. "You cannot, can you?"

Leena dug the pistol into the hard muscles of his abdomen and was gratified to see his jaw twitch. "Did you know that Lord Avon led the Wake?"

Even if she could not kill St. Silas, Leena would do everything she could to wrestle some secrets from him, to gain a modicum of power. Otherwise she would choke on her own continual helplessness.

A glimmer of amusement flashed through St. Silas's dark eyes. *He was enjoying this.* "Aye, I knew."

Leena had never stood this close to a man before, but she was so caught up in the moment she did not notice that her chest was almost pressed against his save for the gun that she held between them. A passerby would think they were two lovers caught in a secret embrace.

How different that image is from this bitter reality.

Leena threw him the same question that Basil hadn't had an answer to. "Who runs the Wake now?"

St. Silas raised a brow and repeated her own words back to her. "No information comes for free. A secret for a secret."

Leena stared up at him in disbelief. "I have a gun aimed at you."

"Yet I feel certain that I am in no danger of losing my life." His gaze was not soft as it roamed her face. "A secret for a secret."

Leena only had one secret left to trade—that ghosts could possess her body when she slept. And she would *never* give him that power, even if it cost her life.

Leena held the pistol firm a moment longer. She could not shoot St. Silas—not when vitality poured out of him like a flood. Not when he was so very *alive.*

A part of her shivered at the punishment that he would soon deliver, although she knew he would not kill her while Lord Avon's ghost remained unfound; that he had made clear.

No, he would make her merely wish for death.

More than ever, Leena desperately needed her actions tonight to result in a victory, or else she would've brought down the Saint's wrath for nothing.

"Why do you seek Lord Avon?" It was the third time she'd asked this question, each time receiving only vague responses back.

His gaze hardened. "As I've said previously, Avon took something from me." Then, as if it was wrenched from him: "Something that has caused my life to deviate from its original path." A frown etched his mouth. "That is all you will get from me, madam, so I would be careful with your next steps."

Leena was grimly satisfied by this, because it was *she* who had received a confession from St. Silas this time, just as he'd forced so many from others.

Just as she'd begun to withdraw the gun, St. Silas's fingers closed firmly over hers.

"Next time—" His voice was rough as he dragged her hand holding the pistol away from his abdomen and toward his chest, right below his heart. He glanced briefly at their intertwined hands, a harsh furrow to his brows. "If you ever desire to kill someone, not merely deliver a flesh wound, aim here." He pressed more firmly still.

"I assure you, sir, this will be the last time." Leena's lips barely formed the words.

He finally released her, but his eyes remained locked on her as if against his will. Leena stepped back, silently returning the weapon, wondering if her punishment would come immediately.

St. Silas took the pistol wordlessly, pocketing it back in his coat. With a final dark glance at her he turned to go, not waiting for her to follow him as he melted into the crowd, his mask firmly back in place.

What Leena had done that night was no small thing. She, Leena—with no name and of common blood—had held the life of the *Saint of Silence* in her palm. For one brief moment, there had been a shifting of power.

Throughout the night, across the streets that pulsed with revelers, in the carriage that descended farther into the mouth of the city, St. Silas's vivid gaze kept dragging back to her—as if Leena's actions had created a new tether between them.

Leena met his glances steadily even if her heart was heavy with uncertainty. Every time St. Silas's eyes returned to her, they flickered with annoyance— *No,* Leena thought jarringly, *not annoyance,* but with a sort of unwelcome realization, as if he was seeing her for the first time.

As if he was unearthing her.

12

WAR'S END

IT WAS AN old Morish proverb:

Silence before the wolves approach is better than the silence afterward.

The next morning, as Leena waited for St. Silas outside the confession room, she expected his punishment. With a heavy heart, she anticipated it.

None came.

In fact, St. Silas regarded her with only indifferent civility; that odd look he'd given her in the carriage the previous night had completely dissipated from his face by morning. He acted as if Leena holding a gun on him was a commonplace matter, not worth even a mention.

She knew without a doubt that it was a charade.

St. Silas didn't forgive. He tended to his wrath like he tended to all his business—quietly, watchfully, until the perfect moment arose. Then he struck like a predator hidden between the vines.

Leena would hold her breath until then.

St. Silas's hair was wet, the thick strands slightly curling at the edges. He still wore his overcoat, the heavy leather boots flecked with mud, and he held a riding crop in his left hand. A newspaper was tucked beneath his elbow.

He did not waste a moment on polite greetings. "The morning confessions are canceled."

This was unprecedented. She didn't dare ask for a free day, knowing St. Silas would never allow this. *Especially* when tomorrow she was due to see Rami. She did not want to remind him of this, especially when she had changed the date without asking for permission.

At her surprised expression, he continued, "There have been riots in Ridgeways."

"Riots?" she said incredulously.

All the city factories were located in Ridgeways, the ever-present soot blackening the bricks until it left the district looking burned. That was where Leena used to work before entering her contract with St. Silas; she'd spent days there bent over scalding laundry basins.

St. Silas dropped the newspaper into her hands. The front page blared:

COMMANDER YOSIF TAKES THE CAPITAL.
Algaraan Malik in Chains.
The War Is Over.

Leena stared dumbly at it, the words blurring in front of her eyes. The war was over? Just like that? The same war that had seen her family forsaken, thrown to foreign lands, her mother buried in strange soil?

It seemed impossible to Leena that it should end with so little prelude, but the article went on to state that Commander Yosif and his fighters had breached the capital, imprisoned the noble families that had not managed to escape the city, and found the Malik hiding in an oil barrel. A few sentences tagged onto the end announced that Commander Yosif would be giving a speech the following morning to outline his plans for a new government.

"Are congratulations in order, Miss Al-Sayer, or commiserations?" There was no real interest in St. Silas's voice as he watched her with his head tilted, hands in his pockets.

He knew her opinions on the war and had heard her whispered words of encouragement to the rebel captain captured within the depths of Newtorn Prison. He knew that treason lay in her heart, her sentiments staunchly anti-monarch and anti-King, but Leena would not give him any more access to her thoughts than he already possessed. Especially the kind of thoughts that would see her hanging from the gallows.

Stiffly, Leena folded the paper and handed it back to him, although she longed to read it again when she was not so stunned. Most of all, she longed to safeguard it as proof that even though she had been born with war in her veins, it did not always have to be that way. That there was peace in her future, as there was for her homeland. That she *would* have peace.

It took effort to keep her face neutral in front of St. Silas's watchful stare, and the small muscles around her eyes ached from it. She circumvented his question with one of her own. "Why are there riots in Ridgeways?"

"Can you not guess?" St. Silas's brows rose faintly, vaguely indicating the newspaper. "Inspiration is a dangerous thing."

Leena understood perfectly.

Still, she wanted to hear it confirmed from St. Silas's mouth. She wanted to hear him say that all the small changes she had noticed lately taking root in Golborne would lead to *something*. That these protests would not falter and be extinguished like her father's hopes of a union. "You think the Mors will one day overthrow their aristos?"

St. Silas must have sensed that Leena was rummaging for his own views on the matter. His smile was brief, a grim incline of the mouth. "Either way, Miss Al-Sayer, I will profit."

She narrowed her eyes at him. "How so?"

He shrugged. "War breeds secrets."

She was no longer surprised that he spoke of bloodshed in terms of commerce, in tallies and profits. "And if war does not come to Morland? If the aristos remain in power?"

"Undoubtedly, I will continue to turn that to my advantage as well."

All Leena wanted to do was return to her chamber and ruminate on this new world she had awoken to. She bowed to him. "If that is all you need of me, Mr. St. Silas—"

"That is not all." St. Silas's voice stopped her before she could make an escape. "Make your way to the carriage, Miss Al-Sayer. We are going to visit Lord Avon's old house in town."

It was an elegant mansion in the exclusive Maybury District, whitewashed, with ivy trailing the bricks and a trim garden with cut hedges. St. Silas had managed to procure an invitation, and he took her through each room over and over again until Leena was so exhausted she swayed on her feet. She'd known from the moment they'd stepped into the house that it was bereft of ghosts, but she'd forced herself to work past her fatigue in hopes that she might be wrong.

All the while St. Silas paced relentlessly on the wooden floors, his steps echoing across the domed ceilings, as restless as a phantom. As the butler gave them the initial tour, his expression grew darker.

"Have you been to this townhouse before?" Leena whispered to him as the aging butler showed them the family portraits of the new Lord Crawford who'd purchased the house in Maybury after Lord Avon's death.

The Saint's nod was short and succinct, designed to repel any further questions.

Still, Leena persisted. "What was the reason you visited the first time?"

He gave her a quelling look, and Leena said no more.

On the carriage ride back to his residence, his mouth was tight with displeasure as the silence grew heavy. He stared stonily out at the rapidly filtering landscape, from the mansions that littered the opulent Maybury District to the throughways that became progressively more cobbled and narrow.

It took longer to return to the Northern Quarters than normal. The soldiers who patrolled the gates between the districts demanded papers from every carriage after that morning's riots. They stopped the carriage whenever they caught sight of Leena's Algaraan features through the window, but waved it on once they recognized St. Silas.

Unsurprised but still annoyed at how being accompanied by St. Silas had made an otherwise horrendous journey smooth, Leena instead focused on breaking the silence with a question that had been plaguing her mind all day. "Are you searching for Lord Avon due to his connection with the Wake?"

The twilight bathed St. Silas's face in a bluish glow. He dragged a hand downward from his forehead to his mouth, and it occurred to Leena that he looked exhausted. She wondered what he did between forcing confessions from his customers, tormenting those who lied to him, and hunting dead nobles.

She was not surprised by his cold silence so she pressed on, listing points on her fingers. "This is what I know so far about Lord Avon: He was the last of the Avon line. He led the Wake for an unknown purpose, but presumably to restore wealth. He was mysteriously murdered—a fact that has been well hidden. Upon his death, he lost Weavingshaw to a Mr. Martin, a tradesman who was able to purchase the estate very shortly after Lord Avon's passing." She looked him squarely in the eyes despite his lack of response, not quite fully believing the next point. "And as far as we are *both* aware, he left behind nothing of value to tether him to this earth—no object or person."

She tugged an escaped strand of hair behind her ear in exasperation before continuing. "And here we reach an impasse. If you remain cloistered in your beastly dark tower, reticent in all your answers, I will have nothing more to go on and we will likely spend our entire lives searching for a ghost that may have never been here to begin with."

If a pistol could not drag answers out of St. Silas, perhaps logic could.

The carriage had, some minutes ago, reached its destination, yet they both continued to sit in the cold, neither one making a move to leave. Outside, one of the horses stamped an impatient hoof on the street, puncturing the silence between them.

All the impatience St. Silas had shown in the townhouse returned, and he glanced at his timepiece as if this conversation was taking up too much of his time.

Leena didn't allow his action to discomfit her. She sat rigid on the seat, waiting for an answer.

When he did give it, it was a single word—as if that could explain everything. "Weavingshaw."

"What about it?" Leena asked over the sudden thrash of rain against the window.

"Lord Avon was going to lose Weavingshaw due to generations of accumulated debt. The lands around the estate are unsuitable for farming, and the waters are too wrathful to fish. Even the coal from the mines is not nearly enough. That's why he created the Wake, to ensure his hold on the estate."

Leena's hand gripped the seat cushion. The rest of her was very still. "He traded prisoners, like *cattle,* for a house made of mortar and stone?"

"The Avons would have sunk to any form of depravity to keep hold of Weavingshaw," he replied, and perhaps by this point he'd heard so many sordid confessions that the degradation of the prisoners didn't faze him. "They consider it the house of their blood."

"I cannot imagine that sort of devotion." Leena was an immigrant's daughter. She'd be lost in the streets of her homeland, a foreigner in the cities her ancestors built.

She thought of Lord Avon's portrait—the golden noble drenched in privilege but who had still been unsatisfied. St. Silas claimed that His Lordship had died from a sword through the heart, and Leena suddenly wished that it had been a convict who had done it. That a disfigured form of justice could still exist.

Riots seemed suddenly to be not enough.

"Then Lord Avon must be in Weavingshaw," Leena said with growing certainty. "I can only imagine how the deceased Lord would feel about the object of his obsession being purchased mere months after his death." She shook her head and continued almost to herself, "If what you say is true, Lord Avon must be irrevocably tied to Weavingshaw—in life and in death."

St. Silas allowed her to muse out loud, his attention focused outside the window, on the gray courtyard alight with a single flickering lamp.

Then he nodded once.

"Martin holds an annual hunting party in a few weeks' time at Weavingshaw. I have already arranged it so that we will go as his guests."

Leena tried to stifle the sudden ignition of hope that flared in her chest. "You've arranged it already? If you have known all along that we were going to visit Weavingshaw, why did you not tell me?"

"I am not obligated to alert you of all my plans, Miss Al-Sayer."

"How have you managed to get an invitation?" Leena asked, but didn't wait for a response. "Let me guess: You have blackmail material on Mr. Martin."

"Does it matter? We will have our admission before the start of winter." His mouth was a thin line. He seemed irritated by her, more than he usually was when she asked questions. In fact, even more than when Leena had held a gun to him. "*Must* you wear that scent?"

Genuine surprise brought her head up. "What scent?"

"The lavender," he said curtly. He did not glance at her, his stare still firmly planted on the gray courtyard outside. "The perfume you've been using to interrupt my confessions."

It was such a sudden change of subject that it took Leena a moment before she cleaned her expression. She *had* worn it in the beginning to spite him, bringing the scent of floral growth to his barren confession room. When she had realized that it did nothing to alleviate the burden of confessing, it had just become a part of her daily morning routine, a comfort amid the fear.

She folded her arms. "If you are implying that I am using it to distract your con—"

"I am not implying it. I am stating it as fact." The words seemed to be forced from him. "I do not condone any distractions in my consultations, Miss Al-Sayer."

"No one has taken notice of it."

"*I* have taken notice. That is enough."

He stared at her for another long moment. "Can ghosts smell?"

She furrowed her brows, unsure what exactly he was asking and for what purpose. "Not that I am aware," she replied slowly.

He acknowledged her answer with a curt nod before throwing the carriage door open, descending swiftly and holding out a hand to her. "Even now," he said, as she took his hand with a gloved palm, his skin still searing through the layers. "You are a distraction."

13

Lord Hargreaves

Somewhere within the north of Morland, in the grand and marbled Weavingshaw, three men met in a room.

The chamber they chose for their purpose was discreet. Not the gilded ballrooms nor the mahogany-lined studies that the ancient house was famous for, but a windowless room that contained only a table alight with tall candles and four seats. The chair at the far end remained empty even after all the men had arrived.

It was Lord Hargreaves who had called the meeting. He held a special interest in the fate of Algaraa, and the report of the Malik's fall had reached him days earlier than the rest of the world. Rather than assembling in his own Hythe House, known for its grapes that made drunkards out of half the kingdom, the meeting was held in Weavingshaw.

The house was isolated upon the grieving moors, desolate in its loneliness, and he knew the northern winds would keep their secrets buried.

Years had passed since Lord Hargreaves had last visited Weavingshaw, back when the estate had still belonged to Percy. He and Percy had been only boys when they had sat in this very room, plotting to restore their crumbling fortunes, and Hargreaves felt the stirrings of unease at being here again.

It had been a decade since Percy's funeral, but his presence still saturated Weavingshaw—so strong Hargreaves thought he might choke on it.

Hargreaves grappled with this feeling of doom. He was no longer a fresh-faced boy; he had now inherited the viscountcy after his father's death. But he would not allow the tragedies of the past to mark his future.

Percy's linen shirt had been drenched in crimson. He looked down at it mutely, touched his abdomen, then looked back up at Hargreaves, his eyes beseeching.

For years, Hargreaves had had to learn to speak casually while hiding the blood that stained his skin. His voice was calm when he asked the two other men in the room to sit.

Directly to Hargreaves's right was Lord Kilworth. Once the second son to an earl, Kilworth had been set to receive only a paltry country manor while his twin brother, born just a few minutes earlier, was deeded the entirety of the title, lands, and fortune, as was the law.

The Kilworth twins had shared the same shock of red hair, the same pointed chin and freckled skin, but while the eldest had been handed a silver spoon, the younger twin had been force-fed resentment. Hargreaves still remembered the night George Kilworth had come to him—his words slurred, his tall leather boots still splattered with fresh animal blood courtesy of the hunt they had attended earlier—and uttered the five words that would allow Hargreaves to manipulate him from then on: *I should've been the heir.*

It was Hargreaves who had then suggested to Kilworth, a few months later, that a drop of poison be slipped into his twin's nightcap. And when Kilworth had finally inherited his brother's title and the several strategic lands outside Golborne that would be most useful to Hargreaves in the future, Hargreaves had made sure Lord Kilworth would never forget to whom he owed his loyalty.

Lord Kilworth's voice was already hazy from alcohol. *Goddamn drunkard.* "Still with the old traditions, eh, Charles?" Kilworth asked Hargreaves, waving a hand at the chair left empty. "How long has our good friend Lord Avon been dead?"

Hargreaves spared him a long glance, and Kilworth shifted beneath the look.

"Yes, Percy has been gone for many years, but it was *he* who created the Wake. We keep this seat empty to honor him," Hargreaves said with finality.

"Percy betrayed the Wake in his final days," Kilworth insisted. "He turned against us. Why should we still honor him?"

Kilworth's belligerence irked Hargreaves, but he kept his expression tepid. "*Bless* the dead."

Lord Kilworth's mouth twisted, but rather than respond, he took another swig of the amber liquid in his glass. "Dead or alive, Percy still has his grip on this group of ours."

Hargreaves had always wondered why Percy had named their group "the Wake." He used to think it was merely boyish fancy, a macabre name picked on a whim. Now he knew better.

It had begun with just the two of them: Hargreaves and Percy—only schoolboys at the time. Over the years, they had acquired and disposed of people according to their usefulness, the Wake now branching out to encompass a sovereignty of men, wealth, and trade.

Still, the day the Wake was founded was a vivid memory for Hargreaves: the creaking dorm rooms in Hardwick's Boarding School, the two boys repeating the oaths they had ghoulishly created, the red leather diary in Percy's hand. The goal had always been simple: to restore their dying bloodlines to their former wealth and glory.

Percy's father, the 15th Lord Avon, had gambled away what was left of the family fortune, leaving his son to inherit a Weavingshaw drowning in debts and disillusionment.

It didn't matter that Hargreaves would inherit the viscountcy and the riches his father had safeguarded for him. He was a *half-breed,* born to a Morish father and an Algaraan mother. Even as a child he had known his very existence was a jest among his peers, and that respect must be taken by other, more ruthless, means.

Before he met Percy, Hargreaves had been relentlessly tormented by the other aristocratic boys at Hardwick's. Then golden-haired, blue-eyed Percy—who wore his popularity like a sheen—had reached out a hand.

Everything had changed that day. No one had dared to taunt Hargreaves after that.

They had been only children back then, but the oath Hargreaves had sworn with his boyhood friend still wore heavily on him, like hooks that sank into his skin and ripped out flesh every time he shook them away.

Percy had laughed when Hargreaves came to give his condolences. Percy always knew how to make his presence felt; even his happiness carried claws. They had only come of age that year, wild boys who trawled the seedy streets of Golborne with the heedless abandon known only to those born with privilege.

"My father's dead, old boy," Percy had said, grinning blithely. "Congratulations are in order, not commiserations. Say, what do you think of going up to Weavingshaw? That land is mine now, completely and utterly. We ought to baptize it anew." Percy was so earnest Hargreaves should've known then that there was something amiss.

Percy was never earnest.

"Bless the dead." Hargreaves uttered it like an oath for the second time. It had been more than twenty-five years since Percy had rejoiced at his father's death, ten since his own, but the memories came back to Hargreaves so vividly now.

"Weavingshaw hoards ghosts," Percy had once told him. "I'd much rather it collected wealth instead."

He was right about the ghosts, for Weavingshaw seemed to have collected the remnants of Hargreaves's drowned wife as well.

He carried her with him always, but here at Weavingshaw—a

magpie's nest for the dead—he swore he could hear her humming in the next room. That he could feel her thick hair between his fingers. Her touch on his cheek.

Couldn't save her, couldn't save her, couldn't—

They'd never had children. His dear Gemma. She'd told him she couldn't before they'd wed; she'd never received her monthlies. Yet he had loved her past the point of madness, past the need for heirs, past the completion of his bloodline.

Percy had always called him a fool for that. Bloodlines *must* be completed.

It was one of the few times he and Percy had disagreed.

John Martin, the third member of the assembly and the smallest in stature, was known to invest wildly, and he speculated even more. His clothes were impeccably cut, the high-collared jacket tailored to fit his bullish form perfectly. His nose stood crooked on his face, and his accent still held traces of the backstreets of Golborne where he used to run barefoot as a child.

Martin was a social climber—any blueblood could smell the *new money* wafting off him—a mere tradesman with an excellent head for business. Factories were dotted all over the country bearing his name, but Hargreaves knew that Martin would not be satisfied until he entered into the last echelon of society that had been barred to him: the ranks of the aristocracy.

Knowing his immeasurable wealth, Hargreaves had allowed Martin to buy his way into the Wake.

Martin had purchased Weavingshaw shortly after Percy's death nearly a decade ago, but everyone still referred to Weavingshaw as Avon land. It had been that way for nearly nine hundred years. It felt almost obscene to rename it now. Yet by not leaving any viable heirs, Lord Avon had left Weavingshaw defenseless, to be purchased by *anyone* with money.

"Let's not distract ourselves from our purpose today, gentlemen." Martin cleared his throat. "We've all read the news: The Algaraan Malik has fallen."

Hargreaves knew that if he had not been present, Kilworth and Martin would've exchanged a few choice words about the barbarity of the Algaraans.

As it was, they both turned a pointed gaze on him.

Before answering, Hargreaves poured himself a drink from the decanter. "Undoubtedly, war is coming." He put the decanter down. "How can it not? It is inevitable that the Morish commoners will look to their neighbors in the west and wonder if their own aristos can burn the same way."

"Can you be so sure?"

"You should be glad, Martin." It was Kilworth who answered the tradesman with soft mockery. "There's money to be made in times of war. Plenty of opportunity for a businessman like yourself."

An ugly pink trailed up Martin's thick neck. Hargreaves didn't intervene; there were more pressing matters on his mind than Martin's hurt pride.

"Algaraans—not to be insulting, eh, Hargreaves?—are a passionate sort," Kilworth continued. "Mors—from the chimney sweeps all the way up to the factory owners—are a practical people. Loyalty to our King, and to the nobility who serve the King so righteously, is in our blood. Rebellion won't happen here."

A headache swirled behind Hargreaves's eyelids. He never suffered fools.

"Our King is infirm," Martin argued. "Everyone knows that His Majesty has taken to his bed, and the young prince is still on leading strings." He ignored Kilworth's sneering protests. "His Highness is *no longer* the strong leader that is needed to guide this country through these times of uncertainty. In fact, he makes the aristos look weak. I've heard a few other tradesmen remark that it no longer makes sense to have a country ruled by those with noble blood when it's the factory owners who possess the most significant amount of wealth."

"Do you also share these treasonous thoughts?" Kilworth asked Martin with disgust, anger making his freckles brighter. He never hid his distrust of Martin, revolted by his lowborn dreams and the way the tradesman vacillated between penny-pinching and displays of crass, vulgar wealth.

Martin negotiated like a boxer in stock meetings, ruthless in his acquisitions and cruel with his workers. Despite that, he still possessed an inherited awe of the gentry, and an obsession with the differences in breeding. "Of course I do not," Martin seethed. "My daughter will soon marry the son of a Baron, then she will bear him heirs. I am safeguarding the birthright of my future grandchildren."

Hargreaves allowed himself only a small smile. It was *he* who had arranged the nuptials, by threatening the Baron that if he did not agree to the alliance, then Hargreaves would expect the payment of all the money the Baron owed him in one fell swoop.

Through this marriage, the power Hargreaves gained over Martin was considerable.

"The Malik's greatest mistake was that he underestimated the working class. He could not control them even with the skilled Morish soldiers our King sent to aid him." Hargreaves brought his wine back to his lips, but it now tasted bitter. "Our way of life—the life of the ruling class—is quickly vanishing. *We must not let this happen.* Anarchy will be the result."

Apprehensive silence met this statement.

Martin broke it. "Who will follow the Malik once they execute him?"

"Commander Yosif will attempt to form a government, but he is inexperienced, and vultures are plentiful," Hargreaves said. "The entire country will soon be destabilized, and a civil war will likely ensue." The pause that followed was loaded. "That is why we *must* crush any and all rebellious sentiment among the Mors before it festers and infects this beloved country."

"If it comes down to bloodshed, to us versus the commoners . . . could we win?" Kilworth brushed a handkerchief across the beads of sweat collecting on his forehead.

"Has the Malik kept his head?" Martin murmured.

Kilworth flushed but doggedly continued. "Will our own Morish army fight for us or for the crudes?"

"Most soldiers come from working-class backgrounds," Martin responded. "Lest we forget, the army turned on the Malik near the end. That is how they lost the war."

That was the crux of Hargreaves's problem—one that had caused him many sleepless nights. Without loyal soldiers, the ruling class would crumble, and Hargreaves would find his own head placed on a spike outside the palace.

A breathless whisper from Kilworth. "Then what must be done to stop this rebellion?"

"As they say, George: *Silence before the wolves approach is better than the silence afterward.*" Hargreaves had always understood that to control a man, he must first learn his motivations and act accordingly. Power was an almost physical object to the men sitting beside him, hoarded like gold, stored within their marrow, passed down from father to son.

Hargreaves was different. He didn't crave power, nor fame, nor excess. He wanted stability. Perhaps it was misguided patriotism for a country that shamed his mixed heritage, but he'd seen what war had wrought upon Algaraa. He also knew that these reasons wouldn't sway the rest of the members of the Wake, so he tugged at their fears of the powerful becoming powerless.

And yet, Hargreaves, for all his insight, had still been blind at the most essential moment—blind to Percy's faults, blind to his own wife's misery, blind to the secrets of the Limitless Vessel.

A knock on the door.

The butler entered, a shiver in his voice as he announced: "Lord Calligan, House of Fray."

Sudden tension filled the room. Both men swiveled around to look at Hargreaves. His face didn't twitch beneath the weight of Martin's accusing look nor Kilworth's palpable disgust.

Lord Calligan Fray was ushered in, and there was a clatter of chairs pushed backward as everyone in attendance rose.

Lord Calligan brought with him a presence of dread; *their* kind always did. His face carried no color beneath the flickering of the candlelight, his waxy skin taut across his cheekbones like animal hide unnaturally stretched. His fingers were disproportionately long enough to choke a man using only one hand. Distantly, Hargreaves heard Kilworth smother a gasp when he beheld His Lordship's eyes, the dark entirely overtaking the white sclera.

He had fed recently.

Hargreaves heard Kilworth mutter a prayer to the Saints beneath his breath: *Lead us away from the influence of demons.*

Demons.

Hargreaves ignored Kilworth and inclined his head in welcome. "Lord Calligan. What a pleasure to see you aboveground. I trust your journey has gone well?"

The man who had entered the room—if he could even be called that—dismissed the rest of the party disinterestedly and took a seat at the last remaining chair.

Hargreaves's face remained mild, but he felt a shadow of foreboding at seeing Percy's seat occupied. Lord Calligan sat next to Martin, who attempted to inch discreetly away from the newcomer. If Calligan was offended, he didn't show it. Instead his lips twitched as if he could taste something in the air, then his pallid face split into a wide smile.

"Sit, my friends," Lord Calligan suggested. He spoke in a clear, well-bred accent. Still, there was something odd about his voice, something elementally *wrong*—something that should never have been heard within the light of the day. "Lord Hargreaves has told me that you are having trouble with your peasants?" He laughed—a gurgle from deep within his throat, as if the very idea was amusing.

Hargreaves would never have invited this decaying visitor—*this demon*—if he hadn't been confident in his ability to control him. Lord Calligan's one ambition was to inherit his father's dukedom as soon as possible and use its wealth to pay his mounting debts, but the old Duke refused either to die or to lend his son any more money. This left Calligan alone to fight off the debt collectors.

Hargreaves would know. Lord Calligan owed *him* an enormous sum of money as well.

And yet, Hargreaves refused to accept the gold that Calligan continuously offered in an attempt to free himself. Gold was plentiful in Bastmore, the underworld, and worth very little to the demons, unlike the humans.

Indeed, it was far more profitable to entrap Lord Calligan in his debt as long as he could, only accepting the paper money that demons used as currency, knowing that it would be a lengthy time before Calligan could collect such a sum.

Hargreaves hid the gleam of triumph from his eyes. How many human men could say that they had a demon lord indebted to them?

"I'm sure you are aware that rebellion is already stirring, and we must dampen that fire before it begins to burn," Hargreaves explained to Calligan.

"Aye, I've heard. And you require my service?" Lord Calligan murmured, eager. Hargreaves knew that Calligan was searching for any other means to pay off his debt early.

Hargreaves's nod was grave. "Your service would be most necessary."

Calligan waved at Martin to pour him a glass of wine. Begrudgingly, the tradesman did as he was told. "I assume that you'd like to borrow a few of my mercenaries to suppress your people?" Calligan brought the goblet to his pale lips. "I've foot soldiers to spare, enough for an entire army—that's not the problem—but what troubles me is how we'd bring them aboveground. A question which has previously confounded us, *eh,* my lord?" Lord Calligan raised a thin brow. "I hate to beat a dead horse, but it remains impossible for one of my kind to travel without a vessel."

"A vessel?" Kilworth interrupted with a flicker of annoyance at being left ignorant of such crucial information. He'd only been made aware of the presence of demons a few months ago, despite more than two years of devoted loyalty to the Wake. Since then, Hargreaves and Kilworth had argued over their differing opinions on the matter. Kilworth viewed the demons as lesser beings, to be hunted and eradicated before they began to hunt humans, while Hargreaves saw a much higher purpose for them.

"A vessel is a talisman," Hargreaves replied to Kilworth. "A trinket that allows Lord Calligan and his . . . *kin* to leave their world and enter our own freely." Hargreaves possessed two himself, stolen by the men the Wake employed to handle such brutal matters. "There are only a few known to exist, and almost all belong to the demon nobility."

Hargreaves could see Martin's mind calculating, his gaze turned inward. "I am sure I must be ignorant of these matters, but I must ask—can the vessel *you* used to enter this world, my lord"—he turned to Lord Calligan—"also be used to bring a demon army to us?" He paused. "For a price, of course."

Hargreaves commended Martin's turn of mind. He thought like a businessman, relinquishing his distrust of the demons for the greater good of profit.

"Unfortunately, unlike humans—who have no limitations in crossing into the demon world through specified portals—the demons are far more restricted." It was Hargreaves who answered rather than Calligan. "A vessel allows only one demon into our world at a time, and cannot be used in rapid succession or it would drain the vessel of all its powers. Therefore, gentlemen, we are entirely at the mercy of these vessels. Even accessed sparingly, a vessel can easily malfunction and deplete."

"My family possesses a few vessels." Lord Calligan's mouth was pursed. "All belonging to my father, of course. He would not allow them to be used carelessly, and certainly not to benefit humans."

"I do not require *those* vessels." Hargreaves leaned forward, a knife-etch of a smile sharpening his mouth, finally reaching the heart of the matter. "Instead, I have heard tell of a vessel that never tires, that never depletes, and can open portals for hundreds of demons at a time, thus allowing *us* to control the trade between both worlds indefinitely."

"Ah, Lord Hargreaves, I wondered when you would finally learn about the existence of the Limitless Vessel." Lord Calligan let out a low chuckle. "Unfortunately for all of us, it is lost."

Hargreaves kept his expression mild.

You fool, he thought. *I have known of its existence for fourteen years.* Only within the last few months had he finally had a hint about its location, but he could not retrieve it himself without external assistance. He would not have revealed his hand today if he had not required the other men.

Martin and Lord Kilworth said nothing, but Kilworth's face had noticeably paled at the description of the Limitless Vessel and he took a shaky gulp of his drink. He met Hargreaves's eyes with fear at the thought of demons having unlimited access to their world.

Hargreaves shook his head slightly, his own eyes flashing a warning to Kilworth to hold his tongue.

The astonishment on Martin's face was slowly replaced with an appreciative gleam. "That would mean a fleet of demon soldiers at our command."

Calligan flicked a hand in the air. "Even if we did find it, the fleet would not be under *your* command, precisely."

Martin's forehead turned a blotchy red, and Kilworth's hand formed a fist over the table.

"Easy now, gentlemen." Hargreaves let out a small breath. "Lord Calligan, it is incumbent upon me to explain that, should we successfully find the Limitless Vessel, we would pay your demon army through trade, which your island desperately needs, ensuring a constant flow of natural resources. This sort of trade is exactly what your father has been trying to arrange for years," Hargreaves continued smoothly, undercutting the subtle threat beneath his words. "But in return, you will understand that the demon army is entirely under *our* control. We would, of course, *ensure* this through the ancient binding rituals, taking noble demon children under human wardship until the demon army completes all our commands and is sealed back into *your* world."

Such a trade had not been enacted in nine hundred years—not since the Saints had banned any contact with the demons, punishing those who aided the underworld severely. It had become clear very quickly that such punishments had crippled the demon world. Their decaying island could not produce the natural resources needed to survive. Fresh water, wheat, fruit, and vegetables—all needed to be transported from the human world to sustain the livelihoods of the demons.

And, of course, for the noble families, a steady supply of humans to feast upon.

All managed by the Wake.

Many times, the old Duke of Fray—along with other heads of noble families—had met with Hargreaves in an attempt to craft a treaty to increase the flow of trade, but Hargreaves had known that creating such an understanding would strip him of the power he held over them. Instead, Hargreaves had allowed only the Black Market to flourish, where human bounty hunters crossed over to sell their merchandise at extortionate prices, all paying a tax to the Wake.

"Have you taken leave of your senses, man?" Calligan's face lost all amusement. "*Demon children?* Do you know how rare they are? My father would never consent to this."

Hargreaves knew.

The one time he had broached the topic with the Duke of Fray, it had been rebuffed most forcefully. Lord Calligan, however, his son and heir, was a different kettle of fish.

"I understand your fears entirely, Lord Calligan. Especially when one observes how demons do not treat humans with . . . humanity, for lack of a better word. But have no fear. *We* would handle the demon children with nothing but respect and kindness—*in the understanding* that the demons keep their end of the bargain."

Martin interrupted eagerly. "We are speaking now as if there is a possibility that we are able to locate this Limitless Vessel. Is this true?"

Hargreaves leaned back in his chair slowly. "Not yet. But this is why I have called you all here. For the first time, I have an inkling as to where it may be, but we must find a way to confirm its whereabouts and grasp it before anyone else." Hargreaves looked at each one of them carefully. "We need the Saint of Silence."

Before anyone could interject, he continued. "The merchant of secrets has an endless supply of resources to either solidify or refute my knowledge."

Without the Saint of Silence, all of Hargreaves's plans would be for naught. All would be lost.

Kilworth interjected slowly, "The Saint has never worked well with the Wake. Should we forget the several dead men at our door in the last few months?"

Lord Calligan appeared bored with the entire conversation, his attention wavering. "We do not need the Saint. *I* know for a fact that he does not have any useful information about the Limitless Vessel."

Hargreaves's sharp glance fell on Calligan. "You have asked him?"

"Why should I bother with such a thing? That sort of tedious business best suits my father."

"Then I can assure you that the Saint has lied to His Grace," Hargreaves responded evenly.

Calligan's expression changed from annoyance to astonishment. "Lord Hargreaves, I worry you have lost all your senses today. You know he cannot *lie* to my father."

"Nevertheless, I am certain he has."

Lord Calligan opened his mouth to argue further, but Lord Kilworth interrupted before he could, leveling a heated glance at Hargreaves. "I still fail to see why you would be open to their kind coming into our world. They would kill us all in our sleep."

"I grow weary of your interruptions, George. As I have told you previously, we will reach an unshakable agreement with the demons before we commence anything." Hargreaves did not mask the irritation in his voice this time. "Or would you rather see your estates, your beloved hunting grounds, your entire lands in the hands of lowborn revolutionaries? Your head on a pike?"

Lord Kilworth ground his jaw but did not answer further.

Martin narrowed his eyes at Hargreaves. "Forgive me, my lord, but you seem to know a great deal about the Saint of Silence. What else have you kept us in the dark about?"

A recurring nightmare had terrorized Hargreaves's mind for many years. It always began the same way. He dreamed he was in Weavingshaw, and St. Silas was hunting him. Hargreaves would awaken just as St. Silas had caught him and begun to carve an X through Hargreaves's mouth.

After what he and Percy had done to St. Silas, it would be a foolish thing to allow the Saint's power to go unchecked. Especially when Hargreaves knew, with intense clarity, that the Saint of Silence did not forget. That he would seek his retribution.

Hargreaves's smile was mild. "Apologies for my secrecy thus far. I only wished to gather more information before I revealed my plans to you all." He inclined his head to Lord Calligan. "I do wonder if your father could be persuaded to speak to the Saint of Silence again on the matter of finding the Limitless Vessel."

"As I've already explained to you thrice before: First, I have no sway over my father, nor does he care for my opinions. Second, my father has no sway over the Saint of Silence in *any* other capacity. Third, my father cannot be lied to, therefore making the second point moot."

"Then that leaves it to us, gentlemen, to persuade the Saint to work with us." Hargreaves held out his hands. "To do this, we must find a weakness with which to exploit him. Should he turn his formidable resources to helping the Wake, I am sure we will find this vessel before the revolutionaries form any lasting plans. But time is of the essence. Every one of you must be in search of any means, any weakness, with which to blackmail the Saint."

Hargreaves had no faith that this would be accomplished by Lord Kilworth, or even Lord Calligan, who would return to the demon world to live his life of debauchery while making only mild inquiries to his father. Perhaps there was more to be had from Martin, but Hargreaves could not bet all his cards on the tradesman.

Years ago, Hargreaves would've trusted Percy. It had proved to be to his detriment.

Percy had held a red diary in his slightly shaking hand. "It's all here. This will lead us to a vessel that cannot die. The demons foolishly think it a mere broken trinket, but I possess the knowledge on how to revive it. We can control both worlds with this vessel. In demon lore, they call it the Limitless Vessel."

Yet all Percy's secrets had died with him.

The red diary.

The whereabouts of the Limitless Vessel.

All lost in Weavingshaw.

Hargreaves had spent the last ten years searching for the diary, but the estate knew how to keep the secrets of an Avon. Weavingshaw would devour itself before allowing a stranger like him to unveil those mysteries.

He knew only the Saint of Silence, master of secrets, could reveal what the dead had hidden.

14

MR. ORLEY

THAT NIGHT, AFTER returning from Lord Avon's house in town—the night before she was due to meet Rami—Leena awoke to whispers.

She had dreamed of Mrs. Van.

The housekeeper had appeared in a monstrous form. Her eyes, normally cool and impersonal, were forceful—the pupils blown, the black entirely overtaking the white. Her fingers, always so unnaturally long, were wringing themselves.

"Do you wish to harm my master?" Mrs. Van demanded.

Leena felt as if she was being torn apart beneath the housekeeper's glare. She wanted to fall to her knees, but a cold prickle on her neck kept her upright. Gritting her teeth, Leena gathered her strength. "Not if he does not harm me first."

"What are you trying to do, girl?"

Leena didn't answer, but lurched forward. The power shifted between them. There was a sliver of fear in Mrs. Van's face as she took a few uncertain steps back. "Don't—don't touch me."

Leena reached out a hand. There was a secret imprinted on the woman's skin . . . something essential to know.

Mrs. Van staggered, her long fingers covering her face. "Protect him, please protect him. Find Lord Avon. How long must he survive this?"

And when Leena touched the housekeeper's forearm, she understood what bound Mrs. Van to St. Silas. A hidden memory: a woman sweeping the floors before a small, sleepy-eyed boy runs in, crying over a scraped knee.

Mrs. Van disappeared and Leena jerked awake. By then, the dream was only a subtle aftertaste in her mouth, a lingering taste of rot. She blinked, her eyes adjusting to the dark. The only ghost who haunted her that night was a shoemaker who wept as he held up a leather heel to the moonlight, but he stayed beyond the circle of salt. Dim lights flickered through the crack beneath her door, and a sudden fear gripped her. Why was her door ajar?

Had someone been in her room?

Horror tightened her stomach.

Whispered arguments and the sound of pacing carried from the hallway. She listened intently, not daring to move.

". . . leave her be." A harsh voice filtering in and out—St. Silas, uncharacteristically furious. "You should have sought my permission—"

Another voice responded, pleading. Mrs. Van. "It had to be done . . ."

Leena strained her neck but could hear no more. Quietly, she slipped from her bedcovers and crept toward the door until she could hear the housekeeper's voice once again.

". . . she took something from me."

The pacing stopped. She heard his disbelief. "From you? How is that possible?"

Just at that moment, Leena rested her foot on a loose floorboard and a loud *creak* sounded. She froze, then cursed herself when she was met with silence behind the wall. She'd no choice now but to make her presence known. Opening the door fully, she was met by the impenetrable faces of St. Silas and Mrs. Van. He bowed to her.

"Have we disturbed you?" St. Silas asked, the previous fury extinguished so completely from his voice that it almost convinced Leena that she'd misheard it.

Then his gaze slid down from her face, his eyes widening, and only then did Leena realize that she was wearing her old nightgown, so thin that it was almost transparent in the candlelight. His throat moved and he tore his gaze away just as she dived behind the door. Utterly mortified, it took all her courage to poke her head back out.

St. Silas's voice was rougher than usual, his eyes still focused on the ceiling. "My apologies, madam."

"You're awake," Mrs. Van said in the long awkward silence that ensued. The housekeeper's body was unnaturally still, like a scorpion before the strike.

"I had a strange dream," Leena replied, her loose hair cascading across her shoulders as she continued to hide behind the door. "Then I awoke to the sound of arguing."

She didn't miss the quick look shared by St. Silas and Mrs. Van. No one asked her what the dream was about. For a wildly paranoid moment, Leena thought it was because they *knew*.

The Saint showed his teeth, his tone persuasive and smooth. "A minor disagreement about household manners. Nothing that should trouble you."

Mrs. Van remained silent.

Perhaps it was the time of the day, or the tendrils of sleep that still clung to her eyes, but the house suddenly felt like a prison, St. Silas and Mrs. Van its guards, and the night a fortress. Leena stared at the long shadows flung from the candlelight, expanding and moving like quivering creatures only brought forth in the dark. Suddenly, she swerved her gaze to meet Mrs. Van's, and the dream came back to her in tidbits. The black, fathomless eyes, the accusing question, the general feeling of *un-rightness* . . . There was something very wrong with Mrs. Van. Something that didn't belong in this world.

She tried to shake the disturbing thought away, but she knew that if ghosts could exist, if those ledgers could exist, then whatever creature—or monster—Mrs. Van was could, too.

"I would like a lock on my door," Leena said firmly, her eyes unwavering from Mrs. Van's face.

The Saint replied without hesitation. "Done. First thing in the morning."

There was nothing else to say. Leena knew that she could not bring up her suspicions without sounding ridiculous, any more than they could convince her that everything was as it should be. Because it wasn't.

Nothing was right within this house.

In the morning, the dream had blurred in Leena's mind the moment she awoke again. Just as she'd given up hope of recalling the dream, a familiar phrase swam before her eyes:

How long must he survive this?

Must *who* survive *what*? St. Silas? He wasn't surviving; he was thriving. He inspired both awe and dread, his business was heaving with confessors, and he was obviously swimming in wealth.

But he wasn't satisfied with any of it. It was an odd thought—one Leena could not dwell on, for it was her agreed-upon day for meeting Rami. St. Silas had not said anything about the change in date; nor had Leena asked. She thought it was one of those times when it was more prudent to beg for forgiveness than ask for permission. She left at dawn. Yet by the time noon arrived, morning had come and gone and Rami had still not appeared.

All thoughts of Saints and the Wake and Weavingshaw had vanished from Leena's mind. Usually, by lunch at the very latest on the day after a fight, Rami would be walking in, whistling and swinging a bag full of coins. Leena lingered inside her childhood home in the New Algaraa District, sweeping the floors again and again in agitation as she waited for her brother to arrive.

But he didn't come.

Rami fought for the worst men in Golborne—the Black Coats—and was completely at their mercy. Working for St. Silas had been a lesson for Leena; she now understood the brutality that existed within the underbelly of the city. Perhaps Rami had displeased the Black Coats, lost money for them—

Perhaps they'd hurt him.

A slow horror spread through her and she tried to swallow the panic down.

Margery didn't know where Leena's brother was, either. The old woman, Tar staining her lips black, only asked Leena if she still carried the timepiece that Margery had given her.

When Leena pulled the gold watch out of her bodice to show her, Margery's eyes fluttered closed, the effects of the drug making her near comatose. "Good. Keep it with you always."

As night fell across the city, fear dogged her steps. She trudged back to St. Silas's residence, hoping that Rami might have misunderstood and would be waiting for her there instead. But only the ghost of the boy dressed in white haunted the steps of the Saint's shop—the same phantom that had led Leena to St. Silas on that first fevered night. She averted her gaze from the boy's right browbone, which had been shattered in his living life. He ignored Leena's questions about Rami, turning away from her in irritation.

It was time to knock on the Saint's study.

He had been there all day, and the door swung open after a long moment spent waiting on the threshold. In that interim, all her panicked thoughts roared through her with force. St. Silas would not help her; she was sure of it. She had interrupted his sessions spitefully. She had not yet found Lord Avon's ghost—the very reason he kept her close.

And worse still, she had told St. Silas, in no uncertain terms, that she loathed him.

Then, salt into wounds, she had held a gun to him.

Leena was sure at this point that St. Silas would derive great pleasure from knowing her brother was missing or dead.

Not for the first time in her life, Leena wished she had more sense and less propulsion to push forward in spite of the consequences, but her foolhardy ways would likely see her in Newtorn Prison—if she survived this contract.

"You are late," St. Silas noted. His quick bow was perfunctory, his tone chilling. "How is your *special friend*?"

"I do apologize for my lateness." Leena barely curtseyed back. "I must ask, have you seen my brother?"

"If I had seen your brother, believe me, Miss Al-Sayer, you would be the first to know." He sat back down at his desk, attention already drifting to the assortment of parchments before him.

She leaned over the desk, ignoring his taunts. She tried to force his eyes away from the ledgers and back to her.

"As you know, Rami's very talented with a sword," Leena said. "Sometimes, to make a few coins, he participates in back-alley fights—fights run by the Black Coats. He told me he had one yesterday and he has not come home since. Even if the match was delayed until today, he should have been home by now. I *know* something terrible has happened." Her fists were clenched so hard over the wooden table that her knuckles turned white. Desperation had led Leena once more to St. Silas's door, and she was sure he would not miss the irony, or the chance to capitalize on it.

St. Silas put his pen down slowly. "Be that as it may, I'm unsure why you've come to see me, madam."

Leena ground her teeth together in an attempt to bar the insolent words that threatened to explode out of her throat, making a hideous situation between them even more impossible. "You're *unsure* why I've come to see you, *the Saint of Silence, merchant of secrets*?"

His expression remained steady and, unlike her, he was clearly in total command of his emotions. "My hand—when it is my own to move—rarely lifts for others. It is how I've survived for so long. So, once again, I ask you: What do you want from me?"

"He is my brother—"

"There are many brothers in the world. I cannot help them all." He looked away dismissively, returning once more to his ledgers. "Let the matter rest. I'm sure he'll wander in at some point."

Leena stared at him. "You mistake me, sir. I've not come for your help. I've come only for information. I would be so very grateful, and *in your debt,* if you were to tell me where to look first. Then that is where I will go."

At her words, St. Silas's eyes drew back to hers, a sudden stillness in his shoulders. "You will go by yourself?"

Leena nodded.

"To the Black Coats?" he amended, as if there had been a miscommunication.

"Yes."

"One of the most violent gangs in all of Golborne?"

Leena nearly replied that she already worked for the Saint of Silence and who could be worse than *that,* but kept her mouth shut. "He is my brother," she repeated staunchly.

His eyes narrowed, as if not quite believing her. "You're either very brave or very foolish."

"Likely a bit of both."

Leena waited for it—his demand for payment. She braced herself, her entire body tense with anxiety. She had nothing left to give him other than the knowledge that she could be possessed by ghosts.

The request did not come.

St. Silas folded his arms. Gone was his habitual sly ease, and a strange tension now rolled from him in waves.

"Orley is the head of the Black Coats. His headquarters are located in Ridgeways. He will know where your brother is." His voice was a challenge, as if he didn't quite believe Leena's intention to go alone.

Leena stood up, swiping a damp palm over her skirt. "Thank you."

She had barely stepped foot into the hallway when she heard St. Silas move to follow her.

"You will go now? At this unsaintly hour?" There seemed to be an underlying sharpness to his question.

She expected him to forbid her from leaving, as he had done previously. After all, she was his ghost-seer and was valuable to him. If he did forbid her, Leena thought with rising panic, there was little she could do to gainsay his command.

Filled with dread, she quickened her steps toward the door before he could stop her. "I cannot wait until tomorrow morning."

His voice was hard, an angry tilt to his mouth. "How will you get there?"

"I'll walk."

"It's raining."

"It won't kill me."

She opened the door to the courtyard, but he slammed it shut with his palm.

Leena waited with a held breath. Now his command would drop. Now he would force her back to her chamber.

It did not come.

Instead, he continued, in barely concealed irritation, "Orley is the worst sort of creature. He will want something in return for any information about your damned brother. What will you give him?"

"For my brother, anything."

His eyes flickered down the length of her body, his eyebrows raised in a silent question. An irate flush rose on Leena's cheeks, recalling in more detail than she wanted to admit the look he'd given her last night when he'd seen her in her nightgown—his tight throat, his burning eyes.

"Not *that*," she croaked, more furious because of how unbalanced he made her feel beneath his gaze.

He stepped forward, looming over her in the narrow hallway. His very presence was a knife. "No, you will merely tell Orley that you can see the dead. The one secret that makes you exceedingly valuable to me."

Rather than answer, Leena turned away once more.

The words seemed driven out of him. "I will go with you."

She lurched to face him, gaping. "*Why*?"

He shrugged his shoulders, an indolent gesture that seemed almost forced. "Protecting my own interests, Miss Al-Sayer. Isn't it obvious?"

The smog from the factories that lined Ridgeways touched everything, smothering lungs and blackening hearts. Shops were shuttered, debris piled on the pavement, and rough sleepers warmed their hands on makeshift fires contained in steel cans. So many of these people, Leena thought, were not Algaraan refugees, but native Mors who did not even have enough coins to house themselves. Little wonder revolution brewed.

Further along the road were the laundry factories, and Leena's hands burned just thinking about the harsh lyes stored there. She credited St. Silas for one thing: She would never have to lean over those steaming vats of water again for as long as she lived.

The carriage stopped at the only establishment that seemed to be thriving at this time of night. Welcoming lights blazed through the windows, and three heavyset men stood guard. A few spirits mingled among the downtrodden, but they were only hazy specters, filtering in and out of existence like dying candlelight.

Once she stepped out from the carriage, a thickly perfumed smell wafted in the air, triggering a memory: Margery sitting in a lonely house as the sugary smoke coiling from her hookah masked the scent of neglect.

Tar.

Apprehension filled her stomach at the realization that Orley's was a place that dealt the drug. Leena pulled Margery's timepiece from her bodice and held it in her hand now as a reminder of her friend.

St. Silas nodded at one of the mean brutes who stood over the entrance, and he let them pass with a bow of deference. St. Silas then led her through a hallway and into a large circular room thick with smoke. Leena froze at the threshold. Tulle curtains hung from the ceiling for privacy, but did little to hide the various men and women lying on beds. Tiny fires burned in hookahs all through the room, small lighthouses leading the blank travelers home.

St. Silas turned to urge her through, but his gaze caught the glint of gold within Leena's clenched fingers. He inclined his head to look closer, but when he saw the name engraved on the cover—*Fray,* in bold cursive letters—he wrenched himself back.

"Where did you get this?" he hissed, startling her from her thoughts.

"It was given to me," Leena replied, astonished, looking down at the timepiece.

"By *who*?"

Leena held it possessively in her hands. It was her one gift from her friend, the old woman's last possession that she had entrusted to Leena. She had often wondered how Margery had got hold of this precious object. Likely, Leena tried to reassure herself, it was a family heirloom.

There was a small part of her, however, that did worry that the timepiece had been stolen, and that part reared its head now, for how could Margery own something so valuable that the Saint of Silence would recognize it? At Leena's first opportunity, the moment St. Silas gave her leave again, she would go back and ask Margery more about the origins of this gift.

Leena quickly hid the timepiece in her pocket and took a step back from him. "Why does it matter who gave it to me? It is mine now and I have not stolen it."

The suspicion on Leena's face caused St. Silas to recollect himself. With a last searching look, he spun away from her. "Then let us not delay any further."

Fray. She also made a note of that name.

Every trivial secret can lead to ruin.

They weaved their way through the multitude of stray limbs and smoking pipes to the other end of the room, then down a long narrow hallway and up several flights of stairs.

The door to the room was unlocked and St. Silas entered without knocking. Taking a deep breath, Leena followed.

She had never seen a more claustrophobic room. It was a magpie's nest of trinkets. By her feet, large wooden blocks with brightly painted letters and pictures lay scattered—the kind used by children learning to read. Vases with decaying flowers cluttered a writing desk. Oddly shaped perfume bottles rested on the windowsill. Above the desk hung a parchment within a gilded frame, only four inky words drawn on the aged sheet:

No Burials for Lambs

Leena's gaze stayed there for a moment—what an odd turn of phrase—but she knew, without knowing how she knew, its exact meaning: *Only lions are mourned.*

On the floor, in the middle of this madness, sat a ridiculous-looking man on a cushion. He was small of stature with hair sprouting from his scalp like weeds, but the bones in his face stood out too far, and the fingers on his hands were unnaturally stretched, curling like a spider's legs. And . . . the pupils of his eyes—fathomless dark holes, expanding, the whites no longer visible . . .

Yet within seconds, the man's eyes were back to normal, leaving Leena to wonder if her mind was playing tricks on her in this drug-filled den.

Then she thought of Mrs. Van. She and this man shared the same look, the same abnormally curling hands. A wave of nausea unsettled her.

Orley is the worst sort of creature.

Her panicked gaze met St. Silas's, but there was neither confirmation nor denial in his look.

"Mr. St. Silas? What a pleasure," said Orley, his voice unnaturally high. He bowed his head while still sitting cross-legged. St. Silas did not return the formality, and neither did she.

It was odd to Leena that any sort of pleasantries could still be exchanged between these two men. Orley had sent spies after St. Silas, and St. Silas had disposed of those spies. While they each sidestepped these recent bloody events, they still hung in the air like smoke. "And who is this beautiful young lady?"

"She is under my protection," St. Silas said. His voice carried an unmistakable warning, and Leena narrowed her eyes at his choice of words. "She has come to ask for a favor."

"Does the young lady not speak for herself? Or has the . . . er . . . *good* fortune of being under your protection robbed her of that ability?"

"I speak," Leena interjected. During their exchange, her attention had been momentarily diverted by a ghost that appeared by Orley's elbow. A boy wearing a servant's livery. His eyes were hollow, his movements twitchy—as if he craved something he could not taste in the afterlife. "I am looking for my brother, Rami Al-Sayer. He is a duelist who competes in fights hosted by your gang. He had one yesterday, but he has not yet returned."

Orley scratched his arm. "Ah, yes, the cripple?"

"I do not like that word," Leena snapped, her eyes burning. "He is a sword fighter who has never been beaten."

Orley's face once more curved into a wide-toothed smile. He seemed to enjoy her offense.

"That's his problem, dearie. We instructed him to lose the fight yesterday, but he went against our orders. One particularly wealthy tradesman was very keen for that match to be fixed against Rami, and he would've rewarded us handsomely for it. Yet your brother decided his *legacy* mattered more than our profit. A pity."

Her head jerked. This was the second time loyalty to a *legacy* would be someone's undoing. Maybe the destitute Al-Sayers had more in common with the Avons than she'd first thought.

She wanted to throttle Rami, and she would when she saw him next. How dare he compromise their future and her only family for an ideal?

The ghost of the servant-boy jumped from foot to foot, and Leena stared at him longer than she should have, her mind blank with worry. Their eyes met. His mouth fell open and he pointed at his chest as if saying: *You can see me?*

Leena wondered if he could be a useful asset. Haunting the leader of the Black Coats must mean he overheard important information, so she gave a short nod.

"Will you tell me where he is?" Leena asked, still staring at the boy.

It was Orley who answered. "Unfortunately, my dear, my customers require the strictest of confidentiality—"

She cut him off impatiently. "What is your price?"

He wagged one long finger. "From you, nothing. No offense, but, lovely though you are, you are of little importance to me."

She knew that this was precisely why St. Silas had elected to come with her, but his demand for caution did not matter. Her brother's life lay in her ability to bargain for it—and she *would* bargain, once again, with whatever she had. "I do, in fact, have a payment that you'll never receive from anyone else—"

"*I* will tell you something, Orley," St. Silas interrupted smoothly, a hand in his pocket.

Leena's eyes widened and Orley gasped. The prospect of a secret from the Saint seemed to excite him beyond measure. Even the ghost of the servant-boy jolted, shrunken eyes widening in shock as he stared intently at St. Silas. Distantly, Leena wondered if this ghost had been one of the Saint's confessors in his previous life.

She looked up at St. Silas mutely. *Why . . . ?*

"Protecting my interests," he reminded her flatly.

It wasn't an act of kindness; it was an act of commerce.

Orley began without hesitation, licking his lips as if preparing for a meal. "Tell me something that has wounded you."

The Saint was still for a long moment, his countenance carefully remote. Then he tilted his jaw upward, exposing his throat and the thin pink line that ran in the shape of a knife's blade. He'd taken the request literally, confessing the history of something that had left a scar on his body, although Leena didn't think Orley had meant it in that way. "Courtesy of a mother whose son went mad after confessing to me."

Orley's tongue poked out as if tasting the air. "How old were you?"

"A few days past seventeen. I'd only just begun my business."

Leena's gaze sharpened on him, but the Saint's attention was on Orley, not a flicker of emotion crossing his face. He was carved from stone, unwavering, dark brows set and firm, corrosive eyes that knew how to conceal every shift of expression.

"What did you do to the mother?" Once more Orley's eyes seemed to expand, the dark overtaking the white entirely, before constricting suddenly—though Leena told herself shakily that it was likely a trick of the candlelight.

St. Silas's drawl was bored. "I took the knife from her."

"And then . . . ?"

Leena held her breath as she waited for his answer.

"It is not relevant."

Orley edged forward, a frustrated notch puckering his cheeks. "Then you've delivered an incomplete payment." This exchange baffled Leena—why was St. Silas's own confession important to Orley, and why did he consider it incomplete?

St. Silas's mouth curled into impatience before he molded his face into indifference once more. "That is all; I merely took the knife from her. Make no mistake—rarely do I forgive any threat against my life."

Very briefly, the Saint's eyes pierced Leena.

Yet he'd forgiven her. She'd pointed a pistol at him and he had not punished her for it. Perhaps even the Saint of Silence had rare inclinations to mercy.

Leena wanted to continue to think of him always as a beast. Any shred of kindness attributed to the Saint would discolor the image she'd built of him in her head. She understood monsters—their selfish wants, their relentless desires. It was the monsters that flickered in and out of humanity that could never be accounted for.

It was for this reason that the next question burst from her own mouth, even though she knew such interruptions usually brought the wrath of St. Silas down upon her. "How old was the son?"

She imagined a young boy sitting on that wooden seat in the Saint's confession room, sobbing as his secret was written in the ledgers, the pain ripping through him with jagged cruelty.

His answer surprised her. "Older than me." Then, as if sensing where Leena's mind had taken her, he met her gaze again. "I do not take the confessions of children, Miss Al-Sayer."

She filtered through all the confessions she'd witnessed, and she was shocked to realize that she'd never once seen a child cross the threshold into the Saint's shop.

Orley continued in a low whisper. "Do you regret reaping the confession from the son? Do you ever feel any shame?"

St. Silas showed his teeth. "If it is shame you want, Orley, you *won't* get it from me."

"Such a waste," Orley whined. "I cannot get a feel for you at all. Why such a hard shell? The girl might've proved to be more delicious."

"You are likely very right. Unfortunately, you've lost your opportunity to find out." St. Silas's smirk was obvious, but for the first time since she had entered his employment, he touched her intentionally, laying a warm hand at the base of her back.

Standing in that claustrophobic room, surrounded by Orley's life trinkets and a young, pained ghost, Leena felt choked. It was almost natural for her to step back into St. Silas's hold, allowing herself to be grounded by what felt like the only other living, warm thing in the room.

St. Silas flashed a surprised look at her unexpected reaction before once more schooling his features into nonchalance.

Leena could not silence the echo of St. Silas's secret reverberating throughout her skull. For a wild moment, she wished that he'd never confessed at all.

She cleared her throat. "Tell us about Rami now."

"Ah, yes," Orley said in the tone of a child who has lost a game. "He forced our hand, you see. We had to teach him a lesson."

"What have you done to him?" Leena demanded, taking a panicked step forward.

"Are you asking if my bruisers mean to keep him alive? How should I know? It's up to the tradesman who asked us to fix the fight," Orley replied, his attention already slipping away from the conversation. "Frankly, this whole affair has already bored me."

"Where have they taken him?" Her voice cracked.

"The place we use is an abandoned cottage on the edge of Bromley Forest. It is a few minutes east of Wringer's Pub."

"Who was it that wanted the game fixed?" St. Silas was already half turned toward the door.

"Tsk, tsk." Orley waggled his eyebrows. "For that, I will need another payment."

St. Silas's voice was mild. "No matter. I shall soon find out."

The servant-ghost raised his hand in a farewell and Leena acknowledged him with another nod.

But before leaving the cluttered room, Leena looked back toward the hanging parchment once more.

No Burials for Lambs

Grimly, Leena knew this to be true.

15

The Burial

THE COTTAGE STOOD on the edge of the woods, its boards rotted from years of neglect, the steps broken, the rail missing, paint peeling from the beams. It had taken less than an hour to reach the fringes of Bromley Forest. During the carriage ride, St. Silas had turned to Leena. "No burials for lambs?"

Leena was so preoccupied with thoughts of Rami, she hadn't realized that she'd been muttering that phrase beneath her breath mindlessly over and over again. "It was written on Orley's parchment—the one in the gilded frame."

She didn't miss the furrowing of St. Silas's brows. "There was nothing written on that parchment."

Leena stared at him. "There was. I saw it."

He looked oddly at her. "I've been in that room many times. I have never marked it before."

"Perhaps it is new?"

"Perhaps . . ." Although his tone was veiled, he did not comment further.

"How does your confession act as payment for Orley?"

Unsurprisingly, his response was unforthcoming.

Before she could question him any more, they had arrived at their destination.

Leena and St. Silas now stood at the edge of the clearing in front of the cottage, eyes alert to any movement within. Nothing stirred. All was quiet.

"A loaded peace," St. Silas murmured, retrieving his pistol. It was one of those new broad barrels—a recent invention that gave the shooter two bullets before the weapon needed to be reloaded.

"Where are the Black Coats?" Leena whispered.

He shook his head and began making his way through the clearing. "Let's find out."

They reached the cottage unchallenged, and the horror of what might be waiting was almost too much to bear. She peered through a muddy window into what looked to be a sparse reception room, and gasped when she saw a lone figure tied to a chair.

Rami.

He barely moved.

"Ah, so we've located Al-Sayer—alive, fortunately—but where are the others?" St. Silas drawled, looking over her shoulder.

No footsteps approached them. No cries of warning. A crow cawed. A few raindrops scattered across the roof. But they were otherwise alone.

That notion was oddly terrifying.

Leena wet her dry lips. "Perhaps they've already gone. Let's finish quickly."

The front door was left slightly ajar. The cottage consisted of only one large room, empty save for a few chairs left askew.

Leena wanted to rush in, but St. Silas stopped her with one hand. With his revolver outstretched, he made long strides around the room. Finally, when he was sure they were alone, he waved her through.

She knelt by her brother and shook his shoulder. "Rami? Wake up. It's me."

He stirred.

"L-Leena?" His eyes were bloodshot and bruises peppered his jaw.

She slumped in relief.

"Rami . . ." she repeated, tugging the rope that bound him to the chair.

Sudden alertness passed over Rami's face. He jerked in his restraints. "*Leena?* Get the hell out of here! My captors have only gone temporarily, but they'll be back soon."

St. Silas stayed near the door, unconcerned with Rami's welfare. "How many men are there?"

"Of all the people I expected to rescue me, you were last on the list." Rami threw St. Silas a broken grin, his teeth bloodied. "Can't say I'm not pleased to see you, though."

"Can't say the feeling is mutual. How many men are there?"

"Two," Rami said, and he winced when Leena pressed on his chest. "Mackenzie Crane and his new favorite, a boy named Burr."

St. Silas seemed to recognize both names.

Leena clawed at the ropes, but they would not give. "Your sword, Rami. Where is it?"

Silence. A heaviness in his voice. "They've taken it."

Baba had traded his wedding band for that sword, which had become an extension of Rami, like a limb that existed outside of his body. By taking it, they had effectively amputated him again.

"I want to kill them." Leena's angry breaths came out in white swirls of frost.

A small dagger was thrust into her hands. She turned to see St. Silas. "Direct that anger and make it useful."

She grasped the knife and slashed through the ropes. Rami stumbled forward, collapsing onto his knees. She took his arm and attempted to drag him up, but he was too heavy for her.

Watching them struggle for a minute, St. Silas sighed and put his arms around Rami, supporting him through the door and onto the overgrown lawn outside the cottage.

They halted at the sound of approaching footsteps on the path leading from the woods.

"Our hosts have rejoined the party." St. Silas dropped Rami unceremoniously on the ground before steadying his revolver. "Stay behind me."

Not daring to breathe, Leena held the dagger tightly in shaky hands.

St. Silas reached into his pocket and threw Rami his spare pistol, and her brother took it in a firm hand.

Stepping into the clearing were two figures. One was a large man whose rough skin told of years of fast living, his fingers sparkling with jeweled rings. The other was a reedy boy whose growth looked to have been stunted by hunger. They both wore coats of the darkest fabric. Mackenzie and Burr, presumably. The boy was already holding a revolver pointed directly at St. Silas, and Rami's sword was buckled about his waist.

"Ah, what a welcome," the older one, Mackenzie, said. When he smiled, his mouth was crammed with gold teeth, terribly done, the canines crooked, the central incisors slightly too long. Leena suddenly remembered what Rami had once told her about Mackenzie, that he pried the gold fillings from the people he'd been hired to intimidate. "'Pon my soul, has the Saint of Silence come to visit us?"

"What *soul*?" Leena snapped from behind St. Silas.

Burr unlocked the pistol, the noise deafening in the still forest.

"Put it down," St. Silas ordered, his lazy command spearing through the frosty night air.

Burr didn't respond, but his pointed face had paled.

"Keep steady," Mackenzie warned Burr, his tone somehow managing to be both oily and inflamed. "No honor among thieves, eh, Saint?"

St. Silas cocked his own pistol. "Oh, there is certainly honor among thieves. I, however, am not one, so I do not need to trouble myself with such trivial things."

Rami spat blood on the grass. His own weapon shook. "Shoot 'em and let's end this, Saint."

Burr jerked his head at Rami, his pointed face twisting into a bitter snarl in the moonlight. "If we don't deliver him beaten and bloody to the tradesman, we don't get paid, and neither does Mr. Orley."

"And a growing boy needs to eat," Mackenzie added, placing a hand on Burr's shoulder.

"This has all begun to bore me," St. Silas said, his posture unwavering. "Tell us who the tradesman is, and perhaps I'll consider avoiding all necessary organs when I shoot."

"How generous," Mackenzie drawled. Then his eyes fell on Leena and his smile widened once more to reveal his stolen teeth.

She didn't understand the reason behind that smile, didn't hear the silent figure creeping up behind her until she felt the hands wrap around her throat.

A gasping scream tore from her.

Leena clawed at the hands holding her in a stone-cold vise. Distantly, she heard her brother shouting. Black dots clouded her vision. Her lungs ached.

She couldn't breathe she couldn't breathe she couldn't breathe—

She was going to die.

Tortured animal panic took hold of her, and she jammed the dagger into the soft flesh of the intruder's abdomen. She heard a grunt, but her captor's fingers didn't loosen. She was sinking . . . *deeper* . . . until a voice cut through the waves threatening to drown her.

"Tilt your head to the left," St. Silas's voice ordered calmly. "There's a girl."

As she obeyed, a shot whizzed by her ear. If she'd turned her cheek a fraction of an inch at the wrong moment, the bullet would have sliced her flesh into ribbons. The clasping hands released her, then the dull thud of a body hitting the floor could be heard across the clearing.

She gasped for oxygen. Yet again, blood was everywhere. On her hands. In her hair. On her shoes.

"Very close shot, Saint," Rami yelled furiously, gun still pointing toward his captors. "You could've easily killed her!"

"Yet I didn't," St. Silas responded curtly. "Do not lose your focus, Al-Sayer." The barrel of his own revolver instantly returned to the two Black Coats. "Are you hurt, Leena?" he called back, keeping his eyes locked on the two bruisers.

Her voice came out raspy from her raw throat. "No."

There was a split-second silence, as if St. Silas wanted to turn around and check for himself, but he refrained. "Did you not know of a third?"

Leena wasn't sure whom he was speaking to until Rami responded. "I didn't see him."

St. Silas continued, now addressing Mackenzie. "The only reason you aren't shot within an inch of your life, Mackenzie, is because I want you to reveal the identity of the tradesman who hired you. I would be willing to let you live when I am content that I have received no lies."

Mackenzie's smile had vanished. Anger flashed in his eyes.

"You killed Adam," Burr said with bewilderment. A muffled sob broke Burr's voice, his large eyes wild in his young face. "They killed Adam, Mackenzie."

"Shoot, boy," Mackenzie yelled savagely.

At his order, another shot rang out, and Leena ducked her head.

A choked scream.

When Leena dared to look, it was Mackenzie on his knees, his right hand held before his face as if to block the shot. It had not. The bullet had torn through the tendons and fascia of his palm, a gaping bloodied hole now in the center of it. More gruesome still, the bullet had sliced his ear, only a torn lobe hanging by a thin thread of skin.

Mackenzie's agonized screams filled the night air.

St. Silas looked at Mackenzie as if assessing his own aim. "I would have preferred to see your *full* ear on the ground, but my angle was slightly off-center. Apologies." The Saint sounded almost contrite.

Burr, whose horrified eyes ricocheted between the Saint's gun and his bleeding master, was very aware that two guns were still pointed at him. Without any further show of bravery, he dropped his own pistol and turned his palms up in surrender.

"Who hired you?" St. Silas asked unhurriedly, as if he was having a pleasant conversation with an old friend. He walked toward the revolver on the ground and pocketed it.

Burr's lips barely moved in response. "M-Mr. Martin."

"How uninspired." Although this revelation astonished Leena, St. Silas seemed unsurprised. Were they speaking of the very *same* tradesman who now owned Weavingshaw?

"Yes, sir. That's all we know, I swear," Burr stuttered.

St. Silas assessed the boy and the moaning Mackenzie dispassionately. "Leave, before I fancy shooting your remaining hand. Or practicing on the other ear."

Mackenzie, still clutching his gaping palm, staggered to his feet. But just as he and Burr turned to leave, St. Silas stopped them. "The sword. Give it back."

Both Al-Sayer siblings jolted.

His chin quivering beneath the glare of moonlight, Burr unsheathed the sword from his hip and threw it toward them on the grass. No one spoke as they watched the two Black Coats disappear through the winding woods.

"Thank you," Rami said haltingly. His head swayed, and he grimaced as he attempted to stand on his own.

Leena could not look away from the body that lay unmoving by her feet, the blood staining the grass a midnight black. She still held the dagger in her hands, and she had to consciously uncurl her stiff fingers to let it go. In the span of less than a month, two Black Coats had lain dead at her feet. But this time, she'd had a direct hand in it.

She brought a fist to her forehead to block out her panic.

"Leena, are you all right?" Rami tried to make his way to her, but collapsed. She turned to the sound of her brother falling, eyes swimming, landscape blurring. She wanted to ask if he was well, but the words lodged in her throat painfully.

Leena staggered toward her brother just as St. Silas pocketed Rami's pistol before hoisting her brother up with a hand below his shoulder, guiding him along the path back toward the carriage.

Leena picked up Rami's sword and walked closely behind them, the moonlight now starker than ever.

She could finally admit that a part of her was not sure that she or Rami would have survived the night, and they certainly wouldn't have done so without the Saint. It was a bitter truth to carry—far heavier than the sword in her hand.

They returned to the carriage. Arthur, who drove St. Silas's team, was discreet, and he wasted no time in helping St. Silas lift Rami into the carriage. He didn't remark on Rami's battered appearance nor the blood that soaked Leena's sleeves. Within minutes of settling him in, Rami had fallen into the deep sleep that follows a shock, his breathing coming fast and short in his chest.

"We must bury the body," Leena whispered, turning to view the clearing. It hurt to speak.

She felt St. Silas still.

When she turned to look at him in question, his eyes were made darker by the filtered moonlight. "Leave it. The Black Coats will find him in the morning."

Leena remembered how the Black Coat's flesh had felt as her knife serrated it, like cutting through silk.

The frayed control she held over herself was unraveling. The Saint did not understand; she *must* bury the body tonight. If her hand did not mold itself over the handle of a shovel now, it would forevermore carry the feeling of the knife instead.

"Tonight." She did not recognize the near-hysteria in her own voice; very rarely had she ever felt so undone. "Tonight." She swallowed again. "You can leave. I will go back."

"He is dead." St. Silas's voice was flat. "It will keep." She knew that tone well; there would be no arguments that would sway him. Nothing that would shift his forceful eyes.

For the second time that night, without waiting for his permission, Leena jumped down from the carriage.

His iron grip held her steady. "What if I forbid you?" His eyes were hard, but there was a crack in his voice.

Her own voice was unsteady. "Then I will return, even if you drag me back and lock me in my room. I will force my way back to bury him."

"Your misplaced sentiments are foolish," he gritted out.

She put her hand over his clasped fingers. "Let me go."

"Or else?"

"Or else I will never speak of Lord Avon again, contract or no." She was unwavering, her brows drawn and set on her face. "Some things are worth the sacrifice."

They stared at each other for a searing moment.

"The burial—" he began, before cutting himself off harshly, abruptly releasing her.

Finally, St. Silas let out a staggered breath before dragging his hand through his hair. It was such an uncharacteristically human gesture it made Leena pause. If she had not known better, she would have said he was angry. No, not angry—*agitated.*

The only reply she got was an imperceptible nod of his head. Without waiting for her, he headed back toward the clearing.

With one final worried glance at her brother, who still lay deeply asleep, Leena followed.

The bullet had hit the corpse in the middle of his forehead, an unsurprisingly perfect shot, and the river of blood and brain matter concealed his face from view.

Leena preferred it that way.

"Is his ghost with you?" St. Silas broke her heavy thoughts, his voice oddly quiet.

"No," Leena whispered, making another careful search. "Thank the Saints."

They found a wooden shed with an assortment of garden tools, including two rusted shovels. The rain had softened the soil. St. Silas rolled up his sleeves and began digging without prelude, the hard muscles of his back coiling with every mound of soil he lifted. Exhausted, Leena worked beside him—albeit at a slower pace, in spite of her best efforts to keep up.

A few times she glanced over at St. Silas. He worked almost mechanically, a distant look in his eyes. Even in her haze of misery, she could not account for his strange behavior.

The task was long and arduous. The earth beneath them was not meant to be a burial ground, and it opposed their unsaintly digging.

"Speak." So focused was Leena on her task that she thought she had imagined St. Silas's voice. She paused and turned to him, but he did not stop, hard eyes fixed on the earth before him.

"I beg your pardon?"

"Speak. Say anything. I cannot abide the silence."

Leena's mouth parted, both weariness and confusion making her slow to react to his words. But as her focus cleared, she regarded the rigidity of his expression and understood his unsaid meaning—*I cannot abide the silence while I am creating this grave.*

After another long, searching moment, Leena murmured, picking up her own shovel again: "Chapter Seven: The Rosethorn. The Rosethorn is native to colder climates, found most notably in the meadows of the Aksari Mountains, blooming in early spring and thriving until midwinter. Its petals are a curious mixture of red and orange, giving it a sunset glow, which helps keep insects active through the winter . . ."

Leena could see the text as if *A Guide to Botany* was open before her. She was sitting reading to her mother, legs swinging beneath her on the crooked chair, the soft breeze bringing in the smells of salt and cooking. There was warmth. And there was love. And she had not been cold or afraid or heartsick.

"Will I never hear the end of that blasted book?" St. Silas finally replied when she took a pause, but when she glanced at him the tightness around his eyes had abated a little. Leena was glad, without knowing why, that he did not look, for a moment, like a ghost himself.

"It is customary for the people of the Aksari Mountains to plant Rosethorns over the graves of loved ones," Leena continued, "symbolizing that if such a flower can endure the harsh winter of the mountains, so can the spirit find peace in the coldness of the earth."

This time St. Silas did not comment.

They continued—Leena reciting, both shoveling—until they'd dug a rectangular hole deep into the ground. Streaks of sun began lightening the sky and birdsong filtered through gaps in the trees—which seemed an odd contrast to the grimness of grave digging.

"Enough." St. Silas finally put his shovel down. He wiped his forehead with the back of his hand, leaving a streak of mud by his left brow.

St. Silas dragged the heavy body across the grass, a trail of blood behind him. With one final push, the body fell into the grave like a disjointed rag doll. The corpse's head hit the ground first, with a sickening thud.

"Wait," Leena cried. "We are the only witnesses to his funeral. We *must* say something."

"I caused his death, Miss Al-Sayer," St. Silas said, with another twist of his mouth. "I do not think this man's main concern would be whether or not his killer says a few kind words over his grave."

She flinched at the word *killer.* Taking a deep breath, she said a phrase in her father's language—a common saying to send off the departed.

May your soul no longer crave the soil.

"That sounds similar to what you said in the prison." St. Silas's voice held guarded curiosity. "Is it a prayer?"

Leena looked at him, surprise on her face. "You remember what I said?"

"I did not understand it. Both sounded . . . final."

Turning back to the grave with stinging eyes, she whispered, "Of sorts. Both are goodbyes."

That distant expression returned to St. Silas's face. When he looked back at the dead man, it seemed to Leena as if he was not quite seeing him. Then he picked up the shovel and started throwing dirt over the grave. "You're shivering. Let's finish."

She was shivering, but she was not surprised that he had noticed. As always, very little escaped him.

They began to make their way back after the last drop of soil fell onto the heap. Just as they crossed the clearing, Leena turned to have one final look at the grave.

She halted, sweat breaking out on her forehead.

A ghost stood over the mound. An Algaraan, barely older than Rami. Blood pooled from his forehead, and his abdomen bore the mark of Leena's dagger.

"Miss Al-Sayer, what is it?" St. Silas was beside her, his sharp tone silencing the birds.

She brought a trembling hand to her eyes. "The boy we killed—" She could barely speak over her own heartbeat. "He looks like Rami. He's half starved, he's *young*—"

St. Silas's eyes flickered to where Leena's gaze was trained, but he clearly saw nothing. "Look away from the dead." His own voice sounded suspended between concentrated control . . . and a fiercely buried lack of it. "We had no choice—"

Leena shook so hard that she could not focus on St. Silas's words, her eyes still trained on the phantom that now lay weeping over his own grave. "No, *he* didn't have a choice," she replied brokenly. "That is what happens to people who look like me. They take our homes, they take our fathers, they take the very food from our bellies—"

"He tried to kill you. It was either be slain or *live*." His voice tightened as he looked at the nothingness, jaw rigid. When he glanced down at her still-pale face, he added, "He was a Black Coat."

It was no real comfort to her that the young dead boy had been a gang member. "Rami could've easily been a Black Coat." The metallic taste of copper coated Leena's tongue. "The Black Coats are filled with immigrant children—children whose homes could be found on the opposite end of a closed fist—"

"I understand—"

"No, you don't understand. How could you?" Her cheeks were wet, the cold air biting her face. "You are Morish. The soldiers on the street stop to interrogate me daily, but they bow to you. The color of your skin, the tenor of your voice, even your accent, all proclaim your right to exist here, whereas anyone who looks like me—like *that* boy buried in this unmarked grave—is *wrong*. He never had a fighting chance." The rise and fall of her chest felt like she was squeezing air through clogged vessels. "It is beyond you being the Saint of Silence. You belong to this land, hold superiority in it." She wiped her face with her dirt-crusted sleeve. "You always have a choice."

St. Silas looked away from her, his stare now locked on the rising sun behind the treeline. The hard lines of his throat worked, as if he was trying to swallow down words—or memories.

When he spoke next, his voice was carefully detached, his expression fixed. "I was very young when I buried my first body. I was sobbing so hard I could not hold on to the shovel." His voice barely changed, but she caught the fragmented borders of it anyway. "Believe me, Miss Al-Sayer, I also had little *choice* then." His stance was rigid, muscles coiled, as if he still held that same shovel. "The boy I buried was fourteen. I was twelve. The earth was not soft."

Leena stared at him in astonishment, feeling a sudden, visceral, burning shame. The need to desperately take back her words rose through her like a tide. At twelve she had been holding her father's hand, eating *halwa* on lazy summer days, not learning her way around a grave.

But Leena's tongue didn't know how to form words of remorse, so instead she continued to mutely watch St. Silas. She found he was staring back, equally wordless, equally weary.

"Survival is a sordid business." There was an odd aloofness in his voice, as if he was not speaking to her.

His choice of words did not immediately make sense to Leena, and it took her a long moment to realize that the Saint of Silence was attempting to *comfort* her.

She could not explain why such an unexpected act of kindness brought forth another rush of tears. She pressed her closed fists against her eyes, turning away rapidly, unable to reply; her aching mind could not lift the weight of so much heartache.

Leena's blurring eyes returned to the grave they'd left behind. The ghost of the young Black Coat was gone, and she was relieved that he hadn't lingered to haunt her.

St. Silas's voice when he called for them to continue sounded distant in her ears, but she managed to put one foot in front of the other to follow him through the clearing. The birdsong continued, drowning out her thoughts and all other sounds of the forest, a symphony of farewell.

16

Theodore Daye

INSOMNIA ONCE AGAIN settled behind Leena's eyelids.

It had been one week since the events at the cottage, and the days since had passed slowly. She'd seen death before—multiple times, in fact—but never had such a direct hand in it. Her skin still smelled of burial.

In the rare few hours when she was not busy looking after Rami, she could not find rest. She searched for a way to stop her consistent deliberations. Amid the usual assortment of ghosts that lingered around her in the late hours, Leena paced, she read, she even sewed—anything not to face how skewed her life had become.

Why, Leena thought with a groan, pricking her finger for the fourth time, did his voice and shadowed face keep finding a home in her late nights?

But, of course, she knew. She knew *exactly* why.

She was contrite—and her contrition would not allow her the respite of sleep.

She had given him little choice that night but to help her bury the young man, threatening him with the one thing he wanted: finding Lord Avon's ghost.

And she did not need to be a palm reader to be able to see, with sharp clarity, that burying the body had pained him.

Speak, he had said.

The methodical, detached way he had dug, the grinding of his jaw and the untethered look in his eyes spoke of a wound he was resurrecting alongside the thick, iron-rich earth.

Giving up with disgust, Leena threw her embroidery onto the bed, instead choosing to vigorously brush her hair for the third time that night. She stared at the mirror without seeing her reflection.

It was no wonder the look he had given her as he'd told of the boy he had buried at twelve spoke of *laceration.*

She'd forced a confession from him, just as she had seen him do to so many of his customers. The only difference was that all of his customers came willingly, lined up for hours, and knew the price they had to pay, yet their reward was ample.

That night, St. Silas had paid the price without the reward. And that was what troubled her—the fact that she'd *taken* the choice from him.

It made matters worse that the ghost of the servant-boy—the very same one she'd acknowledged in Orley's office—had begun to follow her. He stood by her bed, watching her from outside the salt circle. That first night, it had been him, the weeping cobbler, and an old woman whose clawed hand begged for offerings. The second night, it had been only the servant-boy and the weeping cobbler. The nights after that, it was only the servant-boy. His twitchy, gaunt face molded into a smile of greeting every time Leena stumbled out of bed, and she stared in amazement at the emptiness of her room.

"Are you keeping the other ghosts away?" Leena asked in awe.

He bowed, as if she was a lady and he was her servant.

"How do you do that?" she begged. "Can you teach me?"

He pointed toward his chest and nodded, then pointed toward Leena and shook his head. She understood. He could better control the dead because he was one of their number. Leena, who was still living (even though she didn't always feel like she was), could not choose her hauntings.

She rubbed the sleep from her eyes, feeling slightly deflated. "Will you keep the other phantoms away from me at night?"

Leena had asked this without any hope, as the ghosts never did what she wanted, so was startled when the servant-boy nodded. She stared at him, her heart pounding in her chest.

"Thank you," she said haltingly. She had never thanked any of her phantoms before. He even turned around when Leena dressed—unlike a few of her leering ghosts, who forced her to change while under the covers, stripping her of her dignity.

This morning, she had a sudden desire to humanize the ghost, so she did something she'd never done before. She asked for his name.

She found yesterday's newspaper and ripped out the margins, quickly writing the letters of the alphabet in as big a font as she could within the tight space.

"Point to the letters and tell me your name," Leena told the boy, hoping that he knew how to read.

The ghost furrowed his brows, his lips mouthing the letters as he painstakingly pointed them out. It was clear he knew how to spell his name and very little else.

Theodore Daye.

Leena smiled. "Thank you, Theodore Daye."

Suddenly shy, the ghost dropped his gaze, tugging at the collar of his livery.

"How do you know Mr. Orley?"

A shivering fear transformed Theodore's face, and he backed a step away.

Leena understood.

She thought of Orley and Mrs. Van—their creeping long hands, their expanding eyes, their overwhelming presence—so inhuman, so *other*. It had become an obsession of hers, even as she spent her time tending to Rami alongside Mrs. Van. The housekeeper had proved to be an essential asset in the sickroom. Her knowledge regarding herbal remedies far superseded Leena's own, and they spent the long hours boiling broths and preparing poultices.

A tepid understanding had arisen between them.

Yet although she was grateful for the housekeeper's assistance, all her previous misgivings about Mrs. Van still lay like a hard lump in her throat. In those wakeful nights, Leena thought of the dream she had had—*How long must he survive this?*—and she could not shake the feeling that it was essential that Mrs. Van confirmed Leena's suspicions. That if the Saint dealt with *other* creatures, then to be left in the dark might prove dangerous for her and her brother. Especially in her hunt for Lord Avon.

She found Mrs. Van in the kitchen. Leena seldom wandered in there, it being the domain of the stern housekeeper, but it was surprisingly cozier than the unlived-in state of the rest of the house. The fire in the grate was welcoming, the herbs procured from the market hung by the window wafting scents of lemongrass, and somewhere a kettle had been set to boil.

Mrs. Van was finely mincing roots with an experienced hand. She turned at Leena's approach and wiped her bony fingers on her apron. Theodore Daye followed closely behind her and planted himself in the open doorway.

"Miss Al-Sayer," Mrs. Van said, briefly curtseying before adding the roots into a mortar.

Leena smiled tentatively. "Rami's been complaining that you are going to bully him into good health."

"It is as the master wanted," she said, but the corner of her mouth lifted.

"Where did you learn about healing?" Leena asked.

Mrs. Van crushed the roots into a fine paste. "I've lived many lives."

"Any of them good?"

"This one is," she replied softly.

Leena slid onto a stool and began to peel the potatoes Mrs. Van had left soaking in brine.

"Do you know why Mr. St. Silas hired me?" Leena asked.

The crushing sound of mortar and pestle stopped. "He has not told me. The contract forbids him."

"Ah, yes, his contracts. How he enjoys those." The potato slipped from Leena's hands and the knife almost slid into her bare skin. "Would you like to know why?"

"If you are willing."

"Will you answer one of my questions in return?"

The kettle whistled.

Mrs. Van seemed to think for a moment. Then she nodded slowly.

"The reason Mr. St. Silas hired me is because I can see ghosts."

A moment passed. Mrs. Van blinked. Theodore Daye nodded as if he already knew this.

"Ah."

"That's exactly how he reacted."

"And he believes you?"

"I've passed his tests."

"Then it must be so." Mrs. Van's long fingers played with a brooch pinned to her lapel. "A long time ago, there used to be many who claimed to be able to speak to ghosts. I've never heard of one who is able to see them. Still, I'll trust the master's judgment."

"How do you know him?"

Mrs. Van sighed, and went to remove the kettle from the fire, pouring Leena a cup. "Is that your question?"

Leena nodded.

"I worked for his father, and his father before him . . ."

They stared at each other. Leena's heart thudded.

"How old are you?" Leena whispered. The other woman's face was oddly devoid of wrinkles—stone smooth, but aged in the same way bricks and boulders age.

"Very old, Miss Al-Sayer. Now drink your tea. Your brother needs tending."

Leena could not stop shaking as she went to see Rami. She couldn't quite believe what she'd heard, and for one moment she'd desperately wished that Mrs. Van was lying. Life was tumultuous, and the one surety was that it eventually ended. To think that a creature like Mrs. Van could live and live and . . .

It was madness.

Theodore Daye followed her, his ghostly form flickering in and out like a mere trick of the light. It was also madness that Leena could see phantoms. It was madness that the dead did not always die.

She swallowed—but what did that make Mrs. Van?

More important, what was St. Silas dealing with?

Rami was sitting up in bed; he had been given a chamber near her own. The bruises had transformed from a garish purple to a fading yellow. His left eye was still bloodshot, although less so, and he could now open the curtains without wincing at the bright light.

It had been a rough week—and at the worst of it, Rami had cursed her when she'd suggested sending for the doctor.

"No doctors," he'd yelled on that second night. His forehead was burning by then and he'd begun to hallucinate, thrashing so violently that Arthur had to be called to restrain him. Once he was subdued, Mrs. Van had shoveled a sleeping draught down his throat. Just as Rami's eyelids became heavier and his words slurred, he had tugged Leena's arm. "No doctors . . . *please.*" There was such desperation in his voice that she couldn't refuse.

The last time Rami had seen a doctor was for his amputation. They couldn't afford the anesthesia, and the surgeon wouldn't take Baba's shoes or Leena's faux jewelry as payment. It had to be done without. Rami had been awake throughout the entire operation, witnessing his own butchering, falling into unconsciousness only afterward. Baba had wrapped the limb in newspaper and taken it to the cemetery, and Leena knew that Rami had never forgotten that a part of him had been buried while he slept.

"You look awful," Leena said—the same greeting she had given him every morning for the past week. This time, her voice shook with the weight that now plagued her mind, and she felt sick with it.

"Still have all my teeth," was his usual response.

Leena had already told him of all the events leading up to her contract. His eyes had blazed when he'd heard of Leena bargaining her secret for Rami's medication, the fire growing even steadier when he heard the details of her contract. *The Saint will have to employ me as well* was all he said. *For as long as you are indentured, Leena, so am I.*

Leena didn't know if her brother would be allowed to stay; St. Silas had already stretched his mercy to the limit by allowing Leena to shirk her duties to care for Rami.

Rami noticed her pale, trembling face, and he told her to sit on the chair beside the bed.

"What's happened?" he asked, holding his ribs and grimacing as he turned to face her.

A part of Leena was afraid that Rami might not believe her. That if she accused the housekeeper of being *another creature,* he might give her that same pitying look as her neighbors. She didn't think she could bear that.

"Are you thinking about the Black Coat you buried at the cottage again?" Rami asked. "Has his ghost come back?"

That was somehow easier to speak about. "No, not again," Leena said quietly. "Do you remember what Margery used to say?"

"What did that old bat used to say?" Rami hated *all* their neighbors.

She threw him an irritated look. "She used to say that it was bad luck for the old to bury the young."

His mouth twisted. "It's all superstition, Leena. He would've killed you and not suffered your death as you are suffering his."

She let out a shaky breath, still feeling overwhelmed.

Rami frowned as he pulled a piece of loose thread from his coverlet. "You shouldn't have been there."

"Did you think no one was coming for you?" She watched his profile carefully.

The thread snapped in his hand.

After a long moment, he said, "I knew you'd come. That's the only constant."

They had very few constants in their lives. They had both been forced to learn how to rebuild too early and too often.

"Why did you refuse to throw the fight?" The question had been beating Leena's chest throughout the long nights spent watching over his sickbed.

His tone dripped with wrath. "Because devil take them, that's why."

She stood up in a huff. "I could throttle you!"

"Get in line, then," he snapped.

"You're a fool, Rami. And your foolish ways will kill us." She crossed her arms. "What will you do if Mr. Martin tries again? If the Black Coats try again?"

The bruises on Rami's face made him look like a ghastly, twisted reflection of himself. "I'll make them pay."

Leena turned and walked out of the room, slamming the door in the process.

Leena's mind was a chaotic swirl as she left Rami's room. What she needed was a semblance of her routine, repugnant to her though it was. For that, she would have to find St. Silas.

She'd only seen him in passing during the week since Rami's kidnapping. He had left a short note informing her that she would be excused from the duties of the shop while she tended to her brother. That was a courtesy any factory Warden would rather drink poison than give to their workers. For that, at least, Leena respected him. While the Saint was demanding, she had come to find he was also fair-minded with all his employees.

Now that Rami was very much on the mend, she could no longer continue to take time off from both her contract and the hunt. So it was with deep reluctance that Leena knocked on the door of the Saint's study.

"Enter," St. Silas commanded. He was sitting behind his desk in his usual fashion, piles of ledgers stacked on one side, accounts and papers filled with scribbles on the other.

He didn't look up. "You may leave the tray and go, Mrs. Van."

"I've not brought food, I'm afraid. You ought to keep a tin of biscuits in here somewhere."

At her voice, his head jerked up, and she was startled to see dark-gray shadows underneath his eyes. Otherwise, he was as immaculate as ever as he stood to bow to her.

"Miss Al-Sayer." He assessed her wordlessly. His gaze lingered on her neck a moment too long.

"It does not pain me any longer," Leena offered quietly.

"I didn't ask." And yet his sharp glance returned to her fading bruises once again.

Leena nodded, averting her gaze momentarily, fixing on the desk's curved edges. "I only came by to say I am ready to begin our search again. Rami is almost out of his sickbed and no longer needs to be nursed around the clock."

"Good. If that is all?"

She didn't leave. "I also wanted to thank you for giving me time away from my duties to care for him. That was very generous of you." She paused, tugging at a button on her dress. "The Black Coats will be looking for my brother, but they cannot touch him *if* he is to be under your protection."

She could feel St. Silas's gaze burn into her, although she didn't return it.

"If you let my brother stay"—her eyes flashed to meet his—"I will work harder to find Lord Avon. I will—"

He held up a hand, and Leena fell silent. "If I do not have to hear or deal with your brother a moment longer, then he will be permitted to work alongside Arthur as a bruiser."

Relief flooded Leena like a tidal wave. "Thank you, sir. He will not disappoint."

"Your brother—for all that he is an impetuous fool—is talented with a sword. But mark my words, any sign of rebellion"—he slanted her a look—"the *Al-Sayer* rebellion—and he will be gone."

He did not respond to her further show of gratitude.

She turned to go, but when she opened the door it was to see Theodore Daye waiting for her. On peeking inside, the young ghost startled visibly, his eyes fixating on something behind her. Leena first thought that he was looking at St. Silas, but she quickly followed his gaze and saw that it was Lord Avon's portrait that had captured his attention so keenly.

"Do you know him?" Leena whispered, not wanting to startle the phantom.

"Know who?" St. Silas responded, not looking up from his work.

"Do you know Lord Avon?" she repeated gently.

The ghost's mouth opened in his thin face and he nodded slowly.

Leena's heart jumped.

"Is there a ghost here, Miss Al-Sayer?" Suddenly St. Silas was beside her, peering urgently into the nothingness.

"Yes, a boy who claims to know Lord Avon," she continued to whisper, not taking her eyes off the phantom in case he vanished.

"Who is this ghost?"

"His name is Theodore Daye."

She felt St. Silas stiffen beside her, a strange energy radiating off him like a building storm.

"Theodore . . . Daye?" St. Silas looked disturbed, so far removed from his normally languid manner that Leena threw him a questioning glance. "Describe him, Miss Al-Sayer. The ghost."

Leena furrowed her brows. "A boy around fourteen, wearing a servant's livery. Hair as fair as wheat. The color of his eyes is difficult to say, but I think they were once blue. I've seen him only in the past week."

St. Silas stared rigidly into the absence where Leena could so clearly see Theodore, now looking back at St. Silas with equal intensity.

"Can he summon Lord Avon?" Although the question was meant for Leena, it felt as if St. Silas was speaking directly to the phantom.

Leena had never met a ghost that could call forth another spirit, but she asked anyway.

Theodore Daye, his mouth a firm line, nodded once more.

"He can," Leena gasped, barely believing her own words. "*How, Theodore?*"

He pointed toward Lord Avon's portrait, indicating specifically the red book in the noble's hand.

"He's signaling to that book that Lord Avon's holding in the portrait."

St. Silas inhaled roughly. "The red diary."

"What red diary?"

"It belonged to the First Marquess of Avon. Now a lost family heirloom."

"Why haven't you mentioned this heirloom before?" Leena asked him sharply.

He met her accusing stare with stoic eyes. "It's being mentioned now."

She turned away from St. Silas in anger, focusing once more on the young ghost. "Can you confirm that you can bring Lord Avon to us if we have the red diary?"

He nodded slowly.

Leena didn't know if she could trust him; she'd never trusted a ghost before. But she remembered the way that Theo had warded off the other ghosts that haunted her, protecting her while she slept. That he had the power to do so was unique. That he wanted to help Leena was even more novel. She decided that she had no choice but to trust him.

"Do you know where the diary is now, Theodore?" Leena asked eagerly, but she already suspected the answer.

He gestured toward a stray piece of paper on the Saint's desk. Leena understood, hurriedly followed him to the desk, and began scrawling all the letters of the alphabet. With his tongue pointing out of his mouth in concentration, the ghost carefully pointed at the letters.

B—R—A—M

She turned to St. Silas. "He's spelled your given name."

The Saint said nothing.

W—A—V—N—G—S—H—A—W

Then, as if this act of revelation had fatigued him, the ghost nodded once more at her before flickering in and out, finally disappearing entirely. She hoped with all her might that this was not the last time she would see him.

The air felt like it had been extinguished from the room. Even the light from the burning fireplace seemed dim now, the magnitude of what she'd learned dulling it. It was a confirmation of what Leena already knew—*it all led back to Weavingshaw.*

She turned to St. Silas, eager to see his reaction.

"He spelled out Weavingshaw," she said. But if she expected the Saint to share in her excitement, she was disappointed. He'd already sat back down behind his desk, his attention not on his work but rather staring blankly at the fire, brows drawn together, the shadows beneath his eyes even more vivid.

He looked suddenly bloodless—*bled out*—and Leena knew with certainty that the mention of Theodore Daye had opened an old wound.

Slowly, and a little hesitantly, Leena walked around his desk. "How do you know Theodore Daye?"

He didn't answer, but his eyes jolted away from the fire to meet hers. With effort, his expression turned deliberately remote once more.

Because she could not force a response from him, Leena began to think aloud, trying to sort through her thoughts. She'd spent long hours theorizing about why St. Silas was chasing Lord Avon. Was it for an unsettled debt? Hidden treasure? A way to make amends to the dead? A way to take retribution on the dead? None of it seemed plausible. "Were you a servant at Weavingshaw as a child?"

His brows rose faintly, a familiar sardonic lilt to his voice. "Interesting hypothesis, madam."

"Is that a yes or a no, Mr. St. Silas?"

His gaze fell back to the ledgers encircling the study in another stretch of silence, then to his own timepiece hanging from his waistcoat.

"Will you call me Bram?" he asked instead, his voice uneven, once again bordering on the edge of *something*. "I've rarely heard my own name said back to me. Not since—"

Theodore Daye.

She tried not to rear back in astonishment. There was an intensity of emotion to St. Silas that she had never witnessed before, and there was now no doubt in her mind that the young Theodore Daye was the catalyst for this, dragging behind him a past she had no insight into.

Bram.

The name sounded in her head, and she tested the contours of it, wondering if it would turn into poison if she swallowed it. It felt as foreign to her tongue as some of the Algaraan words she'd practiced from her vocabulary books, the consonants at war with each other.

There was no peace to be had from that name, only invasion.

"I am safe here, sir, on the other side," Leena finally replied, quietly, eyes not quite meeting his own.

"And what side is that?" His voice was strained.

“Where you are a formidable and uncompromising employer. And I a . . .” Leena’s gaze did not waver from its focus on the point of his collar. She was not yet ready to acknowledge to herself that here sat before her a man blindly searching for a tourniquet with which to stem his bleeding, much as they did in wartime before they had to amputate.

“. . . ghost-seer,” he finished. Leena’s eyes shot to his, but before she could comment, he pointed toward the door, effectively dismissing her entirely from his presence. “I have private business to attend to tomorrow. Then the day after I will be taking a short trip outside of Golborne. The shop will be closed until I return. Your duties can resume then.”

17

The Injured Boy

Leena saw St. Silas from the landing early the next day.

He was exiting his study, followed closely by another man. A tradesman, Leena guessed from the man's clothes, well made but functional. It was at odds with St. Silas's manner of dress, always darkly elegant, the superior quality of fabric molding precisely to the broad contours of his shoulders, the waistcoat tapering to his narrow hips. For one unchecked moment, Leena allowed her eyes to follow the hard lines of his body, now pausing for a moment on the large hand that had lingered protectively on her lower back in Orley's office.

She pulled her attention back to her surroundings, acutely aware that she was falling into such foolish thoughts more and more lately.

Leena loitered on the top step, hidden within the shadows. The conversation she had had with St. Silas the previous day was still heavy on her mind, and she'd been hoping to avoid him that morning to allow things between them to settle back into their usual habit.

The tradesman stopped at the threshold, swiping a hand through his thinning hair. "I trust in your discretion, sir, and I have no doubt you will guard my secret well."

St. Silas only took confessions in his study from a select few. Leena was rarely privy to those conversations, but sometimes he made her watch unobserved, searching for any phantoms that may have haunted those valuable customers.

St. Silas's bow was polite.

Leena had seen this before; cruelty always followed his civility. "I am the very soul of discretion, Mr. Marlow."

Mr. Marlow released a long sigh. "You do intend to send one of your men today to clean up the mess? I cannot have the other servants stumbling upon the scene. It would cause a scandal, not to mention the magistrate might become involved."

"My deepest sympathy," St. Silas murmured. She almost wanted to shout at the tradesman to look closer into St. Silas's expression; his eyes were hard, without a sliver of pity. "Have no fear. I shall attend to the matter myself."

While the tradesman found comfort in St. Silas's words, Leena knew this for exactly what it was—a threat. Her feet were rooted firmly to the ground as the tradesman walked the expanse of the hallway, before exiting through the back door to the courtyard. St. Silas stayed standing by his study, all hints of a polite smile vanishing from his mouth, retribution in his harsh stare.

Suddenly, St. Silas looked up at her in the stairwell, her hand firmly gripping the banister. He did not look surprised by her presence. Any evidence of what had occurred between them last night was gone from his face.

"Any ghosts following Marlow?" was all he asked her.

Leena shook her head. "What do you have planned for him?"

"How do you know I have any plans for him?"

"You are hard to read," she said quietly, "but your eyes do not always contain themselves."

His brows shot up. There was a tension about him, passing and subtle, the muscles of his jaw taut, before his countenance turned cool. She could tell that what she'd said had momentarily disconcerted him. The Saint of Silence was the one to devour secrets; it was clear that he derived no joy from the fact that she also watched him.

"Madam," he said, bowing once to her before continuing down the hallway, following Marlow like a beast trailing blood.

She was awoken in the middle of the night by a hurried knock on her chamber door.

Leena was out of bed instantly, not bothering even to greet Theo Daye as he stood at the edge of the salt circle, before rushing to unlock the latch and swing the door open. Mrs. Van stood on the threshold, also in her nightclothes, looking less stern with her hair braided to the side rather than in her habitual tight bun.

"Is it Rami?" Leena asked, her heart straining in her chest.

"No, he sleeps soundly. It is the master. He has sent word that he will need our urgent presence in the kitchen."

"At this hour?" Leena's eyes swerved to the heavy grandfather clock in the hallway, but she could not see the hand within the dim light of Mrs. Van's lantern. "It must be near midnight."

"Only just after." Mrs. Van nodded at her nightgown. "Make haste with your attire, Miss Al-Sayer. The master does not like to be kept waiting."

While the rest of the house was frigid, the kitchen was warm, a healthy fire spitting from the grate. Leena rubbed the sleep from her eyes, but the bone-deep fatigue still clung to her, giving the night a disorienting edge. The housekeeper had given her a moment to change, and Leena had shrugged into one of her favorite faded cotton dresses, wrapping an apron over the front.

She wasn't sure what they were waiting for, but she rushed to help Mrs. Van light the tallow candles, filling the kitchen with a steady, pulsing glow. Just as Leena lit the last wick, she heard heavy footsteps in the hallway.

She let go of the box of matches and nervously reached for her copper coins, jumping when the door slammed open.

The first thing Leena's exhausted mind noticed was the blood. So much of it. All over St. Silas, staining his white-collared shirt and his waistcoat a deep red. For one stunned moment, she could not move, her gaping eyes unable to comprehend what she was seeing.

St. Silas tore through the kitchen, his movements fluid and unimpeded, and she released a deep breath when she realized that he was not the one who was injured.

"Quickly." His command was swift. "Where can I put him?"

Leena's eyes fell to the bundle he carried in his arms. She staggered closer, her thoughts passing through her mind like bullets slowed by water.

The bundle stirred. A whimper escaped, then a small childish sob.

"On the table." Mrs. Van hurried to strip the cloth off the aged wood.

Carefully, St. Silas eased the weight onto the table.

It was a boy, not much older than seven, wrapped in St. Silas's coat.

Leena could not tear her gaze away from the boy's pale skin, mottled with bruises shaped like handprints—over his brow, on his neck, trailing beneath his clothes. His shoulder was fixed at an awkward angle, the bone jutting from the socket. Small whimpers racked his body.

Leena was sure that she must've walked into a nightmare.

A flicker of movement by St. Silas's shoulder caught Leena's horrified gaze.

A ghost stood over the boy.

It was clear that the phantom had returned not to comfort the living, but to rage at them. It took her turbulent mind a second to recognize him as the tradesman from that morning, Mr. Marlow.

Mr. Marlow's ghost flared with fury. Even in the dim light, Leena could see the phantom's clothes hung off him in a bloodied mess.

St. Silas's dagger was lodged in his chest.

All at once, the tradesman's words came back to her: *You do intend to send one of your men today to clean up the mess?*

She had thought the worst of St. Silas's reaction that morning. But that same burning anger St. Silas had shown then now thrummed through Leena's own veins, and she could not stop the accusation pouring from her mouth. "*You* did this to him!"

The entirety of Leena's livid focus was on the ghost, and she did not notice St. Silas and Mrs. Van momentarily halt, turning to stare at her.

"No, madam." St. Silas looked at her with an expression he had never worn before, but his tone was cold when he replied, jerking her attention away from the phantom that hovered over him. "While I cannot usually fault your reasoning, I'm afraid you are wrong on this account."

Leena blinked, unsure what he was speaking of, her gaze returning to Mr. Marlow's phantom, who watched the child with dark hatred.

She jolted into action once Mrs. Van called her name sharply.

She aided Mrs. Van in removing the coat from the boy, revealing stretches of skin marked only with pain. Leena's one small comfort at the awful scene before them was that there existed no better healer and apothecary than Mrs. Van with her endless supply of strange herbs, rare medicinals, and thick books lining the kitchen cabinets. If there was ever a chance for amends, the child would find it here—ironically, in the Saint of Silence's own residence.

Leena's hands shook as she unbuttoned the child's shirt collar, wincing whenever she caused the boy to shriek. Hot tears formed at the back of her own eyes and she could not speak past the lump in her throat.

"Who is he?" Mrs. Van asked, and Leena had never heard such strong emotion waver her voice before.

"A servant-boy." St. Silas's voice remained steady. His back was bent as he held a strip of gauze to the boy's forehead, stemming the bleeding from a deep gash across his scalp. The firelight cast St. Silas's face in shadow, and Leena could not read his expression, but his shoulders were coiled as if he was ready to fight again. "He had accidentally broken one of his master's vases while polishing it. Clearly, his master was not the forgiving sort."

"Please . . . please . . ." The boy's lips barely moved as he spoke, but Leena could not catch what it was he asked for.

"Do not be afraid. Your master is dead now." St. Silas's voice did not sound like his own—or not like what Leena had ever heard from him. "The dead cannot bother the living."

Then St. Silas caught Leena's eyes briefly, as if to say, *The dead cannot bother* most *of the living.*

St. Silas's words seemed to bring a measure of comfort to the child, for his whimpers quietened momentarily. When the boy did speak next, his voice was a barely formed whisper. "Will you please . . . continue . . . the story . . ."

Leena had long abandoned undoing the buttons, and was now cutting through the boy's shirt in order to view the extent of the damage to his shoulder, but she stumbled and leveled an astonished look at St. Silas.

St. Silas's mouth was a grim line. He did not return her look this time.

"I will continue, but first you must drink this," St. Silas said, taking the vial of sleeping draught Mrs. Van had concocted earlier. With rare trust, the child did as he was told, choking as the bitter liquid slipped down his throat.

For as long as Leena lived, she would never forget St. Silas's deep intonation threading through the room as he wove a story of a girl named Kit who had grown up in the crags of the north, secretly raising wolves despite her clan's objection to such creatures. Leena had never heard this story before, but it had the cadence of a folk tale—something that had been passed down for generations. She wondered if St. Silas had learned it while sitting on the knee of his own mother or father. Leena caught only fragments of the plot as she focused on her task, but his voice acted as a metronome to Leena's and Mrs. Van's work—a rhythm that kept the wild beats of her own pulse steady.

It was a softness that was entirely at odds with St. Silas's unyielding nature.

This entire night had been a revelation for Leena—an excavation of St. Silas, as if she'd seen him for the first time unburied and alive.

Leena could not help but throw quick, searching glances at St. Silas, who did not return her gaze. He had begun to clean the gash on the boy's scalp with alcohol and gauze. The boy attempted to stay still as he listened, but tears made dirt tracks down his face.

"You are very brave," St. Silas interrupted his story to inform the boy, his large hands working deftly to tie the bandage after Mrs. Van had applied her salve.

Through his tears, the child stared up at St. Silas, and the look he gave him made Leena bite her bottom lip painfully.

St. Silas paused as well, then gave the child a smile that was entirely disarming. "Certainly braver than I am, for I have been known to turn my crumpets at the sight of blood."

The turn of phrase made the child's smile widen, before wincing in pain.

"Leena—the Deathgrips," Mrs. Van instructed in a hurried whisper.

Deathgrips.

A Guide to Botany swam before Leena's eyes as she rushed for the glass canisters in the larder, grabbing a fistful of violet flowers before reaching for the pestle. She crushed them into a fine paste, all the while remembering the passages she'd memorized as a child: *Deathgrip has anti-inflammatory properties and can also be used to draw out infection in small quantities.*

It was not lost on her that on the night St. Silas had chosen to tell a story about a girl saving wolves, Leena was preparing a paste that was widely known to be lethal to the animal; its other name was *Death Comes to Wolves.*

St. Silas resumed his story as Leena worked on the paste and, once that was finished, she began cutting long strips of bandage before Mrs. Van could ask her. She and the housekeeper had fallen into a natural rhythm while nursing Rami, and Leena had learned enough to predict Mrs. Van's wants.

When the shoulder needed to be set, it was St. Silas who held the boy down. He interrupted the story again only momentarily to tell the child what needed to be done beforehand. The boy gave a shaky nod. The sleeping draught had begun to take effect, his eyelids heavy.

"Good lad," St. Silas murmured, nodding to Mrs. Van to begin. Then he continued the tale, his voice holding the same calmative depths that set all their disquieted hearts at ease. "Kit had turned to her father, the chieftain, ready to face her punishment for defying his orders and saving the gray wolf. Her mother sobbed as her father told her that she would be forced to marry an outsider and banished from the clan . . ."

The boy screamed as the bone snapped back into place.

Leena worked around Mrs. Van, wrapping gauze around the boy's shoulder and arm as nimbly as she could to stabilize the joint. Not long after that, the boy fell into a dreamless state, and St. Silas lapsed into silence as he released his hold on the boy, the story of Kit and her beloved wolves still echoing in the room.

As Leena tied the final knot, her glare returned to the phantom in unrestrained triumph.

Mr. Marlow's ghost appeared disturbed, his hands clawing at his sides.

"Yes," Leena snarled. "He will survive."

It was Mrs. Van who answered, not the ghost. "I believe so. He is young; his body will heal." She looked up at St. Silas. "We will need to send him to a convalescent home while he recovers."

St. Silas nodded. "In the morning. Let him rest here until then."

Leena's mind swam with the only picture she'd seen of a convalescent home, drawn in a newspaper once. Such homes were often located by the sea for the healthy treatment of lungs and joints. They were wildly expensive, and usually only accessible to the wealthy.

The ghost did not seem pleased by this news. In fact, waves of fury tore through him until his entire outline began to dim, turning fainter before he disappeared into nothing.

Leena wanted to celebrate the news of this ghost's vanishing with St. Silas and Mrs. Van, but she remembered abruptly that he had been visible only to her.

Her eyes flashed to St. Silas in sudden understanding, the words she had said returning to her with force: You *did this to him!*

The look he'd given her.

St. Silas had thought that she'd accused him.

18

The Courtyard

LEENA COULD NOT bring herself to leave the steady warmth of the kitchen, even after the child had been transported to a more comfortable chamber, to be further watched over by Mrs. Van.

Instead she stood there, staring vacantly at the curved basin in the sink where Mrs. Van had instructed her to wash her hands. St. Silas had left a few minutes ago, when everything had begun to settle and all there was left to do was mop the blood from the floors. The water was now a murky crimson, still disturbed and sloshing at the rim from how violently Leena had scrubbed her skin clean moments before.

It all reminded Leena too much of the night Rami's arm had been amputated. She half expected to turn and see the surgeon packing his tools in a leather case, either too busy or too uncaring to wipe the remnants of Rami's blood that clung to the dull blade. It was a staggering relief that when she finally did look up, it was only to find Mrs. Van returning to inform her that their young patient was settled.

Throughout this hideous night, Mrs. Van's face had worn a look that was both deeply ancient and maternal, and Leena felt an odd homesickness settle in her chest without knowing why.

Mrs. Van caught her yawning. "Off to bed with you, madam."

Just as Leena gave an incline of her head and was about to sweep from the room, Mrs. Van's voice stopped her one last time. "Rest. You deserve it."

Leena halted at the threshold, nearly swaying from exhaustion, unable to find relief in Mrs. Van's words. This night had been long and brutal—the kind that would live in her mind in sharp detail even as other memories faded—but it was not yet over for her. Not until she spoke with St. Silas.

It was some minutes before Leena found him.

At first, her weary feet had carried her to his study out of habit rather than thought. Before she had even lifted her fist to knock, she knew it would be vacant inside.

As Leena stood staring at the doorknob, there was a merging of two realities behind her eyes—the past in which Rami had had his arm amputated on the kitchen table, and the present in which a boy had been healed on one. She remembered that it had been Baba's arms that had carried Rami that time. Now it was St. Silas who had lifted the child, shepherding him from a house that would've seen the boy buried unmarked and forgotten in a field.

Moments passed in which Leena remained lost in her recollections. Finally, she stepped away from the study, heading instead toward the back door that led to the courtyard. She'd always hated the enclosed square cut entirely from stone with no flowers to soften its harsh exterior. Ruthlessly trimmed trees provided cover from the prying eyes of the neighbors and the streets beyond. If not for the single lantern that was lit in the center of this shadowy place, it would have been engulfed in complete darkness, for morning had not yet arrived.

As she made her way outside, Leena remembered that after the procedure had finished and Rami had finally fallen asleep, she had made Baba chai. Although her father's blue-collared shirt had still been coated in blood, he had taken the chai outside to the front stoop of the house. She would never forget the way he had held the glass without once bringing it to his lips. The pads of his thumb and index finger must have been blistering from the heat, but he did not put it down. She didn't think he had even noticed the burns on his fingers as he inhaled the crisp spring air. To Leena, it had looked as if he was trying to expel the poison of that night from his lungs.

That was why she was not surprised when she found St. Silas in the courtyard.

He was leaning on a windowsill beneath the sloping rooftop, sheltered from the rain that was slowing to a drizzle, giving the night a stonewashed smell. The dusky air roughened his skin, bringing slashes of healthy color to the sharply angled bones of his face, lending him a jarring vitality on a night Leena was sure was filled only with ghosts.

He had changed from his bloodied clothes, abandoning the waistcoat and wearing only a white muslin shirt undone at the collar, the sleeves rolled to the elbows, showing muscled forearms corded with veins.

Leena halted in the doorway, briefly bewitched by the way he looked standing within the moments between darkness and daylight. She was surprised to see a cigarette in his left hand, the very same kind imported from Algaraa; she had never seen him smoke before.

It was nearly unfathomable to her that even St. Silas kept bad habits to distract his restless mind. From the start, Leena had viewed him more as an executioner than a man, uncaring about whomever he dropped the ax on, lethal past the point of being human.

To see him this way, a cigarette held between slightly unsteady fingers, made him look like a touchable version of himself. Leena, whose bruised heart had been fractured and split open this night, wanted to find a shred of comfort in these changes.

The last few hours had bound them together in ways that went far beyond the words of a contract. Leena had known it would be like this from the moment she had seen St. Silas drenched in blood.

What she didn't know was what would come out of this unholy bond. Already she felt the ropes between them chafing, creating friction where there had been none previously.

"It is late," St. Silas said drily, without looking at her, his gaze still intent on the courtyard woven in fine mist.

"It is early." Leena nodded at the cigarette. "I did not think smoking was a distraction you partook in."

He glanced down at the cigarette in his hand dismissively. "Only very rarely." He finally lifted his eyes to hers and his smile was faint, more a jeering twist of his mouth. "I tend to look for my *distractions* elsewhere."

Even though she should, by now, have been used to St. Silas's implicit provocations, Leena still flushed deeply.

She could no longer deny that she was aware of him as a man. Even his voice, deep and full of inflections, did not seem strange to her anymore, in spite of all the distance that stood between them. And it would never feel strange again—not after he had used it to ease the hurt of a child.

Within the gloom of the night, St. Silas's eyes lingered on her with an almost begrudging fascination. He dropped his spent cigarette and stamped it beneath his boot, jerking his expression into indifference. "After all the time you've spent in my company, I am surprised that such trivial comments *still* send you blushing, Miss Al-Sayer. Should you see the actions that inspire such words, I believe you would perish."

It was not hard for Leena to imagine St. Silas captivating any woman he should choose with his magnetic allure, his devastating beauty. For even a brief moment, she imagined that she, Leena, could be the sole object of his intense focus.

More heated than ever, she turned her face away.

He gave a short laugh. "Go to sleep, Miss Al-Sayer."

I cannot, Leena thought to herself, even though she knew he was mocking her. Not until she made things right.

She didn't know how to start without sounding banal or insincere. She took a deep breath, her mouth opening and closing uselessly, before she finally managed a trivial, "Are you well?"

He raised his eyebrows at her, already in the process of lighting another cigarette. "Depends. Are you willing to make me feel better?"

His voice, husky and seductive from overuse, kissed along her skin, raising goosebumps in its trail.

In some ways, this was *exactly* the St. Silas she was used to. He was trying to disquiet her, to frighten her away, because he also felt the bite of the tether between them tightening. He wanted to return to their old dynamic just as she did—where he was the Saint of Silence and she was his ghost-seer—but Leena no longer thought that was possible, no matter what she'd said the previous night.

Ever since St. Silas had buried that young Algaraan Black Coat at her pleas, something had been growing between them, slow and lingering, unnoticed by either of them until it had spread. Tonight was its crucible—for it either to burn or to solidify. It seemed to Leena that they both danced around these two eventualities, unsure which one of them would lead to ruin.

"Does that mean you are not well?" It took a shoring of strength for Leena to continue onward with the conversation, despite his attempts at evasion.

St. Silas didn't immediately answer as he inhaled again from his cigarette. "If you are unwilling to come into my bed, Miss Al-Sayer, then I strongly suggest you go to yours."

Leena only just managed to keep her voice steady. There was a rawness to him tonight that was utterly new—or perhaps not new, but previously *hidden.* Whether it stemmed from the act of saving the child or the accusation he thought she'd made against him earlier, she did not know. Especially as he'd admitted to not taking confessions from children. This realization softened her look. "You are very frank tonight."

"I find the need for tact has worn itself out this evening."

He didn't look worn out, Leena thought to herself, watching him from beneath her lashes. Instead, energy poured from him in floods, and she could almost see his mind working. The only hint of fatigue was the darkened smudges beneath his eyes.

Sometimes, she had caught him looking exhausted, but he seemed to work past even that. In the very early mornings before the start of their consultations, she'd often seen him returning from what looked to be vigorous exercise at the gentlemen's club, sweat darkening his hair to a midnight black, his muscles strengthened and defined from endless activity, before he disappeared into his private rooms, undoubtedly for his bath. His energy was ceaseless, and not for the first time did she wonder if he ever slept.

Leena fought through her own growing response to him, because she knew it was becoming very dangerous. "I will leave you now." She curtseyed. "I have only come to rectify what I said earlier—"

"There is no need," he cut in without expression.

"It was not you I was speaking to."

"Was it not?" Still that aloofness.

"No. I saw the ghost of the man who beat the boy standing over him. It was to *him* that I made the accusation."

There was a breath between them. Whatever she had said seemed to momentarily arrest him. Finally, he ground out, "Is the ghost with you now?"

She shook her head.

He watched her for a long moment from behind the thin tendrils of smoke. In the cluster of trees that encircled the courtyard, she heard the first trills of birds. Soon, the city would start to awaken, rousing its inhabitants and forcing them from their beds. All of that seemed to Leena like a faraway thing—as though the city might stir in the background, but she would always be here standing in a courtyard just before dawn, beside a man who was neither friend nor enemy.

It was not lost on her that, twice now, the awakening world had witnessed something unchangeable shifting between them.

St. Silas's next question surprised her. "Why is it so vital that you correct my assumption?"

"Because it is the truth," Leena replied stubbornly, although the way his eyes had sharpened on her face made her nearly doubt it. It was not curiosity in his expression, but a harsh inquisition. It was clear he was not satisfied with her answer.

"Could it not wait?"

She was confused now. It felt as if they were speaking of two different topics, and she was scrambling to link them together. "Could what wait?"

His gaze snaked down the entire length of her, the cigarette all but forgotten in his fingers. "You haven't even given yourself a moment to change. Blood still stains your hemlines. You have not slept. Yet it took precedence that you find me at the first opportunity, to tell me that I was mistaken about your opinion of me. That you knew I had not harmed the boy."

The porch had become a precipice. If she took a step either forward or backward, she would fall. Still, for better or for worse, she marched on. "I could not sleep otherwise."

"Why not?" St. Silas's question did not hold a sliver of softness. It was hard and bludgeoning, forcing an answer she did not know how to give.

Leena did not respond, wrapping her arms around herself to stave off the chill, her head turning to view the sky, which was just beginning to lighten.

"Miss Al-Sayer." He said her name impatiently. "*What* is your opinion of me?"

He was a grave robber digging through the soil for the truths she had buried inside her body. But he would not have that truth. Not when he was so unforthcoming with his own. "Why does it matter *to you* what my opinions are?" she responded.

From her peripheral vision, she could sense St. Silas's displeasure with her in the way he dragged at his cigarette. She expected him to reply with a cutting laugh at the idea that her thoughts would hold any importance to him. She expected his mockery. With a raised chin and turned gaze, she waited for it.

It did not come.

Instead, he said, "If you return to your chamber, will the phantom you saw tonight be waiting for you there?"

She narrowed her eyes, trying to find hidden meaning behind the sudden change of subject. Suspiciously, she said, "No. He disappeared once he saw that the boy would live."

St. Silas nodded. "I'll escort you there, then."

He walked past her toward the door, terminating the conversation.

Leena's voice stopped him. The words seemed to be pulled out of her throat by some foreign power beyond her control. "I think, Mr. St. Silas, that a part of you wishes you had never made this deal with me."

He halted, then slowly turned back to face her. "Is that so, madam?"

"I think you may even regret it."

His smile was indulgent. "You claim to know my regrets?"

The outside world dimmed to Leena. It was near morning, the night a wash of blue in the sky. Carriages had begun to line the main walkways, the sounds of rattling reins and scattered hoofbeats broke the silence, but this went unnoticed by both of them, hidden away as they were in the enclosed courtyard.

"How long has it been since you allowed someone to be as close to you as I am? To see you day in and day out?" she continued when he did not reply. "Can you not guess what I've learned about you?"

His smile dropped into a snarl. "Enlighten me."

This hearkened back to the conversation they'd had on the day Leena had touched the ledgers. Except, instead of circling each other, bloodthirsty for signs of weakness, now she was shying away from the things that were causing him pain. And what a stark difference that was.

"You do not document in your black ledgers every confession." She tightened her arms around herself. "For some—the vulnerable, the infirm, the mad—you let them leave with compensation but without the pain."

"It is to save space in my ledgers."

"You never recorded *my* confession," Leena persisted.

"Because your secret is mine to do with as I please." His answer was just as reticent.

"Your servants are loyal to you. Mrs. Van would likely lay down her life for you."

His nostrils flared. "I pay them well."

Leena continued. "Yet there are many secrets about you, Mr. St. Silas, that are still unclear to me. I do not understand why you collect confessions, where you get the money to trade for them, or even how you can cause such misery to your customers without ever touching them." She did not miss the way he inclined his head closer to her to catch her words. "But there is one undeniable truth about you."

"Pray tell." Although he tried to keep his gaze steady, the intensity of it still bled through.

That you, despite all the indifference you pretend, are just as affected by these confessions as I am.

That realization struck her so hard she was sure the force of the blow would leave a physical ache. How had she not seen it? Had she been focusing so much on her own inclinations, on what she *wanted* to see of him?

Leena ran a hand through the loose strands of her hair that had escaped her pins. St. Silas followed the movement with his eyes.

This interaction had turned to wildfire; it scalded her skin. Leena was a fool for allowing it to ignite—not when she was still determined to break her contract, not when Rami was now also at the mercy of St. Silas, and not when her father remained imprisoned.

This had all gone far enough.

Leena smiled up at him suddenly, her voice teasing. "One undeniable truth I have learned about you, Mr. St. Silas, is that you always take two spoonfuls of sugar in your coffee. Which is surprising."

St. Silas stared at her for a moment longer.

"Why"—his voice had still not lost its gravel—"is that surprising?"

Leena could've walked back to her chamber now and severed this current between them, hoping to save whatever control over herself she still held. Yet she could not leave this rare and unguarded look on his face—not when she felt just as unraveled. "Because I never see you eat or rest. Because you have endless and brutal energy. Because you almost never give in to sweetness."

His sharp focus never wavered from her face. "Oh, Miss Al-Sayer, I would *love* to give in to sweetness."

Leena's wild heart, nearly beating out of her chest, knew in a way only a woman can that he was not speaking of anything but her. The very real fact that she was *not* frightened by the idea terrified her.

There would be no sleep for her anymore. Not tonight.

He must've seen her bewildered look, for another slow smile crept across his face, transforming his harshly handsome features into something almost otherworldly. "Do not be frightened, Miss Al-Sayer. I was only curious, nothing more." He threw the end of his cigarette on the floor, turning back to the door. "You only take your coffee black. What does *that* say about you?"

"Well, it *should* say that I am unsentimental, but I am not."

That halted him again. It seemed that twice now curiosity had got the better of him. "How so?"

"Tonight felt like the completion of a circle." She shook her head. "I wasn't allowed to be with Rami the day the surgeon came. That's always lived with me. Tonight, I . . ." She trailed off.

The silence was soft.

"You did well, Miss Al-Sayer." The acknowledgment of her service was also a stark difference for him, when only a few weeks ago he could not speak enough of her uselessness.

The words were like a balm, releasing a ghost she did not realize had haunted her ever since that day Rami's arm was amputated.

It took a moment before she could speak steadily again. "Thank you. You did well, too. Without you, the boy would be dead."

He bowed—one of the few times he'd ever done it without a trace of mockery—but he stilled when he looked up at her again.

When he spoke next, St. Silas's voice was low and rough. "You should be wary of how you are looking at me."

"How am I looking at you?" Leena asked softly, arms still wrapped around herself in a protective gesture.

"Like you no longer loathe me."

PART TWO

The Revelation

19

The Binding

St. Silas knew how to be a ghost.

Just as he knew how to make his presence felt, feared—a shudder in the spine, a dread in the bones—he also knew how to be invisible. When he walked in Bastmore, the underworld, he kept to back alleys, hands shoved in pockets, gait fast. It was not because he feared the other world—*boyish fears belong in the past*—but because he understood the practicality of moving unseen.

The sky was ink by the time he reached the Duke of Fray's estate. They didn't name estates here in the underworld. Bad omen, they thought, to give an object such power. Instead, everything was possessive. It was the Duke of Fray's township. His Grace's mansion. His servants.

The boys all in white? Yes, they are His Grace's boys.

It was here that St. Silas had been presented at twelve years of age, alongside Theodore Daye. Previous to that, they'd grown up like brothers, playing soldiers on the rocky beaches to which they were both born. Theo was a year or two younger than him, though his exact age was unknown—he had been abandoned on the steps of Weavingshaw as an infant—a perpetually gaunt and skinny boy no matter what he ate.

Theo's greatest misfortune had been knowing St. Silas, for he was traded alongside him.

For years, St. Silas had buried and burned all the memories. Hearing that name again had jarred him, awakening an old beast.

Theo Daye had died, and St. Silas had lived.

Theo should not have died—he had been nearing the end of his contract—but the Duke of Fray's feeding always intensified near the end. Desire to bleed his boys dry, until they were shaking corpses—anything to prolong the Duke's life by even a few more days. This was how Theo had died, weeks away from the termination of his contract, when freedom and another life *almost* awaited.

With effort, St. Silas locked away the remorse of hearing Theo's name once more; that sort of rawness was a weapon down here. Instead, he organized his emotions, setting the expression on his face to mirror mild contempt.

St. Silas lifted the stone knocker and looked toward the canals that circled the township like a writhing snake pit as he waited for the footman to answer the door. The air smelled stale here, the island in a constant state of decay. It was those damned waterways, releasing the odor of rot and churning bodies. His clothes would have to be burned once he returned home. The demons never seemed bothered by it. They bathed their babes in the freezing water on their seventh day of life. He'd seen them plunge the screaming infants in by their heels before dragging them out again, like a second birth. To his knowledge, no baby had drowned yet from the practice. Children were rare here and kept tightly to their mother's breast.

"I'll never understand how humans treat their young," the Duke had said to him once. St. Silas had been a boy then, only a few months trapped in the underworld, still clutching at the straws of his old life that burned at his fingertips. "I have been to your world a few times—always a dreadful business—and it shocks me to see the state of your children.

Barefoot. Dirty faces." He fingered St. Silas's white collar—part of the pristine porcelain shirt and trousers he and the rest of the boys were forced to wear. "How blessed you must feel to be here."

St. Silas was only twelve at the time, but he already knew to bend his neck to hide the malice in his eyes. "What a blessing indeed, Your Grace."

The Duke's estate was cut entirely out of stone—a complicated maze of hallways that extended beneath the ground; every corner, every stairwell, every doorway a marvel of architecture. Gold was worth very little here, as common as iron in the above-world, although the demon nobility guarded it very carefully. They knew what gold meant to humans, how the promise of it could lure anyone into signing impossible contracts. It was how St. Silas continued his trade. All the candelabras and sconces were molded from it. Colored glass windows reflected halos on the floors. All was aesthetically pleasing, all was artwork—and he would set fire to it gladly.

His eyes barely flickered past the rows of paintings hung on the walls of the east wing; he'd seen them so often the bloody depictions had little effect on him. The pictures showed the Morish Saints in various forms of tortured death—all poetic embellishment, and all of it a lie. The demons were not fond of the Saints and wished to rewrite their shared history.

With relish, St. Silas remembered the Duke of Fray's white-faced fury when he had first heard his name, St. Silas—a derivative of the Saint of Silence.

"Stupid, foolish humans." His Grace's lips had curled with disgust. The Duke of Fray had been a young lordling when the purging had happened nine hundred years ago. He was the last remaining demon to remember that time, and he never forgave the Saints for slaughtering the demons who had lived in the above-world. "The Saint of Silence was the most depraved of them all. He used to drag demons from their beds and burn them alive."

"Did he?" St. Silas had murmured, with a slight lift of his brows.

Of course he had known this, just as he had known that it was the Saint of Silence who had curtailed the demons' reach. Back then, there had existed far more vessels, allowing the demons to easily cross between worlds without hindrance, lying with humans and stealing their resources. Above all else, they feasted on human emotions to prolong their lives and replenish their powers. Now, with many of the vessels destroyed by the Saints, only the demon nobility could afford to keep a steady stream of humans to feed upon. The rest of the demons had to contend with shorter lifespans, their powers to curse limited, their impotency made visible.

"It was my father who had the Saint of Silence's tongue cut off and his mouth scarred." The Duke of Fray's bony fingers swiveled the silver ring he wore on his index finger. "He should not have been so merciful."

"Mercy is a failing," St. Silas had agreed mildly.

The Duke of Fray had leveled a long look at him. "Do you pray to the Saints?"

"I do not pray to them, Your Grace."

"Why not?"

"They are not sinless," he had answered, and the Duke of Fray seemed satisfied with that.

He had not been lying; the Saints were fallible. St. Silas had acquainted himself with the long and bloody history between the Saints and the demons, perused books and translations from both worlds, and he had always reduced that history to the same conclusion. The Saints had been too staid in their dealings with the demons.

Brutality should always be met with worse brutality.

A servant led him into the Duke of Fray's invalid room now, and on admission St. Silas's face retained only a mild interest.

The Duke's room was a collector's box of trinkets, as demons always hoarded. Jewels were woven into the blankets and wallpaper, which would have been dull without their rarity. The ceiling was covered with the delicately carved mourner's masks from every funeral the Duke had attended, and the floor was littered with baskets filled with painted fans, gold-encrusted jewelry, and silk wraps.

The clutter, which seemed to satisfy the Duke's vanity, offended St. Silas to his very core.

"Your Grace." St. Silas bowed. "I trust your health has been good?"

The Duke of Fray seemed not to have moved an inch since St. Silas had last left him months ago. He'd been dying slowly for years, and His Grace resisted that soft decay at every turn. Lord Calligan Fray—his son and heir—had high hopes that his father would not last the winter, but St. Silas was not so easily fooled.

The Duke sat in a plush chair with a throw tugged across his shoulders. His parchment-white throat, aged and spotted, peeked out of a scarf wrapped tightly around his neck, but his eyes were as alert as the day St. Silas had been presented to him all those years ago. There was a simmering danger about him, like a father who didn't need the excuse of drink to beat his younglings.

"My boy." His Grace beckoned him forward and St. Silas sat on an adjacent chair with practiced ease, a deceptive languor. "You have come to see me at last. Must I wait so long between visits?"

"I have been working, Your Grace." St. Silas's tone was thick with false graciousness.

The Duke grunted. "Indeed, your work has made you quite infamous. Your reputation has reached even my debauched son; he has been asking after you. I was tempted to invite him into our consultations, but I do not think he yet deserves such a . . . treat."

St. Silas mentally filed the telling information that Lord Calligan was inquiring after him. Their contract forbade anyone but the current Duke of Fray to hold any power over St. Silas, and only in specific ways. St. Silas had been collecting information about each of the Frays, so he knew that Calligan's debts were long and enduring. That Calligan was asking about him now, after so many years of neglecting his duties as future duke, meant one thing: Calligan was debating whether to ask St. Silas for a favor. And when that moment came, St. Silas would be ready.

"I am here to serve," St. Silas murmured.

"Is that so? Then what have you brought for me?"

St. Silas withdrew his leather gloves from his pocket, and his jaw tightened when he realized he was missing the left one. Instantly his face flattened once more as he took out the black ledger next, keeping it carefully away from his bare skin.

These are no ordinary books. Have you cursed them somehow to inflict such evil?

St. Silas continued seamlessly, his voice always smoothly apathetic, every aspect of his emotions hidden, his thoughts a blank canvas. Impossible to feed on. "A few secrets to strengthen you."

"I do feel a chill today," His Grace said. As always, a silver cup-and-saucer set was placed beside them on a side table. St. Silas's expression remained neutral as he poured the Duke a cup of lukewarm tea and stirred in a teaspoon of sugar.

One undeniable truth I have learned about you, Mr. St. Silas, is that you always take two spoonfuls of sugar in your coffee.

"Good boy," the demon said, gripping the cup with elongated fingers. "Now read aloud."

St. Silas didn't need to be the one to read the secrets for the Duke to feed. One of the servants could've done it just as easily. Or His Grace himself.

No, it was done as an act of power exerted over St. Silas—an act of degradation.

"As you please," he said, as if indulging a small child. The Duke of Fray shifted, discomfited by the subtle amusement in his tone; St. Silas never gave him the satisfaction of his anger.

He handled the ledger with his gloved hand.

He read the secrets, the tragedies, written in his own practical script. The captured emotions within those ledgers, the ones he'd withdrawn so meticulously—the grief, the shame, the agony. The ledgers were demon-crafted, created using a powerful ancient curse that only a few demon nobles could enact, which bound and trapped emotions in physical objects. In a desperate bid for his own survival, after seeing all the other boys in white either buried in the soil or the ocean, St. Silas had devised the idea to feed the demons through secrets rather than the emotions stolen from his own body. Trapping the secrets in the ledgers would mean that the Duke of Fray could feed from an entire city, no longer needing to be confined to the seven boys he used to keep.

It had been a successful bid.

With every secret released, St. Silas saw the physical effects it had on His Grace: the faint wash of pink that now colored his pale skin, his back straightening away from its previous hump, his tongue snaking out of his thin lips as he fed with greed, his pupils expanding to hide the whites of his eyes.

It was a reminder to St. Silas that the reason the Duke of Fray continued to live was because of him. Because of what *he* fed the Duke. The irony was never lost on him that St. Silas prolonged what he wanted to kill.

"Halt," the Duke of Fray said suddenly, a grimace twisting his face.

St. Silas raised his brows expectantly, but he felt a dullness in his chest.

"Yes, Your Grace?"

"That secret you fed me just now was a lie. It held no emotion."

St. Silas paused, glancing at the paper. Although he was very accomplished at discerning lies, and had made his reputation widely enough now that most wouldn't even attempt it anymore, a few still slipped through the net. He would cross-reference his notes to see which customer had dared collect his coins and confess a false secret. Arthur would deliver the false confessor to him for retribution. Or perhaps the Al-Sayer boy, now.

"Bram, Bram, Bram." The Duke of Fray shook his head. "You know that I do not take kindly to liars."

"A virtue, Your Grace."

The Duke paused, his eyes flickering to the timepiece on St. Silas's chest. "You were always guarded, even as a child. The other boys . . . what a sight you all were, dressed in a sea of white. How I miss it. I used to smell their fear from across the canals, but not yours. Never yours." He sighed, and the throw fell from his shoulders, revealing a wasting body that yearned to have been buried decades ago. "A secret for a secret. Your deal with me still stands."

St. Silas bowed his head again. "At your service."

He had been young the first time the Duke fed on him. At the time, it had felt like a *loss,* an *undoing,* a *death.* Something had shifted inside him that day. No longer was he the young child who had entered the stone halls of the Duke's estate, but anger and vengeance and survival wrapped in a boy's skin. He had learned to control his emotions. Knew when to hide them, and when to reveal them. From then on, any secret he fed to the Duke was an emotion he had *chosen* to give. Nothing could be stolen from him without his permission again.

St. Silas plucked one of the glass ornaments from the side table—a cube that reflected a beam of light across the walls—and played with it carelessly. "Nearly two weeks ago, I shot a boy in the forehead."

"And do you regret it?"

It is customary for the people of the Aksari Mountains to plant Rosethorns over the graves of loved ones, symbolizing that if such a flower can endure the harsh winter of the mountains, so can the spirit find peace in the coldness of the earth.

"I do." St. Silas threw the trinket in the air and caught it with ease. "I've never cared for violence—as you are aware, Your Grace. Still, it was necessary. I always do what is necessary."

He fed the Duke the remorse that had been wrapped around his throat for the past fortnight.

St. Silas clenched the glass cube in his bare hand as the emotion ripped through him, and when he looked down he noticed that he'd cut his palm. A trail of red dripped down his wrist. Discreetly, he hid it behind his back. The wound didn't matter to him because it was over. St. Silas had revealed only as much as he'd intended to reveal.

"Why did you feel it was necessary?" the Duke prodded, searching for a way to prolong the feed.

Leena.

Her name came to him with so much force that he could not bar it this time. It filtered through. The Duke grasped at it, leaned forward, excitement curdling his face.

"What was *that*?"

St. Silas did not allow a break in his composure; years of experience had taught him to keep a firm hold on himself. "Your Grace?"

"I tasted an odd feeling from you, something completely foreign to your nature. What was it?"

St. Silas's glance was half lidded. "Ah, that. I've hired a new secretary, Your Grace."

The Duke leaned back. "And what is she to you?"

Demons understood lust, cravings, beauty. Any other emotion would pique the interest of the Duke.

St. Silas shrugged his shoulders, but his bleeding hand formed a fist behind his back. He had learned the trick of lying to the Duke of Fray years ago, even when the rest of the boys in white had never been able to achieve such deception—to their detriment. To their demise. "A pretty face to keep around until she wears out her welcome."

Maskless, standing within the revelry of the Festival of Demons, she stared at him, wild hair unbound, eyes large and flared with emotion, mouth inescapably full, the gun still held to his abdomen. It was not the first time he'd marked how beautiful she was, but it was the first time he'd resented it.

The Duke's expression was oddly speculative. "Have you bedded her yet?"

"Not yet," St. Silas responded stoically, ruthlessly quelling the images that flashed through his mind at the Duke's question. He did not have the luxury of his thoughts carrying him *there,* not while His Grace watched him carefully.

That speculative light never left the Duke's eyes. "Bed her, if you desire, but a word of caution: It will not serve you to become fond of her. Do not forget your loyalties to me."

St. Silas wanted to bare his teeth at the Duke.

Instead, he inclined his head. "We have unfinished business, Your Grace. I've had plenty like her before, and never have I let myself lose focus." He tapped his gloved hand on the ledger. "And the proof is here."

Oh, yes, St. Silas's *business* would not be finished until the Duke lay in his death shroud.

His Grace assessed him with narrowed eyes for another moment before nodding slowly. "You may continue, Bram."

"Will you call me Bram?"

"I am safe here, sir, on the other side."

An unfamiliar feeling had risen in his chest then: humiliation.

In a moment of rare weakness, on that night when Theodore Daye had reappeared, St. Silas had wanted to hear his own name said back to him—and not by a demon who held power over him, but by her.

The old Duke leaned back once more in enjoyment as St. Silas read.

Finally, just as he turned the last page, the Duke's eyelids began to droop, and he heaved a sigh as if he'd just finished a satisfying meal. Years had been scraped from his face. He held out his hand, showcasing the silver ring that he wore on the knuckle of his index finger. "Come, bid your farewells. Leave with health."

With his bleeding palm, St. Silas took the Duke's hand. Schooling the disgust that threatened to curl his lips, he placed his forehead on the ring.

The Duke smiled. "As always, your payment for the next round of confessors will be delivered to you."

For the first time, St. Silas allowed his eyes to harden as he gave a brief nod.

"Good boy," His Grace said. "You've proven yourself to be an asset. Was I not merciful for having decided to keep you all those years ago?"

"Why should I keep you?" the Duke had asked, barely glancing up from the accounts he was reading. "You cannot meet your end of the deal. You've become useless to me."

Bram stood frozen on the stone floor, his heart hammering. He'd only just turned sixteen. He knew that because he was the only one of the Duke's boys to know his birthday. Even Theo Daye had to guess his age based on the day his mother had left him, like a wrapped parcel, on the steps of Weavingshaw.

Still, despite the turmoil he felt, he'd already learned the trick of turning his voice into a smooth poison. "Let me live, Your Grace. It would be an honor to serve you longer."

The Duke put the accounts down. One long, spindly finger tilted Bram's chin upward, and the glitter from the silver ring mocked him.

"Such beautiful manners," His Grace murmured. "Almost like a demon. But there is something bitter about you, boy, that repels my taste and has the undesired effect of aging me. You have become a burden to me, and I cannot keep you."

"Unbind me, then."

"You have broken your promise to me." He clucked his tongue. "I do not take kindly to liars."

The Duke of Fray had taken everything from Bram. He would not take his life. Bram bent a knee on the cold stone floor and placed his dark head at the feet of his sire. His posture was lowered, but spite kept his mind agile. It was not to the demon he bowed, but to the altar of his own making. The ring on the Duke's finger became his contract, Bram's silence his signature, the demon unknowingly his witness, as he vowed to himself: One day my hands will be stained red by the blood of the Fray house.

"Have I not done everything you have asked of me? And am I not yet willing to do more?" Bram could not stifle the bleakness from breaking his voice.

His Grace's tone flattened, his gaze already drifting away from the boy. "More? What more could I want of you?"

"Secrets," Bram replied, with a wild desperation in his gaze. "I can feed you what you crave. I can make you live forever."

St. Silas rose from his knees, droplets of blood collecting on the floor. No longer was there desperation in his gaze.

He was the danger now.

After St. Silas left the Duke's estate, he made his way through the township. The lamplight created distorted waves on the canals in the twilight; only a few longboats were out. The boat demons cut through the preternaturally still waters with their bony hands dipping in and out like oars.

St. Silas walked behind a funeral procession, but he didn't stall even as the mourners extended burial offerings—sweet biscuits shaped like coal—and burned incense. They wore masks to cover their faces—various exaggerated depictions of grief molded in clay, a carnival of sadness—as the pallbearers carried the casket that would eventually be thrown into the ocean.

Since the Duke's town was on an island without enough land, all the damned corpses were buried in the water—even the nobility. Perhaps that was why the canals, which fed from the sea, always smelled like decay to him. It was this town's only water source. So the broths they made, the tea they drank, even their bathwater came from rot.

St. Silas walked to the docks. He'd need to take a boat to the mainland, to reach the gate that would allow him to slip back into his world.

Once again tonight—unwillingly, forcefully—his thoughts drifted back to *her.*

Turning abruptly on his heel, St. Silas made his way back through the township.

The hill where the two graves lay remained untouched.

St. Silas had marked the spot not with a tombstone, but with a rock he had dragged here when he was sixteen. Eight years had passed since then and still the place was unchanged. Two graves he had dug; two boys who had indisputably died because of him—

Joseph by St. Silas's own hand, a rock shattering his temple, and Theo by the unfortunate luck of knowing him.

St. Silas knelt down to rip out the weeds that had grown over the two mounds. The soil was unturned and undisturbed these last eight years.

From the depths of his pocket, beside where he carried his pistol, he withdrew the stems of two Rosethorns he had purchased from a demon at the Black Market. He placed them on the graves and rested his hand for a long minute beside the orange petals.

Rosethorns are . . .

For a brief and rare moment, he felt the iron grip around his heart loosen. It was a remarkable turn of events that she—half-dead Leena, barely dragged from the hands of phantoms—could create within him an elusive comfort bordering on momentary peace.

He stood up and dusted the dirt from his hands, her face flashing once more before his eyes—this time not a recollection but a fantasy. *Leena, mouth tipped not into a frown but a smile, face edging toward him, his hands reaching . . .*

He clamped his teeth and ripped himself away from the flowers and the grave and the girl.

This would be the last distraction he allowed himself.

Especially now that Weavingshaw lay in sight.

All the oaths St. Silas had made—*he was twelve years old, standing in front of a mirror, repeating the words his father had told him*—every revered promise—*he was seven and holding a clod of earth in a tight, grasping fist*—every murmur of vengeance—*he was sixteen, prostrate, head bowed, pleading for his life from a Duke he vowed to kill*—hung like a loosened noose around his neck. To be suffocated slowly, conscious all the while, memory-eaten, was the worst form of death.

He would not succumb to it.

20

The Prisoner

As Hargreaves made his way to Newtorn Prison, he remembered the night that they'd caught that runaway prisoner, more than twenty years ago now.

He and Percy had been drunk. Too much youthful merriment; Percy had come of age only that year while Hargreaves still awaited his inheritance. Their empty pockets meant they couldn't find comfort at the brothels nor pleasure at the gambling halls.

Hargreaves had stumbled into a hidden alley to spew his guts. Once that endeavor was over, he'd looked up to find himself face-to-face with a gaunt, unwashed man who'd worn the striped uniform of the incarcerated. They'd blinked at each other before Hargreaves sprang up and grabbed hold of the escaped convict's arm. The noise of the scuffle had drawn Percy, and they had caught the stranger in a death grip, pushing him onto his knees. Hargreaves had never forgotten the man's wild gaze as it roved across their faces, looking for a shred of clemency. His skin had been as brown as Hargreaves's own.

Percy had laughed in delight. "An escaped convict. How capital! Shall we tie him up and take him to Lord Shevington's ball?"

Since Percy practically worshipped debauchery, it was left to Hargreaves to be the perpetual voice of reason.

"No, I'll go hail a soldier. He may be a cutthroat—hardly a fitting guest."

The prisoner had begun to speak then, quick words in Algaraan, his eyes fixed on Hargreaves's face.

"What did he say?" Percy asked him.

Hargreaves shifted, irked that he had to be the one to translate. He closed his eyes, trying to make sense of the prisoner's words through the haze of wine. "He denies being a murderer. He stole from an unattended shop till. He's a thief."

Percy watched the man, his eyes slitted from the effect of strong drink. "Let's not be hasty to condemn. Let's consider this man's situation. He might've been starving; to be thrown onto these unforgiving Golborne streets is no blessing, either. It can turn anyone into a desperate creature."

Hargreaves glared at Percy. He knew his friend was neither merciful nor kind. "What do you suggest, Avon?"

"Justice, my friend," Percy responded, raising his hand as if he were standing on a pulpit. "Ask this man how many years he's been sentenced to."

Reluctantly, Hargreaves complied, though he knew it was a dangerous thing to indulge Percy. *What isn't learned in the cradle will be learned too late.*

"Fifteen years," the man responded uneasily, in stuttering Morish.

Percy shook his head. "Is the punishment not too harsh for such a crime?"

Hargreaves gritted his teeth. "Do you suggest we let him go? Likely he's lying; no sane magistrate would give fifteen years for mere robbery. Perhaps he *is* a cutthroat, and the next throat he slits may be ours."

"Of course we won't let him go, but we could grant him a greater mercy," Percy said. "We won't return him to Newtorn Prison."

Hargreaves's stomach tightened. "Where would you take him?"

Percy's pale-blue eyes widened in excitement. "Orley. That old demon told me that the underworld will pay good money for living human bodies to feed on. We can take him down there, allow him to serve just a year with one of the demon nobility—a fair amount of time for his crime—and collect him the next spring. It would be *fair.* It would be *just.*"

Hargreaves swallowed. "I thought we'd put the matter of demons to rest. You are soon to be wed, Percy, too old for these childish fancies. The law may have been harsh, but it's the law."

Percy stared at him, then yanked the prisoner upward by his hair until he was on his feet. "Hargreaves, this is your countryman. He bleeds like you. He shares your tongue. Do you think that a Morish man would have received the same punishment? Yet you allow your kin this unfair fate due to . . . *legalities*?"

Once again, a feeling of annoyance built in Hargreaves's breast at being compared to this prisoner, at being othered by his friend in such a way. Hargreaves was also a noble, and was far wealthier than any Avon had ever been. He had no further kinship with this prisoner than a tepid tie to a country that Hargreaves had never even seen. Why must he be responsible for the man?

But just then the prisoner started humming, as if to calm himself. It was an Algaraan lullaby—one Hargreaves's mother used to sing him to sleep with. It jarred him to hear such a nostalgic tune come out of the mouth of such a despicable creature.

Hargreaves looked at Percy. He knew that the choice was his. If Hargreaves insisted on calling for the soldiers, then that was what they would do. Making up his mind, Hargreaves sighed. "This is the first and last time, do you understand? We take this one prisoner to the underworld, then that is it. No more dealings with the demons."

It had not been the last time.

The Warden greeted Hargreaves now at the entrance of Newtorn Prison. Twenty odd years had passed, and Hargreaves was a middle-aged viscount. Percy was long dead.

"Your Lordship." The Warden bowed deeply before ushering him up a flight of stairs and into his own office. It was a comfortable room, with a scarlet carpet to cushion the hard stone floor, but even here the walls vibrated with the ever-revolving assembly lines that existed within the prison.

"I have five prisoners who I think would be suitable for your . . . ah . . . purposes," the Warden said eagerly, his eyes bulging from his thin face.

Hargreaves waved for him to start, a headache building in his temples. It was a grim business, but one Hargreaves didn't trust to anyone else. Years ago, when the Wake was the only group to be trading in convicts, there was profit to be made. At present the market was saturated with freelance traders who had ventured into the underworld, with the Warden happily taking bribes from any of them who paid in full.

Now Hargreaves only performed this discomfiting task as an act of clemency. While it unsettled him to link himself to these Algaraans, they were still his countrymen, and he now knew how unfairly the law viewed them. It was his personal brand of justice that he took them away from a life sentence here. They could spend only a few years in the demon world before they'd be set free.

Providing they survived it.

Lord Kilworth was the only member of the Wake to have ever opposed the trade of prisoners. He did not view it as an act of mercy, as Hargreaves did, but an unnatural act of human submission to another, lesser being.

"How dare the demons think they could steal from a human? Cow us into compliance, into shells to serve their purposes? Feed on us to grow their own powers, to prolong their lives?" Kilworth's voice had been laced with abject disgust. "Mark my words, Hargreaves, we ought to shoot 'em before they take the notion into their heads to enslave us."

It was a tired argument, one born out of fear. The demons could be managed, could be controlled. Hargreaves had told him that he would manage them.

Kilworth had taken a swig of hard liquor, mouth twisting from the taste. "Beings like that can only be managed through strength. Especially that demon who works for the Saint. I guarantee you she'll know where the Limitless Vessel is. We ought to force the information out of her."

Hargreaves had not bothered to respond, the foolishness of the suggestion grating on his ears. They'd had this argument before, but Kilworth was stubborn in his certainty. The demon servant did not know; neither Hargreaves nor Percy had ever allowed her to have that information.

No, the only person to know the location of the Limitless Vessel was Percy, now ten years in his crypt.

The first two prisoners the Warden presented now were simple cases of larceny that had been given a disproportionate amount of prison time. Hargreaves gave them both three years in the underworld. If they lived through that, they'd earn their freedom.

The Warden turned to him before leaving to bring in the third prisoner. "The next one is the convict you asked for, the father of the Saint of Silence's new companion."

Hargreaves had kept updated on St. Silas. That he had employed a new secretary had not escaped his notice.

"Bring him in," Hargreaves ordered the Warden.

The prisoner entered in chains, his beard scraggly and gray, his steps shuffling. Oddly, he didn't give the same fearful half glances as the other convicts. Instead, his gaze was steady.

"What have you been sentenced for?" Hargreaves asked, eyeing the man with distaste.

The prisoner's Morish was heavily accented. "A lifetime for treason."

Hargreaves switched to Algaraan effortlessly. It was better this way, away from the Warden's understanding. "What sort of treason?"

"I attempted to start a union." The prisoner smiled. "You are *Effendi* Hargreaves?"

Hargreaves inclined his head.

"My dearest daughter worked for you once."

Hargreaves raised a brow. "In the kitchens?"

"She was a lady's companion for your mother. Not for long. Her name is Leena Al-Sayer."

Hargreaves straightened and stared at the man. *A lady's companion? Who worked for him?* He had gone through many lady's companions with his mother as her memory increasingly deteriorated. The name rang a bell in the recesses of his mind—a young girl who had handed in her notice without any explanation. *She* was St. Silas's new companion?

His Lordship studied the prisoner. "You attempted to start a union? For what purpose?"

"For progress, *Effendi.* For better wages, for safer conditions."

"Is that it?" Hargreaves's tone was derisive. "I've seen men like you—men who yearn for destruction, for chaos. You were hoping to start the same revolution that occurred in the homeland."

"Have you called me here to speak of politics?" The prisoner glanced disdainfully at the manacles encircling his wrists. "I used to lecture in history at the Algaraan University. You Morland nobles fear an uprising—and, yes, you are right to fear one. If the Algaraan revolutionaries win the war—"

"They have won. The Malik is soon to hang."

The man stepped back, shock widening his eyes.

"What did you say that surprised him so?" the Warden asked, but Hargreaves ignored him.

"The war is over?" the prisoner whispered, then let out a booming laugh that ended in a coughing spasm.

Anger stirred in Hargreaves's chest at the prisoner's joy. "It is men like you who make orphans. What does Algaraa have to show for its revolution? An unstable country, derided by all. I am trying to set right what you and your kin have done wrong."

"Your kin as well, my lord," the man interrupted him. "Do not forget this. We are countrymen. We share a homeland."

Hargreaves turned to the Warden, speaking in Morish. "Fifteen years in the underworld is fair for this man. That will serve to stabilize his more dangerous sentiments."

The Warden bowed. Just as the prisoner was dragged from the room, Hargreaves called at him in Algaraan, "Are you aware that your daughter is currently working for the Saint of Silence?"

The man started, his face paling under the layer of dirt. "My daughter? *Leena?* You must be mistaken, *Effendi.* I have warned both my children never to have anything to do with that con man."

Ah, interesting. He indicated to the Warden to take the prisoner away. Hargreaves would keep an eye on him in the underworld until he found a use for him.

As the door shut behind him, Hargreaves leaned back and closed his eyes. His thoughts trailed back to that first prisoner they had traded all those years ago, and the memories that had sunk their teeth into him.

Percy, you fool, Hargreaves thought to himself. *If you had stuck with this endeavor, if you had learned to practice economy, if your greed hadn't corrupted you, then you would have kept Weavingshaw. And the Avon line would not have ended.*

Hargreaves was going back to Weavingshaw.

Weavingshaw—where his wife had walked into the ocean. Where he'd met Percy for the last time on that barren field, blade in hand. The same Weavingshaw that had brought them all peace as boys, before taking it back with an unyielding hand.

No, Hargreaves was never to have peace again.

Not after Weavingshaw.

Somewhere far off, he heard a distant scream. It was likely the Warden marking the prisoner with seven brutal letters seared into his forearm: *The Wake.*

21

The Metal Box

WEAVINGSHAW SAT LIKE a wraith upon the moors—an entity that thrived in the dead and decaying season. Leena could not imagine the estate in summertime; likely it would look shell-shocked and glassy-eyed in the growing season. Indeed, from the moment Leena had her first look at the dark house, she had the unsettling feeling that it had fed on its surroundings until it was the last living thing within miles.

Leena *felt,* rather than saw, when they finally entered Avon land. The earth smelled different on this side. Richer, more iron-clad, like it had soaked in the blood of its defenders for centuries and would not let them go. Even the wind was coarser across her cheeks, as if still carrying with it the remnants of sunken ships.

But most of all, it was the howling that jarred Leena. It was widely known that the north was the only land that still held wolves, and their terrible howls pierced her like arrows.

Leena closed her eyes and tried to ground herself in the present, focusing on the sound of her even breathing and the feel of her skirt beneath her fingers.

Yet, in spite of her best efforts, her mind wouldn't be quieted.

Their journey had taken five days.

Thanks to Leena's pleading, St. Silas had allowed Rami to accompany them, as Golborne was crawling with Black Coats who wanted her brother's blood. It was clear St. Silas was dubious at best about bringing Rami, but she had told him that she'd be *useless* with worry over her brother while in Weavingshaw, and would likely need to take to her bed with her nerves.

St. Silas had commented drily that Leena's nerves would likely outlast even him.

It felt like a terrible plan to Leena, knowing they were visiting the estate belonging to the same man who had ordered Rami's beating. Still, she'd rather he stayed where she could keep an eye on him and try to keep him out of trouble. Leena had additionally forced Rami to promise that he would remain discreet and not further incur Mr. Martin's wrath. He did so, but the begrudging way he agreed made her uneasy.

The five days of the journey had been uncharacteristically warm, although the sun hid behind a dense sleeve of clouds and mist. Theodore Daye was her companion in the beginning, but the farther north they went, the more he seemed to fade, nearly disappearing entirely by the fourth day, as if the journey had exhausted him. This worried her. She was afraid that he might vanish completely before he had a chance to deliver Lord Avon to them.

Leena spent most of the trip with her nose buried in her books. She distracted herself with linguistics, translating newspaper articles from Morish to Algaraan, using her aged dictionary as a reference. And all the while terribly missing her botany book.

But it was difficult to concentrate on her handwriting when her mind was pulled in a thousand different directions.

Ever since Mrs. Van had revealed her unsettling age, Leena's nightmares had become disturbed—images of dark creatures with abnormal hands that upset her rest. She'd gone to see St. Silas just after he'd come back from his prolonged trip, but he'd merely laughed at her suspicions.

"Come, Miss Al-Sayer, can anyone be that old?" he'd asked, but the smile had never reached his watchful, half-lidded eyes. "Mrs. Van was jesting at your expense."

He was lying to her.

Just as he stepped around the truth of his ledgers and his own past, St. Silas carried his secrets close to his chest. He was hiding something rotten, a twisted history—one that Leena was determined to find out.

She watched St. Silas through the window now, riding alongside them on a brown thoroughbred. He was an expert rider, in total control of the temperamental beast, and yet there was no enjoyment on his face as he rode, as if he was being *propelled* forward to Weavingshaw rather than leading the way there.

It had been a fortnight since the courtyard, and the time had passed for Leena in a whirlpool of morning confessions and preparations for their journey north. She had heard reports from Mrs. Van that the boy brought to them on that dark night was now recovering well at the convalescent home, and would likely be out of bed in another week. Leena was heartily glad to hear that; at least some good had come of that evening.

But since then, something foreign had lain between her and St. Silas. It took all her efforts not to dwell on this; to name it would have been to give power to it. She did not want St. Silas to hold any more of her than he already had. Already he employed her abilities on his behalf. Already her body seemed to react to his presence. She didn't want him to have command over her thoughts or emotions as well.

They stopped for the nights in various posting inns, where Leena stumbled into the clean sheets, her back aching from the journey. Then, in the mornings, she would sit in the carriage, entirely travel-weary, her hair often still wet and curling from her bath the evening prior. The hours stretched with blinding boredom, and she had begun to miss even Golborne's dirty but familiar streets.

On what Leena desperately hoped was the last morning of travel, she was surprised to see that St. Silas had elected to sit in the carriage with her, no longer in his riding habit but his normal stiff collar and black suit. Mrs. Van and Rami rode atop the box seat; she knew that Rami didn't like the claustrophobic interior of a carriage, especially after his accident. Still, he popped his head through the window.

"You okay, Leena?" he asked her, eyeing St. Silas suspiciously.

She merely waved him away.

She tried to ignore St. Silas, keeping her own head bent over her language studies, but sitting so close to him, even in silence, still brought a startling awareness of him.

They did not speak, but more than a few times she was sure she felt his gaze burn into her. She refused to meet it, pretending to be engrossed in her book. In the moments he studied her, what did he see? Did he notice that her hair was particularly untidy this morning? Or that her dress was wrinkled? Or that she had excellent posture, a habit acquired from when she was a lady's maid?

Still, she ran a discreet hand to smooth the folds of her dress.

The smell of decay thickened the air as they traveled into the moors—the scent of roots rotting, of mildew entrenching itself deep into the frost-ridden soil. Twilight pulled a curtain across the sky, and Leena caught her first sight of Weavingshaw moments before the darkness settled. A single turret—a beacon, a warning. It sent a jolt of fear through Leena's stomach.

On the maps she studied, Weavingshaw was the last human dwelling this far north before the empty expanse of sea. Only a tiny miners' town called Lytham bordered it, and it was still widely considered Avon land, despite His Lordship having been dead for a little more than a decade.

They pulled into the town just as the miners finished their shift, trundling past with soot-covered faces and tin lunch pails. As the carriage passed by, it was clear that the Saint's horses were better fed than the townspeople. The miners stopped to stare at them, their picks and hammers swung over their shoulders, all lined up in a single row. An eerie welcome—but as Leena peered through the dark, she could see that their expressions were not welcoming at all. Their mouths were twisted, their eyes hostile. One spat at the wheels. Another snarled, "Aristo pigs."

Nearly all of them wore a twine of rope pinned to their lapel. A sign of the Rebels.

"They think we're nobles," she said, lurching away from the window, her heart pounding.

St. Silas met the miners' stares as they wheeled past, his posture unwavering, and for a stark moment he looked like an errant noble from a forbidding fortress.

Leena clutched the copper coins between her fingers, a tremor overtaking her body.

"What if they overturn the carriage?" They'd reach Rami first, and he'd barely survived his last beating. Although the bruises had finally faded from his face, she knew that his ribs still ached with every sharp inhalation. He could not afford to be in another fight so quickly.

"They won't. Their anger has not yet surpassed their fear," St. Silas replied, yet he didn't turn away from the miners until they had passed them.

As they progressed deeper into the town, they saw dilapidated houses sunken from years of rain—the broken shingles, the makeshift patches used to cover the leaks.

St. Silas straightened, an odd anger in his voice. "Martin has been idiotically deficient in his duty to his tenants."

Leena turned to him sharply. "How so?"

"Simple attention to the safety of the mines and the houses they reside in would have improved their productivity." His mouth thinned. "And decreased the chances that half these men will end up hanging from a tree for treason."

"This is why," she said softly, "my father wanted a union. In the end, the Mr. Martins of the world always win."

"Victory," St. Silas replied with an edge to his voice, "comes to those who wait."

Leena had no doubt that he was not talking about her father, Mr. Martin, or even the Morish King, but she refrained from saying any more.

Although they were only a few miles from Weavingshaw, St. Silas had decided they would stay for the night in the posting inn that bordered the forest between the estate and Lytham. Leena was eager to press on, her mind returning to the snarling faces of the miners, but St. Silas was firm; they would arrive in the morning.

He seemed oddly cautious about riding toward the estate at night.

The posting inn had a lived-in shabbiness, but the floors were swept clean and the fire roared. The innkeeper's wife met them at reception—a plump lady who spoke in hushed tones, apologizing that her husband was away on business, but promising she would do everything to ensure her guests' comfort. She told them that a few other attendees of the "master's hunt" were also staying at the inn. Leena was not eager to make those guests' acquaintance and hurried past the parlor.

By the time they had settled in, eaten dinner, then retired to their rooms, Leena was exhausted, and she could think of nothing except burrowing into her bed and sleeping until the fatigue left her body. Her bags had been brought up, and the first thing she searched for was her pouch filled with salt.

"No, no, no," she moaned, her heart sinking when she realized she'd stupidly forgotten her precious pouch at the previous inn. With the heavy taxes on exports from Algaraa, the amount of salt Leena needed wasn't cheap and she knew she couldn't ask the innkeeper's wife for such an amount. Leena herself had to save for months to afford it, and every morning she carefully scooped every grain of salt she could collect back into the pouch. All the while, she dreaded the day she'd have to replenish it. During those times when she had no choice but to purchase some more from the market, both Leena and Rami had to live off stale bread and watery milk for at least a week to make up the excess. She'd have to wait until they reached Weavingshaw the next day to procure some more—she was sure such a cost would mean nothing to Mr. Martin, who lived and dined in such a grand house.

Leena sat on the edge of her bed and buried her face in her hands, so weary she could barely lift her head. It would mean having to spend a night entirely awake, fending off ghosts trying to possess her body and do their bidding. Already she had to force her eyelids open.

Theodore Daye hadn't made an appearance since early morning, so she would not be able to rely on him to guard her through the night. Nor could she ask Rami to help keep vigil; he was just now starting to have unbroken sleep as his pain eased.

She must fight her own battles tonight.

When Leena finally did look up, she was not surprised to see a ghost waiting impatiently to be acknowledged.

Leena reared back in shock when she peered more closely at the ghost.

A drowned woman stood before her.

Leena recognized her immediately—the vacant eyes, the dripping clothes, the long wet hair.

Lord Hargreaves's wife.

Leena could not believe that the ghost had found her so soon, before she had even stepped foot onto Weavingshaw land. Leena's eyes swerved to the dim outline of the clock and saw the hand strike midnight. Abruptly, the ghost's outline seemed firmer, a trace of color bleeding through her skin.

The lady beckoned for Leena to follow her away from the warmth of the inn and into the dark night already thick with the prowling of wolves. Leena stood up and shook her head, well aware that she was not yet ready for this meeting.

But the ghost was very insistent, her eyes no longer vacant but flashing with rage.

"No," Leena ground out with frustration. "*Go. Away.*"

Her anger seemed to trigger the phantom. She grew larger, rage twisting her blue-tinged lips until she towered over Leena. Her hands tried to grasp Leena's clothes, her anger so potent that Leena felt it like a shock on her skin.

"Stop!" Leena yelled, tasting something metallic in her mouth. "You don't have power over me. Don't forget that only I can see you. If I close my eyes, you cease to exist!"

The phantom halted, sudden terror in her eyes.

Leena's hand snatched her copper coins but let them go after a moment's deliberation.

She could not shake the sudden fear that this might be her one and only chance to learn valuable information she could trade with St. Silas, who clearly had a vested interest in this particular ghost.

"If I follow you, will you leave me alone?" Leena asked slowly.

The drowned ghost's eyes widened, and she nodded.

Cursing to herself, Leena put on her cloak. Although creeping outside in the night—*especially* in a town with insurrection on its mind—frightened her beyond measure, instinct propelled her onward. There was something here to be uncovered, she was sure of it.

The inn's halls were quiet, save for a rhythmic snoring from inside one of the rooms. She took a kerosene lamp, providing just enough light to see the ghost in front of her. The stairs creaked beneath her boots, but all the armchairs in the parlor were vacant, and the reception desk was empty. On the desk was a vase filled with the violet blooms of Deathgrips. She allowed herself only a brief moment to wonder if this was a northern tradition, to put Deathgrips by the window to keep away wolves, before she grabbed a handful of stems and stowed them in her pockets. She followed the ghost outside, clutching her cloak tighter against the bite of the wind.

It was her first time following a phantom into the barren expanse of the countryside without street lamps or tall buildings to shelter her. Apprehension slithered down her spine, raising goosebumps.

A smooth voice slashed through the darkness. "Fancy a midnight walk?"

Leena froze on the porch steps before swinging her lamp around to find St. Silas making his way back to the inn. She peered closely at him, trying to settle the pulse pounding in her neck. He was in an unexpected state of disarray—mud caking his boots, shirt loosened to the collarbones, sleeves rolled to his elbows, and hands covered in dirt.

"Have you been burying a body in the woods?" she asked, and then instantly cringed even as the jest left her mouth.

He seemed to be in an unusual mood, his eyes bright in the darkness. He ignored the question. "Meeting your *special friend,* Leena?"

The way he said her name made her shiver, and she remembered the force of his gaze when he'd asked her to call him Bram. That sort of informality unnerved her.

Ahead of her, Lady Hargreaves had continued on, so intent on her destination that she hadn't turned back to see that Leena had lagged behind.

She rushed to catch up, calling behind her to St. Silas, repeating what she'd said the last time he'd caught her sneaking out at midnight. "I didn't give you leave to call me by my given name!"

Silence.

Then the sound of St. Silas's footsteps followed her. "Where are you going at this time of night?"

"Perhaps I'm going to see the miners." Leena kept an eye on the ghost who walked ahead of her. "Reassure them that, while *we* are not nobles, they'd still be very welcome to take you."

"The town is the opposite way," he replied drily.

She repressed an exasperated laugh. He was never short of answers.

They approached the dense cluster of trees that St. Silas had told her marked the border of Weavingshaw; Leena hesitated on the edge. The woods were dark, her lamp illuminating only a small area while the rest of the world was hidden, cloaked in a thin mist rising from the ground. Her pockets full of Deathgrips were needless, for the forest was filled with their thick aroma, and even in the darkness their petals were luminescent.

Sensing her hesitation, St. Silas halted beside her. She could feel the warmth of his body next to hers, so at odds with the ghost's chill.

"Can phantoms disturb your sleep?" The lamplight flickered across St. Silas's face, giving him a spectral look.

Leena didn't like how close St. Silas was to the knowledge that phantoms could possess her, so she gave him a half-truth instead. "Not always. Tonight, I had a particularly insistent one." She also chose not to reveal that it was Lord Hargreaves's wife. "This does not concern Lord Avon or yourself, so you're free to go back to the inn."

Rather than wait for his response, she plunged into the forest, her boots snapping a dry twig, her heart racing. Leena was used to being alone with the dead, to having one foot in *their* world, to being haunted forever and ever and—

St. Silas didn't leave, but kept pace slightly behind her.

And Leena was so glad of his presence that it unsettled her.

In the flickering darkness, St. Silas became a silhouette, yet she found this more comforting because she could not see him clearly. It was only for this reason that she asked, "And you? Do you sleep well at night?"

They walked in silence for another stretch. Leena had almost forgotten she'd posed a question before his words came back, guarded, as though by a sentry.

"Sleep is for the dead," he said above the rustle of decaying leaves.

"That's untrue." Leena looked over her shoulder. "Even the dead don't sleep."

Rather than respond, he took hold of the heavy lamp she'd been carrying; her muscles had begun to ache from the weight, her arm continuously dropping down before she jerked it back up again.

The forest smelled of buried and dead things: rotten stumps, decomposing branches, withering plants. Lady Hargreaves seemed at one with her surroundings, as if this was a path she traveled daily, like a pilgrim going to pray. Leena had seen ghosts become obsessive to the point of blindness, unable to see or hear anything while their last wishes remained unfulfilled. Lady Hargreaves showed that same all-consuming fixation, still never once turning back to look at Leena, as if she was compelled down the forest path.

"You let your hair down." St. Silas's voice jerked her from her thoughts.

For a moment, his remark confused her, until she ran a self-conscious hand across the thick curls cascading down her back.

"I was preparing for bed just as the ghost appeared, and I didn't have time to pin it back up. In truth, it needs a cut."

"Do not—" His voice was uneven, but St. Silas broke off before he finished the sentence.

Although Leena took pride in her hair, it was not currently in fashion, nor had it ever been. Never had she received even a half compliment for her wealth of curls before. For an odd, unfiltered moment, she wondered how his fingers would feel brushing through her hair.

Why had he not finished his sentence? She was sure he had been going to say, *Do not cut it.* Did that mean he had noticed her hair and liked it?

No matter how much she told herself that it did not matter what he thought of her features, her hand still smoothed over the tresses again as if he *had* touched her, her mind feverishly turning over St. Silas's incomplete sentence. She knew that a part of her would remember it every time she released her hair before bed, and another part of her hated that he had the power to seep into her recollections so easily—with just two single words.

The scent of salty air reached them. A gull screamed overhead. The trees began to thin, the path now descending a steep slope, the piney forest floor transforming into sand.

Leena halted when she caught her first sight of the ocean. Black cliffs crowded the coast, making her breath catch with their magnitude. Lights shone from Weavingshaw's single menacing tower, watching them from afar like a still vulture.

She had seen the ocean before, of course, but never like this. She'd been to the docks multiple times, but that was only a mess of seamen hauling crates and fishermen weaving nets.

This northern ocean was not beautiful; it was terrible and wild. One wave could engulf a person whole—burst their lungs and bash their head upon the rocks like a monster bent on destruction. Jagged boulders separated the sand from the waves, as if to imprison the sea-beasts that waited in wretched hunger just beyond the shore.

The ghost lingered on the edge of this feral sea. Finally, for the first time since starting this journey, she turned back to look at Leena.

Then Lady Hargreaves's gaze slid to St. Silas standing beside Leena, and her entire body seemed to shudder, her eyes turning ashen. All at once, her outline started to dim, great ripples of emotion flowing off her. What that emotion was, Leena could not say, only that it seemed to distress the phantom past the point of fading.

"Stay." Leena lurched forward, toward Lady Hargreaves. There was a history here; she was certain of this now. She would not lose this one opportunity to uncover it. "I will follow where you go."

Lady Hargreaves turned away from St. Silas, as if looking at him was a punishment worse than purgatory. She pointed fervently at a weeping willow that grew between the jagged rocks, its leaves dipping into the ocean as if it could not decide if it wanted to be alive in sea or on land.

Leena squinted, catching within the moonlight a small metallic box nailed to the bark of the tree.

Leena turned quickly to see St. Silas watching the landscape and then gazing at her with a frozen expression. Sudden understanding dawned in his eyes. "Whose ghost are you following?" he snarled.

She saw him mark the spot where her stare had landed moments before, and her breath hitched.

Without answering, she sprang down the sandy beach toward the tree, desperate to reach the box first.

She heard him drop the lantern and give chase instantly, engulfing them in darkness save for the light of the moon. Her lengthy skirts and thick petticoats impeded her progress, and his far longer legs narrowed the distance between them rapidly.

It was seconds before he grasped her arm, pulling her back. Rather than fighting his hold, she let herself fall against him, pushing him backward toward the ground. Leena landed on top of him with a thud, and, even in the frenzy of their movements, she could not unfeel the hard expanse of his chest and the power of his coiled muscles, making her already pounding heart beat impossibly faster. There was no sense in fighting St. Silas's brutal strength; she knew her only escape must be through other means.

Leena lurched from him, grabbed a fistful of sand, and threw it directly into his face.

Then she ran.

"Bravo!" She heard his voice not far behind her, but she knew she was still holding the lead.

Her hemline was now drenched in salt water as she scampered over the rocks and slippery seaweed, until she reached the weeping willow. She'd been right: There was a small tin attached to the bark. It looked like a postbox but Leena couldn't imagine what one would be doing here in the middle of the isolated wilderness. She opened the lid and reached inside, withdrawing the object held within.

A miniature glass bottle. With two pieces of parchment inside.

She gasped when she saw the preserved parchment, hearing St. Silas's sure footsteps over the rocks just behind her. *How many years had this been here, waiting to be found?*

Moments before he could reach her, she smashed the bottle against the nearest rock and swiftly slid the small parchments deep into her bodice.

There was an instant when both panting parties were staring at the concealed notes in her bosom. St. Silas was the last to look away. "I am not above retrieving that. And it would not be a hardship to do so, Leena. So be a good girl and hand it over now."

For a wild moment, the vision that started with her picturing him running his hands through her hair shifted into something far more potent—St. Silas finding his way through her clothing, St. Silas's calloused hands on her sensitive skin as he pulled the parchments out . . .

Leena shut her eyes tightly and then opened them, as if to ward away the treachery of her own mind when what she really needed was absolute focus to navigate her way back.

St. Silas's stalking gaze did not miss her reaction, momentary though it was. His growing smile was slow and sure, as if he was seeing the same vision flash through his mind as well.

The freezing water beat against her now-soaked shoes, but rather than feeling the chill, her entire body was suffused with warmth.

"You would not dare." Careful not to slip on the rocks, she made to walk past him, trying to collect as much dignity as possible.

For the second time that night he halted her with his hand on her arm. His gaze, made darker by the filtering light of the moon, burned into her. She could not bring herself to jerk her arm away. His touch seared her, and she knew she would carry the remnants of St. Silas all night on her skin.

"Dare me," he challenged softly.

Before Leena could reply, Lady Hargreaves reappeared before her. She began mouthing hurried, anguished words—and when she saw Leena was not reacting accordingly, made a strike for her.

Leena reared back, almost pulling St. Silas toward the jagged rocks with her. His firm hands righted them just in time.

"What do you want me to do with this?" Leena asked the ghost frantically, trying to make sense of the violent gesticulations. "Do you want me to deliver it to someone?" The lady didn't make another attempt to approach, wary of St. Silas's foreboding figure hovering close to Leena. She continued to shake violently. "Is there a name on the letter?"

The ghost's face crumpled in waterless tears, nodding and pointing toward Leena's bodice, then toward St. Silas, and lastly at the stark, distant presence of Weavingshaw, thumping her heart three forceful times.

Then, as if she'd finished a great and grim task, Lady Hargreaves shuddered before fading into nothing.

Leena stood very still, the salty droplets beating against her cheeks like small painful kisses. Lady Hargreaves had been her first ghost—her first introduction into the world of the departed, her first realization that she would never find true peace among the living. And now she was gone, and Leena was not sure if she would ever see her again. Had Lady Hargreaves's phantom finally been released?

St. Silas took her by the arm and led her steadily up the cracked rocky path onto firmer ground. Leena kept turning back toward the sea, as if searching its depth for answers she could never have.

"It was Lady Hargreaves you just saw, wasn't it?" St. Silas's voice when he spoke next was slightly rough, like he too was battling emotions he was trying to bury.

It was a peculiar sensation to have St. Silas a witness beside her in the presence of phantoms, watching her as she wrestled over secrets with beings that he could not see. To him, there was only nothingness.

"Willing to make a deal?" She walked toward the fallen lamp, seeing if she could revive it for the journey back.

"You want to know about the Wake?" His impatient voice carried easily above the waves.

"Yes." She turned, only to find him nearly at her back, his voice sounding far more distant than his presence.

"The Wake was created by Lord Avon." He took the lamp from her hand, shaking the sand from its surface and reigniting the flame. "He traded prisoners to restore his fortune."

"I know that. I want to know who runs it *now.*"

St. Silas's expression blackened. "So that you can offer yourself in exchange for your father?"

She kept quiet, masking her surprise at his astuteness by continuing to stare back at him with bright, defiant eyes. It was none of his business what she wanted to do with her future. Once she found his ghost, she would be free to pursue any life she chose.

His jaw worked. Then he turned away from her abruptly and began climbing up the path toward the forest in long strides, the lamp still clenched in his hand.

"So you will not tell me anything about the Wake, then?" She ran after him, the wind carrying tendrils of her hair into her face.

"No, madam." His tone held a warning.

She was taken aback by this. She had gambled on the fact that St. Silas had a very vested interest in the ghost of Lady Hargreaves. She'd seen the despairing way the ghost had reacted to *him.* That St. Silas would waste such an opportunity, when he wasted very little, was unfathomable to her.

In the silvery light cast by the moon, Leena angled her body toward the sea to retrieve the parchments from her bodice, in case St. Silas turned and saw her efforts.

The first parchment had bonded to the second one and protected it from the elements, leaving the first one ruined and entirely illegible, and the other preserved. Leena had to rip them apart to separate them, and mourned the words lost on that first letter.

She tore into the second one.

It was addressed to someone, but the ensuing years had stripped and faded the name. She broke the seal and unfolded it with frozen fingers, relieved to see that the inky scrawls inside were still legible.

I know what you've done and I know the evils you have dallied with—and that poor boy, what has he ever done to you?

You have brought me to visit this cursed estate for months on end, and I've begun to believe that we're all cursed. All those who set foot on these marbled floors, all who breathe this moorish air, all who have eaten its food—we are all cursed.

Weavingshaw has fed on us, and I curse your eyes for having brought me here.

That was all.

A dam of guilt burst in Leena's throat. She'd taken the last words of a dead woman, reading them like a voyeur peeping through a curtain. She felt numb all over. *Was this letter intended for Lord Hargreaves? And what had he done to deserve such a bitter parting note?*

Her brows furrowed further. And who was *the boy*? What had been done to *him*?

She looked up to see St. Silas standing under the awning of a tree, waiting for her. She was too far away to read his expression, but his silence had teeth. Leena made her way toward him slowly, calculating what she had to do.

"If you won't tell me about the Wake, then tell me about Mrs. Van. The *truth* this time."

She waited, her face raised toward him. The lamplight bathed both of them in a yellow glow, giving her the feeling that, beyond this sphere of light, the world was locked in eternal sleep.

His glance fell to the letter in her hands, and he didn't start walking away again as she expected him to. "Mrs. Van is as preternatural as your phantoms."

Leena held her breath. "What is she?"

"I trust her with my life."

"Yes." Leena accepted this, but still persisted. "*What is she?*"

"A demon."

With blood pulsing wildly in her ears, Leena tried to hold his gaze as her sleep-deprived brain worked rapidly. *Was he lying?* No, she could not forget Mrs. Van's appearance in her nightmare: the expanding eyes, the long fingers, and, most important, the years of life that Mrs. Van had accumulated.

To most people, Leena would be considered utterly mad for seeing ghosts, although they were her daily truth. So why shouldn't other supernatural creatures also exist?

But *demons*?

If she had not been standing by St. Silas, she could've sworn the ground was shifting beneath her, a formidable crack forming underneath, dragging her down to an unknown abyss where nothing was what it seemed.

"Is Mr. Orley a demon as well?"

Another nod.

"How did you get involved with demons?" she whispered.

His mouth turned, and she noticed that his breathing was as harsh as hers. He put out a demanding hand. "The letters."

She gave both to him mutely and watched as he read the second one, her eyes quickening to any subtle changes to his face. When he'd finished, he wordlessly folded it and slipped both into his pocket.

"Are you the boy the letter was referring to?" Leena asked softly. "Lady Hargreaves pointed at you, then thumped her heart three times, as if . . . as if in apology. Is that why you're involved with demons? Are you cursed, Mr. St. Silas?"

He didn't respond, his dark eyes as cold as the mist surrounding the forest. As they began to make their way back through the woods, St. Silas took the lead. She could see nothing of him except the rigid contours of his hard shoulders and the faint glow of the lantern.

It was only a while later, when sleep was as distant as ever for her, that Leena realized—in spite of his steady pace—the hand that held the lantern had shaken slightly all the way back to the inn.

22

MOIRA

THEY WERE NEAR the gates of Weavingshaw.

Leena hadn't yet had her first look at the estate, waiting impatiently as the carriage made its way at a steady pace through the winding roads of the countryside near noon. They all sat within the confines of the vehicle this time, except for Arthur, who drove the team.

Her mind, already so fatigued with several nights of poor sleep, was an echoing chamber of questions.

What were *demons? Had they always existed alongside humans, unsuspecting neighbors and friends?* She threw a discreet look at the stoic Mrs. Van, as if hoping to find all her answers imprinted on her face.

When had humans begun to believe that such creatures were nothing more than superstition? To be remembered only during the Festival of Demons, except by a small few who still kept up with the old prayers?

Sitting directly across from her was St. Silas, but Leena refrained from looking at him entirely.

Their closeness last night seemed to have deepened the distance between them this morning.

Every look he'd given her on the shore last night lay like a burr against her skin. He'd never responded when she'd asked him if he was cursed, but his silence had been as heavy as if it had carried entire cities. She couldn't look at him the same way—not after that letter, not after Lady Hargreaves's striking remorse—so she chose not to look at him at all.

Even though he did not confirm it, Leena was surer than ever that the boy Lady Hargreaves spoke of in her letter was St. Silas. But the rest of the picture remained in utter darkness—most notably Lady Hargreaves's connection to the now infamous Saint of Silence.

It was St. Silas who broke the silence first, always cutting to the heart of the matter. "While we are staying at Weavingshaw, we will act as guests as we undertake our search for the red diary. I will introduce you and Rami as my wards, whom I am leading into society—"

At this, Rami snorted. "You're barely older than us."

St. Silas didn't acknowledge his remark, which was unsurprising as he rarely acknowledged Rami other than to bark out orders. Begrudgingly, Rami had to take it, for otherwise St. Silas might change his mind and send him back to Golborne to face certain death by the Black Coats. That he had even let Rami accompany them was a small miracle that Leena didn't want to shatter.

St. Silas continued. "We must be thorough and systematic in our search. I have determined several likely places where the red diary may be hidden. We will start there."

Leena kept her attention outside the window, watching as gray clouds loomed over them in a menacing fashion, warning them away. "Will Lord Hargreaves be present?"

She felt his gaze burning her averted profile. His tone was mild and impersonal, as if everything that had happened with Lady Hargreaves had been merely a slight deviation on their journey. "I have not acquainted myself with the entire guest list, Miss Al-Sayer, nor am I bothered to do so."

Leena knew with certainty that he was lying.

Until she saw her first glimpse of Weavingshaw, Leena didn't believe in monsters.

The house was immense, and built like a fortress to withstand violent sieges. More than forty darkened windows watched their insignificant carriage pull up to the front, resembling dilated eyes unblinking in silent judgment. Ivy draped the pale limestone bricks, and wild roses tangled up from the soil. The single turret towered over them, parting the mist. To the left were the burned remnants of a crumbling tower, the walls decaying and blackened. Deathgrips, their still-violet petals a contrast to the dull browns of late autumn, grew like a moat surrounding the house, as if to ward away any wolves that might be growling at the edge of the forest.

Stone statues of Saints decorated the balconies and the expansive limestone steps, though Leena had only ever seen them in cathedrals, never houses. Dense ivy crept across the old Saints' bodies, as if binding them to this house. Guarding the entrance, his hands out in blessing, a strip of gauze over his mouth, was the Saint of Silence.

A house as ancient as this, with its foundations watered by Avon blood, seemed more like a creature of flesh and blood than a building of stone and mortar.

It also seemed to be whispering to Leena: *Nothing this lovely could be cursed.* But then, the closer the carriage approached, the more her skin seemed to burn, as if sensing the terrible undercurrent that ran like fire through the house's veins.

"What do you think of it?" St. Silas asked her, his gaze oddly bright.

A shiver went up her spine. "I haven't caught sight of any spirits yet," she said cautiously. "But you must give me time."

He seemed unsatisfied by her answer. His eyes hungrily jolted across the scenery even as a muscle ticced in his jaw.

"Do you hate this place?" Leena asked. After witnessing his

barely suppressed reaction, she had the distinct feeling that there could only be one of two answers here, both polar opposites.

Absolute hate or a devouring love.

"Hatred leaves a clean cut."

Mrs. Van shifted her gaze to St. Silas. Her bony fingers twisted in her lap.

An incomplete answer, but then, this Saint never gave as much as he took.

Leena met Rami's eyes. He, too, looked uneasy, his hand reaching to cover his missing arm. Leena had felt the change since riding onto Avon land—a feeling of desolation, as if the dead had awakened and were stirring to life.

The carriage slowed to a stop on the curved drive, and the main entrance loomed over them.

No one stood outside to greet them.

Not the host, the butler, or even a maid. Leena had witnessed guests being welcomed at Lord Hargreaves's estate back when she had worked for his mother. It had been a spectacle, with all the servants and the hosting family standing on the front steps no matter the weather. On the top floor, Leena caught sight of a curtain being drawn quickly, as if someone had desired to watch them while remaining unseen.

The message was clear: They were intruders. It made sense. St. Silas had very likely blackmailed his way here.

This lack of reception was not insulting to Leena and Rami, who would have preferred entering through the servants' quarters alongside Mrs. Van and Arthur anyway, but cold fury darkened St. Silas's eyes. No longer was he discomposed. Slowly, deadly, like the turn of a snake, he stepped out of the carriage.

"I will let them have their enjoyment," he said with a peculiar twist of a smile, "but it will be short-lived."

Leena and Rami descended after him in silence.

St. Silas pounded on the door, and it swung open within moments to reveal the stoic face of the head footman, who bowed and asked if the gentleman would like to be shown to the master.

Leena felt like a trespasser entering the arched hallways of Weavingshaw. The floors were sculpted from deep-veined marble, and a large Avon crest—of wolf and Deathgrip combatant, separated by a quartered circle—was carved into one of the walls, indented so deeply that it would have been impossible to remove without toppling the pillars of the house. Leena, who had already seen it in a drawing, halted for a moment to stare.

Here, etched in stone, the wolf looked far more menacing and the flower far more poisonous. As if the empty roundel that lay between them might suddenly shatter and the two meet in earnest.

She felt a sudden longing to reach over and trace the words written at the bottom: *I complete what is mine.*

"Come, Miss Al-Sayer." St. Silas's command startled her from her brief reverie. She turned to find that he had not stopped, cutting through the hall without sparing even a single glance at the dizzying architecture of the house.

As Leena followed, she could see her breath in the frigid air. Once, long ago, during a time when money was never thought of, great roaring fires must've been lit in every room. Now the cold saturated the foundations of this place. Mr. Martin must hold his coins in a tight fist.

They were shown into a study far greater than any Leena had ever seen. In here, a fire did blaze within the grate, oil paintings and finely woven tapestries adorned the walls, and dark wooden cabinets held delicately embossed leather books.

Leena stopped near the hearth in hopes of catching some warmth. Rami still stood by the entrance, staring restlessly at the bay window. St. Silas didn't bother pausing for an invitation; he threw his long frame into the chair in front of the opulent desk and sat with what felt like coiled energy. None of the three spoke, each waiting for the inevitable arrival of their host.

It was not long before Mr. Martin made his entrance, closing the door behind him.

Born into poverty, yet wealthier than a king, a bulldog in a suit—this was how Leena would have summarized their host as she observed him covertly.

His appearance didn't fit the grandeur of this house. Leena could understand the angelic figure of the late Percival Avon possessing such a place, but Mr. Martin inspired no such awe. He was a short man with cauliflower ears, his face round enough to lose any delineation of a jaw and his hair all but gone. He still had the face of a boxer, though his clothes were of the latest cut.

Both Rami and Leena gave a stiff acknowledgment of his arrival, her curtsey only just perceptible.

This was the man who had ordered Rami's beating and his near death. Leena hated Mr. Martin on sight.

Mr. Martin ignored both Rami and Leena, but gave a stiff bow to St. Silas.

St. Silas did not return the bow.

"Welcome, sir," Mr. Martin said, his expression cordial except for the slight twist of his mouth. His accent held traces of the Golborne backstreet alleys.

Mr. Martin barely looked at Leena and Rami. "*Wards* of yours, eh?" His glance landed on Rami a second too long, and Rami stared back with barely disguised hate. "Ah, the sword fighter."

Rami smirked. "Never yet lost."

"May your luck endure, son." If they hadn't known that it was Mr. Martin who had attempted to kill Rami, Leena would have thought he sounded sincere. He sat at his desk, making a show of adjusting his papers. He turned to St. Silas again. "I do apologize for the lack of reception on your arrival; I must've mistaken the time."

In contrast to Mr. Martin's high-handed mannerisms, St. Silas—who moments before had been seething for a fight—was now perfectly at ease.

"Was my letter not precise enough?" A warning lurked beneath St. Silas's airy demeanor.

"Of course it was. But it was the fault of my new secretary, who is not so well trained. I will certainly make my displeasure known." Mr. Martin squinted at him.

St. Silas leaned back casually, looking around the opulent room, then gave a low whistle. "Mr. Martin, you *have* come a long way. I take pride in being the one to have brought you here. I would *hate* for my own secretary to make a similar mistake and release information on my clients that would better be kept secret."

Mr. Martin paled. "I am sure, sir, you would employ nothing but excellence."

What possible secret did St. Silas have over this tradesman? Leena knew without a doubt that such a secret would be life-destroying, and she itched to uncover it.

Just then, a knock sounded on the door. Without waiting for admittance, the door swung open and a ginger-haired man sauntered in. His fine breeding was evident in his bearing and his low bow.

Leena jolted. She *knew* him.

It was Lord Kilworth. The servants of Lord Hargreaves's estate used to call him *the Hunter*, for more reasons than just his proclivity for collecting animal trophies. She remembered with ferocity the sobs of the scullery maid who'd been a victim of his wandering hands.

Mr. Martin made the introductions with a tight frown. "Lord Kilworth, this is Mr. St. Silas, Miss Al-Sayer, and . . . er . . . Mr. Al-Sayer."

His Lordship's gaze instantly landed on Leena, his perusal lingering moments too long on her corseted bodice. Leena knew that look. It was the way certain Morish men viewed Algaraan women—imagining submissive, pliant bodies; desert-brown skin against pale; an exotic adventure to be experienced then discarded.

She met his gaze with frank disgust, and her obvious refusal seemed only to stir him more.

She heard St. Silas slowly rise from his reclined position, deliberately stepping closer to her, a hardness erasing his previous carelessness.

"My ward," he said, a coldness to his eyes.

"Yes," Lord Kilworth said with a raise of his brows. "I had to see the . . . er—*wards* of the infamous Saint of Silence for myself."

Lord Kilworth's eyes flickered over them, their features so out of place, so foreign, in the magnificence of Weavingshaw. What must they think, Leena wondered, of the Saint of Silence bringing Algaraans to this gathering of Morish nobility?

Rami stood staring out the window, but something about Kilworth drew his attention. "I've seen you at the Black Coats' games," he said. "You hunt, don't you? I heard you once telling tale of a boar you'd shot."

Kilworth's pale lips tightened at Rami's casual address. "Aye, boy, I'm a keen hunter." His eyes fell to Rami's missing arm.

Rather than be provoked, Rami turned back to the window, already losing interest in the conversation.

Leena had been momentarily distracted with shooting her brother warning glares: *Do not draw the wrath of the aristos.* But a conversation had been happening in the interim, and when she refocused she managed to catch only the tail end of it.

". . . shown to *separate* quarters." Mr. Martin's expressive glance fell on her and St. Silas.

"Have a care," St. Silas said softly.

Mr. Martin flushed. "As the owner of this fine house, I intend to keep its reputation pristine. You must forgive my caution."

St. Silas's smile was barbed. "Your owning the house alone is a scandal, Martin."

"Sir, I would like to remind you—"

Lord Kilworth barked out a laugh. "The Saint has a secret over you, doesn't he?"

Mr. Martin froze, a hitch forming between his brows. Abruptly he stood up, barely facing St. Silas. "It would give me great pleasure if you would accept my hospitality, sir. In the meantime, we will *both* take our leave now."

It took only a few seconds for Mr. Martin to forcibly usher Lord Kilworth out.

Once the door to the study had closed, Rami plucked up a brass ornament and held it at eye level. "Quite a welcome. At the mention of a secret, *Mister* Martin was tripping over his feet to run out the—"

But Leena was no longer paying attention.

Her eyes were trained on the far corner of the room where a young woman lingered by an empty vase. Another spirit; no human could be that still. She was lovely, clear-eyed, with fair hair and a slight, girlish figure. She met Leena's gaze with keen curiosity, inclined her head at Rami, but paused on St. Silas the longest.

In an instant, she was in front of him. A gentle hand lingered on his cheek, but then the touch hardened.

She was angry. *Furious.*

Her small hands wrapped around St. Silas's throat—a futile attempt, as effective as a ruffle of cool breeze. Her mouth opened and silently she screamed—

Except it was Leena who was screaming as the ghost and Leena became one, and the anger and betrayal the spirit felt now made a home in Leena's chest. It scorched an unbearable heat across her sternum.

Then all was black.

She was no longer Leena. Of this she was certain.

She inhabited another body, another memory. That of the fair-haired ghost.

And standing in front of her was Lord Percival Avon.

Not as a spirit, but with the stunning animation of the living.

Leena sensed the fair-haired girl's physical reaction to Lord Avon, her cheeks flaring when he looked down at her.

"My Lord Avon," she whispered, bowing. The girl's voice was higher than Leena's own.

"Percy," he corrected, with a caress to her cheek.

With a pang, Leena—*the fair-haired girl*—noticed the gold band on his left hand. He followed her gaze.

"I wear it for society's sake. Believe me, I've long forgotten her." Percy's words brought her no comfort, however. He was a flash of lightning that could not be contained, no matter how hard she tried. He held up his other hand to show the silver ring that bore his house insignia. "Ignore my wedding band; pretend it is cast far into the sea. It is only this ring that I cannot be parted from."

"Your family ring," she breathed in awe. Then a sudden thought struck her. "Do you care for it more than me?"

Instead of answering her question, he asked her to play for him.

Leena felt acutely how much this girl wanted to please him; the pain of her devotion was like thorns scratching her skin. And yet the taste of this woman-child's fear was very bitter. Here was an older titled man with vast lands and endless sophistication far beyond her grasp. What could he possibly see in her?

But whenever she played, he smiled. And she would have done anything on this earth to see him smile at her in just that way.

She sat by the piano, her posture straight.

Her fingers skimmed the keys and soft music streamed forth. She knew she could bring her listeners to tears, but His Lordship's eyes remained dry even after the last note faded into silence.

Yet her reward was his hand on her cheek again; she shivered from the contact. "One day, my little one, I will take you to Weavingshaw."

The scene dissolved.

But another image arose. Percival Avon lay next to her wearing only a nightshirt, the firelight catching the gold in his hair and softening the blue in his eyes.

They were in bed.

He loomed over her, large and masculine, and for the first time the girl felt an inkling of fear. She now saw that the muscles of his arms, which had only been used to protect her in the past, could also be used to hurt.

"I'm sorry, my little one," Percy cooed, his blue eyes shadowed with remorse. "Oh, my dearest one! I'm sorry, but he can't know where we've hidden it, and if he catches you, he will do terrible things to you. *I shudder to imagine.*" Here he clutched her close to his chest. "I must save you from the worst of fates." His whispered words landed as a sharp dagger between her ribs. "My sweetest Moira, will you keep this secret for me?"

"I will," Leena heard herself promise in Moira's voice. Her pulse thrummed in her ears—both from his embrace and the passion in his voice.

Percy swept the hair from her eyes. He looked at her deeply and, Moira thought, with some confusion, in sadness.

"I'm sorry, my darling, but I have to be *certain.*"

Suddenly, Percy's hands gripped the delicate curve of her neck, his touch unforgiving and hard, as he squeezed her throat until no more air passed into her lungs.

The shattering clatter of two copper coins striking each other.

Someone humming tunelessly.

Leena drifted in and out of consciousness.

The taste of grit in her mouth. A blistering headache behind her eyes.

"What's happened to her?"

"She fell. I reckon she saw something—"

"Has this happened before?" It was St. Silas's voice, sharp.

"A few times . . ." That was Rami.

Leena tried to tell her brother to refrain from revealing more to St. Silas than he'd already guessed.

All she managed was a raspy plea for water.

Within moments, a glass was tipped gently to her mouth, a few droplets dribbling from her chin. She opened her eyes to see St. Silas standing over her with a glass in his hand.

"More," she pleaded.

He turned to Rami. "Hail a servant to fetch more."

Rami was already making his way into the hall, opening and shutting the door with a slam.

Leena bolted upright, her hands massaging her neck, both the ghost's memory and her own creating a phantom pain. She was lying on the floor; someone had thrown a blanket over her. She jerked around, but the fair-haired phantom was nowhere to be found.

The ghost had left Leena a memory, but it had been so real, so *horrible,* that she felt sick with it. She could not shake the terrible weight of the girl's trust in her lover as he betrayed her. As Lord Avon *murdered* her. All to keep a secret.

But what secret? What had they hidden, and who could not learn of it?

"What happened?" St. Silas asked her quietly.

She couldn't speak. It was the second time Leena had been strangled—once in real time, the other in a distant memory—and both times she had been powerless to stop it. Her hands went to her throat as if to check for bruises. St. Silas didn't miss the gesture; she could see from his eyes that he was already trying to reach some conclusions.

The ghost's invasion left a lingering rot in Leena's body, and she wanted to rip her own skin off. It was all too much.

Demons. Murder. Secrets.

Saints.

"Did a ghost just possess you?" St. Silas pressed. "Is that possible?" His keen mind probed her like he would a confessor, almost reaching the final truth.

She jolted, then scrambled away from him.

Very rarely did this happen anymore—not since she'd discovered the power of her copper coins. Usually she was more vigilant, preemptively sensing when a ghost was gearing up to attack her and striking her coins. This time, she'd been distracted by the phantom's captivating anger, and she'd been too late.

St. Silas must *never* learn how far her ability went, that she could be a channel for the dead. How would he use her then? How many more ways could she become his pawn?

"No," she rasped, wanting to redirect his thoughts. "I saw a ghost—a fair-haired woman. She . . . was very angry with you. I think her anger must have overwhelmed me." Leena touched her own forehead. "She wanted to choke you."

It was the second time since stepping onto Avon land that a ghost had been obsessed with the Saint of Silence. And yet it was more elusive than ever how St. Silas held secrets over both the living *and* the dead.

Leena looked around, her eyes once more roving the room in search of the ghost.

Why? Why was Moira so violently angry at St. Silas?

He didn't look the least disturbed. "Well, evidently she didn't succeed."

"Her name was Moira," Leena pressed.

St. Silas looked sharply at her. "How do you know her name? I thought you said you cannot hear ghosts speak."

Leena's heart pounded in her chest. "I-I saw her name written on a locket she was wearing. I assumed it was hers."

St. Silas looked entirely disbelieving.

Leena scrambled to control the conversation once more. "Well, do you know her?"

He straightened. "There are many waiting in line to wring my neck, madam. Must I be expected to recall all of them?"

"But do you know *her*?"

St. Silas furrowed his brow in thought, then finally shook his head. It was always difficult to read St. Silas, and as always she could not be certain he was speaking the truth.

Leena rose tentatively, smoothing her crumpled skirts. She knew her hair was in disarray, but there was no looking glass with which to tidy it, so she swept a hurried hand across her escaped ringlets.

What was taking Rami so long? Leena desperately wanted to find her room, lie down, and sleep dreamlessly. Her head was throbbing in excruciating pain.

"What would've happened if your brother hadn't handed me the copper coins to strike together?" St. Silas walked toward the door, opening it slightly, but refusing to let her leave.

Leena tensed, not meeting his gaze.

"And what of the humming?" He would not be deterred.

"Can you step aside, Mr. St. Silas? I am very weary and would like to lie down now."

"And if you'd been alone, madam?" There was an edge to his tone that she could not understand and she was too tired to try.

"Nothing would've happened." She sighed, struggling to keep standing straight when her entire equilibrium was in chaos. She didn't appreciate him attempting to drag out her secrets when he held so tightly to his own.

After a moment he stepped aside curtly and let her pass. At first she wasn't sure if he was following her down the corridor or had stayed behind in the study, but his footsteps finally sounded on the hard marble floor behind her.

She needed to find a servant, *anyone,* to lead her to her room before she collapsed.

"Do not go searching for ghosts on your own anymore."

She halted and turned to look at him in astonishment; there was a rigidity to his jaw that amazed her.

"What do you mean? I'm always alone with ghosts."

"Then come seek *me.*" He took a step closer to her, the intensity of his gaze jarringly akin to what Moira had seen when she looked at Percival Avon.

"Come seek you . . . ?" For a moment Leena was not sure if it was Moira's voice or her own that had spoken. "*Why?*"

There was a tense silence, and his eyes held a look that she had never seen before. Then, as if the words had been wrestled from him, he spoke, "Deny it as much as you like. If you are possessed again, it is clear you cannot come out of it yourself—"

"I was not—"

"But I will drag you out—even if I have to perform the exorcism myself."

His words ignited shocks across her skin. If Leena was not careful, she would fall into the same trap Moira had in looking at Percival Avon: feeling utterly protected, *cherished.* That feeling was intoxicating. And Leena would know; only moments before, she had been suffused with it in another woman's memory.

Both men, so different in looks and bearing, and yet sharing the same dark magnetism. Each with the same fierceness in their eyes, declaring a vow that could lead to her ruin.

Leena shook her head, unsure if she was denying Percival, Moira, St. Silas, or herself. "You are mistaken, Mr. St. Silas. I have never been possessed, but I thank you for your words. I will survive to ensure Lord Avon is found, so you should have no fear of our contract ending prematurely." A phrase reminiscent of what he'd once said to her.

She turned to go, shaking slightly.

He grabbed her arm. "*Do* you understand? Come find me."

"*Please,*" she whispered with equal fierceness, unclasping his hand. "What do you want from me?"

The undoing in her voice and the exhaustion in her eyes must have reached him, for he let go and didn't follow her even as she left him behind, standing alone in the marbled hallway of Weavingshaw.

23

The Hunting Party

LEENA AWOKE THAT first morning in Weavingshaw to the sound of howling.

She would later learn that the wolves' calls were ceaseless, a hungry lament. She suddenly felt glad of the Deathgrips that surrounded the house, as if in protection against an encroaching and wild forest.

It took considerable effort for Leena to come down to break her fast that morning. The events of the previous night had stretched her body to its limits. All she wanted was to continue to sleep in her grand guest room, painted in hues of blue and yellow. Yet Mrs. Van's sharp knock and the message she conveyed in short, clipped words—that the *master* bade her a good morning and to please join him downstairs—left little room for argument.

In spite of her fervent desire to separate herself from the fashionable guests, she understood the unmistakable importance of their presence among Mr. Martin's hunting party. Tongues would still wag, no doubt, but they had to try their utmost to keep the true reason behind their presence a secret. And besides, Leena thought wryly, she was already drenched in secrets. Another would not tip the scales.

She met Rami and St. Silas in the hallway, both walking from their own wing dedicated to the bachelors. Rami looked as sleep-deprived as Leena felt, but St. Silas seemed refreshed, immaculately dressed in his habitual dark clothes. Leena had to retie Rami's sloppily done cravat.

While Leena herself looked a far cry from the girl who used to run wild in the refugee camps as a child, she knew that she, too, didn't fit the magnificence of these halls. Yet, she reminded herself, she was here to play a role and to hunt a ghost; everything else was merely a mask.

As she attended to Rami's cravat, St. Silas's eyes skimmed her briefly. Then he nodded brusquely and started to make his way down the hall. She didn't acknowledge his evaluation; the way their conversation had ended last night still reverberated in her head.

The confidence with which he guided the Al-Sayer siblings to their destination led Leena to believe, once again, that this was not his first visit to Weavingshaw. Although he had neither confirmed nor denied it, Leena still wondered if he *had* been a servant here once, long ago.

Leena took a deep breath just as the footman swung open the door to the breakfast parlor.

It was a moderate-sized hunting party, consisting almost equally of lords and ladies. The men were supposed to start the hunt on the first morning of the gathering while the ladies lunched at a picnic on the beach. However, the unpredictable northern weather had plans of its own, drawing dark billowing clouds over the cliffs that released a torrent of rain, preventing anyone from stepping outside.

Meaning the entire party had gathered in the breakfast parlor instead.

Leena was not surprised to find their entrance caused a small stir—or, in fact, the opposite. The room fell into a deep silence as every guest halted to stare at the three of them: brown-skinned Leena, amputee Rami, and, of course, the Saint of Silence.

St. Silas walked toward the breakfast buffet without even acknowledging the shock he had caused, but Leena and Rami stood a moment in acute embarrassment, never before having received such politely hostile stares, a few men offering her barely stilted bows.

Finally, Rami nudged Leena and they both followed St. Silas stiffly.

Slowly, conversation started to resume, although even more hushed and stilted than before.

Eventually, after sitting down as far from the group as possible, Leena began to follow the conversation that was most pressing to them: What should they do with their time should it rain for the entire week?

Mr. Martin, who had pretended to be busy when the Al-Sayers and St. Silas walked in, was now attempting to reassure the guests that there were plenty of activities planned to keep them entertained—including a grand tour of Weavingshaw and its renowned art gallery.

Leena, with her eyes mostly on her plate, didn't at first mark Lord Hargreaves sitting by Mr. Martin's left side, but jerked up when she heard his voice.

"I think this is a splendid idea, Mr. Martin. Our guests, I am sure, would be delighted to learn the great history of this house. We should commence directly after breakfast concludes."

Leena could not look at Lord Hargreaves without seeing his dead wife thumping her heart and pointing toward St. Silas. The words of the letter flashed through her mind, Lady Hargreaves both begging and cursing her husband, unable to reach her peaceful rest until that *something* had been fulfilled.

It was as if Lord Hargreaves was able to read Leena's thoughts, for he turned and looked directly at her with a pleasant smile, and inclined his head a fraction.

She didn't know how to respond. It had been years since she had worked for him, and she was not even sure if he still recognized her as his former employee. So she merely nodded back and turned to Rami.

A portly lord who sat near the window spoke next. "Eh, what say you, Martin, if we were to take a tour of the crypts? They are the oldest in the country, I hear, housing all the dead Avon Lords."

Lord Kilworth, looking irritated, responded, "Impossible! The crypts are the most dangerous part of Weavingshaw. No one has set foot there since—" Leena knew he cut himself off just as he was about to say, *Percival Avon's death.*

Mr. Martin interjected, shaking his head sadly. "I would be more than happy to oblige you, my lord. However, we are in the process of renovating much of the architecture there, as some of the walls are not sound."

Leena heard St. Silas scoff beside her. She turned to him.

If she were to step out of the roles they were playing and observe him objectively, she would have had no doubt about saying St. Silas *belonged* here. The part of the bored gentleman he was playing was done so well she nearly believed it herself. His long frame was draped across his chair in decadent ease, his nonchalant expression flickering between the window and their host in tedium.

And yet she knew, from watching St. Silas so long, that he was not bored. That he was indeed charged with energy. That tic in his jaw, so subtle, was making its appearance.

As breakfast concluded and the guests readied themselves for the tour, Leena knew that she could not excuse herself from this activity. She still had to play her part as a guest—however unwanted—and could not find a legitimate reason to leave and go in search of her own pursuits.

With great reluctance, she prepared herself for the inevitable, and was then dismayed when St. Silas informed her that he would not be joining them for the rest of the day. So now she'd have to tackle the gentry with only her brother on her side.

"Stay sharp," was all St. Silas said to her before he was gone.

Oddly enough, the more isolated Leena felt from the other members of the party, the closer she became to Mrs. Van.

The initial fear and repulsion she had felt for the demon had turned into fascination. That afternoon, after the awkward tour of the house—on which Leena saw all the portraits of the Avons from the first Marquess to the last—all Leena wanted to do was isolate herself in her room. But that was not to be; she would have to make an appearance at dinner. Mrs. Van was already present to help Leena change into her evening dress and to re-pin her curls. The housekeeper proved an extremely talented lady's maid as well, and she'd made Leena look every inch the noble, even if she did not feel like one. Everything Leena wore felt like a costume meant for someone else, and she missed her old cambric dresses.

"The master has told you about me?" Mrs. Van asked as she twisted a gold-filigree band through Leena's hair. She said it matter-of-factly, but her unusual elongated fingers had tightened their hold on the hairpiece.

"Yes," Leena replied steadily.

Mrs. Van's cool eyes met Leena's own in the mirror. "My mother was human, but my father was a demon." She paused. "Are you afraid?"

Leena sucked in her cheeks. She thought of the blood that ran through her own veins, viewed disdainfully as *common* by the nobles, as *foreign* by the Mors—and how, in the end, blood was just blood when it was hemorrhaging.

"No, I don't fear you," Leena said, and was astonished to find that it was true. "In fact, I owe you a debt for curing Rami. You're very talented—at everything you do."

Mrs. Van gave her a small, weary smile, and Leena suddenly felt less lonely in this house filled with ghosts.

24

The Season of Wolves

Over the next few days, they searched for the red diary relentlessly.

To Leena, the challenge felt insurmountable.

The most difficult part was that they had to participate in every scheduled activity organized to entertain the gathered party while still finding time for their hunt. Meaning that she, Rami, Mrs. Van, and St. Silas could meet only very early in the morning or very late into the evening. They only had a week, and it felt to Leena like too little time to search the massive house, not to mention the lands that belonged to Weavingshaw.

It also didn't take long for Leena to notice that Mr. Martin was having them followed. She sensed watchful eyes on her with every step she took, from the footmen down to the gardeners and maids, who seemed to be forever moving from one place to another with their pots and pruning shears, mops and brooms. Even the butler made a few unexpected appearances in places he would usually not frequent. It was an odd feeling for Leena, to be trailed by beings other than ghosts.

Theodore Daye had also made his reappearance, although he

looked more faded here. He took his habitual stance beside her bed—at least Leena had been able to renew her supply of salt, with the aid of Mrs. Van—but he could not answer her questions about the whereabouts of the diary nor lead them to it.

The search began with the obvious places.

On that first day—both after the tour and in the dead of night—they searched the vast library. It was difficult, the wooden shelves weighed down by hundred-year-old manuscripts and leather-bound books. It was also the size of a small marketplace in Golborne. After several hours of dust-infused exploration, all four of them left frustrated and filthy.

It was not there.

Neither was it in the study they were first shown into when they arrived at Weavingshaw.

As Leena and Mrs. Van made their way back from their fruitless search there on the second day, they met Lord Kilworth in the hall. Leena had been avoiding him, but all throughout the tour of the house and gallery the day before he'd found excuses to linger beside her, to brush her shoulder *accidentally,* despite Leena's irritated insistence that His Lordship pay better attention to his surroundings—until Rami had "accidentally" stomped on his foot. That had caused quite a stir.

This time, his gaze was not on Leena but on Mrs. Van. Revulsion twisted his lips, a white fury flaring his nostrils as he bowed to Leena only, his attention lingering on Mrs. Van's abnormally long fingers, then her neck, as if desiring to snap it. Leena felt trickles of fear slide down into her stomach, and she pulled Mrs. Van along as quickly as possible.

"Do you think he knows that you are . . . ?" Leena whispered the moment they were out of sight.

"He must know," Mrs. Van replied steadily. "And he would like to kill me for it."

Leena's heart quaked, her grip tightening on the housekeeper's arm. "Be careful."

A touch of a smile graced the older woman's face before her expression folded into sternness once more. "Where would I be if I allowed myself to fear all the Lord Kilworths of the world?"

On that same day, just before dinner was served and while all the ladies were partaking in their afternoon naps, Leena and St. Silas entered a small parlor that held only Lord Hargreaves reading the paper. Leena watched as His Lordship and St. Silas bowed to each other, muttering polite nothings. It was a mild greeting between strangers, in such contrast to the raw agony of Lady Hargreaves.

"Have you managed to walk the grounds yet, Mr. St. Silas? Even in the rain they are a sight to behold this time of year," Lord Hargreaves asked. It seemed a generic inquiry, but Leena did not miss the sudden narrowing of St. Silas's eyes.

St. Silas looked steadily at Lord Hargreaves for a long, cool moment. "It is the season of wolves. It would be foolish to venture out unattended."

"Ah yes, the wolves. Such . . . terrifying creatures."

"Only to those who have blood on their hands," St. Silas murmured. "Do you have blood on your hands, my lord?"

Lord Hargreaves's regard did not waver. "Not nearly enough to be marked."

"Not yet, at any rate," St. Silas replied succinctly.

Leena had the unmistakable sense of two vicious animals circling each other, searching for weakness before the kill.

St. Silas did not await a reply. He bowed and exited the room, with Leena at his heels.

Still, Leena could not stop herself from turning back to see Hargreaves staring after them, his face leached of color.

Leena felt as if she were caught in the midst of a different sort of hunting party, where both the imagined and the real predator were at their door. She could not repress the question that escaped her lips, one that had been circling her mind for several nights as she lay awake listening to the animals' terrible cries. "Do the wolves ever stop howling?"

St. Silas did not halt his long strides. "Why should they? They have scented blood."

Leena, who had always been a careful observer of people—mostly because she existed on the fringes of their interactions—had begun to silently immerse herself in the lives of the upper-class guests about her.

It was a shocking and liberating discovery to find that, outside the company of St. Silas, the guests did not take any notice of her unless she all but shouted her presence. It was as if she was one of the many servants working silently to keep every function of the day moving smoothly. Leena used this to her advantage as she continued the search for the red diary, listening to the guests in part for clues, and in a larger part out of curiosity.

Several times when she was in one of the great parlors, crouched while rifling through a desk drawer or standing just by the fireplace, she'd been able to overhear the guests' prattle. She'd been privy to the escalating tension between Lord Deverall and Mr. Cotts, pertaining to the horse the latter had bought from the former, which had once been hailed as the Great Thoroughbred but was now limping from an injury that had been suspiciously sustained just after the transfer of funds.

Then there was Lady Margaret Bishop and her daughter, Miss Cecilia Bishop, who thought everything absolutely drab and undistinguished, called Mr. Martin an embarrassment, but secretly wondered if they would be invited for the Early Spring Soiree; they were clearly petrified that they would not be.

There were also several couples Leena tried to avoid, both old and young, who barely exchanged two words with each other, apart from a clipped "Will you stop making a cake of yourself, you old drunk?" and "You grow more tedious with every passing year, m'dear."

It should not, therefore, have come as a surprise when she caught snippets of Lady Beywood and two of her friends speaking of St. Silas. To find that he had immeasurably captivated the female members of the hunting party should not have made Leena feel out of sorts, confused and flushed, but it did.

Yet still she strained her ears to listen as they spoke of his form—tall, athletic, and graceful. Of the deep timbre of his voice; of his smile and the flash of white teeth; of his dark eyes and the thick hair that was cut too short to be considered fashionable and yet still *suited* him. And, most of all, when they spoke of how they felt when he gave them his undivided attention, Leena *understood.*

It felt as if a new moon had decided to orbit their planet, changing the tides and storms forever.

It was those stormy feelings she was struggling with as they spent another fruitless night combing the second half of the great library.

After several futile hours of battling dust and darkness, Leena turned to St. Silas, trying to hide the defeat in her voice. "If we do not find the diary before we depart, we will return to Golborne with nothing." She could not bear the thought of returning to the agony of the confession rooms. Even Golborne, with its stark outline and soot-coated rooftops, seemed like a choked dream from within the splendor of Weavingshaw and its rolling moors. "Where else can we look?"

St. Silas perched on the back of the settee, watching her with an odd look. For one paranoid moment, Leena was frightened he could read her thoughts and all the turmoil she had been combating—especially since Moira's unexpected possession of her.

His answer was slow, his dark eyes unwavering from hers, scrutinizing her. "Weavingshaw has several attics filled with old trunks and hidden crates that must be searched. There are also smugglers' caves inside the black cliffs that have been forgotten for centuries. We will not leave until we have combed through this entire estate."

When Leena did not respond, he crossed his arms. "What are you not saying?"

Leena swallowed. "Nothing."

"Come, we know each other well enough by now. Out with it." His look was piercing, and again she had the disquieting feeling that they were speaking about two different things. She remembered their first night here, his hand on her arm, when he had told her not to search for ghosts alone anymore.

She scrambled for an answer to give him—anything to distract him from the truth. "I find it very hard to imagine that a mere guest, who, granted, may have been here once or twice, would have such specific knowledge of the whereabouts of *smugglers' caves* and *hidden crates.*"

There. She dared him to deny this.

He gave her no answer, continuing to watch her from beneath hooded eyes.

"What are you not telling me?" she persisted.

"What are you not telling *me,* Miss Al-Sayer?" he countered swiftly.

Leena wasn't sure what he spoke of; there were so many secrets that she was now keeping from him. The secret of being possessed, the secret belonging to Moira, and the secret of Leena's growing fascination with St. Silas that seemed to be eating her body alive.

Likely, he wanted to know all three. He wanted to know everything.

St. Silas would never be satisfied until he undid her completely. Until she was as transparent as a phantom, and he held mastery of all her secrets.

Not for the first time, Leena promised herself that that would *never* happen.

They stared at each other for a long moment. Neither was willing to disarm. This was not their first duel—nor likely their last.

"Then we will continue our search, just as we are," she replied after a moment, shifting backward away from him.

He rose from the settee and took a step forward just as she backed away, narrowing the space between them.

"*Just* as we are?" The change in his gaze was rapid, his pupils dilating.

Leena felt her throat constrict—an emotion evoked just from that single look. He was standing close enough that she could see the arched shadow of his long lashes on his cheek, could smell the starch of his collar, the fine earthy cologne on his skin.

Leena felt that the lines that had once been so clear to her when it came to St. Silas were beginning to blur painfully. The intimacy with which she knew him—his looks, his scent, his *lashes*—could not be easily undone from her memory, and her heart responded with a crushing thud.

What was happening to her?

She remembered Moira looking at Percival in the same way, devouring his presence with equal fervor.

Before he had killed her.

For that was how it would always end—at least in Weavingshaw.

After a few heated seconds, she took another firm step back from both St. Silas and her own maddening reaction, her footsteps echoing loudly in the room.

"Yes. Just as we are."

25

Lady Hargreaves

Leena did not sleep easy within Weavingshaw, even with the pouch of salt Mrs. Van had procured for her.

It was on the third night that she dreamed of Lady Hargreaves.

No, not dreamed. Leena *was* Lady Hargreaves, back when she was alive and still known only as Gemma, attending a ball in the first blush of youth, an empty dance card in her trembling fingers. The hundreds of flickering candles made her feel as if the entire room was on fire, the twirling men and women dancing amid the blaze.

Standing beside her was a woman Leena knew instinctively was Lady Hargreaves's mother, her sharp eyes critiquing her daughter's every movement.

"Stand straighter, Gemma," her mother hissed. "No man will look twice at you slouched over like that." She turned away from the girl with a frown, her attention reverting to the gossiping chaperones who sat among the perpetual wallflowers. "What did you say, Lady Grenville?"

"He's not brought *her* with him tonight," Lady Grenville tittered.

"Who?" the dowager sitting next to Lady Grenville asked.

"Lord Avon. This is the third party he's not brought his wife to."

The dowager lowered her voice, forcing all those who wished to listen to crane their necks. "He keeps her in Weavingshaw. It is Avon tradition; she is not to leave until she bears him a babe."

"An heir," Lady Hargreaves's mother corrected.

Gemma felt a sinking dread at the thought of Lord Avon's wife, isolated on those terrible northern moors. How lonely she must feel surrounded by violent waves and rocks, to be brought there as a young wife, then abandoned until she became a mother. Did she miss the girlhood she had left behind?

"It's a shame he married a tradesman's daughter," the dowager continued, her voice croaky with age. "Money or no, the heir's blood will be sullied."

Gemma's eyes roved the ballroom, landing on Lord Avon's golden form. He was surrounded by people, lords and ladies alike, each lapping up every word that left his handsomely curved mouth. A man stood beside him on the fringes of the crowd, both somehow simultaneously within and outside of it. She recognized him as Lord Hargreaves purely from his Algaraan features. She lingered on his eyes, brown and deep-set, a serious tilt to his mouth that offset Lord Avon's gaiety.

Suddenly, Lord Hargreaves's gaze met her own, and she reddened at being caught staring. She lowered her gaze to the dance card in her hands.

Within moments, she felt a presence by her elbow. A deep voice caught her attention, and she dared to lift her eyes to see Lord Hargreaves asking for the next dance.

They were married in the spring.

Images flashed through Leena's mind—at times vivid in color, at other moments blurred and slightly hazy with age. Still, despite the years that had passed, Lady Hargreaves's wedding came to her in sharp detail, as if her happiness on that day had cemented the memory in the ghost's mind.

Leena felt Lady Hargreaves's exuberance as she bound her hand to Lord Hargreaves, the ribbon clasping their fingers together as a priest said a vow to the Saints. She saw Lord Avon standing as the best man. She saw the way Lord Hargreaves looked at his wife, as if entranced. She felt Lady Hargreaves's own response to her husband, the twisting of love and devotion.

She never once saw Lady Avon.

Leena awoke with a gasp, lurching forward, squinting frantically in the early-morning light that broke through the window.

The salt circle remained unbroken.

Lady Hargreaves stood on the other side, wringing her hands in silent entreaty. So, she had not been laid to rest after all. But Theodore Daye maintained his habitual stance beside her bed, guarding Leena through her sleep.

Great emotion rippled from the ghost boy as he gestured angrily toward Lady Hargreaves. The room grew colder, and frost crept over the windowpane. Leena could see her panting breaths as swirls of smoke.

With this drop in temperature, Lady Hargreaves began to dim.

"No . . . Theo—" Leena staggered out of bed, but it was too late.

Lady Hargreaves was gone. Theo had banished her.

"Saints damn it!" Leena cursed.

Lady Hargreaves had not returned to possess her, but to warn her. Even while the salt circle remained intact, ghosts still sometimes left imprints of themselves inside Leena's mind while she slept. Especially here in Weavingshaw, where Leena felt more tethered to the dead than anywhere else. Even now, Leena continued to sense Lady Hargreaves's desperation like a steady hum in her chest, a plea for Leena to do *something,* but what that something was Leena had no clue.

Theo had flinched at her exclamation, and Leena's expression softened.

"I'm sorry, Theo," she said quietly. "I'm not angry at you. You were only protecting me. I just wanted to know what Lady Hargreaves had to say."

Theo nodded slowly, but he had hunched over, his small frame crowded in on himself.

Leena rose from the bed, approaching him cautiously. "I truly mean it, Theo. Thank you."

Theo looked as if he wanted to speak, but, not for the first time that morning, the words of the dead were lost to her.

Leena searched for a portrait of the 16th Lady Avon, Percival's wife, but she could not find it.

The gallery in which they'd had their initial tour was filled with portraits of the Lords of Avon, all blue-eyed, all fair-haired. There was the 1st Marquess—bewitchingly handsome, drenched in light, making it look like the golden glare originated from him. Leena remembered what had been said on that tour: that Weavingshaw's initial purpose had been to be a fortress, Morland's frontline protection from the Casland invaders. When the King had given the property to the 1st Marquess of Avon, it had comprised only the burnt remnants of a house and untamable lands, with orders to ready it as a stronghold.

To Leena, it seemed an impossible task—especially the more she saw of the north. Even the ocean was not safe. She'd caught glimpses of shipwrecks and ruined hulls left on the beach, centuries old.

It *was* an impossible task. The 1st Marquess should've failed, the Avon root cut, Weavingshaw a pile of forgotten bricks.

Yet standing here, nine hundred years later, staring at the portrait of the 1st Marquess, she wondered how he had managed to transform Weavingshaw into this enduring bastion. Beyond the Marquess's handsomeness, the artist had given his face an almost beastly expression, his sharp features molded in cold aristocratic cruelty. Leena felt a quiver race up her spine at the thought of what, exactly, the Marquess might've done to ensure the continuation of his line.

Her eyes then drifted toward the last Lord Avon's portrait, and she could not help but contrast this painting with how he appeared in both Moira's and Lady Hargreaves's memories. He was younger in this rendering, dressed in a crimson hunting jacket with a musket slung over his shoulder. He still wore his silver insignia ring, but the wedding band was not yet on his finger. In Moira's memories, there had been a different smolder to him—a fever that was all-consuming.

That had, in fact, consumed Moira to her death.

All four of them met in the same gallery that evening.

Leena, Rami, and Mrs. Van had spent the afternoon scouring the attics as the rain persisted outside, unveiling trunks filled with clothing from centuries past: dusty dresses with wide hoopskirts; linen pantaloons; musty, white-powdered wigs. There were also other hidden treasures, but the diary was not one of them.

St. Silas had returned from the smugglers' caves in a foul mood, his wet hair plastered to his forehead in thick tendrils, mud caking his boots. "I found only boxes of old rifles," he told them grimly.

"What's next?" Rami asked, loosening the cravat at his throat in frustration.

"The crypts." St. Silas's gaze flickered to the portrait of Lord Avon, his first acknowledgment of the painting since his arrival at Weavingshaw. "Tonight we go to find Percival Avon's tomb."

26

The Crypts

The crypts were hidden deep beneath Weavingshaw—cavernous and seemingly endless, with sudden drops and blind ends, deadly as a devil's fist.

"They were designed by the First Marquess of Avon," St. Silas explained as they descended the steps to the cellar. "He was a paranoid man. He kept all the heirlooms, as well as the family mausoleum, down there."

Rami seemed entirely unimpressed with the 1st Marquess of Avon. "Why go to all that effort?"

"He feared grave robbers, so he constructed crypts that would be impossible to traverse without a map."

"These family heirlooms," Rami said, "must be worth a fortune if he had to build a city under Weavingshaw to protect them."

St. Silas's mouth twisted without humor. "That's the irony. It would be his own ancestors—penniless and desperate—who robbed his tomb."

It was half past two in the morning; not even the servants stirred when St. Silas led the Al-Sayers into the wine cellar. Lining the walls were stacks of wooden shelves that must've held countless bottles of wine once, but which were now empty save for dust. Each of them carried kerosene lanterns, but they provided only a weak defense against the encroaching darkness.

St. Silas walked the entire length of the cellar, inspecting each shelf. Finally, he tapped one booted foot on the floor and a hollow thud resounded.

"Here it is." St. Silas knelt down, swinging open a concealed door. The hidden latch was nearly indistinguishable from the rest of the tiles, easily missed in the dim lighting.

Rami shone his light into the passage, revealing winding stairs that descended into pitch-black. "Steep."

Leena peered as well. The entrance looked like an open mouth, framing the steps like teeth, waiting to swallow them whole.

St. Silas pulled Rami back just as he was beginning his descent. He took the lead instead, his lantern illuminating the path onward. Leena went second, and Rami brought up the rear. There wasn't a railing to hold on to, just a stone wall that grazed her palm whenever she used it to steady herself.

"Do you have a map?" Leena asked, no longer able to stand the silence.

"Last step," was St. Silas's only response as he tilted his lamp downward.

His reticence worried her more than his answers.

The ground leveled as they walked a long stretch of passageway, the light from their lamps pooling in the crevices of the curved ceiling. Here, even the scurrying of small rodents was magnified. They passed a doorway barred with metal railings, a rusted padlock still hanging from the handle, and Leena shuddered to think what lay behind it.

St. Silas seemed to know which direction as if by instinct, taking turns without a moment's hesitation, although each passage shared the same rough-bricked outline.

". . . a cold finger,
That's where the ring will go,
Merry in the ground,
We'll toast her shadow . . ."

Rami's voice weaved through the darkness, reciting an old Golborne tune often sung during the Festival of Demons to keep the spirits at bay.

"The sound of a dying cat would be a marked improvement." Leena could hear the abject disgust in St. Silas's voice, but neither he nor Leena told Rami to stop. Perhaps he was as glad of the break in the silence as she was.

They walked for another long spell, the darkness sitting heavily on their chests. Evenly spaced torches jutted from the walls, and Rami reached to kindle one with his own light. The sizzle of the flame meeting the wick was loud within the narrow hall.

St. Silas whipped round, a harsh command wrenched from his mouth. "Rami, step back!"

"Wha—?" Rami began to ask, but it was too late.

An explosion erupted behind her, where Rami had been standing moments before.

Instant. Thunderous.

Leena felt her body hurled against the stone wall, St. Silas's unyielding arms confining her in place. The debris flew around them, but she remained untouched. St. Silas pulled himself away from her only when the silence overtook them.

Heart hammering, Leena pushed forward past St. Silas, shouting her brother's name. Images of Rami's body strewn on the floor, charred and lifeless, flashed in her mind. She staggered toward him, horror rising in her chest with every second in which he didn't answer.

"I'm here, Leena. I'm all right." It was Rami's voice, corporeal through the thick haze. "It's just smoke." He let out a loud cough.

"Lucky for me, or I'd be dead." Another cough. "Or have lost another hand in a completely unrelated accident. No one would believe that story."

She grabbed his arm and they stumbled through the smoke together, holding their breath until they cleared it. Rami cleaned the soot from his face with the back of his sleeve, leaving streaky residue over his cheeks. The entirety of Leena's back was a grit-covered mess from the wall, and her hair was ashy, as if she'd powdered it in the old fashion. St. Silas had been far enough away from the initial explosion that it hadn't affected him at all.

"Are you all right?" St. Silas lifted his lantern to Leena.

"Yes." She flushed. "Thank you for your assistance." St. Silas did not respond, his assessing eyes searching her. She tried to wipe her face free of dust. "Rami was behind me when the explosion occurred. What happened?"

"The explosive mechanism from the hidden trap must have backfired, so only smoke was released." St. Silas began relighting Rami's and Leena's fallen lamps. "You were lucky. Some of these traps are too old to function properly. The next one might not be so forgiving. Do not touch *anything* without my explicit command. And don't light any of the torches; they are all designed to explode."

Both Leena and Rami looked outraged.

"You could've warned us!" Rami took back his lamp with more force than necessary.

"Consider yourself warned." Without another glance at either of them, St. Silas pressed forward, and the Al-Sayers had little choice but to follow.

Leena was not sure how much time passed. The crypts felt as if the hours didn't reach them, as if time itself stood still, too weary to progress in these decrepit halls. They had entered the crypts shortly after half past two; surely they must have been walking an hour at least. She hoped that they were not too far from their destination.

Just as she was about to ask St. Silas, who always carried his timepiece with him, she felt a wet trickle slide down her nose. When she wiped it on her sleeve, she found blood.

Leena drew back in surprise. She thought she'd been too far from the explosion for it to have caused any damage, but the bleeding would not stop.

First it was the left nostril. Then it was the right. Then it was both.

Carrying the kerosene lamp prevented her from searching her pockets for her handkerchief, so she used her sleeve to stanch the flow of blood.

Gradually, the passage narrowed until they were forced to walk shoulder to shoulder with the walls. Both St. Silas and Rami dipped their heads to navigate the low ceilings. And all the while, Leena silently tried to control the bleeding, irritated with her body's response. First, she had lost control with Moira and needed to be rescued, and now she was injured and risked slowing them down.

Then Leena began to taste the metallic acidity of blood at the back of her throat. Stubbornly, she tried to swallow it down, but the backward flow from her nostrils had intensified, making her choke.

The hall expanded suddenly into a large cavernous space just as Leena dropped her lamp and began coughing up blood.

She couldn't catch her breath, and tears were welling in her eyes from sheer terror. This was the third time she'd experienced the feeling of being choked to death.

St. Silas was beside her in an instant, tension tightening his face.

"What is it? What's wrong? You are hurt," he demanded, bending near her as blood splattered on his collar.

Rami wasted no time in reaching into her pocket and thrusting two copper coins toward St. Silas.

St. Silas understood and struck them together furiously.

The blood flow stemmed instantly, and Leena was able to grasp her first gulp of air after what felt like years.

"Are you possessed? *Is she possessed?*" St. Silas turned to Rami once he was more certain that Leena could breathe.

"I don't know," was Rami's frantic reply. "Leena?" He reached into his pocket and handed her his handkerchief.

She didn't immediately respond as she wiped her nose and chin. She was unsure if she had been possessed. It hadn't *felt* like a normal possession. She had been mistress of her own faculties throughout, she had been grounded in her surroundings and could control her own limbs without resistance.

And yet—

It was as if something had been hemorrhaging her from the inside, turning her vital organs against her.

It was certainly not the explosion that had caused it, as she'd first predicted, but perhaps *something* had awoken because of it.

She brought a shaking hand to her forehead.

"Leena?" St. Silas urged.

"I'm here. It's me," she responded, removing her hand from her forehead in an attempt to regain some control.

St. Silas and Rami exchanged doubtful looks.

"Where did you hide the parchment that night we met Lady Hargreaves?" St. Silas asked, his intent gaze never wavering from her face.

Leena's eyes swung to his, and even in the dimness of the corridor, her cheeks were red. "Of all the questions in the world," she began in outrage, "*this* is the one you choose?"

St. Silas looked more reassured, helping her up with a rare grin. "It's the only one that came to mind."

"Of *course.*" She continued to dab the handkerchief on her clothes, the blood entirely soaking the white fabric. St. Silas handed her his own without another comment.

Once they began walking again, Leena could not focus, her mind shifting from horror to abject anger. How had she found herself, in the span of less than a week, at the mercy of two otherworldly creatures?

She was now certain that although she had not been possessed this time, *something* in these crypts was trying to harm her. Why else would it have responded to the copper coins? Whatever *it* was, it was likely drawn to her in the same manner as the spirits aboveground. And yet, the ghosts—more often than not—had some purpose in finding her. It seemed to her that the creature in the crypts had only one intention: to harm her. But *why*?

"Where *did* you hide the parchment?" came Rami's suspicious voice, breaking her thoughts.

She was glad of the shadows within the crypts, hiding another infuriating flush. St. Silas tactfully didn't answer.

She paused. "In a hidden pouch," she responded vaguely. "Where else?"

She could see St. Silas's shoulders silently shaking ahead of her, and she longed to bare her teeth at him.

Leena had the lingering apprehension that whatever had tried to choke her was following them, and that the copper coins had deterred but not vanquished it. She felt a real fear that the crypts held more than the Avon family's final resting place. She tried not to alarm the others, but she furtively threw glances around her with every turn of the passage.

It was the footsteps that had Leena jumping forcefully.

All three of them instantly halted.

There was no mistaking it—footsteps not far behind them.

St. Silas hissed for both of them to extinguish their lamps, keeping only his lit. For a wild moment, Leena thought it was the creature coming back to fulfill its purpose with her, but no. As she listened closely, the footsteps sounded human. Rhythmic and heavy.

They ran.

Struggling to keep their own footsteps quiet, St. Silas led them farther through the maze of passages. The sound of oncoming steps was farther away now, but still present, the stone walls echoing them as if they were coming from all directions.

Ahead of her, St. Silas swerved around tight corners, across identical paths, and down a flight of stairs. Not once did he waver in his direction. Behind her, she heard Rami stumble.

"Don't turn back," Rami warned as he picked himself up, abandoning his lamp.

St. Silas finally halted in front of a doorway. Leena could not control her own raspy intake of air as they stopped behind him. Unlike the other wooden or metal doors they had passed, this one was carved from pale limestone—the same material used for the entirety of Weavingshaw's exterior. The Avon crest was carved into the center. A wolf. A Deathgrip. And, between them, a circle and a cross.

I complete what is mine.

"We've arrived." In spite of their sprint, St. Silas's breathing remained even. "Welcome to the Avon family graveyard."

He rammed the door open with his shoulder. The lock must've been broken years ago, for it gave way easily. The expansive chamber was made of the same limestone, spanning the floor and vaulted ceiling. Only the tombs were made of dark stone, and there were at least eighty of them dotted across the room, safeguarding the decomposing bodies of the nobility.

They were eerie in their stillness.

Grim statues of old Avon lords watched them, their faces frozen in expressions of disinterest and old-blood superiority, spider's webs collecting across their bodies. A silver shield carrying the family crest gathered rust by Leena's feet.

"We bury our dead in the ground, wrapped only in sheets." Rami looked around in distaste. "We see it as a homecoming."

Leena understood what he meant. The word for death in Algaraan also meant *return.* This place felt unnatural, a stalling of time. It was as if the aristos thought they could curb the decay of death by enclosing their corpses in marble. In her peripheral vision, she saw St. Silas's head turn searchingly as he took in the chamber, his chest rising and falling.

Leena also searched for spirits, but it was oddly barren for a place full of the dead. At the far end of the chamber, she spotted a pianoforte, the black and white keys gleaming in the dimness. *Why was there a piano in a crypt?*

She squinted . . . Yes, she could see a sitting figure playing it, but no sound emerged from the instrument.

Finally, a spirit.

She could never mistake the distinctive features of Moira—not after the events of the possession.

The sound of approaching footsteps broke the silence. Either the footsteps were following them, or they had the same destination. It didn't matter which at this moment; the priority was to remain undiscovered.

"We have nowhere else to go." Rami reached for the hilt of his sword, looking at the closed limestone door in apprehension. "Could we hide behind the tombs?"

St. Silas pulled out his pistol, also aiming at the door. "They've come with lanterns. Our shadows will reveal us."

Leena turned frantically to Moira. "Help us."

Both men looked at her in surprise, but she ignored them, her entire attention focused on the spirit.

Moira regarded her for a long moment as if debating her request. Then she tilted her head toward St. Silas.

"I will owe you a debt. Please help us," Leena pleaded.

Slowly, Moira nodded. Then the spirit walked toward one of the gray tombs near the entrance, her hand banging soundlessly on a stone cover.

Leena understood.

"The tomb," she gasped. "We can hide in there."

St. Silas remained rooted to the spot even as Rami ran toward the tomb. "*No*," he ground out.

The approaching footsteps, accompanied by a glow of bright light, were more distinct now, directly behind the door.

"Help me lift the cover." Leena threw her entire weight on the heavy lid. A leak in the chamber ceiling had damaged the outer facade of the tomb, making the deceased's name impossible to read. It could not have been Lord Avon's tomb because, when they managed to slide it open, the interior was empty.

Still St. Silas stood motionless where he was, pistol clenched tightly in his hand. "I'd much rather fight."

Leena threw him a sharp glance, but there was no time to ask any questions. "What are you doing?" She grabbed him by the arm and tugged him toward the tomb, but he would not budge. "*St. Silas!*"

". . . the tomb—" His voice was strangled.

"Will be *our* final resting place if we don't move now." Leena spoke between her teeth, pulling at his hand with all her strength. "Don't force your haunting on me."

At this, he startled and stared down at her. Swallowing harshly, he nodded. Leena wasted no time in following him, squeezing herself into the tight space, wondering how they'd manage to fit all three of them in.

"Come on, Rami," she urged, her breathing harsh.

Rami shook his head even as he started to move the cover above them. "Someone has to push the lid over you."

"No—"

"I owe you both, for that night with the Black Coats."

"Rami—"

"Don't worry," he said, with the glint of a feral grin. "I'll find somewhere to hide."

"*Rami*—"

It was too late. He pushed his weight against the stone lid, plunging them into darkness save for a tiny slit for air. Rami extinguished the last remaining lamp, then came the sound of scattered footsteps running.

Silence.

Leena counted her own wild heartbeats.

One. Two. Three—

Sudden brilliant light speared the space between coffin and lid.

Voices.

Leena prayed furiously that Rami was hidden.

She was aware that she was pressed closely against St. Silas as the tomb seemed smaller than average, designed to fit a small person—*a child*?

St. Silas took up most of that space. Her cheek lay against his hard chest while she continued to count with the rhythm of his breathing. He was warm, in a way that made Leena want to tunnel closer to him until he had suffused her entirely. Without realizing it, her hands were gripping his shirt as if her body was afraid to be torn from his, and she had to consciously unlatch her fingers.

Seven. Eight. Nine—

Leena was not expecting the distinctly rough voice that echoed in the chamber to be that of Mr. Martin, followed closely by Lord Kilworth's. She stifled her gasp against St. Silas's shoulder.

". . . Orley offers the best guarantee. I won't go over his head for some harebrained scheme of yours."

A cultured accent, slippery as oil. *Kilworth.* "Why go through a middleman? Why sell the Tar to the Black Coats when it was *your* boat that took the risk to smuggle it, and it was *my* capital that bought it in the first place?"

Leena's brows shot up. *Tar?* They were smuggling *drugs*?

Martin snorted. "Can *you* package that Tar and convert it from powder to liquid? Bribe the soldiers to look the other way? Will it be yourself who is selling it on the streets?" He cleared his throat—a loud wet sound that echoed. "Stick to hunting, Kilworth. Do not overextend yourself."

A tense silence.

"That's *Lord* Kilworth, Martin," His Lordship corrected disdainfully.

A pause, then Martin's reluctant apology.

"Show me the supply," Lord Kilworth interrupted. His footsteps sounded very near their tomb. Leena held her breath, wondering where in this vast chamber Rami was hiding, and whether it was good enough to keep him out of trouble.

A scuttle. A harsh grunt. Then the sound of stone grating against stone—the lid of a tomb being pushed open.

"It's all here, and it'll fetch a good price." Martin's voice was low, but Leena didn't miss the admiration in it. "I know it would've saved us some time had we kept the supply in the smugglers' caves as you requested, my lord, but the low oxygen in the vaults will keep the Tar exceptionally pure."

Leena looked at St. Silas.

She expected him to be listening with his usual predatory intent; what she didn't expect was the change that had overtaken him. Even within the thin slash of light creeping through the slit, Leena saw that his face was stripped of color and his body was as rigid as a corpse.

She remembered his uncharacteristic reluctance earlier when she had pointed to the tomb, so at odds with his usual decisive manner.

Was he afraid of enclosed spaces?

Leena nearly banished the thought; the dreaded Saint of Silence was not afraid of anything. Still, when his eyes met hers, there was a wildness in his gaze.

Deliberately, she reached through the dark to find his hand. She heard his sharp intake of breath, then his fingers tightened around hers crushingly.

Outside, she heard a smattering of piano keys, then a tune being played. Lord Kilworth cursed a few times when he hit the wrong note.

"Aye, I'll send for the Black Coats to retrieve this delivery soon," Martin said over the din. "A shipment this large should pay off both of our debts by the end of the month."

"By the by, how much money did you lose betting against that cripple?" Kilworth asked casually.

Leena clenched her teeth. She *hated* that word.

"Enough. Coupled with the collapse of most of the mines I've invested in, as well as the end of the Algaraan civil war and any arms deals I had pending, my coffers have run desperately dry of late. I must gain it all back to remain the master of Weavingshaw."

The music abruptly stopped. "Oh my. You have not been investing very wisely these days, Martin." Kilworth had a smirk in his voice.

"I would say the same for you, *my lord.*"

The loathing between the two was exceeded only by their need for each other.

The sound of the lid being pushed back over the tomb was grating. Both Martin and Kilworth could be heard making their way back toward the entrance of the chamber, their voices fading.

Then they were gone.

St. Silas and Leena lay in darkness, neither of them moving to untangle their hands. St. Silas's breathing had slowed, but the fierce grip of his fingers didn't relax.

"Are you frightened of enclosed spaces?" she whispered to him.

His hand reluctantly let go of hers just as the lid above them was suddenly slid back by Rami. "No. Not small spaces."

Leena blinked into the light of the lamp that Rami had relit.

"Are you both well?" he asked, helping Leena out of the tomb.

She nodded.

"Where did you hide?" she asked him.

"They kept the door open," he replied. "I hid behind it."

"Clever," she remarked, looking back to see that St. Silas had already climbed out. He stood forlornly beside the tomb, keeping his back to them.

Her heart ached a little for him. She didn't know the reason for his paralyzing fear, but fear like that was not a stranger to her.

Then come seek me.

It was the first vow he had given her without demanding anything in return—to tether her to this world when she had every fear of leaving it.

Silently, she returned that vow.

She looked once more at the tomb's lid, and this time she noticed that an old Saint was carved into the stone. *A woman holding an olive tree.* She squinted, trying to recall what that represented, but was unable to remember at this moment. She would mark the drawing in her notes to research later.

To Leena's relief, she could not find Moira near the piano or anywhere else in the crypt.

Rami walked with a caged energy toward a tomb at the far end of the chamber. There was a type of madness on his face—the kind that wears the same face as anger but stretches further, coarser, as if desiring to set the whole world on fire.

A sudden fear gripped Leena at Rami's expression. "Don't further tempt Martin's wrath."

Rami spared her only one look—a look so full of bitterness that it sucked up all the air in the room. Rather than responding, he pushed all his weight into sliding the lid of the tomb aside, revealing rows and rows of tightly woven burlap bags inside.

Rami whistled. "There is enough here to buy all of New Algaraa District and the people inside it."

Leena also stared. "You could buy all of *Algaraa* with this."

Before Leena realized Rami's intent, it was too late. His hand was already at the hilt of his sword, unsheathing it in one fluid motion, and bringing the blade down against the sacks, spilling the white powder inside like an offering.

"What are you *doing*?" Leena jumped at him, attempting to grasp his arm, but he wrenched away from her. "Martin is already suspicious of us. He will gladly see us hang for this!"

Rami continued his slicing, tendons taut at the neck—up and down, up and down.

St. Silas's long strides cut across the crypt, but by the time he grabbed Rami by the collar and threw him to the ground, it was too late.

White powder had spilled everywhere, like blood let on a battlefield. Humidity would render the drug useless. No buyer would touch it.

"You've just signed your death warrant," Leena exclaimed, bringing her fist down on Rami's chest. He grunted, but dodged her next hit. He brushed at the powder that coated his jacket white.

"Martin already wants me dead," Rami responded. "At least now I've earned it."

St. Silas's expression was grim, standing over the white powder like freshly fallen snow. "No, you've just condemned us all."

Rami halted, his brows tightening. "Martin won't return to the crypts so soon. Very likely that trade with the Black Coats won't occur until we are back in Golborne."

"For your sake—*for all our sakes*—let us hope so." The somber foreboding didn't lift from St. Silas's eyes as he turned away. "Come. Let's find Avon's tomb."

Leena also swerved away from Rami, so furious she could barely see straight.

"I am heartily sick of these caves," she spat.

They spent half an hour searching through the stones. Some of the tombs were so aged that she could no longer read the engravings.

It was Rami who ended the search.

"I found it," he shouted.

St. Silas was at the far end of the room, and it seemed as if he hadn't heard. Unable to wait another moment, Leena and Rami pushed open the lid, heaving from the effort, and looked down at the mass of skeleton and dust. All that youthful vitality, that power that had emanated from Lord Avon, that golden handsomeness, was now but a crumpled heap of bones.

Then she remembered the soft look in his eyes moments before he had strangled Moira, and she thought that decay was too good for him.

Rami, clearly disturbed, turned away, so Leena was left alone with what used to be Lord Avon. She bent down, staring into the skull with gaping holes for eyes, and whispered, "Come find me. You have left the living in unrest, so come find me and settle your debts."

The corpse didn't stir. Leena's eyes raked through the rest of the tomb. It was empty.

"It's not here." Bleakness broke Leena's voice. "After all that, the diary *isn't* here."

27

The First Promise

No one spoke as they traversed the passages from the Avon family resting place back toward the cellar. The mood was somber, and Leena could not stifle the horrible dejection she felt. They'd found nothing, and, what was worse, Leena was now in debt to Moira.

Saints above—and that ruined Tar.

Leena knew with dark clarity that the discovery of the spoiled drug would be fatal. She prayed that they were all back in Golborne before this could happen.

They turned a sharp corner where the corridor forked in two directions. It was similar to the rest of the passages that St. Silas had led them through on their arrival, but this time he hesitated. He swung his light from the left to the right, observing each passage carefully, then shook his head.

"Are we lost?" Leena asked.

After a moment of deliberation, he started forward. "This way."

They took the left.

The smell of still water and mildew began to emanate from the walls and the ceiling. Somewhere far off, the sound of falling water droplets echoed.

Leena halted suddenly.

A cold sweat broke out across her forehead.

That creature was back, stalking them in the dark.

She dropped her lantern to reach for her copper coins, striking the metal together once, twice, three times. Ahead of her, both St. Silas and Rami turned sharply at that now familiar sound.

This time, the coins had no effect.

Her shaking eyes became unfocused as the creature's dark power intensified, swallowing her up. She clawed her nails down the flesh on her arm to keep herself conscious.

If St. Silas or Rami was trying to speak to her, hold her, shake her, she had no awareness. All her focus was on the overwhelming energy scorching inside her.

She finally understood that it was a demon and not a spirit that lurked in these halls, older and more powerful than Mrs. Van or Orley.

The demon tugged at her consciousness, and she fought it—wildly, desperately—the demon rearing back as if surprised by her ferocity.

Do not think I've forgotten that you tried to bleed me dry, she snarled at it, even as the demon tried to cudgel her body into submission.

If there was such a thing as wrestling internally, Leena was doing it with savagery. They struggled brutally until there was a momentary lapse in the demon's power—long enough for Leena to claw a memory from it.

The 1st Marquess of Avon resembled Percival in every way except for the scar that ran across his left cheek, giving him a piratical look. He stood in a large chamber that looked to be an extension of the crypts. Within this chamber lay an expansive and utterly still lake. The Marquess seemed to be conversing with the black waters. There was no mistaking the ritualistic nature of his movements as he slashed his palm with a sharp knife and let the blood drip into the dark pool.

"I promise you, in Avon blood," he said hoarsely, "that every Avon after me will be your servant, will do your bidding, and will lay eternal devotion at your feet. In exchange, you will protect Weavingshaw, ensuring that it remains loyal to the Avon line only. An enduring fortress until the end of time for any Avon blood to come."

It was as if the water pulsed in response, and the Marquess's blood was absorbed into the heart of the lake like a promise—like a sealed contract.

Starkly, another image arose, from centuries later:

Standing in front of the same lake was Percival Avon, blue eyes wild. "Stop feeding on us. For the love of the Saints, stop feeding on us! Haven't I given you enough?"

His desperate screams seemed to bring the demon pleasure. The creature tasted it with rapture, the sweetness of his despair deeply satiating.

Then a third memory— No, not a memory—a hungry desire:

Leena saw herself being pulled into the depths of the lake.

Choking. Spluttering. Airless.

The demon had been starved for the last ten years, unable to feed once the Avon line was extinguished.

For the demon, Leena was not as delicious as an Avon, nor as lasting, but she would do—her soft body rare in its openness to total possession and therefore domination, something he could not enact upon the other humans living above the ground . . .

The demon viciously wrestled the image back from Leena before she could see any more.

It's too late, Leena thought maliciously. *I have seen enough.*

A feeling of warped victory washed over her. This demon was expecting the same submission from her as from an Avon.

You are angry that there are no more Avons to feed on, and your power is curtailed. She wanted to choke *it* just as it had tried to do with her.

She felt the demon's rage. *What Percival Avon left behind is enough to feed on for all time,* it replied in a threaded whisper.

As quickly as it had tried and failed to possess her, it withdrew.

Leena felt the shift in power as she regained control of her limbs and her focus. Her eyes unclouded, she found herself in the exact spot in which both the 1st Marquess of Avon and Percival had stood while bargaining with the demon.

The black waters of the Hall of the Lake stretched before her. She intrinsically knew the name of this hallowed place, a remnant piece of knowledge left by the demon.

No longer were the passageways of the crypts made of stone, but instead of cold marble that curved into a large, yawning chamber. The ground gave way to a sudden pool, expansive and seemingly endless. A simple wooden raft was moored by the shore, the paddles slung over its sides, the wood suffering from years of neglect. Sculptures bordered the water—three grand men who must've once been lords of this land but were now crumbled relics: One was missing a head, the other an arm, the last a leg. Soft black waves swirled in the lake, beckoning her forward.

Rami and St. Silas were only seconds behind her, stopping abruptly at the entrance when they first caught sight of her and the lake.

Before they could say anything, she turned to them with her palms up. "It's fine, I'm sorry, it's fine, it's me—and before you say anything, Mr. St. Silas, I claimed to be visiting a *special friend* on that night you caught me sneaking out of your house."

At this point, both Leena and St. Silas knew that she could become possessed; all that was lacking was her confirmation, which she still held on to. Should she validate his suspicions, there was no going back.

Still, she could see the palpable relief on both their faces upon hearing her words.

She wanted to tell Rami that this was the first time she had been able to fight off a possession without the help of salt or copper coins, but she could not do so now—not when the watchful presence of St. Silas hovered close.

She walked toward them, away from the lake and the disfigured statues. "There is a dark energy here that I . . . sensed. It isn't a spirit; it's a demon. Weavingshaw's entire foundation is built on a promise to a demon."

She remembered her mama's warning: *Beware the promise of Weavingshaw.*

"For Saints' sakes, *demons*?" Rami's fingers shook slightly as he tugged back his hair. "Do demons even exist?"

St. Silas's eyes bored into her own. Reading his expression was like looking through an off-kilter mirror—the picture wavering, transient, only a reflection of light and shadow. He would never reveal more than he intended to.

"Tell him," Leena commanded.

He didn't respond to her order, merely picked up his lamp and turned back toward the path. "If you are well enough to continue, madam, then we had better make our way back. It's nearly dawn."

Leena caught up with him. "Did you hear what I said? Weavingshaw's existence is intertwined with demons. One cannot exist without the other."

He continued walking. "Will this help us find Lord Avon and the diary?"

"No, but—"

"Then it is entirely useless information."

She watched him walk ahead in surprise. No information was useless to the Saint of Silence . . .

And that in itself was a telling sign.

28

The Old Housekeeper

Leena felt as if she was on borrowed time, her thoughts always trailing back to the ruined Tar sitting idly in the crypts, waiting for Kilworth or Martin to discover it. Every hour seemed both a blessing and a misery, a countdown to an inevitable reckoning. They had only two more days until they returned to Golborne, and she was unsure if she wanted the time to pass quickly so that she could save her brother, or slowly so that she could find the diary.

And now the business with this horrid hunt.

When she'd woken up on the morning of the sixth day, Mrs. Van had notified her that Rami and St. Silas had already departed for the hunt, this being the first morning when it wasn't raining heavily. She knew that both Rami and St. Silas were loath to waste a precious day when they were still no closer to finding the diary, but they had to keep up appearances for the other guests.

She could not bear to just sit and wait for them to return. Ever since she had successfully prevented the demon from possessing her body, Leena was suffused with a new energy. Never had it occurred to her that she would one day be able to fight these beings and *win*, when she'd only ever lost before. This triumphant milestone had given her a newfound confidence in herself that she had rarely experienced in the last three years.

Leena could also not shake off the surprise that St. Silas had not questioned her ruthlessly about the demon she'd found hiding in the crypts. She wondered if it was because *he'd already known.* In fact, she was certain of it. But, as usual, St. Silas would not divulge any more information than was absolutely necessary.

It was a harder task still to explain to Rami the existence of demons. She was not sure she'd succeeded in that endeavor, for her brother had walked off exasperated and suspicious.

By the time Mrs. Van had helped her dress and styled her hair, she'd made a plan to ask Arthur to drive her down to the miners' town. She didn't relish going back there, remembering the angry faces of the villagers, but she also had a purpose. Through Mrs. Van, she had learned the whereabouts of Percival Avon's old housekeeper, now in the late stages of memory impairment. It was useless to ask any of Martin's current staff about Percival Avon, because they were all newly hired.

She hoped that the old housekeeper might be triggered to remember any useful information that could help guide their search. In truth, since the disappointment of the crypts, they'd reached an impasse.

She sat on the box seat with Arthur, her hair tucked into a woolen scarf. Arthur's red nose looked ready to fall off from the chill. She'd asked Theodore Daye to come along as well, hoping that he might take strength from being outside Weavingshaw. His poor face seemed even more gaunt these days, his eyes turning empty within the marbled house.

Sitting beside her, he flickered in and out like a candle. Her heart sank; she'd never allowed herself to worry this much over a ghost.

"Don't dawdle too long, miss," Arthur said as he spat out a wad of chewed tobacco onto the ground beside the carriage. "Something's brewing in that town."

"I know," Leena said. She was aware that Arthur had acquainted himself with the local alehouse, likely listening to stray pieces of gossip and reporting back to his master. "Is the entire town owned by Mr. Martin?"

"Aye, but they ain't too fond of him." Arthur snapped the reins. "I'd sooner sell my mother off, bless the dead, than go down those mine shafts. They're built on volatile land, but Mr. Martin refuses to reinforce the beams, making the descent real dangerous." Arthur's mouth twisted in distaste. "At any moment the caves may give way, burying everyone inside alive. And the air down there is as thin as a fish bone."

"Are most of the townspeople miners?"

"Aye, ma'am, and a miner's life is short and starved. And even after, Martin will not suitably compensate for their deaths."

Leena shivered, feeling not for the first time that poverty still shaped the Algaraans and the Mors in the same way.

"You seem to know a great deal about this mining town, Arthur," Leena ventured.

He looked away momentarily. "My father was a miner, may the Saints rest his soul."

Leena was startled, but held her expression well, murmuring the proper words to rest the dead.

Arthur tucked his hat low over the descending cold. "Do not look so crestfallen, ma'am. The townspeople have taken heart from the Algaraan revolution, and not a single one of them has been to the mines in the past few days. Although . . ." He paused and, after her plea to continue, reluctantly added, "I hear that Martin's thinking about sending in soldiers to curb any dangerous ideas of revolt."

Leena's eyes widened. "Soldiers? For this small town? Isn't it a little much?"

"This entire country is dynamite," Arthur said, "waiting for the first spark."

She thought of her baba, how they'd beaten him down, crushed the spirit of the union to destroy it. "They'll kill them, Arthur," Leena whispered. "They'll kill them for this."

Arthur patted her shoulder reassuringly. "I reckon they have more fire than you give them credit for, ma'am." Still seeing the frown on her face, he flashed a silver-toothed smile. "Aye, don't fret. You'll be miles away by then. I'm going back tonight myself; the boss wants me to keep an eye on the shop."

Her safety was not the reason that Leena felt restless, but she refrained from expanding, as they'd almost reached their destination.

The town's streets were empty.

It was not for Sweeper's Cough, Leena knew, for the northern towns were too isolated to catch the raging infection.

Only the bakery, the church, and the posting inn were in decent condition. The rest of the houses were dilapidated, the roofs sunken from years of rain, yet the front steps were swept clean and the gables painted. Newspaper lanterns—likely made by the children—hung from the thatched roofs to welcome the winter celebrations. A few curtains shifted as they passed, and small pointed faces peered at them from darkened windows. Nailed onto every door was a single sheet of paper, and Leena read the first line aloud before stopping herself: *By Order of the King . . .*

Leena didn't need to read any more. She wondered how many of the townspeople were literate. She thought of her father being read his prison sentence in a language he could barely understand.

The housekeeper's cottage was the farthest down the lane. She left Arthur waiting on the street, rolling tobacco, as she went to investigate. Theodore Daye accompanied her, his steps slow and dragging, but he refused to go farther than the porch. The cottage was as run-down as the others, but this one seemed to be suffering a worse form of neglect. The windows were unwashed, the paint flaking. When she knocked on the door, the broken hinges made it swing open of its own accord.

"Who is it?" a croaky voice inquired.

Embarrassed by the intrusion, Leena stepped over the threshold. The cottage had only a single room, with a bed pushed to one side, a cramped kitchen tucked in the corner, and an armchair in which sat a shrunken old woman. It was surprisingly warm inside, with a hearth that boasted a large fire and several logs of wood piled high.

"Who is it?" the lady vaguely asked again.

"My name is Leena Al-Sayer, madam. May I come in?" Leena hovered in the doorway. "I've come down from Weavingshaw to ask you a few questions about Lord Avon."

"You've come from the House?" the old woman asked, beckoning her inside, the word *house* uttered with reverence. "Leena . . . is that a foreign name?"

"Yes, madam. Algaraan," Leena replied, approaching closer to the armchair.

The old woman's expression turned distant. "His Algaraan Lordship used to visit the House often. He was a great friend of the master."

Lord Hargreaves, Leena thought. Once more his name had been mentioned alongside that of Lord Avon, adding weight to Lady Hargreaves's embedded dreams. "How long did you work at Weavingshaw?"

The housekeeper wrenched her head up. "What happened to the Algaraan lord?" She gripped Leena's arm, her taloned fingers digging into her skin. "That filth, that half-breed. Curse him! Curse him! May he rot!"

Leena lurched away. The old housekeeper no longer looked as harmless as she had initially appeared, her white hair wild across the visible area of scalp, spittle forming on her thin lips.

Her heart beating faster, Leena tried her questioning again. "Why do you hate Lord Hargreaves?"

But the housekeeper continued as if she'd not heard. "How I grieve for the House, all alone on the moors. First they took the boy, then the master."

Leena stared blankly at her. "Who took the master?" But then she paused, a sudden sinking feeling in her chest. "What boy?"

"*What boy?* His Lordship's son, of course." The old woman rocked back and forth. "Oh, by the Saint of Lost Children. Oh, by her olive trees . . . keep him safe."

Saint of Lost Children? Olive trees? Leena remembered the empty tomb, her hands cold.

She'd never known Lord Avon had a son. Her gut twisted and she didn't realize she had taken a step toward the woman.

St. Silas himself had confirmed that the Avon line had died with Percival . . .

By that point, there was no one left in this world to inquire after him.

His words on her very first night of employment rang in her ears.

St. Silas had lied.

Of course he'd lied—just as he had hidden so many other things from her.

Leena could not avert her gaze from the old woman's face.

"How old would the boy be now?" Leena whispered, but the woman continued with her jumbled speech.

"They told everyone that he was missing, but I know different. *They* took him."

"Who took him?" Leena insisted, trying to keep pace with the conversation that was rapidly falling out of her grasp.

The woman leaned forward, baring teeth that were surprisingly strong and white. "The Wake."

Leena's breath caught. "Why would they take the boy?" Her hands gripped the fabric of her dress until her knuckles turned white. "Is Lord Hargreaves in the Wake?"

The old woman kept rocking back and forth. "They took him, that little darling."

Leena knelt by the woman, urgency welling in her throat. "What was the boy's name? *What was his name?*"

The woman continued to mumble.

"Please," Leena pleaded. "Try to remember. What was the boy's name?"

The old woman's foggy gaze landed on Leena once more. She tenderly brushed a curl from her face.

"You are beautiful," she said vaguely. Then her eyes fastened on the golden chain around Leena's neck, pulling at it gently to reveal Margery's broken timepiece with the name *Fray* engraved on it.

The old woman abruptly rose, as if seeing Leena's timepiece had triggered a lost memory. She walked toward the hearth where a small box lay, opening it carefully. Turning, the old woman showed her an identical timepiece, and Leena could not hide her surprise.

"Where did you get this, madam?"

The old woman found her chair again, looking down at the watch vacantly. "From Lord Avon, weeks before his death. He entrusted me with it, for I am his most loyal servant." The old housekeeper exhaled a harsh breath. "*Mrs. Graham,* he said, *do not be afraid of Weavingshaw and keep its secrets safe.*" One wrinkled hand touched her mouth. "*Mrs. Graham,* he said, *I trust you with my life.*" She closed her eyes briefly, as if petrified she would lose a memory she held with every heartbeat. "*Mrs. Graham,* he said, *never let Lord Hargreaves come upon this. I have . . .*"

When she opened her eyes, there were tears in them. She blinked as if through a dream.

Leena wanted to reach for her and hold a hand to her scrawny shoulder in comfort, but dared not, for she did not know if the old lady was speaking from a memory, a nightmare, or confusion, and whether she would reject such a gesture.

And yet, Leena knew she had been right to follow her instinct to visit the old housekeeper. There was something here that was vital for her to know. She could not understand why Margery would possess the same timepiece or what her purpose had been in giving it to her for safekeeping. She cursed herself for not carving out time as she had wanted to do to question Margery.

"I understand," Leena responded slowly. "May I see it?"

The old woman handed her the timepiece freely. Leena stood to inspect it better by the fire. It was identical to hers, down to the elegant letters of the inscription: *Fray.*

But just below that was another engraving, this time the letters rough and uneven, as if someone had done it in a hurry:

Avons can cross.

When she unlatched the cover, she found to her surprise that the clockface went up to thirty-six rather than twelve, or eighteen, as Margery's did. She could not account for this strange style of clockwork or for its purpose, for it was clear it did not tell the time. But it was equally clear that the discrepancy was deliberate, and not the mistake she had once assumed from Margery's timepiece. Here, like Margery's, a single hand was positioned at zero.

Leena peered intently at the woman, whose attention was now on her own hands. Before the old lady could mark her actions, Leena switched the two timepieces, returning Margery's to the box while keeping Lord Avon's.

She knew she would later feel the remorse of her duplicity, but for now she composed her features as best as she could, returning to the old housekeeper's side.

The old lady's eyes suddenly seemed very focused as she stared back at Leena. For a moment, Leena thought she looked as if she had full capacity of her senses, so watchful was that look.

"He came to see me." The old housekeeper gripped Leena's hand once more. "His Lordship still hasn't forgotten me. He sat and spoke with me. He filled my shed with chopped logs. The master has always been kind to me."

Leena swallowed. Was the old lady alluding to seeing Lord Avon's ghost? Or was this another distant memory?

Careful not to disturb her flow of speech, Leena prodded, "Is it Lord Avon you speak of, madam?"

"Yes, of course—who else would I be referring to?" the old woman scoffed, releasing her hand.

"But, madam, Lord Percival Avon has been dead these past ten years."

"Well, of course he has; I was at the funeral. I speak of Master Bramwell, the new Lord Avon."

Leena's reaction was visceral. The humming in her ears, the pallor of her cheeks, the heaving of her breath were all entirely beyond her control.

She hadn't anticipated this revelation, and yet she had known it deep in her gut. Maybe she had known it since the moment she'd seen St. Silas enter Weavingshaw, absorbing its energy in hungry gulps.

The sixth sense that led her to see ghosts had already warned her that the master had come home.

29

The Winter Sea

LEENA STOOD AT the fold where the ocean met the land, the salty water beneath her boots retreating and advancing—not a dance but a war. The savagery of the waves created ridges and footholds on the black cliffs, battering the stone into submission.

Leena had gone to the rocky beach after she'd returned from the old housekeeper's. After Theodore Daye had bowed his head when she'd asked him if the blood that ran through Bram St. Silas's veins was Avon blood. After she'd stood on the pale limestone steps of Weavingshaw, her chest aching, nearly suffocating, as if the estate was bent on stealing the breath from her lungs.

She could not bear to be on Avon land a moment longer.

But no matter how far Leena walked—toward the forest, toward the ocean, toward the cliffs—Weavingshaw's silent tower still watched her. Even here, as the seawater licked her hem and the wind whipped her hair, she felt its bedevilment.

Leena thought of St. Silas's expression as they arrived at Weavingshaw for the first time—not hatred as she'd originally assumed, but an intermingling of wrath and a fierce, all-consuming devotion.

She'd likewise noticed the ease with which he walked the marbled halls, his odd familiarity with the house's secrets. And yet, his passion clearly stretched past the stone halls of Weavingshaw. She could easily remember his simmering anger at the mistreatment of the miners—all tenants on his land.

Even the ghosts in and around the fortress seemed to crave a closeness to St. Silas, their hands outstretched as if he were a life source, welcoming him home.

The wind stole Leena's gasp as she remembered the empty tomb . . . *St. Silas's* empty tomb . . . the one she'd forced him to hide in. How it had paralyzed him, and how she'd entirely misunderstood the reason for that disturbance.

Leena knelt down suddenly, splashing freezing water onto her face, inhaling sharply from the glacial temperature.

Percival Avon's son.

But they were a study in opposites. There was nothing of St. Silas in Lord Avon's golden features. Lord Avon exuded vitality; St. Silas was cut from menace.

No. Leena remembered that there had been one striking similarity. Percival Avon's voice had had the same smooth masculine intonation as St. Silas's own—used to tempt, to seduce, to ensnare.

The voice had entranced Moira, raising a bloom in her cheeks as he called her *my little one*—mere moments before he had strangled her.

Emotion tore through her, as serrated as a knife's edge, leaving jagged scars in its path.

She could not tear her eyes away from the dying sun, its orange light a distorted reflection upon the heaving waves, the endless seething sea. The gray clouds loomed, a prelude to another storm. The shrieks of the seagulls surrounding the shore sounded like battle cries. Somewhere far off, she could hear the rumble of thunder. Now that Leena had learned to listen, she swore she could hear the distant cries of wolves.

She stood motionless as the freezing tide brushed her hemline, the arctic temperatures expanding her anguish until she felt she might go mad with it. With shaky fingers, she bent down and undid the laces of her boots before sliding down her stockings. Even that was not enough. Leena wanted to be lost within the elements, to submerge herself in the water until she felt awakened by it, far away from the entombment of Weavingshaw.

She thrust off her overcoat, throwing it behind her on the hard sand. One button followed another as she flung her dress where her coat lay. It was a greater struggle to undo the stays of her corset, but years of experience made her fingers deft with the laces. She almost ripped the delicate threads of her petticoat in her haste to be rid of that, too.

She stood shivering in her lace-woven undergarments, covered only by a simple white cotton chemise that offered little protection against the battering wind, and she could not remember a time she had been so bare in the outdoors. She gasped from the chilling bite of the ocean as she took her first steps into the water. It was a sort of liberation not to be pulled down by her heavy skirts as she advanced farther, the chemise only long enough to cover her thighs. Her arms were also free, catching goosebumps from the bitter wind. It was not eerie, but *right,* that Leena was the only warm creature in a barren land, surrounded by the shadows of cliffs and jagged rocks.

Within moments she was waist-deep, the waves crashing and breaking against her body as if intent on claiming her as one of their own. She closed her eyes, wishing the cold would breathe life into her, reminding her that she was a living thing that had not yet yielded to death.

Leena had an urge—not for the first time in her life—to scream into the wind. It shredded through her lungs, and the sea swallowed her howls, welcoming Leena as another shipwreck on the shores of Weavingshaw.

She only stopped once she remembered Percival Avon screaming wildly—pleadingly—before a black lake. She didn't want to tether herself any further to the Avons when she was already so deeply entrenched.

The Saint of Silence—Master Bramwell—My Lord Avon.

The raw edges of her body sensed his presence on the beach before he had even spoken.

He called to her.

She did not turn.

"Leena."

His voice evoked within her relief and heartache in equal and unforgiving measure.

She shivered—not merely from the glacial water that had bled all the color from her skin, but from his voice as he said her name. Still she did not turn back, her gaze pinned on the looming waves that surrounded her.

"Leena, look at me."

He was closer now, his command cutting through the burgeoning storm.

Finally, fighting the sob that had curled in her throat, she turned to him.

Fully clothed, St. Silas had come into the water after her, his dark riding coat undone and whipping in the wind. The light of the setting sun was at his back and it looked as if his entire outline was on fire. For a moment, he exuded the same force—*the same holiness*—as Percival Avon.

Once more she felt like Moira—her heart aching at the feral beauty that was the Avons.

He continued when she did not speak. "Have you been possessed?"

Slowly, Leena shook her head. Before he could ask, she said quietly, "You take two spoonfuls of sugar in your coffee. I do not."

Leena was aware she must look every inch a madwoman, standing in her underthings in the winter sea, hair coming undone from the braid that had been coiled atop her head, the long tendrils whipping about her neck and waist in a frenzy. She could forgive him for thinking she was possessed, for she must truly look a ghostly sight.

She refrained from folding her arms to cover herself, knowing that her white chemise had become see-through where it made contact with the water, her skin now exposed to the intensity of his focus.

From the moment she'd turned to face him, St. Silas's eyes had darkened. And even from where she stood she could see his harsh swallow as he nodded his acknowledgment.

Then, as if his gaze could not contain itself, it dropped to outline the soft contours of her body.

The way he was looking at her evoked within Leena a strange alchemy. It made her feel both afraid of what was to come and yet *longing* for it with fervent urgency.

"I can see every—" He swallowed again, his tone rough. It was as if he could not look away, and he did not.

Her own voice cracked. "I did not expect anyone to come upon me here." Even though he was still near the shoreline, she felt touched by his gaze, her body kindling in spite of the cold.

The tails of his dark coat floated about him as he stood nearly thigh-deep in the violent waves. His boots were no doubt a better defense against the icy temperatures than her bare feet, and for a moment she envied his dry undershirt, the thick woolen protection of his coat. And most of all, she envied that he was more in command of his surroundings than she.

Leena could see it now, the way the land rose and fell under his mastery.

Their differences had never been so apparent, standing there as they were within the tumultuous ocean: the control he wielded, the noble blood that flowed through his veins, his strong and rugged form a battlefront against the wind—a sharp contrast to Leena, who was stripped to the elements and flooded with the remains of the dead.

"Why are you here?" Still, his voice was raspy.

Leena could not answer him, unable to explain the insanity that had forced her to plunge into the glacial ocean. At her unblinking silence, a troubled frown had begun to breach his expression.

"Come out. The tide is rising." He reached a hand toward her, and, in that one movement, he looked like a conqueror on a savage shore. He had brought war with him, and that invasion would reverberate through her body until he had changed the map of her. She would not survive him.

Instinctively, she allowed the harsh waves to pull her backward, shouting to be heard over the crash of water. "I've learned something today."

He did not step back, nor did he waver. Instead, he stalked toward her, the sleek, rigid lines of his body parting the angry waves, the civilized attire he wore a poor disguise for the hunter beneath. "What have you learned?"

"Something about you."

"Leena—"

"Something about your birthright."

St. Silas halted then, watching her alertly.

Slowly, he read the secret that had shrouded itself on Leena's face, and he dropped his hand.

He knew.

She opened her mouth to speak, but he stopped her.

"Do not." There was a harsh warning in his eyes: *Do not name me.*

It was at this moment that the sky opened up, releasing a torrent of brutal rain, drenching them even further.

She plunged toward the shore, already wishing herself a thousand miles from the turbulent ocean and back on dry land where she had as firm a hold as he.

But her bare foot caught on a rock wedged deep within the shifting sand just as she began to move forward, and she plummeted back into the ocean until she was fully submerged in salt water. The cold was so overwhelming that she felt caught in its icy teeth. She fought to right herself, panicking when she could not tell where the ground and the sky were.

Strong hands pulled her out in one powerful motion.

"I have you; be calm." Very rarely had Leena felt such instantaneous relief as when St. Silas took hold of her, lifting her so that he carried her cradled to his chest, one arm supporting her head, the other beneath her knees.

His long strides cut through the fierce tide, bringing them back to the sandy bank. He paused for a moment to retrieve her shoes, before continuing against the strong gale. Even though he carried her flush against him, Leena could no longer see him clearly in the tempest. Still, her obscured vision transformed the hard lines of his throat and arms into a lighthouse, anchoring her in this storm.

St. Silas led them away from the beach, toward the jagged cliffs and to a narrow opening that would have been impossible to see from the oceanside.

A smugglers' cave.

Despite her better judgment, Leena allowed her head to burrow against the hard expanse of his chest, both in comfort and in a rare rush of vulnerability.

She felt St. Silas pause for a moment at her unexpected surrender, looking down at her. She refused to meet his gaze and, after a moment, he resumed his pace, but his fingers tightened on her.

Not wanting to ruminate on what he must be thinking, Leena concentrated on his scent instead: woodsmoke from the hunt, fresh washing powder still clinging to his shirt, and the sandalwood from his shaving soap. To be so near to him was an intoxication. Already she felt her senses begin to blur in an embittered defeat.

Leena fought against it, until she heard his voice rumbling through his chest. Perhaps she imagined him speaking altogether; perhaps it was the beat of her own heart that she heard.

I cannot surrender, Leena.

Leena did not know if she imagined his words, if they were the echoes of the storm, or if her own toiling mind was creating phantoms that were never there.

Still, she did not dare look up at him. If she did, she was afraid to confirm what a part of her had already known standing on Weavingshaw's shore: that he saw her as another siege he would have to withstand.

That he *would* withstand her.

Leena shut her eyes tightly, trying to swallow the rawness of that reality.

When she finally dared to lift her head, it was to see they had entered the cave, leaving the downpour behind.

30

The Cave

It felt like they had entered another world. Instantaneously, the cacophony of the storm dimmed, the curved walls of the cave offering them shelter. To her right were stacks of old, abandoned crates, the hinges now coppery with rust. It was dry inside, but her breaths still came out in white puffs.

It took a long moment before St. Silas put her down on her feet, and she had to overcome the feeling of being adrift without his arms around her. Her teeth still chattered even though the cave was warmer than the ocean.

St. Silas had already taken off his coat, handing it to her slowly. "Should anyone cast doubt on my being a gentleman . . ."

She threaded her arms through the sleeves, once more wrapping herself in his scent, before throwing a slanted glance at the man himself.

He is unguarded, Leena thought to herself in bewilderment, for when she did meet his eyes again, it was to see a flash of possessiveness mark his glance as he absorbed her standing wrapped in his clothing, her frame all but lost in his overcoat.

Leena could not articulate why she felt warmth spread across her chest at his look, nor could she stop it.

He turned abruptly away to face the mouth of the cave, loosening his wet cravat. The well-defined muscles of his back shifted fluidly while he stripped himself of his waistcoat, leaving him in only his damp linen shirt. Leena tried not to stare, but she was sure she wore the same look on her face as the one he had given her on the shore. She was glad he was turned away from her.

Thinking of the shore brought back to her mind the compulsion that had led her there in the first place.

"Thank you for your help earlier. I do not—" Leena flushed. She desperately wanted to be calm when she spoke of the revelation that had flung her into the ocean in the first place. It took great effort to keep her voice measured. Already he thought her wild, and there was no need to press that point further. "I do not regularly frequent the outdoors in my . . . my . . ."

He turned to face her once more. "Undergarments."

"Chemise—it is called a chemise, and it is meant to be—"

"Transparent?" His voice was strained again.

It was her turn to look away, eyes lifted to the ceiling in an effort to contain her embarrassment.

"It is not transparent. Only the water made it . . . made it so." Leena tried to subdue her rising panic, but, by the Saints, just *how* much had he seen?

She raised herself to her full height, once more attempting a dignity she did not particularly feel. "Can we please refrain from discussing my . . . my clothing any more?"

"Certainly. Although I thought we were discussing the lack of it." Still she did not look at St. Silas, but she heard the laugh in his voice.

Hearing him like this, the shades of reservation and composure usually hovering between them cast away, Leena almost convinced herself that she *could* let go of the turbulent emotions welling inside her.

She almost convinced herself that the battlegrounds had all been laid out—that the battle had already been fought, and it had nothing to do with her.

It mattered little that Leena knew St. Silas's secret, that he was the 17th Lord Avon. It changed nothing within their contract and her task remained the same.

And would it not have been easier if they could have stayed in this moment, pulsating with fragility and humor and something as yet unnameable between them, away from dangerous and painful truths?

Yet Leena, who had never learned to walk away from the things that could hurt her, could not walk away now.

He watched her with his arms crossed across his chest, eyes nearly lost within the shifting storm-wrought shadows of the cave. She wished she could ask him to step into the light.

Whatever levity had existed between them had transformed, replaced with the revelation that weighed them both down, waiting to be voiced.

"Then forgive me for my breach in good manners on several occasions today." She gave him a deep curtsey and, when she rose, she met his shadowed glance. "Most notably that I did not sooner make my bows to the master who has come home." Still she did not evoke a response. *"My Lord Avon."*

Silence—so searing she felt the stab of old wounds.

"You found Percival Avon's ghost?" he asked sharply, the sudden flash of lightning once more revealing his angular features and rapt eyes.

"No, I have not found him." But she understood better why he had been so eager for this quest, for this particular ghost.

His father.

With that confirmation, St. Silas schooled his face once more, wearing the same expression he used when taking his confessions—a studied casualness, as if he was an indifferent observer to someone else's misery.

Then he did something that Leena didn't expect.

He smiled, dark eyes suddenly dancing as if they were once again sharing a jest. He narrowed the space between them in two long steps. "Miss Al-Sayer, you are still shaking." His voice was laced with silky concern. He reached for her frozen hands and cupped them in his own, bringing them close to his mouth to breathe on them. "Never mind all of this. Come here—I shall warm you."

A charge went through her the moment he touched her, and she forced herself to jerk away from him.

What St. Silas did not realize was that *she,* too, had begun to know him, to unravel the workings of his mind as perceptively as he saw hers. He was trying to make her doubt her own convictions by distracting her. This was the Saint of Silence as he was, layers of subtle manipulation to conceal the truth.

"I am warm enough without more lies," she said, her anger once more building in her refusal to be diverted by him. "You are Percival Avon's son."

The smooth smile dropped. His eyes were alert again, their dark flecks enhanced in the storm's gloom.

"That changes nothing."

"It changes *everything,*" Leena whispered fiercely, head tilted upward to meet his, to ensure that he didn't mistake the earnestness on her face. "You are master of the last fortress in the north; all the land until the sea is yours by birthright. Your father was Percival Avon. You come from a lineage as old as the First Marquess of Avon, traced back nine hundred years."

Another sudden blaze of light, then the distant roll of thunder. The electricity in the air coursed over her skin again, raising tiny hairs at the back of her neck.

She felt exposed under St. Silas's eyes, every pore on her skin vibrating under his focused attention, until she felt as charged as the lightning.

"What do you want from me, Leena?" The sudden change from

his indifference—the fervency with which he asked the question—roared in Leena's ears. She remembered when she had asked him that exact question not long ago, how it had torn through her own throat and left blood marks from how badly she'd wanted to know.

"The truth," she responded, just as low. "Nothing else."

He returned her curtsey with a low bow of his own. Even as he did so, his eyes lingered on her neck, sliding momentarily lower, his pupils dilating.

"The Seventeenth Marquess of Avon, at your service." He even spoke like an aristo. She'd always wondered about his cultured accent—his voice a drawl, like wine spilling into a glass, while Leena's tongue gnashed at her *R*s and tasted her *T*s like grit. "Does it displease you to find out I am an Avon?"

"No . . ."

"Are you angry?"

"*Anger is a very useless emotion,*" she gritted back—the same words he had used on her long ago. "No, I am not angry. I am not even angry that you withheld this information. I would be a hypocrite if I were to deny that we all have painful secrets we wish to hide." Leena could see that he had not been expecting that answer, but she pressed on before he could interrupt.

"Do you know about the Avon curse? Do you know what the First Marquess of Avon promised to the demon living under Weavingshaw?"

There was no change to his expression; it was as if they were merely speaking of polite nothings over dinner. "This is the history of my lineage. I have known it since I was old enough to speak."

She could not keep the astonishment from her voice. "So if you *knew,* why are you looking for a way to reclaim Weavingshaw? No, do not deny it; this entire hunt for your father was always about taking back Weavingshaw."

"Because it is mine." The words were not a statement but a proclamation of war.

The rain outside had sharpened its onslaught, breaching the defenses of the cave, a few droplets reaching them. It had turned into sleet. Soon, it would start to snow.

Even as they argued, Leena was aware that St. Silas's gaze struggled to remain on her face, continuously dropping below her collarbones before jerking up again, and her face flamed. But still she persisted.

"It was also Percival Avon's," Leena returned, and the hollow cavern twisted her words into a dark echo. "And I saw a memory of him standing over the lake in the crypt, *pleading* with the demon to stop feasting on him."

St. Silas shrugged, not at all disturbed by that knowledge. "My father was a weak man. He could not control the demon, so it controlled *him*—to his demise. I will be different. I will curtail the beast underneath, eradicate it in time."

She stared at him uncomprehendingly. She could not understand this ferocious tether to a land, being perpetually unmoored herself.

A refugee was just another type of ghost.

Leena shifted her bare feet against the hard rocks in frustration, her entire body tense with thought.

St. Silas had been watching her movements in silence, his eyes slightly out of focus as he once more traced her soft outline in the dimming light.

"If this is to be a fair fight"—his voice was gruff, that unguarded look in his expression again—"then my concentration cannot be shredded to pieces." He reached for Leena's coat buttons and roughly fastened them, one at a time. "This cannot remain open."

It took all her strength not to redden further as she stood rigid, allowing him to perform the task intently, not daring even to breathe.

The intimacy of having a man—*this* man—slowly fasten the buttons of his own coat on her, his hands large and focused on their task, caused a maddening havoc to momentarily overtake her mind.

She let out a staggered exhalation. His gaze pinned itself to her mouth before he abruptly dropped his hands and stepped away, a high color on his cheeks.

"Did you not hear what I just said?" When Leena spoke again, she sounded hoarse to her own ears, even as the threads of frustration still tugged at her. "The First Marquess of Avon made a contract—*bound by blood*—that every Avon henceforth would be irrevocably tied to that cursed demon until it killed them. And that includes you."

The return of the resolute gleam in his eyes told her what his silence did not—that he would not give up Weavingshaw even if his own death walked hand in hand with it.

For a moment, they were engulfed in the sound of crashing waves and violent wind.

Leena could not stop herself this time. She turned away from him first and started to furiously pace the tight enclosure of the cave. She found an old, corroded kerosene lamp. The oil in the reservoir was depleted, but she opened the cap to check, just to have something to do.

She heard his movements as he came up beside her, gently taking the lamp from her hands and putting it back down on the ground.

"How did you find out?" he asked, and Leena knew that the mild curiosity in his voice belied a much deeper void that he needed to fill.

She withdrew the timepiece and thrust it toward him. Leena still could not understand the meaning behind these timepieces—why Margery and Lord Avon had both possessed one—but she sensed that this was not the time to question St. Silas. The moment Leena returned to Golborne, she would go to Margery and demand some answers.

"*Avons can cross*," Leena said. "The old housekeeper—*your* old housekeeper—told me that the current Lord *Bramwell* Avon had visited her. That was all." The night they had both followed Lady Hargreaves flashed into her mind with clarity. When she had met

St. Silas just outside the inn, boots caked in mud, cravat undone, mood alight. He had been returning from his visit to the housekeeper. And, as the old lady had boasted, had restocked her firewood while he was there.

St. Silas took the timepiece, staring hard at the engraved message for a long moment, before giving it back to her wordlessly. "That is not all," he said roughly. "You've been watching me like I'm one of your phantoms."

"My phantoms," she whispered, clutching the timepiece in her cold fingers, "are far less stubborn, reticent, guarded, unholy . . ." *Bewitching,* she thought desperately, remembering Moira again and her destruction at the hands of an Avon man who put Weavingshaw above all else. "If you continue down this path, my lord, it will not be long before you *become* a phantom, and I will have to spend my days trying to release you."

The return of the intensity in his eyes was so harrowing that Leena brought a hand to her chest to steady the ache.

His words were slow, guttural. "Is that why I found you half frozen in the ocean? Because you are afraid you will grieve my loss?"

She could not tell a convincing lie; of that they were both certain. It was not only her voice but also Moira's, spanning across a decade, that at last answered, "I would grieve it."

His eyes flashed. But there was no satisfaction in his look, no victory, only *starvation* for more.

"I won't come back to haunt you." He made this vow like it was a cursed thing, burning his tongue on its way out. His head imperceptibly tilted toward her as he drank her in, his eyes lingering on her lips. "The contract forbids me to."

She didn't take a step away this time. Her pulse pounded, and she imagined what it would feel like if he closed the space between them, if his unyielding mouth met her own. If this would soften the iron of their bitter contract.

She was deaf to the sounds of the downpour calming and the

snow finally starting its descent, nor did she see the last orange rays of the sun break through the black clouds.

Leena, who had never been kissed before—not while ghosts haunted her every step—wanted to experience for the first time in her life the abandon of doing something she *wanted.* Not for survival, not because it was the right thing to do, but because she *needed to.*

Yet his mouth never met hers.

St. Silas jerked away before it could happen, his breathing ragged. He dragged a hand down his face. For a moment, he looked undone. Conquered.

Like *she* had bewitched *him.*

"*This* can't—" The words tore from his throat unevenly.

Leena stared at him, her own breaths harsher than normal.

She brought a quick hand to her lips as if they were bruised. In spite of himself, he followed the gesture, his eyes darkening—swallowing her whole.

Leena turned away from him, toward the opening of the cave, looking at the sea that had begun to soothe itself after its show of righteous fury. She struggled to keep her tone brusque; it was an insult to them both to pretend after what had occurred between them. "I won't tell a soul of what I've learned today."

She could feel his stare burning into her profile. "Not even the Wake?" he asked quietly, knowing that a promise from her would mean a betrayal of her father. Leena felt her gut twist at his words. The Saint of Silence was a powerful man and notoriously reclusive. Any secret about him could surely be used as a bargaining chip with any group that wanted power over him.

Leena also knew, with a certainty that dug deep into the marrow of her bones, that she would never do this, and that was *precisely* where the pain was seeping from. "What did the Wake do to you?"

He didn't answer. Even now, he kept his secrets close to his chest.

"It was Lord Hargreaves and your father. They were the Wake."

All of Leena's questions and the unsolved riddles written in her notes started to fall into place. She looked at St. Silas with both dawning understanding and wretched sympathy. "The Wake traded in prisoners." Her hand stung with the urge to reach out to him. "Did they also trade you? Did Lord Avon trade you—his only son, *his only heir*—to a demon?"

"Promise me, Leena, that you will not seek him. Hargreaves." His voice was at war with his body. Leena could see he was trying to sound calm, but the clench of his fist and the hardness of his shoulders gave him away.

She continued, unable to comprehend the cruelty of his past. "Is that why you have those ledgers? Is that why you collect confessions? For *them*? For the demons?"

He took her by the shoulders, his thumbs brushing her collarbones. "*Promise me.* Do not seek the Wake."

The horror deepened in her throat, scorching her. She could not tear her wild gaze from the ferocious set of his face.

Leena could not find a homeland on any map, but she'd found it in her father's booming laugh, in his kind hands, in the brown eyes she'd known from the moment she was born. And what St. Silas was asking of her would inevitably turn her into an exile again.

He shook her lightly. "Not *just* for my sake."

"I promise never to reveal a word about you." Leena repeated the oath in a whisper, much like kneeling at the altar before a holy Saint.

His words were vehement, a low command. "Promise for yourself."

She stepped away from him, already feeling the loss of the warmth of his hand on her skin. She walked toward the light snow, the dropping temperature sending goosebumps over her spine.

She was silent as she bent forward, slowly unlacing the shoes that St. Silas had brought with him from the beach. It was only when she wore them that she turned back to face him once more. "You seek to reclaim a home, my lord. Well, so do I. But I won't seek the Wake until we've concluded our business." She nodded at him. "We should head back now before it turns fully dark."

He didn't immediately follow her into the open air. Leena took her first steps into the freshly fallen snow, the twilight obscuring her footsteps as she started to climb her way back, her heart immeasurably heavy.

What she left behind in that cave was yet another promise—to herself this time—that she would *survive* this, no matter how painful, no matter how never-healing the wound would be. Unlike ill-fated Moira, she would eventually walk away from Bramwell Avon without turning back.

PART THREE

THE RUIN

31

The Hall of the Lake

AVONS CAN CROSS.

St. Silas understood.

The message had been left for him by his father. Whether it was meant as a warning or a guide, it did not matter. What mattered was the diary. What mattered was finding Percival Avon's ghost. What mattered was Weavingshaw.

At dawn on their final day, St. Silas went to the crypts alone.

He had learned the trick of the passages as a boy, and it was deceptively simple—one right turn for every three left ones. To survive, do not light the sconces. Do not open the barred metal doors. Do not cross the lake.

He'd made a mistake a few nights ago, and Rami had nearly been maimed. Leena had nearly been possessed. The rational side of his mind—the one that schemed and plotted—could not help but be fascinated by how attuned she was to the remnant powers left by demons. The other side could not forget how pale she had looked as she fought the possession. How the fear had burned his own throat. It was that part he tried to deny, to starve out, to extinguish. It was that part that would kill him if he allowed it.

He would not allow it.

The Hall of the Lake was undisturbed since they had left it last: the black waters, the penetrating darkness, the disfigured statues, the single raft. It was demon-made. He'd spent enough time in the underworld to recognize the distant hum of *their* power, that sharp current in the air, so foreign, so *wrong*.

He'd felt it the moment he'd set foot here once again, for the first time since the age of twelve: the land humming beneath his feet, the hush in the trees, as if the very house had been plunged into worship by his arrival. Of course it was. He was an Avon; this was Weavingshaw. They were one and the same.

This land could have only one master.

The lake would've drowned Martin had he attempted to cross it.

It would've drowned anyone who was not an Avon. *Demon-cursed.*

St. Silas understood that now, when before his father's obsessive warnings to never cross the lake had seeped into his consciousness. He should've known never to heed his father's word.

Martin could light a thousand fires in Weavingshaw, but the estate would remain cold to him. It was the demon that controlled that.

St. Silas knew snippets of what was inside the red diary. He was keen to see if there was anything more in there that could be of use.

The book told of his family history. Of how the 1st Marquess had brought the crypt-demon to Weavingshaw, how its magic had wrapped around the estate, protecting and shielding it from the rough elements that threatened to destroy it daily. The north had been a different landscape nine hundred years ago, when the 1st Marquess was deeded the estate by the King. It had been meant as a punishment; the 1st Marquess had displeased the King by trifling with his favorite mistress. Weavingshaw had been a fortress back then, the last defense before the sea, invaded countless times by the neighboring warlords who hailed from across the rough waters.

Seven times Weavingshaw had been burned to the ground, and rebuilt every time anew.

Each time more savage than the last.

The demon had put an end to that forever.

St. Silas stood in the Hall of the Lake now, watching the still black waters beneath him, staring at his reflection distorted in the ripples.

It was in this exact spot that his ancestor, the 1st Marquess, had made the original bargain: The demon would protect the house against any foreign invaders who desired its complete annihilation. In return, each new Lord Avon must swear fealty to the demon, promising to remain on the land, to bear sons to continue the bloodline—and, above all, to always feed the demon.

If the contract was broken, if the Avon line died out, Weavingshaw itself would crumble. The great house would turn into dust on the moors.

St. Silas hadn't yet performed the ancient act of binding himself to the demon; he'd been taken away as a child before he could. And he could not do so now while still indentured to the Duke of Fray, for he could not serve two demons at once.

St. Silas took off his jacket, rolled his sleeves to his elbows, and left a single candle burning on the shore.

No matter how intently he looked into the lake, he saw nothing but the empty expanse of water, the demon hidden deep within. Still, he felt its presence—a coiling energy that darkened these walls. This energy could not feed on St. Silas without the initial rites being performed, and it was for this reason the demon had chosen to feast on Leena instead.

It did not succeed, he thought savagely, and not without a hint of pride.

His thoughts returned to Leena's turbulent face in the cave, asking him to abandon his tie to Weavingshaw forever.

If St. Silas chose never to perform the ritual, then the demon would starve itself to death, destroying Weavingshaw alongside it. He could never abandon what was in his blood.

Already, without the rightful master ruling these vast lands, the demon had weakened to such an extent that it had allowed the likes of Martin to enter its halls, invading Weavingshaw just as decisively as the warlords of the past.

St. Silas would find the red diary, and then his father's ghost, whatever the cost might be. The seething anger that St. Silas had subdued violently over the years whenever he thought of his father simmered to the surface now, engulfing him with disgust. There would be no sentimentality when he finally saw Percival's ghost, no words of endearment traded.

His only goal was to establish from Percival how to break the contract that had indentured him to the Frays eleven years ago—a contract forged by Percival's own hand.

Once his bond with the Frays was finally broken, St. Silas would return to Weavingshaw as the rightful lord, reclaiming it from Martin by any means necessary. He would then cut his palm over the lake, allow the blood to drip into the water, tying himself forevermore to the demon and to Weavingshaw.

Then he would force the demon's demise, eradicating it from these stones once and for all, purging Weavingshaw and resurrecting it anew.

St. Silas turned to the raft bobbing up and down on the water. The small craft might have been brightly painted once, but the ensuing years had stripped the color away. It creaked beneath his weight.

He took a candle with him, but it snuffed itself out every time he tried to light it on the water. St. Silas cursed low under his breath: *Damned demon.* The only remaining light was the tiny flame left on the land. Otherwise, he was completely blind. It made no difference if he shut his eyelids or opened them; darkness was a sentry down here.

The raft glided through the waters. He rowed forward, entirely sightless, the only sound the slap of the oars hitting the water. The hum of the current grew louder, and he knew that he was approaching the place where the power was concentrated.

His thoughts drifted to *her,* as they often did now.

Leena knew he was an Avon.

She also knew about Weavingshaw's demon. It was the risk he had taken, allowing her to be close. He had known from the outset she was clever, but as he got to know her more, he felt an odd pleasure at knowing exactly *how* clever she was.

Her knowing who he was hadn't been factored into his plans. He had been a fool for thinking he could keep her in the dark until they found Lord Avon's ghost.

Still, he would shift and adjust. Take what was needed, leave what wasn't. Do what was necessary for himself and for the tenants of his land.

For Weavingshaw.

I will have to spend my days trying to release you.

He had stepped closer to her in the cave, his entire focus narrowed to the blush of her lips and how he wanted to submerge himself within her—to taste her in decadence, in starvation. The silhouette of her soft curves even now played across his vision. If what he could see was enticing, what he *imagined* was devastating. He had wanted to shred to pieces the overcoat that she was wearing, or kiss it in gratitude for covering her. Had it not been there, there would have been no secret, no request she could have made of him, that he would have denied.

He cursed under his breath, low and harsh. *How,* he thought, *had she attained such previously unattainable power over him?* He was not at all comforted by the fact that she did not know it yet. He was sure, sooner or later, he would reveal himself.

With effort, St. Silas restrained his thoughts.

He would be damned if he were to go further with Leena while the contract still stood. The power shift between them was too great, and he did not want her to feel the weight of it forcing her choices. If she chose him, she needed to do it of her own volition, within her own freedom. He would not touch her until then.

He, himself, lived under the cruel hand of a contract, and he knew what it meant to be choiceless.

St. Silas glanced behind him. The candle's light was now a mere speck. If that guttered out, then he would lose his direction. He'd never known this sort of blindness—the kind that had depth, that swallowed, that smothered. It was a trick designed to tug at the bleakness that rested in the consciousness of every human. To tempt them into the water.

Everyone except an Avon.

The crypt-demon needed the Avons.

St. Silas had heard stories of what Weavingshaw's demon had done to his grandfather—slowly feasting on his soul day by day, until three decades later his grandfather had lost all semblance of himself, locked in his own head, wandering the grounds in madness and despair.

His father had told St. Silas once, when he was a child, that the Avons' sacrifice was worth it, for the endurance of Weavingshaw.

The demon living in the crypts was a rare breed, unlike the ones St. Silas had dealt with in the underworld. Most demons fed on emotions, ultimately leaving the bodies of their victims hollow husks, or killing them outright if fed on too much and too quickly.

Weavingshaw's demon fed on the mind, implanting obsessions and delusions instead, plunging the Avons into eventual madness. In exchange, the Avons prolonged the demon's life by allowing it unrestrained access to feast on them.

The 1st Marquess of Avon had been an intelligent man and he had known how to guard himself, eventually succumbing to death before he succumbed to madness.

St. Silas's grandfather had not been so strong—although he had managed to avoid complete insanity until streaks of gray threaded his fair hair. In contrast, Percival had been weak, and, even as a boy of twelve, St. Silas had seen the first fledglings of paranoia beginning to unsettle his father.

St. Silas knew that Weavingshaw's demon could never easily plunge him into submission, into madness, unlike the majority of his bloodline.

If St. Silas had been a weaker man—if he didn't strive endlessly—the underworld demons would have fed on him until depletion years ago. He would've been long dead. Buried in that cursed ocean that surrounded the Duke of Fray's estate with the other boys dressed in white.

He saw them now.

It was the demon magic warping his mind; this he knew. He stared hollow-eyed as the young boys now marched across the water.

There was Joseph, the eldest of the group, still smooth-faced.

Hector, who cried into his fist at night while everyone else slept.

Theodore Daye, who had had the misfortune of being St. Silas's servant, indentured to the demon alongside him as a parting gift from Lord Avon.

He'd forgotten the names of the rest. They had blurred over the years, becoming echoes of themselves, haunting no one, not even St. Silas—the only one of them to have lived.

But he saw them now.

They were all just children. He hadn't realized it at the time. Not given the way they'd clawed at each other for survival.

In the beginning, St. Silas had been a lordling among street urchins and pickpockets. The Duke of Fray had paid him special attention at first—perhaps to reward him, perhaps to punish him—but it had stoked the hatred of the other boys. *Except* Theo Daye, who was now dead because of him.

It had disturbed him that Leena saw Theo's ghost, forcing St. Silas to reckon with a past that he thought he'd already sealed over long ago.

He'd been twelve when Joseph had forced his head into the underworld canal and held him down until his limbs weakened, until black dots clouded his vision. Until the water's rot had baptized him anew. Baptized him *worse.* It was Joseph whom St. Silas had killed with a rock to the brow in that final fight for survival.

And it was Joseph he'd dug a grave for, because he couldn't stand the thought of a human buried like a demon.

St. Silas's muscles stiffened as he forced the raft away from the boys standing in a motionless row. Their faces were expressionless, six heads turning as they watched him go. There was accusation in their silence.

No, that was just the cursed waters, feeding on the jagged edges of his memory.

Instead, St. Silas imagined the Rosethorn taking root in the hard soil atop the two burial mounds, digging deep and reaching the dead beneath, speaking a language of comfort that had once been foreign to him.

Once more he felt the vise around his chest ease. He continued to row forward.

St. Silas thought he'd see his father next; it seemed the exact sort of maudlin nonsense that the demon craved. Or even hallucinations of Lord Hargreaves and Lady Hargreaves, and the many nights he'd spent as a small boy in Hythe House when his father went away. Hargreaves teaching him how to shoot or toasting him as he declared, *To the youngest member of the Wake.*

Perhaps he'd hear Lady Hargreaves's soft southern lilt as she sang him a lullaby—the closest thing he'd had to a mother in that cold house.

The fact that Lady Hargreaves had drowned by her own hand meant only one thing to St. Silas—that Weavingshaw had also gripped her. Whether it was anger or madness or guilt, St. Silas would never know, for he had been traded before he could ever find out. But the ache of her loss was far more potent than the loss of Percival or even the mother he could not remember.

And still, he would row past.

But they didn't come.

Instead—

"It's not intuitive, is it?" a soft voice said from behind him. He turned around, his hand already resting on the barrel of his pistol, but he halted. Leena sat in front of him, knees drawn close together in the tight confines of the raft, her hair spilling onto her shoulders.

He stared at her.

"The demon's magic," she amended. "It's not very intuitive."

"Isn't it?" he asked in a low voice.

Her head jerked as if she'd seen something in the edge of her vision; he'd seen her wear that expression before, when a phantom appeared. Fear scrunched her brows, her chest rose and fell—and suddenly, without warning, she buried herself into his chest.

It is merely a hallucination. He knew that the scent of lavender that enveloped him was not real.

Still, his arms tightened around her in spite of himself, and he felt the warmth of her body even through the layers of clothes.

She was dressed exactly as she had been at the Festival of Demons, save for the mask. Her curls swept down the length of her back; he remembered how his hands had burned to entangle themselves in their softness even then.

Leena looked up at him from beneath thick lashes, her eyes earthy brown and wide—that searching look, soft as thistles, a dagger to his chest. Haltingly, she placed a hand on his jaw. He swallowed. His muscles tensed, not daring to move, as she brushed her lips against his.

A tether broke inside him.

He leaned forward, one palm slamming on the wooden seat by her hip, the other drawing her closer as he took her mouth with his own, just as he had wanted to in the cave. She tasted like sweet sorcery—maddening him, enshrouding him. He pulled away to take a deep inhalation, burying his forehead into her neck, trailing kisses across the soft skin.

He felt the vibrations from her throat as she spoke. "I won't leave you behind, Bram. I'll stay with you."

He stiffened.

Those were not her words but the vows of the demon, dragging out his deepest desires from when he had been a boy of twelve, left abandoned in the underworld.

Suddenly, jarringly, he released her, taking one last look at her smile—as if she trusted him, as if seeing *him* was happiness—before he pushed her over the raft's edge and into the fathomless waters.

The vision of her shattered like glass, plunging him into darkness once more.

St. Silas didn't linger any longer. It had not been his Leena. He forced himself to keep his gaze steady and row, not to look down, not to *make sure* . . .

Time moved differently down here. Perhaps he was only on the lake for a few minutes; perhaps hours passed. But he finally felt a jolt as the raft hit the shore on the other side.

This time, while on land, the wick held its flame. More statues littered the place, the stone facades aged with algae and dirt, nobility left to decay. He tied the raft to the arm of a Lord whose jaw had crumbled into dust, leaving only parts of a lip still frowning. The flame flickered in and out, collecting shadows on the wall, while he navigated the stone floors and disintegrating relics. His steps echoed. There was no Al-Sayer here to sing folk songs, and St. Silas kept silent.

At last he came to a raised platform at the far end of the room. He knew what he'd find before he reached it. He climbed the steps, his boots thudding against the marble.

A tomb lay in wait.

"Bravo," St. Silas murmured. He felt the electric hum in the air again, the demon's power so condensed his skin felt feverish with it. He circled the vault, his brows furrowed as if trying to decipher a puzzle. The stone felt real beneath his hand, the rough texture familiar, scraping the calluses on his palms. There was no name on the lid.

It could be his father's. It could be his own.

Swallowing harshly, he pushed on the lid. The color drained from his face as the smell of spoiled meat enveloped him. His father's corpse lay inside—not a smiling skeleton, but a bloated, mangled body that still retained its flesh. He was only recognizable from the tufts of still-golden hair crowning a face half eaten by rats and maggots, the sinewy muscle glimmering underneath, the eyes blue and gaping. A sword had pierced him in the chest, plunged so deeply that only the bronze hilt showed. Nestled between the corpse's folded arms was the red diary. All St. Silas needed to do was move the arms and grab the book.

He knew it was not real. His father's actual remains lay behind him, in the family crypt. He knew that this was another layer of the demon's magic, convulsing his mind, consuming him.

Still, St. Silas stood paralyzed.

You were always guarded, the Duke of Fray had told him once, *even as a child.*

He could not force his hand to move.

Such a waste, Orley had said. *I cannot get a feel for you at all.*

Fear constricted his lungs, a slow asphyxiation.

Do you tear hearts for a living?

A change overtook him. The terror receded. His expression flattened, blackened—a derisive curl to his lips, a cold fury in his eyes. St. Silas's own promise, the one he had made when he was sixteen years old, head bent as his life was debated by the Duke of Fray, rang louder than the rest.

He would not falter.

Reaching out, his actions firm and steady, he took the red diary. The crypt and the image of his putrefied father shattered into nothingness.

A demon's trick.

There he stood—Bram St. Silas, Bramwell Avon, waist-deep in vows, in vengeance, born to privilege, marked by brutality. There he stood, the Saint of Silence, triumphant in the dark.

32

The Slaughter of Sheep

It was twilight, and snow had begun to fall in earnest.

Rami exercised in the courtyard, far away from the flutter of departing guests and carriages rolling through the broad iron gates. Most of the hunting party had bid their farewells and the gentlemen's chambers were empty.

St. Silas had been absent for nearly the entire day. They still hadn't found the damned red diary, and he understood that they could not afford to remain much longer than tomorrow morning. Already, they were overstaying their welcome.

He sheathed his sword and stood motionless in the remnants of twilight. Although there were no city noises to distract him here, an uneasy silence made his ears ring.

He *hated* Weavingshaw.

It never failed to elicit a phantom ache in his shoulder, forcing him to recall the sawing of the surgeon's blade. As if Weavingshaw *itself* was a knife, hacking at its occupants slowly. He felt its presence even now, breathing down his neck.

A sudden noise disturbed the hush.

Running footsteps, then Rami was wrenched back to see Martin hovering over him, his face quivering with rage.

Rami swallowed, and he knew with utter clarity that the ruined Tar had been discovered. His grip tightened on the hilt of his sword.

He'd really thought that they would be out of Weavingshaw by the time the Tar was found. There was no reason Martin should return to the crypts to check on the drug so soon after his previous visit. Still, he cursed his own rash actions.

Martin was standing so close that Rami could see the bone protruding from his nasal bridge, healed improperly from a past break. His voice was grating, his pale lips barely moving. "You. Did. It."

Rami kept his face neutral. "Did *what*?"

A sudden blow struck the side of Rami's head, quick and thunderous, causing his vision to erupt in black dots. A boxer's punch, full of weight. Rami swayed slightly before regaining his posture, unsheathing his sword in one fluid motion.

Martin held a pistol.

Rami froze. He wondered briefly if his sister would hear the shot.

"I won't even grant you a burial, boy." The light caught the metal of Martin's weapon, glinting in the thin mist that encircled them.

Rami sneered. "What does it matter? I've already ruined you."

A smog of aimlessness had enveloped Rami ever since his father had been taken away. The only emotion that pierced through that smog was anger. He leaned into it now. "What will you do, *Mister* Martin? Will you crawl back to the Saint of Silence and reveal another secret in the hopes that he will save you? Just so you can continue play-acting nobility? You're nothing but dirt to them."

The pistol unlocked.

"I'll take you back to Golborne in chains," Martin vowed. "To decay in Newtorn Prison."

Newtorn Prison.

That place followed Rami in his waking hours and in sleep.

Every migrant boy knew the contours of that place, felt its dreaded presence looming over them, like a voyeur watching their every move. To grow up always being the object of observation, every word accounted for, every move condemned. A part of Rami always knew he was a criminal before he'd even committed the crime.

Martin's smile was slow and nasty. "You were always going to end up there, boy."

Rami tightened his grip on the sword.

"Really, Martin, you cannot perform an execution in the middle of a courtyard. Very bad manners." A smooth voice cut through the tension, and they both whipped around to see St. Silas leaning against one of the parlor doors. He still wore last night's clothes, now uncharacteristically disordered—the cravat lost and the collar loosened. He held his own pistol in a relaxed grip. "Think of the mess."

"This is not your fight," Rami snapped.

"To my dismay, it is," St. Silas replied easily.

Rami nearly groaned in frustration.

"My patience has frayed with this boy, Mr. St. Silas," Martin growled. "You have all entered my estate uninvited, through sheer force and blackmail."

Martin pointed toward Rami with the pistol. "Your *ward* has cost me an immense fortune—*again.* You cannot deny me the right to punish him as I see fit. Damn Newtorn Prison; I will hang him myself, here on the steps of Weavingshaw."

"You forget yourself, Martin. The boy is under my protection and therefore cannot be touched."

There was a loaded silence. Martin's shoulders visibly tensed, his jaw jutting. "If your entire party is so inseparable, then you will all have to partake in this punishment. No one is leaving before I am recompensed."

Martin's words sent Rami's heart pounding wildly in his chest. Never once had he thought that the retribution would touch more than just him. Leena swam before his vision, face pinched with worry every time he left the house late at night and came back disordered and bruised. To think that she would be harmed because of his actions was a twisting knife.

St. Silas pushed himself off the door and started to make his way down the stone steps. He casually stood beside Rami, pistol still very much in sight.

"Do you know, Martin, a few days ago I had an inkling that it might come to this. Hence, I've taken the liberty of sending my man down to Golborne with a sealed envelope containing a detailed description of your *very kind* hospitality as well as certain other . . . facts about you." St. Silas's drawl never wavered, and Rami could not tell if he was lying or speaking the truth. "Should I not return as expected, these *facts* will be on the front page of every newspaper in Golborne."

Martin stood arrested, paleness marking his brow.

The Saint continued, his smile deepening at the signs of the tradesman's distress. "Well? What will it be, Martin?"

"I will not let him go, Mr. St. Silas." Martin's voice swelled with the wealth of wrath he was trying to tamp down. "Of course, sir, you are free to go *after* the boy's execution"—he hesitated at St. Silas's raised brows—"to ensure that you will not rally any outside help for this criminal."

He was sealing them all in Weavingshaw. Suffocating them. Even though they were not all going to be put to death, they were all going to watch Rami die, and for Leena that would be another kind of death.

Rami's grip on his sword was so tight it was nearly bruising. He hated how right Leena had been down in the crypts, begging him to be cautious, to think.

The smile on St. Silas's lips was fixed, his eyes watchful.

With desperation, Rami's mind filtered through options for another escape. "A duel, then, Martin. At dawn, to allow you the chance to take revenge upon me."

Martin's laughter echoed in the courtyard. "Do you take me for a fool? To accept a duel with Golborne's finest swordsman?" His laughter dropped. "And deprive myself of the sheer pleasure of watching your neck snap in two? I think not, Mr. Al-Sayer."

Had Rami's punishment lain in Newtorn Prison, there *may* have been a chance to escape, but to concede to Martin's demand now would mean Rami would never step foot outside of Weavingshaw again. His sister's face once more flashed through his mind, eyes alight with laughter. She might never smile again after this.

More frantic than ever, his mind leaped to St. Silas, his eyes very briefly darting to the man standing in front of him. Was there *anything* the Saint of Silence could do to get them—*him*—out of this? Clearly the threat of revealing Martin's secret guaranteed only St. Silas's safety, but surely there must be something else?

Arthur? No, damn it, he had gone ahead to Golborne. And St. Silas had brought no other staff with him save for Mrs. Van, trusting no one else in the search for the red diary.

There really was no way, Rami thought, his chest airless. Bleakly, he replied, "I accept on one condition: that you let my sister leave with St. Silas unharmed." When he saw Martin was going to interrupt, he raised a hand. "Yes. *After* my hanging."

"I have no ill will toward the rest of your party. *Afterward,* they may all leave. That includes you, sir." He looked at St. Silas with a slight smile. "And as I will ensure this unfortunate business will be concluded quite quickly, you should reach Golborne in plenty of time to . . . er . . . reassure your man of your safety."

It played, Rami thought with disgust, perfectly into Martin's hands. He would have executed Rami and safeguarded his secret in one fell swoop.

"While I salute your . . . generosity in allowing the rest of us to leave unaccosted, there is"—St. Silas began indifferently, as if he were speaking about the weather, not the lives of the four of them—"another option. You may not accept a duel with Rami—sound reasoning—but perhaps dueling with me might be a better choice."

Martin's entire body stilled, his gaze shifting from Rami's flushed cheeks to St. Silas's carefully neutral eyes. The astonishment that played across Martin's face was slowly replaced by a speculative gleam.

"To clarify, sir, it would be *you* who would fight, not the boy?"

St. Silas bowed his head.

"What would be the terms, then, Mr. St. Silas?"

"If I win, we dismiss the matter of the ruined merchandise entirely—and myself, my servant, and my wards are free to leave your pleasant company unimpeded."

"And if you lose?" Martin prompted.

"I would imagine that is self-explanatory. If I lose, I will die—and all your secrets die with me," St. Silas responded smoothly.

Martin didn't lower his gun from Rami, but his entire posture seemed to vibrate. He released a staggered, disbelieving exhalation. "What will happen to the envelope you've given to your man if you are slain in this duel of honor? Your absence would mean he would go on to publish my secrets to the world and ruin me."

"My man, Arthur, takes orders from only three people in the world. Myself and my wards." St. Silas shrugged. "Should I . . . unfortunately perish in our duel, then upon the safe arrival of *both* my wards in Golborne, they will instruct Arthur to cease all publications about you."

Rami's head whipped toward St. Silas. *What in* damnation *was he playing at?* Arthur would never listen to either him or Leena, unless—*it had to be*—it was St. Silas's way of ensuring that if he died, the Al-Sayers would still reach Golborne unharmed.

It was obvious St. Silas did not care a fig about whether Rami lived or died, but it was clear to Rami that even St. Silas, shrouded in reclusiveness and reticence, was softening toward his sister. No, more than softening—*yielding*.

Martin seemed to be considering this new proposition carefully. "Swords, then, at dawn."

St. Silas pocketed his pistol. "I feel sure, Martin, that I do not need to question your integrity with regards to tomorrow's affair."

Mr. Martin huffed. "Are you casting doubt on whether I will participate in an honorable duel, Mr. St. Silas?"

"Your outrage does you credit. My doubts are now laid to rest."

Rami looked at St. Silas carefully, yet neither doubt nor reassurance was shown on his closed face. Rami was suddenly gripped with panic. In all the fear of being hanged and the subsequent life-and-death exchanges, he had not thought, for a minute, that Martin might play dirty.

But of course he would, lest Rami forget the wood cabin and Mackenzie Crane.

Damnation.

But St. Silas already suspected this, and was likely making plans based on those suspicions.

Mr. Martin jerked his head in assent, but he did not look any happier. He then turned to Rami. "Throw your sword to the ground, Mr. Al-Sayer. You will be kept locked in your room as leverage, to ensure the duel takes place."

Rami had no choice but to walk forward toward the entrance to the parlor. As he passed St. Silas, he was subsequently patted on the shoulder in what seemed uncharacteristically like comfort. Then, just before St. Silas turned to go, he murmured low enough for only Rami to hear, "If you see Leena, do not inform her of the treachery Martin will likely attempt tomorrow. Otherwise, she will try to follow us in a misguided attempt to help."

Rami nodded tightly. That was exactly what Leena would do, should she suspect Rami's life was in danger.

As Martin led Rami away, he felt abruptly like a sheep being led to slaughter.

33

A SAFE PASSAGE

LEENA WAS ABOUT to encircle her bed with salt when a knock came at her door at a quarter past one in the morning. She'd stayed awake later than usual in the despairing hope that Lord Avon would come forth, but he remained bitterly elusive.

She looked inquiringly at Theodore Daye, who had taken his usual position beside her bed.

She opened her door to find St. Silas darkening the threshold.

She hadn't seen him save for briefly this morning, and a part of her had wondered if he'd been avoiding her since the cave.

She moved to let him in, grateful that she was still dressed in her yellow cotton skirt and that her hair was not a complete mess, still in the pins that Mrs. Van had painstakingly woven through her curls before dinner.

St. Silas had never visited her in her chamber; for him to be here must mean that there was something urgent to be said. His gaze dropped to the salt pouch in her hands, but he did not comment.

There was a grimness in his eyes tonight. Wordlessly, he stepped inside and withdrew a palm-sized book from inside his coat.

"The red diary," Leena gasped. "How did you—?"

"The Hall of the Lake. *Avons can cross.* Call your ghost," St. Silas responded succinctly.

Leena stared at him. She imagined St. Silas rowing across those dark waters, entirely unaffected by the coiling energy—so potent, so corrosive, enough to drive a man to drown himself. Leena herself had felt the demon's powers, felt its attempt to force her into submission, and she knew she would have succumbed to it had she been on the lake.

That St. Silas had survived simply because he was an Avon was nearly unfathomable—especially when she'd felt the demon's craving for Avon blood.

Although Rami was her brother and there was very little she kept from him, she had not told him what she'd discovered about St. Silas in the cave. But after the Tar incident, her faith in Rami's ability to keep a calm head was shaken. She could not trust he would not accidentally or purposely release such knowledge.

Before Leena could question him further, Theodore Daye had already stepped forward and motioned for Leena to place the book on the floor. The ghost knelt beside it, one hand grazing the scarlet leather exterior. He stayed in that position for a long time; Leena had never seen him so still. His movements were often jerky, his skin itching, as if on fire.

"He's here," she whispered, not taking her eyes off Theodore.

The temperature in the room dropped. Goosebumps trailed her spine. Thin sheets of ice crept across the windowpane.

Finally, Theodore Daye stood up. He turned to the clock that hung on the wall, pointing toward the twelve o'clock position.

"Will Lord Avon's ghost appear tomorrow at noon?" Leena asked.

Theodore Daye nodded.

Of course, it would be either noon or midnight—those witching hours when the separation between the dead and the living was thinner, and ghosts seemed able to take a step into their world more easily.

Leena's eyes swerved to the clock again; it was now half past one in the morning. It could've been tonight. They had been so close.

"Where will Lord Avon appear?"

Theo pointed to this room.

"Here? In this chamber?" Leena clarified.

Another shaky nod.

She explained all this to St. Silas, who nodded briefly but did not say more for a few moments.

Leena sensed that the stillness around St. Silas was merely a prelude, as if he was trying to speak in a foreign language but didn't know how.

She stayed quiet, folding her hands in front of her, patiently waiting.

"Is Theo still here?" St. Silas finally murmured, staring hard at the nothingness she'd been speaking to.

"Beside me," Leena responded softly.

He nodded, his jaw ticcing.

Another silent moment. "Will you tell him something for me?"

She noted the color on his cheeks even as he was trying to control the look in his eyes. "You can speak to him yourself. He can hear you."

St. Silas jerked at this. It was as if he had never contemplated the idea that he didn't need Leena for his voice to breach the boundaries of death. He nodded imperceptibly. "Theo, I wish I could've done something different. I am sorry."

Leena looked between the two of them: Theodore Daye, still a boy of perhaps fourteen, stunted by death, stood in jarring contrast to St. Silas, who was so vitally *alive.* Never had she seen the disparity between the living and the dead so starkly.

Theodore Daye's eyes widened, as if this apology had been a strike and not a balm to him. He pulled at his hair, his entire body shaking, and the temperature of the room dropped even further. Then, as if he could bear it no longer, he disappeared.

"Theo forgives you." Leena had no regrets in uttering this falsehood, not allowing herself to assess why she needed St. Silas to believe this.

"You have a terribly honest face, Miss Al-Sayer." The words St. Silas had first used to describe her still echoed today.

Leena desperately wanted to ask St. Silas who Theodore Daye was to him and why he was apologizing to the young ghost. But Leena knew that there were secrets better left untold, buried deep within the chest like a second heart.

In the silence that ensued, St. Silas picked up the red diary, slipping it into his coat pocket again, before he turned toward the window, the snow obscuring the glass and the light of the moon.

"You need to prepare your bags tonight. Immediately after Theo summons Percival, we will be leaving." He continued to stare out of the window as he said this. "However, should we meet any . . . complications beforehand, do not wait for Percival. Leave as soon as you can."

Leena's mind was working rapidly, trying to make sense of what he was saying but failing to understand the reason behind the sudden urgency suppressed by his seemingly calm tone. She had already known that they would be leaving Weavingshaw as soon as Percival's ghost was found, but this new shift—for St. Silas to willingly abandon his plan before its completion—was no less than astounding.

"Mrs. Van has been given instructions that—unless I tell her otherwise and we are able to await Percival—she will collect you shortly after dawn to return directly to Golborne." He turned away from the window to look at her once more. "I do not trust Martin. Mrs. Van knows the halls of Weavingshaw unquestionably. She will be able to lead you out and into the pre-arranged carriage without being seen."

"Wait—"

"If I do not meet you in Golborne," he continued, as if not hearing her interruption, "you will find in the bottom drawer of my desk an envelope. That is yours."

"*Wait,*" she interjected forcefully again. "The way you are speaking, it is as if you're expecting an execution of some kind tomorrow. What's happened to make you speak this way?"

He didn't respond immediately.

"My lord," she insisted, walking up to him. "*What* has happened?"

His face was blank. "There will be a duel tomorrow at dawn. I have every confidence that it will end in our favor and we should continue with our plans as before. However," he said slowly, "I am also preparing for the . . . unexpected."

Leena absorbed his words. "The Tar has been discovered, hasn't it?" An angry flush crept across her cheeks. "Where is Rami? Allow me to kill him before the duel tomorrow. This is the fault of his rash, impulsive behavior!"

"He is currently locked away, and he is to have no visitors tonight, but he is in no danger," St. Silas replied. Then, after another pause, "He will not be fighting in the duel."

She reared back. "*You* are fighting in his place?"

"I told you from the very beginning to leave your brother behind, but I've learned now that telling you anything will result in the opposite happening." It was not quite laughter in his eyes, but something close to it.

Leena did not find humor in this.

A hundred questions filtered through her mind, but the inescapable one was *why* St. Silas would take the place of her brother, especially as Rami was no favorite of his.

"Why are you fighting instead of Rami?"

St. Silas shrugged. "I've been waiting for a chance to dispose of Martin."

"Why?" she persisted, although a part of her already knew the answer.

He raised his brows at her. "I do not think you will like the answer."

"For Weavingshaw?"

"For Weavingshaw."

The flames were roaring in the fireplace, but in spite of it, Leena felt chilled.

She nodded once, turning to look at the drifting snow outside the window. "Is the duel won at first blood?"

Leena, from having Rami as a brother, knew the rules of combat. There were two eventualities, agreed upon before the fight took place: The duel would be concluded either when the first blood was drawn, or when one fighter was dead.

St. Silas's answer was swift. "Do I look like the sort of man who stops at first blood?"

Leena emitted a humorless laugh. "No, you do not."

"And so I repeat: If I am slain, Mrs. Van will be one of the first to know the outcome, and all three of you must therefore abandon the search and leave immediately."

Leena had an image of St. Silas lying on a patch of isolated moor. The hot blood leaving his body would melt the surrounding snow, until the soil was seen beneath. She gasped at the image and, not for the first time, fought to hold back tears. She wished they were all far away from Weavingshaw.

He saw the look on her face, and his hard eyes softened imperceptibly. "Upon my return from the duel, which is far more likely, we will have the luxury of awaiting Percival's ghost undisturbed."

Leena's eyes snapped to him. "If Mr. Martin is slain, would Weavingshaw finally be yours?"

"It is a start." The look that came upon St. Silas whenever she challenged him about Weavingshaw was always the same: warlike, blood-filled.

"Is it swords or pistols?" she asked after some time.

"Swords."

Unease filled Leena's chest. It was widely known that St. Silas was an extremely deadly shot. His sword work, on the other hand, was nowhere near as exceptional as Rami's. This would put him at a disadvantage—especially as she knew that Mr. Martin, while he had also been cultivating his boxing career, was also known as a ruthless swordsman.

Leena started to pace, as she often did when trying to steady the hum of her fears.

"Leena." St. Silas watched her turn about the room for a further few moments, finally halting her with a light touch on her elbow. "Do not be afraid. I vow that, whatever happens, you will come to no harm."

"It is not myself I worry for," she replied distractedly.

"Rami will also be safe."

Leena turned swiftly to look at him. Was it not obvious? In her every expression? In the way she now looked at him? Had he, the Saint of Silence, cunning and perceptive, a reaper of secrets, not seen the confession so openly written on her face?

Her mouth was dry when she spoke, choked with emotion. "For your sake, I worry also."

Even *that* was a sliver of what she felt.

Suddenly, all the unsaid things between them ignited to the surface, unable to find a home in the choked silence.

He nodded once, tightly.

Then, St. Silas did something that she did not expect.

Slowly, he reached into his hidden coat pocket to withdraw a rectangular object. At first Leena suspected it was the red diary again, and she gasped when she saw *A Guide to Botany* in his hands. His steady gaze did not leave her face as he handed it to her.

She stared wide-eyed at it for a moment, disbelieving. She had thought it burned, fed to the fire, another past memory cremated.

The blue cover, still so familiar to her heart, was intact, and she could see no sign of missing pages. Without the book, the sound of her mother's voice had been extinguished to a faint murmur, but now it roared back to life—a beloved and much-missed melody.

With slightly shaking fingers, she reached for it.

His voice was low. "I restitched the first three pages." His eyes were dark with repressed emotion. "I wish I had never taken it from you."

Leena opened the cover reverently, and almost let out a peal of laughter when she saw the pages St. Silas declared to have burned in the days of their first confessions.

She traced the bumpy but small stitches over the spine that kept the first three pages intact. They were not sewn like a seamstress would sew a garment, in continuous stitches, but as a surgeon would sew a wound, with urgency, with precision, battling to keep the blood within.

"You did this yourself?" she asked softly.

The muscle in his jaw worked. He gave a brief nod.

With her heart in her throat, Leena had sudden images of St. Silas in his study, setting aside the endless tasks always demanding his attention to do this. His brows would have been furrowed in concentration as he bent over the pages of *A Guide to Botany*, weaving the small needle in and out with his large hand, before cutting the thread with his teeth.

"Where did you learn to sew?" she asked through the lump in her throat.

He gave her the first smile of the evening. "You and your questions."

She smiled back. "You and your non-answers."

He huffed out a laugh. "If you must know." He stepped back and did yet another unexpected thing. He removed his jacket and began to unbutton his waistcoat. As he did so, Leena's eyes widened with his every movement, unable to tear her gaze away.

"What . . . ?"

He freed his white linen shirt and pulled it from his trousers, revealing the rigid expanse of his abdomen. He seemed carved from stone, all hard, brutal muscles, causing the long and irregular scar that stretched across his right ribcage to appear more startling. "Before Mrs. Van, there was only Arthur and I. There were some fights that did not require any suturing. And some that needed to be done in the darkness, with nothing but a small candle and a sharp needle to stem the flow."

"You did this yourself?" She found herself asking the same bewildered question twice, almost reaching out for him, barely stopping herself in time.

His eyes followed her hand, and it took him a long moment to answer. "Yes."

"You are a man of many talents, Lord Avon." It took all Leena's self-control to place her hand back in her dress pocket, where she clenched it into a fist.

His eyes moved from her face and landed on the large bed behind her. His color heightened, and he tore his gaze back to the falling snow outside the window.

Fire scorched her veins.

For the first time since knowing St. Silas, it was a marvel to realize that, here in her bedchamber, they both saw the same thing, *imagined* the same thing, and were caught in the same impossibleness of it.

He did not say anything further as he righted his clothes.

"Do not give yourself cause," Leena finally said hoarsely, "to bleed again."

His only answer was silence.

Then St. Silas took out his pistol. "One last thing."

Her nerves caught in her chest; there was too much uncertainty tonight for Leena to be able to reason her way through it.

She remembered the last time she had held his pistol and what the result of that had been.

So much had changed since the Festival of Demons. In regard to Leena. In regard to *him.*

"You remove the safety like this. Be mindful of the jar to your shoulder when it fires. Hold your stance firm so you do not fall back. You have two bullets before you have to reload."

Her mind swam at the surreality of the night—at the fact that St. Silas was teaching her how to shoot.

"I will not need—" she began, but he grasped her hand and clasped it firmly around the pistol, holding it tightly there for a moment. Lightning coursed through her at his touch, almost painful in its intensity, but she did not pull away. "When you aim, make sure you aim two inches above your target for best accuracy. If you can, toward the heart."

Next time—if you ever desire to kill someone, not merely deliver a flesh wound, aim here.

She tried not to sound afraid. "It is as if you're saying goodbye."

He gave her another slow smile. "Don't aim the revolver at me."

Reluctantly, he let go of her hand.

Another heartbeat between them, reverberating through the walls of the chamber. She understood what he was doing even if he did not speak it. He was ensuring she had a chance—a safe passage home.

Instead of turning to go, St. Silas reached out and carefully unfastened the pins holding her hair, letting them clatter to the floor one by one. He watched the curls tumble to her back, and for a moment, under the glimmer of the candlelight, there was no mistaking the look in his eyes.

She could not say or do anything to stop him; tears obscured her vision.

He did not deny it. It *was* a farewell.

Roughly—as if having to extricate himself from the image of her standing before him, hair unbound, the unsaid goodbye flickering in her gaze—he turned toward the door.

"My lord, I ask you again: Do not bleed and do not give me a reason to use this. Come back so that I can return it to you in person," Leena said to his retreating back.

He exited the room quietly, leaving her to the silence of the gun.

34

The Motherless Boy

On the night before the duel, Leena did not encircle her bed with salt.

She understood the risk, felt the fear of being possessed curl in her stomach, but her desperate need to find any means to help outweighed the consequences. *Especially* on this night, above all others, as her brother and St. Silas readied themselves to face the sword.

"Lady Hargreaves," she whispered into the empty room. Theo Daye had not re-emerged and, for the first time, Leena ushered in her own haunting. "Return. Finish your story."

It took some time before Leena's restless mind fell asleep, the copper coins nestled in her hands.

When sleep finally took hold of her, she dreamed of Lady Hargreaves.

It was only a few months into the marriage when Lady Hargreaves felt the first inklings that something was not right.

Her husband was often busy. This was not unusual; he was an important man, with estates and lands to oversee. It was the host of men who entered his study at all hours that bothered her—some of them of the undesirable sort that made the skin crawl on her neck. There was that loathsome Orley, with his long, trailing fingers and expanding eyes. And, almost always, there was Lord Avon.

Lady Hargreaves disliked him most of all.

Lord Avon had a way of speaking that was designed to smooth and manipulate any obstacles from his path. She had seen him twist the truth, threading wrong into right, turning water into wine. She'd seen the influence he had over her husband.

Oftentimes, she'd catch the tail end of their conversation.

". . . if His Grace is to continue business with us, we must provide him with more boys. He won't take prisoners; says that their emotions are tainted." That was Lord Avon.

Lady Hargreaves stopped in the stairwell to listen. Frightened, she wondered who these boys were. A shiver overtook her spine.

"I do not like this, Percy." Her husband's tone was uneasy. "We are walking down a path of no return."

She heard the disappointment in Lord Avon's voice. "Hargreaves, these boys are from the workhouses. They are half starved, the refuse of society. We are giving them a chance . . ."

Their voices began to drift down the hall, and Lady Hargreaves could hear no more.

Later that night, as Lord Hargreaves prepared for bed, she asked him about the conversation she'd overheard. While it was custom for husbands and wives of the nobility to sleep apart, her husband never followed that rule. She'd heard some of the servants remark upon it, but she paid no heed, preferring the way her husband's body felt cradled by her own.

He looked momentarily taken aback that she'd overheard them, then his voice turned mild as it always did when he tried to hide something. "It is nothing, my dearest Gemma. Do not trouble yourself over such petty matters."

Lady Hargreaves shook her head, putting down the brush she'd been running through her hair. "Be wary of Lord Avon, my love.

He cares about nothing save Weavingshaw and begetting an heir. The way he keeps his wife all alone . . ."

"Do not speak of what you do not understand." It was the first time her husband had spoken sharply to her, and Lady Hargreaves halted, her fingers still clutching the handle of the brush.

When her husband saw the hurt on her face, his expression softened, and he leaned across to brush a kiss over her hair. "I apologize for speaking to you in such a boorish manner, my love. It is only that Percy is my oldest friend, and he has had some unfortunate luck."

"How so?" Lady Hargreaves asked tentatively. She'd heard rumors, but she'd often dismissed them as idle gossip.

Her husband reached for her wrist, his eyebrows furrowed as he concentrated on unbuttoning the cuffs of her nightgown. Goosebumps pebbled her skin at his touch. "Excuse the vulgarity of my frank speech, but Percy married his wife for the money her father had promised him. He owned a shipping company." He took her other hand, undoing those buttons as well. "A few days into the marriage, it was revealed that all of the money that had been promised to Percy was gone. The girl's father had made some bad investments, and a ship he'd been counting on to restore his wealth had sunk in the Westin Ocean a day after the wedding. When the girl's father learned of this, he suffered a heart attack, leaving all his debts to poor Percy."

"That's terrible," Lady Hargreaves said, as her husband moved on to the ribbon at her neckline.

"It is worse than terrible. If Percy does not find a way to restore his wealth, he will lose Weavingshaw. He will die before he allows that to happen."

"What about those boys Lord Avon was speaking of? The ones that *His Grace* wanted?"

Her husband paused, the white ribbon caught between his thumb and index finger. Once more, his voice turned mild. "A Duke has offered Percy a few coins to find him some suitable servants, that is all." He leaned toward her when he saw the worried notch on her brow, tucking her neckline lower. "Come, let us forget all of this. Percy already has a wife to content himself with. Let me content myself with my own wife tonight."

The boy was motherless.

Lady Hargreaves held the babe in her arms, fascinated by the dark wisps of hair that fell over his brow. She hummed to him, the young master Bramwell Avon, relishing the way his tiny fist held her finger.

"He grows well." Her husband had paused at the threshold, watching as she rocked the sleeping baby back and forth. "He's a handsome lad."

"Takes after his father." Lord Avon was steps behind him, a smile crinkling the corners of his eyes. Lady Hargreaves watched him covertly beneath her lashes. There was no grief on Lord Avon's face, no remnant of feeling from his wife's passing only a few months prior, during childbirth. Not a single mention of her name. Even the black he wore did not resemble mourning attire, cut impeccably in the latest fashion.

She gripped the baby tighter to her chest. "I think he takes after his mother."

She didn't miss the narrowing of Lord Avon's blue eyes, nor the way he took the boy from her, anchoring him to his own chest, his hand possessively snaking over the sleeping infant.

"He is an Avon through and through," was His Lordship's only reply, as if the boy had been born in isolation, from a single line. A motherless child even before birth.

Lady Hargreaves's delight expanded the more she watched Bram grow.

He was a quick learner, and he understood the world in different ways from the adults around him. He would notice small details that escaped everyone else's attention—that the tonic Lady Hargreaves had each morning to calm her nerves made her drowsy and dazed, or that the parade of men who entered Hythe House always left with a brand on their forearm: *The Wake.*

Bram was only seven when he asked her about the Wake, and when he saw Lady Hargreaves freeze, her eyes wild with fright thanks to all the things she'd seen and heard over the years, he learned not to ask again. Her husband and Lord Avon had begun to take the young master into their meetings, excluding Lady Hargreaves on the other side of the closed door, and she knew that they were molding him to one day inherit it all.

She watched with growing dread the way Lord Avon treated the child. He was not a neglectful father, nor even a cruel one, but he was forgetful. It was obvious he loved the boy, taking great pride in both his intellect and handsome features. But Lord Avon was prone to taking long trips, leaving the boy either with Mrs. Van, the governess, or at Hythe House with Lady Hargreaves.

When he returned, he'd whisk the boy back to Weavingshaw, and Lady Hargreaves felt the gap in her chest grow wider at Bram's absence. Sometimes, her husband would accompany Lord Avon on those trips north, and every time he returned from Weavingshaw, Lady Hargreaves sensed a change in him. Something dark had rooted itself in her husband's chest and he barricaded himself for longer in his study.

Bram also returned changed.

Childhood seemed to fall off him quicker, leaving behind something ancient and cold. He still knew how to smile at her in that boyish way that had always charmed her, but she'd seen the way that smile dropped the moment she turned her head. All the unease Lady Hargreaves felt seemed to build and build with each passing hour until she felt smothered beneath the weight of it.

But . . . her husband still visited her at night. Lady Hargreaves told herself that she could live with the disquiet she felt during the day if it meant she could have those nights with him.

Just before Bram's twelfth year, her husband took her to spend the summer at Weavingshaw.

It was her first time at the estate, and Lady Hargreaves longed to see the land that had captivated the child she'd grown to love with her entire being.

The estate was beautiful.

But it seemed to *hate* Lady Hargreaves beyond compare.

She felt suffocated within the house. Sometimes, she imagined the walls were closing in on her, depriving her of breath. During the nights, even though she could see her husband's sleeping form beside her, she felt cut off. Isolated. Without shelter.

She pretended happiness for Bram's sake. She could clearly see that the boy's soul was embedded within Weavingshaw, spellbound by it. From the window, she'd once watched as Bram and his father walked the lands with holy reverence, cutting through the Death-grips that grew in a tangle around the estate, both reaching down to grasp a piece of earth in their cupped hands. It was clear in their movements, the broadness of their shoulders, the angle of their jaws, even the slant of their brows, that they were father and son. Lady Hargreaves wondered how she had ever thought that Bram would inherit his looks solely from his mother; it became unmistakably clearer with every year that he had the Avon bearing in spite of the darkness of his hair and eyes.

During those sweltering days, she and Bram left notes for each other in a postbox they had nailed to a tree beside the wild beach. She would hum to him the same lullaby she'd sung to him as a babe.

Bram was always a quick child, sharp and observant, and she knew that he'd also started to notice the odd changes of behavior that had begun to unsettle his father that summer.

Paranoia had taken hold of Lord Avon, His Lordship's eyes growing increasingly suspicious by the day, his words piercing as if he suspected everyone of some nefarious purpose.

Their once humor-filled dinners had gone silent.

Her husband would sit in seething silence, throwing guarded glances at Lord Avon every now and then, as if searching for a shred of recognition in his oldest friend. More than once, Lady Hargreaves would hear their muffled, angry arguments as she listened in at the closed study door.

Her husband never answered her questions, only stating that he and Lord Avon had had a disagreement—one they would resolve in time.

She should've known something was wrong when Bram turned to her one morning as they walked the length of the beach, his eyes flickering in the direction of the house. "It's worth it, is it not?"

Lady Hargreaves shaded her eyes from the overbearing sun. "Is what worth it?"

"Weavingshaw," Bram said, as if speaking to himself. "It's worth everything."

Lady Hargreaves never let go of the regret that she had not bitterly disagreed with him that day. That Weavingshaw was not worth everything. That it was not worth him. That it was *never* worth him.

By autumn, the boy was gone.

He was taken, her husband had told her softly. *Kidnapped.*

He muttered excuses for his disappearance, but Lady Hargreaves was deaf to it all, her grief its own monster. She begged: *Find him, please find him, that poor motherless boy.*

But no one went looking for him.

And through it all, her husband forced her to remain at Weavingshaw. He told her that they could not leave when their business was unfinished. What that business was, he did not disclose—despite her wild pleading.

No longer did Lady Hargreaves allow her husband into her chamber. Every night he knocked on her door, and every night he found it locked.

The less anyone in that house spoke of Bram's disappearance, the more she began to *hate* her husband. As the months passed, she watched as Lord Hargreaves's bond with Lord Avon snapped, deteriorating into a frenzy of distrust and anger.

Now the silence during their dinners was choking.

During one such night, Lord Avon had suddenly stood up, slamming his hands on the table.

"Leave, Charles. Leave this house—I command it."

Lord Hargreaves paid him no mind as he continued to slice his roast. "I will not, Percy. Not until you return what you have stolen. It belongs to the both of us. That was the agreement."

Stolen? Were they speaking of Bram?

Lady Hargreaves eyed them both carefully, but it was clear they were not speaking of the missing son. Her heart cracked at this realization.

Lord Avon's face flamed. "Without Mrs. Van, you know everything is worthless."

"Then we shall find her," Lord Hargreaves continued, putting down his knife and fork. "Until then, Percy, we will not leave."

Vaguely, Lady Hargreaves realized that she had not seen Mrs. Van in some time—not since Bram had also been taken. She wanted to demand answers; she wanted to stand and scream until her ears bled. But Lady Hargreaves only kept silent, wondering why no one commented on the dying woman at the dinner table.

Lord Avon sent for his mistress to be brought to Weavingshaw.

Moira. She was a slight thing, with shy eyes and a girlish figure. She played the pianoforte beautifully. Distantly, as if through a haze, Lady Hargreaves noticed one evening that the girl wore the Avon ring on her left hand.

She heard Lord Hargreaves's whispered accusation to Lord Avon as they sat listening to the girl play. "You've married her, haven't you? Does she know where you've hidden it?"

Lord Avon's voice was a snarl. "You won't find it, Charles. Weavingshaw will keep my secrets. So will the new Lady Avon."

Lady Hargreaves listened quietly as the young Lady Avon's fingers skimmed over the keys, and she felt a fierce regret for this girl. There was nothing she could do. Nothing anyone could do.

Weavingshaw had already condemned them all.

A week had passed, and the new Lady Avon was nowhere to be found. No one dared utter her name.

Lady Hargreaves was unsurprised.

Nor was she surprised when she saw Lord Hargreaves ride out at dawn to meet Lord Avon, a sword at his hip.

She waited for him at the edge of the forest, away from the watchful eyes of the servants, and he came staggering back at noon, blood staining his shirt. His eyes were red-rimmed.

When he saw her, he let out a sob. "I've done it. He's dead. Percy's dead." He reached for her, clinging to her neck, burying his face into her shoulder while she stood motionless. He babbled nonsense. "I had to . . . Percy has grown in power since the trade . . . the Limitless Vessel . . . he would've destroyed us all. You've seen him, Gemma, the way that paranoid ideas have begun to breach his mind? The Avon curse has rotted his brain. He could not have . . . *I should not have* . . . allowed him . . . such influence . . ." He continued to weep like a child. "Speak, my love. Please—say something to me. I cannot stand your anger anymore."

"And Bram?" she asked quietly, her voice steady.

He did not look at her. His response came after a shuddering moment. "Gone. With Percy's death, he is gone."

Anger welled up in Lady Hargreaves's throat, and she pounced on her husband, clawing at his eyes. *"I know you did it! You son of a bitch! You did something to him!"*

Lord Hargreaves did nothing to defend himself. He merely placed his bloodstained hands over his head, repeating the words over and over again as if in a trance. "They are both gone. Can't you understand? I had to do it."

That night, Lady Hargreaves filled her pocket with rocks. She paid one final visit to the postbox she had used to hide small gifts for the child she had once loved fiercely. That she still loved fiercely. She left two letters—one addressed to her Bram, and one to her husband.

She would no longer tie her fate to that of a murderer.

Then, her eyes dry, Weavingshaw at her back, she walked into the ocean.

And even *that* did not release her from this cursed land.

35

A Duel of Honor

He is late.

Lord Hargreaves stood waiting beside Martin on the fringes of a flat meadow. The carriage was settled nearby, the horses' wide nostrils venting puffs of steam into the crisp air. In the distance, he could hear the howling of wolves deep within the forest. It sounded much nearer today.

Hargreaves tried to shake away the feeling of disquiet he always experienced at the ever-present snarl of wolves, as if they sensed his thoughts and were ready to tear him limb from limb. Even ten years ago, when he'd stood rooted to this very spot, he'd heard them, his heart pounding with urgency, as if they smelled the blood that marked his betrayal of one of their own.

He looked over at the Al-Sayer boy now to distract his thoughts. He stood with one foot tied to the single shriveled tree that broke the landscape. Dispassionately, Hargreaves noted the bloody marks and bruises the boy carried; it was clear Martin had beaten him ruthlessly.

The boy's injuries did not stop him from pacing in an arc in agitation, as far as his rope allowed him, marking footprints in the frost-covered ground.

The land around them was a barren wasteland, just outside Weavingshaw's boundaries, the soil too hard to grow anything other than weedy grass.

Hargreaves's thoughts could not contain themselves this morning. It was as if the landscape had refused to change in the ten years since he had last been here, when he had met Percy for the last time, sword in hand.

He'd *had* to draw Percy out here, even with the dangers lurking near the edge of the forest, for he could not have touched him within Weavingshaw's domain.

The irony was not lost on him. Hargreaves had chosen this very meadow once more to meet Percy's son, as if the Saints wanted him to complete the cycle. He would not admit even to himself that he was afraid that Weavingshaw would still do everything in its power to protect its young master, even if he had yet to swear fealty to its walls, for it still recognized Avon blood.

It was a few minutes past dawn when he heard the horse's hooves pounding on the frost-hardened ground. At moments like these, Hargreaves could see nothing except the similarities between father and son.

The way they both rode a horse masterfully, the roll of their shoulders, their height, even the eyes—glacial, hateful, *cannibal* eyes, despite their difference in color. For an instant, Hargreaves was not sure if it was Percy who had, after all, been resurrected from his grave.

If not for the dark coloring, which Bramwell had inherited from his beautiful, doomed mother, then Hargreaves would have bent his knees and prayed to the Saints for bringing back the dead.

And yet such prayers would never be accepted. He could never forget that it was he who had joined Percy when they took young Bramwell to the underworld on his twelfth birthday, one hand on each of his shoulders, steering him to sign his name on the contract.

The boy had been shaking so hard his signature came out scrawled and illegible, and he'd been forced to repeat it.

"For Weavingshaw," Percy had told him.

"*For Weavingshaw,*" the boy repeated.

Hargreaves had knelt down to look Bram in the eyes. "We will come back for you. I promise."

They hadn't.

Over twelve years, the boy had grown into a man under the glare of demons. They had fed on him; that was clear. Hargreaves knew the look of someone who had been fed on often. That he had survived so long—under the merciless dominion of the Frays, no less—was unfathomable.

But in truth, it was fortunate that the boy had not died.

Since Percy's death, Hargreaves had spent the last ten years searching in vain for the Limitless Vessel. Finding it would have at least given young Bramwell Avon's sacrifice *purpose.*

He and his men had swept every inch of Weavingshaw, save the parts of the crypts that were barred to him, but the estate hid Percy's secret.

Except for Mrs. Van, who had disappeared for years before re-emerging at the elbow of the Saint of Silence, Hargreaves had interviewed every servant who had worked at Weavingshaw within the last two decades. All of them were worthless—*except* Avon's old housekeeper, whose mind had been spoiled long before the Limitless Vessel was traded for Bram.

In desperation, Lord Hargreaves had had his men search the old housekeeper's cottage a few months ago. He'd found the timepiece there. Percy had always favored Mrs. Graham above all other servants. Even when her mind became demented, he still had a fondness for her and ensured she was looked after until his death. One half of the mystery was revealed to Hargreaves the day he gave the locket back to the old woman, knowing it would not be long before it was found again. His plan only grew from then.

Hargreaves was once more brought back to the present by St.

Silas dismounting the horse, patting the animal's muzzle with an absentminded hand. He didn't seem surprised that Martin had chosen Hargreaves as his second.

A surgeon was deliberately not present this morning—though it was one of the criteria for all duels of honor. Hargreaves knew St. Silas had noted this obvious breach of the code, but said nothing. He did, however, observe Rami tied like an animal, and a cold anger darkened his face.

"Not *entirely* honorable, I see," St. Silas drawled.

"Do not be concerned, Mr. St. Silas. This is only to ensure that all parties remain on the premises until the completion of the duel," Hargreaves replied mildly.

Ignoring him, St. Silas walked toward Rami, his sword ready to cut the rope.

Hargreaves didn't want this to be a massacre. A duel *must* take place. He needed St. Silas to be desperate, not dead.

Not yet.

"Unfortunately, you have not given me a choice, Mr. St. Silas. I will be pointing this pistol at Mr. Al-Sayer's head throughout the duration of your duel." The click of Hargreaves's gun put an effective stop to St. Silas's determined actions. "However, as long as the duel is kept *clean,* and you emerge the winner, both yourself and Mr. Al-Sayer will be free to leave without any further delay—as promised."

St. Silas and Rami exchanged a hard look, but not a surprised one. Hargreaves would once have despised a man who did not respect the code of honor that would have ensured a fair duel, but he was now desperate and short on time.

Hargreaves had already warned Martin that he did not care about the ruined Tar. His sole focus was to retrieve the red diary and the secret it held, pertaining to the whereabouts of the Limitless Vessel. Hargreaves was never going to allow St. Silas or his *wards* to leave Weavingshaw.

St. Silas gave Martin a curt nod to commence.

"Your pistol," Hargreaves commanded St. Silas. "Throw it here."

His mouth hard, St. Silas pulled the revolver from his pocket and threw it toward Hargreaves's shoes. Hargreaves bent to retrieve it, hiding it in his own coat.

The snow had begun to fall in earnest now, coating the lapels of St. Silas's dark jacket.

Beside him, Martin stood at the ready, silently unsheathing his sword.

Martin was an expert swordsman, and he knew it. Wordlessly, he stood in position, the blade held aloft.

St. Silas, his expression as icy as the surrounding frost, mirrored Martin's stance, his own sword held in a firm grasp.

"At your marks, gentlemen." Hargreaves's other hand reached for his sword hilt just as his fighting hand held firm to his pistol, still pointing at the Al-Sayer boy. "One, two, three . . . Start!"

The clash of steel resonated—so man-made, so misplaced in this barren land.

Both men were vicious, their thrusts slicing through the air, their boots struggling to gain purchase on the new snow. Hargreaves watched for a moment, wondering how long Martin could last.

Their breathing created white frost clouds in the air, and all around them was silent.

Even the wolves had ceased their howling, waiting for the victor to be declared.

Hargreaves was not a swordsman, but it was clear that St. Silas was winning.

Martin was an older man now. His footwork had slowed, his breath tearing out in gasps. And although St. Silas's attacks lacked the rhythm of a highly trained swordfighter, his energy was undiminishing, and his strength clear. More than once, he forced Martin to reel backward under the power of his assault.

Hargreaves began to wonder if the rumors that swirled about the Saint of Silence's lack of proficiency with a sword were deliberately untrue, likely put about by St. Silas himself to gain an advantage . . .

Percy's linen shirt had been drenched in crimson. He'd looked down at it mutely, touched his abdomen, then looked back up at Hargreaves. His eyes were beseeching—

It was time.

Hargreaves deftly put away his pistol and switched his sword to his dominant hand, his boots crunching the frost as he walked to the two fighters. St. Silas's attention was focused on Martin's strikes, leaving his back entirely exposed. Hargreaves knew that the Al-Sayer boy was watching him, but it was too late now.

Hargreaves readied his sword, the murky sunlight glinting off the steel.

"St. Silas, your back!" Al-Sayer shouted.

St. Silas turned—too late. Hargreaves had already lurched forward, slicing a jagged tear along St. Silas's left flank.

A grunt.

St. Silas's weapon clattered to the ground as he clutched his side, pain twisting his face.

It was done.

Despite Hargreaves giving clear orders the previous evening for Martin to cease his attacks once Hargreaves struck, Martin still made a final charge toward St. Silas, lifting his sword with deadly intent.

Hargreaves should have predicted this. Martin was now enthralled by the idea of St. Silas's death, burying all his secrets with him.

A gunshot sounded, shattering the air like glass.

Beside Hargreaves, Martin crumpled sideways onto the ground, blood pouring from his shoulder in rivulets, marking the snow like a butcher's stockroom. His body lay unmoving, and Hargreaves could not say for sure if he still breathed.

Reckless fool.

Hargreaves did not spare Martin another glance. Alive or dead, he never suffered a fool.

Instead, his attention swung back to St. Silas, who had withdrawn a second pistol hidden inside his right boot, holding it in one hand and his wounded side with the other. Smoke still coiled from the muzzle, from the shot that felled Martin.

"Drop the sword," St. Silas said, punctuating each word like an attack.

Hargreaves allowed the blade to fall from his hand, the crimson on the steel splattering the snow. He knew that he should've searched Bram at the start of the duel for both the red diary and a concealed weapon, but being so close to such a ferocious beast, even with a pistol in his own hand, did not bode well for Hargreaves. Instead, he'd waited until he had a chance to weaken St. Silas entirely. A hidden weapon complicated Hargreaves's plan, but did not ruin it.

In his peripheral vision, he saw the Al-Sayer boy drop to his knees, stretching his arm to reach for Hargreaves's discarded blade.

"My apologies, Bramwell," Hargreaves began. St. Silas's eyes hardened at the use of his given name.

St. Silas struggled to his feet, the pistol still firm in his hand. "I have one bullet left, Hargreaves. I would be very wise with my next words, if I were you."

The snow had begun to fall with force, as if attempting to shroud their shame.

"My sword—the very same one that sliced you—was coated with rare demon poison." Hargreaves watched St. Silas's expression, but there was neither a flicker to his eyelids nor a tightening of his brows. If he was afraid, he did not show it. "Without the antidote, you will be in your grave in less than a week."

Silence.

The weight of Hargreaves's own actions bore down on him. For a moment he did not see the Saint of Silence, but a small child with two missing front teeth, showing him the birdhouse he was building in a tree.

Then St. Silas barked out a laugh, jarring Hargreaves, raising the hair at the nape of his neck.

Even facing death, Bramwell was more fearless than his father.

"What will you tell me next, Hargreaves? That only *you* have the antidote but require something in exchange for it?"

"The red diary." Hargreaves locked the image of the small child away into the recesses of his mind, instead looking unblinkingly at the man before him. "Your *ancestor's* red diary."

St. Silas was motionless, the gun unwavering in his hand, the vicious laughter still in his eyes. At this revelation, the Al-Sayer boy froze, still on his knees, still trying to reach for Hargreaves's discarded sword.

"Then we shall drop all pretenses," St. Silas murmured, inclining his head in a mock bow. "Why is it that you want the Avon diary?"

Hargreaves stepped forward once more, but halted as the gun moved from his chest to his head. He raised his palms like a priest granting a blessing right there in the cold wasteland of the meadow. "To help you, Bramwell. I promised you that I would bring you back from the demons twelve years ago, and I will. But I cannot do so without the Avon diary."

"Your notion of *helping* is quite skewed, my lord. Do you poison all those you desire to help?" St. Silas's smooth voice, so similar to that of his father, continued to carry hints of savage amusement.

The Al-Sayer boy had finally reached the sword, slicing the rope around his ankle in one fluid motion. Freed, he did not hesitate to press the poisoned tip against Hargreaves's own collar.

"Shall I run him through, Saint?" the Al-Sayer boy spat.

Hargreaves's face remained mild, although he felt the first inklings of apprehension settle in his chest. "I would not do that—"

"Yes, yes, I know." St. Silas cut him off. "*The antidote.* I do not doubt, however, that I can procure it very easily in Golborne, so your existence is entirely useless to me." He turned away from him, locking his pistol. "Run him through, Rami."

Although it was the Al-Sayer boy who was holding the blade firmly against his skin, Hargreaves didn't lift his gaze from St. Silas. "Have the demons ever told you how to break your indenture?"

A sudden stiffening to St. Silas's back.

"You do not know," Hargreaves continued, undeterred. "That is why you are searching for Percy's ghost. You wish to ask him what it was he traded his son for all those years ago, so that you may trade it back for your freedom. Am I not right?"

"Of course you are right. You were there, after all." St. Silas unlocked his pistol again, but kept it aimed at the blood-splattered snow. "And I venture to guess that you know *exactly* what object it was that you sold me for. Am *I* not right?"

"I am surprised you did not come to me sooner, Bramwell. You know that as your godfather, I would've given you the information you sought unhesitatingly."

"What a fool I would be to return to the man who would, it seems, go past selling me to outright killing me." St. Silas released another cold laugh. "After all, look at where we are now. Poisoned, with only a week to live."

"What has happened today was done out of necessity, as was the case twelve years ago." Hargreaves did not allow the emotion of bartering off the young Bramwell to overtake his voice now. "But you were never alone. We had allowed that servant-boy—Theodore Daye, was it?—to accompany you."

"Ah, yes. Theo and I were the first real taste of human *currency*. The Wake then found it had a ferocious appetite for it." If St. Silas's look had been vicious before, it was past malevolent now. "I hear your business is flourishing, my lord."

What would be the difference, Hargreaves thought, *if the prisoners rotted in Newtorn Prison or rotted with the demons? At least with the latter, their sentence would be magnanimously reduced.*

"I am surprised you know so much of the goings-on of the Wake. We do try to keep our . . . business tightly sealed, especially from the disreputable Saint."

The Saint raised his brows mockingly. "If that is the case, I highly suggest you shoot Orley in the face, for he has been most obliging in trading your secrets with me."

Hargreaves did not let his growing irritation show. He knew Orley had no allegiances to anyone, not even to the gang he ruled, and was as likely to work with a person as to slit his throat. Still, he had served his purpose.

"You are very right: Orley is unhinged. But for the right price, he is still willing to be of service. For example"—Hargreaves knew he was going to take special delight in this revelation—"he has been controlling poor Theodore for a very long time. Upon my instructions, Orley sent Theodore to appear before your Miss Al-Sayer, claiming to possess the ability to bring forth Percy's ghost."

Hargreaves marked the blazing fury that hardened St. Silas's dark eyes. "Let me guess—to lure me here to find the red diary for you?"

Hargreaves released a long, almost apologetic exhalation of breath. "Percy's ghost was never coming to save you."

With interest, Hargreaves looked for any show of dismay in Bramwell's face. There was none; only a jeering indifference. Hargreaves shifted, halting when the pistol focused on his chest.

"And yet," St. Silas continued, "you still fail to mention why you have such a fascinating obsession with the Avon diary. It leaves one almost . . . in sympathy for all your efforts over the years."

It was Hargreaves's turn to bark out a laugh.

"I doubt you show sympathy for anyone, Bramwell, and least of all for me."

St. Silas did not respond, waiting patiently for a reply.

When there was no immediate answer forthcoming, the Al-Sayer boy's voice cracked in the air. "You know about Leena's . . . ability?"

The boy pressed the sword more firmly into Hargreaves's exposed neck, almost drawing blood and wounding him with the same poison that now coursed through St. Silas's veins.

"Mr. Al-Sayer, I would strongly suggest you drop the sword. Your father's life depends on the choices you make now," Hargreaves said.

The Al-Sayer boy stilled. "What do you know about my father?"

Hargreaves was struggling to think past the tip of the poisoned blade tight against his neck. "Lift your blade if you desire an answer."

After a pause, the sword was edged slightly away.

"He is a prisoner." Hargreaves's reply was curt. "Under the explicit watch of my guards."

Taking hold of the conversation once more, before the Al-Sayer boy did anything reckless, Hargreaves spoke directly to Bramwell, finally reaching the heart of the matter. "You cannot kill me, Bramwell—if not for the antidote, then for the very real fact that, in the entirety of the human world, it is only *I* who knows how to break your demon contract."

St. Silas still seemed unimpressed. "In which case, there are many ways to drag secrets out of a body that do not amount to killing him."

"Torture?" Hargreaves asked, once more assaulted by recollections of Percy, who also would have sunk to any form of depravity to keep hold of Weavingshaw.

St. Silas brushed the snow off his jacket in an unbothered gesture, but the other hand still holding the pistol was white-knuckled and tense. "Being left to the demons, *my lord,* makes you demonlike yourself."

"But forcing answers from me in such a manner will still take time. Especially"—Hargreaves spoke easily, belying the threat beneath his words—"as Miss Al-Sayer is back at Weavingshaw with no one but Kilworth to offer . . . protection."

St. Silas stilled, an arrested expression on his face.

"What did you say?" he whispered softly.

There, the crack in the formidable armor. Hargreaves's eyes blazed in triumph.

Hargreaves had observed—with rapidly growing interest—the interactions between St. Silas and the Al-Sayer girl. At the best of times St. Silas was difficult to read, but there were moments—as she was leaving the room, as she smiled up at him—when his eyes could not hide themselves, watching her in unmistakable fascination.

"Indeed, Kilworth could not stop speaking of her. I have grown weary of hearing him obsessively describe the color of her lips, the long, slender neck that had him . . . well . . ."

St. Silas crossed the space between them in two long strides, pulling Hargreaves out of Rami's hold by the collar and brutally smashing his forehead into Hargreaves's nose, before shoving the muzzle of his pistol against his temple, all but cracking the bone with its force.

The pain was instantaneous and shocking.

Hargreaves had never felt anything like it. The ridges of his nose shifted, fire burning through the rest of his face with agony.

"If you lay one finger on her, I will make certain your decaying flesh will be a feast for the wolves." St. Silas's words were a snarl. "Kilworth I will personally gut."

Hargreaves spat blood on the snow. "I have no doubt you are true to your threats. However, I urge you to exercise restraint. I have sent for the assistance of several Black Coats; they will be here imminently—perhaps within the hour."

Ignoring him, St. Silas roughly patted Hargreaves's jacket until he found both hidden guns, pulling them out and throwing them toward the feet of the Al-Sayer boy.

"Ready the carriage," St. Silas barked toward Rami. "*Now.* Your sister is left alone with that reptile."

Then, rearing back, St. Silas brought the barrel of his pistol down hard against Hargreaves's skull.

Another strike of pain erupted across Hargreaves's head like an earthquake, and he collapsed onto the ground with his cheek pressing painfully against the ice.

"Do not think," St. Silas said softly, "that I have been complacent or forgetful in those years I've been the Saint of Silence. I was always going to return for you."

In spite of the blood flowing through his teeth, Hargreaves smiled, the ghost of memories soothing the throb behind his eyelids.

"You are your father's son, Bramwell Avon, and you are a neck running toward an ax—just as he was."

Bram spat inches from Hargreaves's head where he lay prostrate in the snow. Then, distantly, Hargreaves watched the blur of St. Silas's leather boots recede toward the carriage.

The clatter of carriage wheels struck the ground

The horses surged into motion.

They were gone.

And Hargreaves remembered that it was in this exact spot that Percy had drawn his last breaths.

36

Lord Kilworth

Until the break of dawn, Leena kept vigil.

She had awoken with a gasp after Lady Hargreaves's revelation, only to find the ghost still at the edge of her bed. Her eyes were harrowing. She gave Leena a nod as if to say: *That is all. Release me. Release the boy.*

Then she disappeared.

Leena bit back a sob, but tears still streamed down her cheeks as she thought of St. Silas as a boy.

No one looked for him.

Leena's chest heaved.

What had changed between Percy and Hargreaves that the latter had killed the former? What was this power that Percy had amassed?

Snow fell outside her bedroom window, wet clumps collecting on the glass. Leena had just managed to gain a hold on herself when her door opened, allowing Mrs. Van to enter. She stood staring down at Leena, the angles of her face made sharper in the daylight. Leena rose rapidly, her eyes red-rimmed. If Mrs. Van noticed, she did not comment.

"Any news?" Leena clenched her hands.

The frown deepened. "None yet. It's still early."

"You look worried."

Mrs. Van didn't respond. She busied herself by relighting the smoldering embers in the fireplace. Leena was just about to open her mouth again when the bedroom door swung open with a slam.

Leena jerked to her feet, a tide of hope rising that she might see Rami or St. Silas on the other side.

In shock, she stared at Lord Kilworth swaying on the threshold. He stumbled forward, the tip of his nose as cherry red as his hair, a rifle hanging loosely in his hands. Leena's eyes jolted to meet those of Mrs. Van, who gave only a single shake of her head in warning.

"*Keep watch, Kilworth. Nothing more.*" His Lordship's voice was dangerous, his speech slurring. "Damn Hargreaves—*that halfling*—and damn the secrets he keeps. Eh, I'll keep watch."

He staggered backward, then pounded a fist on the doorframe to steady himself, the vibrations shaking dust from the ceiling. The astringent smell of alcohol reached Leena's nose as she stood frozen in place.

His Lordship's body, normally sleek and fit, seemed larger within the frame of the doorway, blocking their only exit, the rifle swinging back and forth in an arc.

He leered toward Leena, his face splitting into a sickening, lopsided smile. "I'll have the truth out of you, pet. Everyone here knows that this business of you being the Saint's ward is a sham. Have you been fuc—"

"My lord!" Mrs. Van interjected angrily. "That is enough. You will not speak to my charge—"

"*Nasty demon.* How dare you address me?" He pounded the rifle on the floor. Once, twice, to the inflections of his voice. "I. Know. What. You. Are."

Mrs. Van's mouth flattened.

Kilworth continued to slam his rifle closer and closer to Mrs. Van's feet.

An overwhelming thought flashed through Leena's mind. *He desires to hunt her like prey.*

"Did you know, m'dear, that the Saint deals with demons?" Lord Kilworth turned to Leena with a short, humorless laugh. "Do you have any idea what you've set foot into?" He shook his head. "Ask the Saint why he collects secrets."

Leena felt the pistol St. Silas had given her nestled in her pocket, but she could not reach it while Kilworth kept a grip on his rifle.

He leaned closer, lifting one sweaty palm toward her. "But perhaps you do not know who the Saint truly is and require some assistance to escape his clutches. Consider my hand a helping one."

Leena slapped that helping hand away.

"Touch me and—" she warned viciously, but the harsh slam of the rifle against the floor silenced her. Both she and Mrs. Van jumped backward, startled by the dull echo of metal on wood.

Then, almost tenderly, Kilworth turned to Mrs. Van and lifted her chin with the butt of his gun. Leena imagined the shiver of cool steel on her own skin and seethed in fury.

"You've fed on humans before," Kilworth said softly to Mrs. Van, disgust curdling his face. "I know that look. You see our despair and make a feast out of it. What is it that your kind says—*joy tastes bitter*? You ought to be executed for your crimes." He glanced briefly at Leena. "You may go, chit. The demon stays with me. I have the notion that she may hold the answers to a few of my most *pressing* questions."

Leena could not say at what point she had stopped viewing Mrs. Van as something *other.* Nor could she forget how tirelessly Mrs. Van had aided her in nursing Rami back to health, or all those mornings when Mrs. Van had taken particular care with her curls. All the meals she'd cooked for them back in Golborne. The broths. The pots of tea.

"Make it fair," Leena said quietly. Her pulse bounded. "Give us a head start. You've always wanted to hunt one of *her* kind before, haven't you? Now is your chance."

Kilworth's bloodshot eyes didn't fall from Mrs. Van's face. "I've always wondered if *they* bleed like us." The allure of the hunt had given him a wild look, as if he was already in the forest, smelling his prey.

He lowered the rifle and slammed it again on the floorboards. *Thud. Thud. Thud.* "I will grant her five minutes."

Neither Mrs. Van nor Leena moved.

"*Now.*" Kilworth's eyes were on the clock above their heads. The rifle continued to slam its rhythmic beats.

"Go," Leena shouted.

When Mrs. Van didn't move, she grabbed the other woman's arm and forced them both through the door. Lord Kilworth's attention was still fixed on the clock, his lips moving imperceptibly as he counted down the seconds.

Leena stood at the threshold of the room. Her mind focused. Her blood slowed. She grabbed hold of the pistol in her pocket, drew it out, and unlocked it.

Then, holding the weapon in a death grip, she aimed the muzzle at Kilworth and fired.

It jarred her shoulders and she fell back against the bedroom door. But St. Silas had warned her about this, so she was prepared for the pain.

The shot echoed across the winding halls of Weavingshaw like a scream.

Then Leena's heart dropped.

The kick of the pistol had been too much. She had only managed to clip Kilworth in the ear, blood dripping from the cut in a trickle, the bullet implanting itself instead in the wooden post of the bed.

Kilworth's face twisted with sudden fury.

In one practiced motion, his rifle swung toward her, his finger hovering over the trigger.

Leena lurched out of the way as the bullet whizzed by, missing her by mere millimeters.

She and Mrs. Van bolted.

Leena's bare feet pounded against the floorboards, with Mrs. Van only seconds in front of her. As they slipped down the stairs, Leena turned back to find that Kilworth hadn't yet followed them. A sinking sensation descended in her chest when she realized that he was waiting for them to leave tracks. That he was *still hunting them.*

"Outside?" Leena whispered, but Mrs. Van shook her head.

"He's planning on that. He'll shoot at us from the window."

The ceiling above them creaked—the hollow thud of the rifle striking wood.

Terror built behind Leena's eyes. She looked for a phantom to lead them out, a servant to offer help, but for the first time in a long time the house was completely bereft of any living or dead creatures. She didn't have time to question this stark emptiness, her mind intent entirely on survival.

Scrambling, she tore through the drawers of one of the long mahogany tables lining the hallway until she found a lamp and a box of matches. She motioned for Mrs. Van to follow her, retracing the same steps St. Silas had taken when he'd led them toward the crypts. They moved fast and silently, ears pricked for any approaching footsteps.

They climbed down another flight of stairs to the wine cellar.

Leena fell to her knees and scrambled across the room, frantically patting for the latch hidden within the floor.

There—the trapdoor.

Leena paused before lifting it open, her heart hammering in her chest as she recalled the demon lurking in the dark. But she had triumphed over it. She reminded herself of that.

"What are you waiting for, girl?" Mrs. Van urged from behind her.

Still, Leena could not move. Was she creeping toward a new danger? A *worse* danger?

Somewhere above them the sound of footsteps—slow and sure, the march of an executioner.

She swung open the latch.

A voice in her head screamed at her to turn back.

Mrs. Van held the lamp, the light reflecting halos on the ceiling as they made their descent.

Finally the ground leveled out. A long hall loomed ahead of them, black and beckoning.

Mrs. Van gripped Leena's arm painfully, her eyes almost wild with animal fright. "Where have you taken us?"

Leena hesitated. "Do you feel the presence of the demon as well?"

"In all the years I worked here previously, I never set foot in the crypts." Mrs. Van let go, leaving welts on Leena's skin. "It's not right, what they've done to this place. It's not right."

Above them, the trapdoor slammed open.

Lord Kilworth had found them.

Not caring to keep quiet anymore, they bolted down the length of the crypts' maze. The uneven floor was rough on Leena's feet, and she felt the sting of cuts forming.

Neither Leena nor Mrs. Van needed a map to traverse the sudden twists and turns. They were both attuned to the dark presence that saturated these walls and urged them forward, toward the heart of the crypts.

Finally, the stone walls gave way to a great marble chamber, desolate and empty, the light from their lamp reflecting off the black waters. All around them pale statues watched, almost hungrily.

The Hall of the Lake.

They stopped, gasping for breath.

They had nowhere else to run, and the sound of Lord Kilworth's relentless footsteps followed them.

Leena stood in front of the lake, eyes blazing at the black waters, the demon's energy coiling against her skin.

"Help us," she demanded. "Help us and I vow to protect the last living Avon."

There was no response from the demon, but she sensed its anger toward her, furious that she had refused to submit to it.

Thud. Thud. Thud.

Kilworth was close.

Leena turned quickly to Mrs. Van, who stood with her gaze trained on the dark expanse of the lake. "Do you trust me?" Leena asked.

Mrs. Van jerked as if breaking from a trance, then gave Leena a firm nod.

"Pretend you are prey," Leena whispered furiously to her. Before waiting for the other woman's response, Leena ran to hide behind one of the statues near the entrance, both the cloying darkness and the sculpture's stone body concealing her from view.

Thud. Thud. Thud.

The strike of a rifle on marbled floors, the echo magnifying the sound until it was an assault.

Lord Kilworth stood by the entrance.

His walk was slow, predatory, stopping steps before the water. Kilworth didn't look at the lake, nor at the magnificence of this room carved from marble. The blood continued to trickle from his ear, marking his collar red.

He lifted the rifle, the barrel pointed toward Mrs. Van.

"Where is the Saint's whore?"

Leena's fingers tightened around her pistol. She had one bullet left. She could not miss this time.

Mrs. Van didn't lift her hands to plead. She merely stood there, posture unwavering, cheeks sunken and hollow. "I told her to leave me."

Kilworth laughed. "It will be my pleasure to find her next, then. After I rid this world of one more demon."

At his words, Leena stepped out from behind the statue, still unseen. Sweat slid down her back as she lifted her arm.

"You were once Percy Avon's servant, weren't you?" Kilworth spat, covering the click of the pistol unlocking. "Any inkling of where he has hidden it?"

Leena paused, gun held aloft.

"Hidden what?" came Mrs. Van's stoic reply.

Kilworth's laugh was sharp and acidic. "You may have lied to your master, but you will not lie to me, demon. The Limitless Vessel. Where did Percy hide it?"

Mrs. Van stared at him, chin lifted—unanswering, unmoving.

The Limitless Vessel? Leena didn't have a chance to dwell on Kilworth's odd ramblings. The gun was heavy in her hands—

St. Silas's words came back to her with force—*aim two inches above your target . . . toward the heart.*

This time, Leena pointed the barrel toward Kilworth's scapula.

His Lordship's entire attention was fastened on his prey as Leena again fired the gun.

When the bullet implanted itself in Kilworth's chest, forever severing the connection between heart and arteries, His Lordship's gaze was still fastened on Mrs. Van.

He didn't scream.

By the time his body fell into the black waters, Lord Kilworth was already dead.

37

Detritus Poison

Leena's eyes remained fixed on the lake, but Lord Kilworth did not rise.

A sudden nausea gripped her, so strong that she bent down and vomited forcefully. After a moment, she rose up shakily and wiped her mouth with the back of her hand.

"It is done," Leena stated hollowly. She didn't know if she wanted comfort from the other woman or confirmation.

Mrs. Van responded evenly. "Aye, but it had to be done."

Leena turned away from Mrs. Van, beginning to walk back the way they'd come.

Several weeks ago, Leena had been in a starkly similar position: both times pointing a pistol at a man. She was so heartily glad that she'd lowered the gun during that first episode, that she'd spared St. Silas's life, just as she was glad she'd had the nerve to fire this time.

As St. Silas had once told her: *Survival is a sordid business.*

Kilworth had his burial—just not underneath the ground.

May your soul no longer crave the soil.

The grazes on her feet began to ache, but she ignored them. Mrs.

Van followed her, and for a long while the only sounds that echoed were their own footfalls.

Leena finally broke the silence, turning to Mrs. Van. "What is the Limitless Vessel?"

She remembered Lord Hargreaves had also mentioned the Limitless Vessel on the day he'd killed Lord Avon in Lady Hargreaves's recollection—that it was the reason he'd murdered his oldest friend.

"I do not know," Mrs. Van replied slowly, as if she was deep in thought. "But we must tell the master of Kilworth's last words. We must tell him soon."

It took some time before they emerged from the wine cellar into the morning light. Leena had been too blind with worry to take note of the passages as they ran from Kilworth, but Mrs. Van's mind was sharp, and she'd had enough foresight to memorize their exact route and lead them back.

Leena was surprised that it was still early daylight. Surely years must've passed since Mrs. Van had come into her room that morning?

She searched for Rami and St. Silas in the emptiness of the halls, but even the servants seemed to be gone. They made their way toward the grand entrance, stopping in front of the door that opened to the outside world.

They were not there.

Leena's heart sank, St. Silas's clear instructions ringing in her ears. If he was not back shortly after dawn, Mrs. Van and Leena were to make their way back to Golborne directly—without him. Rami, she knew, was still locked away.

St. Silas did not realize that Leena had never had any intentions of leaving without him.

She glanced at the grandfather clock. Distantly, her mind absorbed the fact that it was another three hours before Lord Avon was due to appear.

Not that this mattered anymore. She felt a crushing despair at just how close they had come to finding Lord Avon's ghost.

But there was no time for that now.

Leena turned to Mrs. Van urgently, knowing that there would be consequences from her sudden change of plans. "We must ready the carriage and go find Mr. St. Silas and Rami before making our way back to Golborne."

Mrs. Van shook her head, gripping Leena's arm. "That is not what the master instructed."

Leena pulled her arm back. "I am well aware of Mr. St. Silas's plans. However, he is not here to enforce them, and we are not leaving without them."

The tiniest flickering of a smile appeared on Mrs. Van's lips before the older woman's face turned blank once more. "First, shoes."

It took them less than five minutes to collect their necessary belongings. Mrs. Van had found for her a small leather satchel, and Leena packed *A Guide to Botany* and the old housekeeper's timepiece. Then they made their way down the steps of Weavingshaw's grand staircase.

Once more, Leena felt a stirring of foreboding at the emptiness of the house. "Where are all the servants?" she asked Mrs. Van as they left the house, the crisp air like a knife to Leena's lungs. The snow had reached her ankles as she bounded down the curved driveway, heading toward the stables where they would hopefully find a carriage ready.

"At the miners'—" Before Mrs. Van could finish her sentence, they heard the rattle of wheels on the drive.

They froze. Leena's pulse thrashed in her ears.

A gilded carriage came from the forest at breakneck speed, the horses shooting dangerously across the path. Whoever held the reins was an unsteady driver, the entire vehicle jostling up and down.

Leena and Mrs. Van lurched toward the banks of snow on the side of the road, missing the iron of the horses' hooves by seconds. Just as the vehicle passed, Leena saw a familiar figure on the box seat, back hunched over in concentration. She heard the figure shouting her name.

"Rami!" she yelled, racing after the carriage, nearly slipping on the ice in the process.

Rami's lip was split and fiery contusions spread across his cheek. "Leena!" he called back, and tugged on the reins with a hard wrench, forcing the horses to halt. "Where's Kilworth?"

"Dead." It was Mrs. Van who replied before Leena could.

"Where is St. Silas?" Leena countered.

"He's inside the carriage. Get in quickly; we are being pursued." Rami's eyes were hectic, peering wildly at the road behind them. "The Black Coats are not far behind. We must make a head start before they arrive."

What on earth were the Black Coats doing this far north?

Mrs. Van was faster than Leena in following these instructions, jumping to sit beside Rami on the driver's seat. She took the reins from Rami, who was struggling to control the two horses single-handedly.

Leena barreled inside the carriage, her shoes slipping on the icy step. Mrs. Van set the horses flying before Leena had even shut the door.

It took a moment for Leena's eyes to adjust from the blazing brightness outside to the dimness within. Eventually, she was able to focus her vision enough to see St. Silas sprawled across the seat, a pool of crimson spreading beneath him.

As Leena's eyes frantically assessed him, St. Silas returned her searing appraisal with one of his own.

"Is that all yours?" she demanded, moving closer to inspect him in the flickering sunlight.

"Are you well?" he interrupted. His eyes were steel. "Did he hurt you?"

Leena's eyes widened in shock. *How had St. Silas known of what had so recently transpired between her and Kilworth?* "I am unhurt."

Her gaze raked him again, focusing on the blood. She reached to unbutton his waistcoat, but he stopped her, covering her hand with his own, holding it just over his heart. She could feel the drumming of his heartbeat against her palm. "Where's Kilworth?"

Leena kept her tone brusque, although memories made her stomach knot and her throat constrict. "I shot him dead with your pistol."

"There's a girl," he whispered softly—the words an echo of the first time he'd said them to her, what felt like centuries ago. "Fearless Leena Al-Sayer."

Leena did not look at him, but her fingers shook as she continued to unbutton his waistcoat. The burden of Kilworth's death lay like a stone on her heart, and yet St. Silas's words were like an ax shattering that stone.

"Is this blood all yours?" she asked again.

"Afraid it is," St. Silas said, almost apologetically, trying to catch her eye. "I'd be much obliged if you kissed it better."

Leena paused in her attempts to remove the layers of his clothes and glanced up at him drily. "If you are well enough to jest, then surely there is no cause for concern."

"Who said anything about jesting?" His eyes ricocheted between pain and laughter.

The carriage swerved through the uneven terrain, jolting Leena against St. Silas's wound, causing him to inhale sharply.

The white shirt beneath had already adhered to the wound. Grimly, and without giving him a chance to realize what she was about to do, she ripped the fabric that clung to the gash in one fluid motion. The clenching of his knuckles was his only reaction to the pain.

Leena blanched at the sight of the wound, which scored between his ribs and his hip on the left side.

It was horrific.

The blood streaming from the severed skin seemed endless.

More gruesome still were the spidery black lines that emerged from the center of the wound, spreading outward. Leena had never seen such markings in her life.

St. Silas watched her face carefully, his eyes half-lidded. "Demon poison."

Leena wrenched her gaze to meet his. *"Demon poison?"* she cried, fear racing down her spine. "What is the treatment? This does not look—" Her tone faltered, mind racing.

"Easily procurable in Golborne," he replied without hesitation.

Golborne—that was five days' carriage ride away. "Will we have enough time?" she asked frantically.

"You worry too much."

Leena ignored his attempt at lightheartedness. "How did you get injured with demon poison?" She wasted no time in tearing thick pieces of fabric from the hem of her dress to create bandages. The wound needed pressure immediately to stem the bleeding.

Leena heard Rami curse just as the carriage jostled precariously on the ice, tipping them leftward before righting itself once more and continuing forward.

St. Silas could not immediately answer as she began to swiftly wrap the gauze around his abdominal muscles. His eyes tightened briefly with every pressure she exerted on the wound, but he said nothing to stop her.

"We have Hargreaves to thank for this," St. Silas finally responded after he had caught his breath. Though it obviously caused him pain, he moved slowly to pull back the curtains and look out the window. "We are not moving fast enough."

"*Hargreaves?*" Leena echoed, her mind reeling back to the memories that Lady Hargreaves had left. A missing child—who was not missing at all, but a man now, bleeding in front of her. "Why was Hargreaves at the duel?"

Another perilous lurch. This time, Leena was more prepared, holding on to the cushioned seat tightly.

Leena could now see that they'd passed the forest surrounding Weavingshaw. In the distance, she could see big plumes of smoke rising from the miners' town, but she didn't have a moment to wonder about the cause.

"Hargreaves wanted the red diary for the Wake." St. Silas tried to sit up straighter, but Leena pushed him back, continuing to wrap the bandages firmly.

"Why?"

"He very rudely did not specify his reasons."

"Have you read the diary? Could there be anything in there that could capture his interest?"

His mouth was a firm line. "There are few passages, mostly mundane accounts from the First Marquess of Avon. The rest of the pages are blank."

Blank?

"Do you think Lord Hargreaves knows this?" Leena asked.

"I doubt he does," St. Silas said, gazing down at her hands tying the bandages. "My father must've fooled him into believing that it held vital information."

Leena held her misgivings. If the red diary retained benign, mostly blank pages, would this be enough to capture Percy back from the dead?

Leena looked back out the window, her mouth pursed. They'd just entered the moors, leaving behind Lytham and Weavingshaw's ever-watching tower.

He continued softly. "There is something else, something about Theo—"

Horror descended into Leena's stomach with St. Silas's brief but concise explanation of the events leading up to the duel. His expression remained neutral throughout, his voice continuing in that same slow cadence.

Warring emotions played through her chest: hurt on St. Silas's behalf, fury at the betrayal of the boy-ghost who stood guard over her bed each night, and shame that Leena had led their entire party to disaster on Theo's word.

She felt like the worst sort of fool. Tears pricked the backs of her eyes.

St. Silas must have marked the expression on her face, for he opened his mouth to say something, something soft and careful—

—but he was cut off by the deafening screech of wheels, followed by the snap of breaking metal.

This time, the carriage didn't correct itself, instead plunging into the snowbanks with force.

Leena was thrown forward toward the window as the carriage fully overturned, her back painfully crashing against the glass panes.

Stillness.

Leena blinked through the confusion, trying to gain a sense of orientation, instantly looking for St. Silas. Before she could utter a word, the carriage door—now where the ceiling had been—flew open, and Rami's panicked face appeared.

"Are you two all right?" he cried, eyes jerking between the two of them.

St. Silas slowly straightened beside her, his hand spasming across the site of his wound, jaw tense with pain.

Relief flooded Rami's face when he saw them both begin to stir. "The wheel of the carriage had broken and I couldn't stop it from toppling over into an icy ditch." He helped Leena exit the carriage first, followed more slowly by St. Silas. "Hurry. We must move fast."

Mrs. Van helped Rami unharness the horses, but her attention kept slipping back toward the road. "They are not far behind."

The snow had thickened. Already the sky had darkened beneath the clouds; only a thin remnant of light remained to guide their way. All around them the earth was covered in white, the snow now up to Leena's ankles, coating the hedgerows and the trees.

Her teeth chattered, more from spent nerves than the cold, but she knew that the temperature would soon drop further. Already the tips of her ears felt raw.

St. Silas was leaning against a birch tree, eyes too bright and slightly unfocused.

She drew closer to him, reassessing him for any new injuries. "Are you all right, my lord?"

He nodded, the flush in his cheeks a contrast to the paleness of his skin.

Leena placed a hand against his forehead, her heart sinking when she felt his temperature scorching.

"You have a fever," she cried in alarm, turning to Mrs. Van. "He says that he has been injured with demon poison—"

"Describe the wound," Mrs. Van demanded.

Leena did so as best she could, emphasizing the black marks emanating from its center.

"Detritus Poison." Mrs. Van's breath hitched. "The antidote is rare."

St. Silas nodded toward Mrs. Van. "Can you make it?"

"I can," Mrs. Van confirmed, "but I must go back immediately to Golborne where my books are. Then it will take a few hours to collect the ingredients."

Golborne, which was five days away. And now their carriage was broken. "How long does he have before the poison reaches his heart?" Leena's eyes swung between St. Silas and Mrs. Van in horror.

Mrs. Van fleetingly looked at St. Silas before answering. "A few days. At most, a week." She struggled to meet St. Silas's gaze. "First, he will swing in and out of acute delirium, and infection will ravage his body, before he falls comatose—likely around the fifth day. I have only ever seen this poison used once. Afterward—"

Mrs. Van stopped, unable to continue.

Leena touched her chest as if her own heart felt the ache of the poison, already preparing for the end.

Coming to Weavingshaw's hunting party, a thousand grim scenarios had played out in her mind. But never once had she seen St.

Silas dying in any one of them—or imagined that the very thought of such a possibility would send her into a premature grief, as if that loss could already be felt.

Leena finally looked at all three of them mutely: Rami, his teeth clenched; St. Silas, poison thrumming in his veins, already ravaged with infection; Mrs. Van, demon-born, whose grim face belied a depth of emotion.

Leena knew with certainty that St. Silas would not last a journey on horseback.

She inhaled a lungful of crisp air, welcoming the way it burned her throat.

Steeling her nerves, she turned to her brother. "Rami, you and Mrs. Van must ride to Golborne now. You will have to push yourself to the limit, but you can make the journey in two and a half days if you ride day and night. You will have to change horses at every posting inn." Leena glanced at the horses. They were carriage horses and would need to be traded for two riding horses at the next town. *That* would slow them down as well. "Once you arrive in Golborne, Mrs. Van will concoct the antidote. Once that is done, you must ride as quickly as you can back to us."

"Where will you be?" Rami asked as he took hold of the horses from Mrs. Van, already preparing for the long ride ahead.

"In Lytham, a couple of miles back. There is an old housekeeper who lives in the center of the town. We'll hide there."

Rami nodded. "You two must not walk back on the road, but circle around the town. I will lead the Black Coats away from you. Mrs. Van will take one horse and I will take the other, so that they may think that we have all gone to Golborne." He paused in the act of knotting the long reins. "If we are lucky, they will not uncover the deception until we are back in the city."

Mrs. Van's gaze raked St. Silas. "He is fever-touched already. Our time is very short—especially as Mr. Al-Sayer will have to travel back with the antidote in this weather."

"You will have to make it, Rami," Leena said firmly. "If not, then I will personally track down Lord Hargreaves and trade the red diary for the antidote."

Leena had seen St. Silas hide it in his coat pocket when they'd struggled out of the upturned carriage.

At this, St. Silas jolted, stumbling forward to grasp Leena's shoulders in a tight grip. There was urgency in his eyes. "Swear to me that Hargreaves will never get ahold of that diary, Leena. It is essential. *Swear it.*"

Leena locked her stare with his. For the first time in her entire life, the lie felt natural on her tongue. "I swear it."

He released her, turning toward Rami. "Here." He thrust out a drawstring pouch, full of coins. "If you need more, Mrs. Van will know where to look in my study."

Mrs. Van took one last look at St. Silas, her stern eyes memorizing the contours of his face, and for a moment it looked as if she was in prayer. Then her straight brows formed a formidable scowl as she swung herself onto the horse.

"I'm sorry," Rami said as he climbed onto the other black gelding, "that you both have to walk toward town in this snow, but this is the only viable way to lead the Black Coats away from you."

St. Silas nodded, his gaze already turned toward the miners' town and the road that lay ahead.

Leena kept the information from Rami tucked away in her mind, unable to focus on it now when so many other problems required her immediate attention.

"Be careful?" Leena implored, looking up at Rami with a lump in her throat. At Rami's short nod, she gave him the satchel in which she'd packed her botany book and the housekeeper's timepiece. "Take this back to Golborne for me."

Rami took it distractedly, glancing at St. Silas for a moment with a hooded expression that she'd never seen him wear before. He shook his head before he bent to her, his voice low so that only she could hear him. "The Saint knew the duel was an ambush from the very first. He knew it was *slaughter.* He still went."

Leena absorbed the words. "Yes, he told me, but what I don't understand is why he would do such a thing. It is very unlike him."

Rami straightened, staring down at her with something bordering on exasperation. He took the reins and turned the horse southbound.

"Rami!" She tried to go around him but he threw her an irritated glance before trotting forward.

"Have you not guessed by now?" The horse grew restless, Rami barely able to restrain it single-handedly.

"Do not play games now."

Rami speared one final glance at St. Silas, before looking back at her intently. "I was going to be executed on the steps of Weavingshaw. The Saint saved me. And it was all for you."

Then he lashed the reins forcefully, a canter turning to a gallop, Mrs. Van following closely behind. Leena watched him go, his words echoing in her ears.

She felt his absence like the cleaving of two branches that shared the same root.

38

The Moors

Rami and Mrs. Van were gone.

Go with them, St. Silas had told Leena.

And miss a walk in the snow? she'd responded.

Only now they walked through a storm.

The snowflakes had built to a crescendo, and they were the only two figures making slow progress against the harsh drifts. The roads were no longer visible, so they relied on the tall blades of grass peeking through the snow to navigate the banks.

The farther they walked, the more Leena supported St. Silas—every step laborious, half stumbling in exhaustion. They had passed Lytham in the carriage, and now walked back toward it, away from the road. It had been only two hours since they'd started their slow progress toward the miners' town, but already Leena felt St. Silas descending further into delirium.

She looked obliquely at him. His expression was stony, long eyelashes tipped with frost, breath clipped in pain.

"What are you thinking of?" he asked her. He was no longer able to maintain his habitual honeyed tones. Now his words were grit.

"I am thinking of you." Leena felt his head turn toward her.

Rami's parting words still tore through her—*all for you*—until they had remodeled her in some essential and unknowable way. She could not think past them—not when she had spent so long *fighting* to survive, not when life found new ways to orphan her continuously. Not when she was so exhausted from always carrying loss on her back.

That St. Silas had deliberately, *willingly,* met the sword for her—

She choked on the thought, felt it expand within her until she was suffused with it from the inside out. She knew she could never adhere to Rami's last caution—to use the inexplicable hold he thought she had over St. Silas to her advantage—and she knew her brother would likely think her a fool for not doing so. But she could not. She would not.

"Leena?" St. Silas's voice broke her from her reverie.

Yet she could not speak of Rami's words to St. Silas, not when she'd not had time to understand them. Not when he'd not admitted to them himself.

Instead, she said softly, "You are suffering greatly, yet you show nothing of it. I was wondering where you learned such a trick."

He didn't respond for a while. The growing fever coming from his skin alarmed Leena more than his silence.

"Tell me," Leena said, thinking quickly, "how you learned to shoot so accurately."

His response, when it did come, was stilted. "It was Hargreaves. We practiced daily when I was a boy."

"Is that also how you learned to ride so well?"

A nod. "Though that was more Lady Hargreaves. She loved horses."

With a choked voice, remembering the memories Lady Hargreaves had left in her of Bram as a boy, Leena asked, "Tell me what your father told the world when Bramwell Avon went missing at twelve years old."

His words came slowly, as if dragged from a deep cavern. "My mother's family was not noble. My maternal grandfather was a tradesman. My father and Hargreaves told society that I had been kidnapped by a few of my grandfather's less savory contacts as a punishment for all the money he'd lost them. They said that they'd thrown every resource into finding me, but they'd been told that I was likely already dead. I think my father always intended to come back for me eventually, to 'find' me—"

"Because you are his son?"

"Because I am his heir," he corrected. "Only Percival was killed before he could."

"That was a very far-fetched story they concocted. Did anyone believe it? Surely *someone* must've gone looking for you."

There was a frown on his face. "Society would believe anything an Avon said."

Leena gripped St. Silas's arm tightly, as if to show him the ache she felt for him. "Lady Hargreaves came to visit me last night. She cared for you. Deeply."

St. Silas stiffened.

A sudden trough in the earth caught them unawares, sending them both flying onto a blanket of snow.

Leena groaned.

Ice clung to her cheeks and fell down the back of her collar. Her stockings were now thoroughly wet, and she reckoned that she had a hole through her left boot.

Beside her, St. Silas lay completely still.

She scrambled toward him, heart thudding. His skin was entirely bleached of color, his eyes closed.

"My lord!" she shouted. "My lord, wake up!"

No response.

She shook him but his muscles were limp, as if he was already dead. "St. Silas . . . *please*!"

His eyelids flickered.

She shook him harder, disturbing the snow dusting his hair.

"St. Si—Bram . . . *Bram*! Wake up. *Please,* wake up."

Something shifted inside her. She could not explain it, only that his name on her tongue felt familiar, as if her body had begun to refer to him as Bram—*not the Saint, not St. Silas*—before her mind had.

His eyes slowly opened, pupils dilated, hazy and unfocused.

Leena let out a small sob. "Bram . . . please, we cannot rest here . . ."

The distant sound of the galloping horses was like a blow. Leena's head swiveled, attempting to locate the noise on the quiet, dark moors, terror gripping her when she realized that it came from the direction of Weavingshaw. And they were not far off.

Had they been too slow? Had the Black Coats already caught up with them?

There was no time to ponder this; they were likely minutes away from being discovered.

"Bram—*Bram,* we must move!" she whispered frantically, trying to drag his body to a standing position, but he was too heavy for her to lift.

He didn't stir.

"If you rise now, Bram, I will tell you *all* my secrets. Every single one."

The sound of the racing horses intensified, and yet she still could not see any discernible riders yet.

She grasped the lapels of his coat, attempting to drag him to a more secure hiding place among the high, frozen grass. All the while, she muttered a string of pleas: "Do you remember I once said I would never refer to you by your given name? I was afraid that I would begin to see you as something other than the enemy. But you're no longer my enemy. You're my . . . my . . ." The horses were nearly upon them now. Her breath hitched, her mind blank with animal terror. "Get up, Bram. *Please.*"

Something flickered in his face—*awareness*?

Suddenly, he lurched up, grunting from the effort. With her help, he heaved himself toward a clump of tall grasses.

Then, with a last burst of effort, Bram pulled her toward him, cradling the nape of her neck between his hands just as the horses approached.

Leena's mind sharpened, taking in every detail around her: the feeling of Bram's arms around her—a safety net all on their own—her own heart clawing through her chest, the taste of fear in her mouth, the sound of the horses' rough breaths mere feet from them.

Would the horsemen notice the footprints in the snow? Would the storm worsen? Was Bram—for now she could think of him by no other name—well enough to continue?

In the silver light of the storm, Bram's eyes were half lidded, feverish, but fully alert. As he watched her, an unidentifiable emotion seemed to be flickering in and out of his face. She couldn't hide from him, not when they were only millimeters apart, so she stared back. They stayed like that during the long, agonizing moments in which the riders approached. She shrank down further, not daring even to pray, ears pricked for any sign that they had been discovered.

The hoofbeats came, then receded.

They didn't move until the only sound remaining was their own harsh breaths.

With reluctance, Leena attempted to extract herself from Bram's hold, but his arms tightened around hers.

His words were feverish. "Say it again."

Leena looked at him in confusion. "Say what again?"

"My name. Say it again."

His gaze was bright and unwavering from her face. Leena's heart pounded.

"Bram," she whispered after a long moment.

"Say it again."

She rose up slowly, releasing his hold on her, unsure why it felt so intimate to meet his eyes while calling him by his given name. "Bram." She swallowed, averting her flushed face. "We must go—"

"And again."

"We cannot delay—"

"Leena." He interrupted her, his voice a hoarse command. "Once more. *Say my name.*"

She stood up, her hands slightly shaking while brushing the snow from her jacket, still unable to meet his unfaltering stare.

The still moors and the thick trees were silent, as if waiting for her next words.

"Bram . . ."

He let out a staggered breath—as if this was the first real inhale he had taken in a long time. And yet the irony that these very breaths were now numbered did not escape her.

Leena banished that thought as quickly as it came, however, and stretched a hand toward him. With her aid, he rose to his feet with a grim determination, swaying for a moment, but then he regained his balance and took a half shuffle forward. Then another, until they set a slow pace again.

Even though it was much harder to walk among the long grass than on the route they had originally been traveling, Leena deemed it safer, as they were far less likely to be tracked this way.

The hours slipped past and night fell and still Leena was not sure they had made much progress. Their speed was painfully slow, and her shoulder had begun to ache from where she'd supported Bram. How far had they been from Lytham when the carriage overturned? Four miles? Five? She'd been too distracted to keep track, and she was now paying the price.

She mourned whatever the distance was ahead, for it was clear that Bram was struggling.

She began speaking again: words and secrets and half-remembered recollections flowing from her tongue. If Bram consumed secrets, then she would feed him all of hers.

He must live.

Leena would do everything in her power to ensure it.

First came the lighthearted secrets. *Those* were easy.

Bram gave an amused huff when she told him about the time she had finished a whole tray of Baba's *halwa* by herself and left it under Rami's bed to incriminate him.

But other secrets followed—less amusing, more poignant.

She told him that all the women in New Algaraa District reminded Leena of her mother. It was the eyes these women carried, filled with a gritty love that she was sure she'd inherited herself. He was listening intently, and she felt triumphant that she'd found a way to keep him conscious through their arduous journey.

She told him of her dreams to be a translator and of her mother's poetry books. She told him of the importance of *A Guide to Botany.*

Then she told him of her love for Baba—though this he already knew. But the secret which Bram didn't know was that she resented him also. That her baba had willingly shattered their already broken family for an *ideal* when he could've so easily stayed—an act that killed her in a thousand ways every day.

"This is the one similarity between our fathers." Bram's voice was distant. "They both traded their families for an ideal."

Leena looked at him with a sharp ache. She didn't like her baba being compared to Percival Avon, but a part of her had also made the connection and grieved it.

Her driving force since signing her contract with Bram had been to find her father and free him, to prevent the Wake from taking him. Now he had been taken, and she was back to the beginning with nothing to trade for his freedom. Yet it was inconceivable to Leena that she would ever trade Bram's secret or his red diary. There was still her own secret to bargain with, but she'd seen what Hargreaves had done to Bram. She'd seen Lady Hargreaves's recollection, and she knew that to trust Hargreaves would be to welcome her own destruction.

Leena gripped the fabric of Bram's coat tighter. It was time she revealed her last secret: that she could be possessed.

That Moira had done so.

The words streamed from her mouth in a torrential flood. She told him of the memory of Moira being choked to death by Percival, days after he had made her the new Lady Avon.

Then she told him of Lady Hargreaves's memories. She told Bram how he had once been loved so fiercely and so fervently that it had reverberated even after death.

When she was finished, there was only silence.

Although Leena knew Bram wanted to disavow his father, the unholy acts of his bloodline would undoubtedly still have an impact on him. Percival had killed a woman, Bram's stepmother, on their marital bed. Just as Leena knew the circumstances involved in Lady Hargreaves's passing were bound to wound him. Leena wished she had never had to tell Bram this, but she knew that secrets to him were sacred—*especially* ones pertaining to him.

His response came after a long moment. "Her ghost . . . was it— Is she now at peace?"

She slanted a look at him, and realized that although he did not glance at her, his eyes were brighter than usual.

"Yes," she responded softly, seeing before her eyes Lady Hargreaves as she'd gifted Leena the last dream, contrasted with the first time Leena had seen her. "Very much at peace."

It was not a lie.

He did not comment any further, but Leena knew that he absorbed it. That, even in the grips of fever, he was turning it in his mind, seeing the tragedy of it from every angle.

They walked in silence again.

It took a few minutes for Leena to realize that Bram's grip was loose on her shoulder as he struggled to place one foot in front of the other.

"Bram," she said sharply, looking up at him. "Bram?"

". . . Yes?" His answer came slowly, as if he was drifting in and out of consciousness.

"Continue speaking," Leena implored. "Anything to keep you awake."

His voice was smoky with the fragmented thoughts of the feverish.

"*He* used to steal emotions from us while we slept," he said, and she felt his muscles tighten. "He especially liked our shame."

She couldn't begin to fathom what this meant to Bram. Who was he speaking about? A demon? What had *happened* to Bram Avon at the hands of this father?

He halted abruptly, his eyes unfocused.

"Bram, we mustn't stop—"

"I didn't think they would abandon me there. I never thought—" He shook his head, mouth hardening.

Leena tried to follow his words. She knew Lord Avon and Lord Hargreaves had abandoned Bram, and dreaded to learn what had happened to him after they had left him. She knew that revelation would be a gnawing, unreckonable truth that would sear her soul.

"I still remember . . . the first time *he* fed on me . . . it felt like a loss. I cannot fling it away." Bram's next words were ignited in fury. "But it will all be mine once more. Everything that has been taken from me will be mine once more."

His attention had slipped from her, fastening on a point behind her shoulder. Leena looked, too, and gasped when she saw the flickering lights in the distance.

She took his hand once more, a sudden urgency in her pace. "Come, Bram. We are very close."

They stumbled forward again, but the nearer they approached, the more Leena began to hear shouts resounding from within the town. Angry, disturbed shouts. Smoke coiled like a warning in the skies, and Leena suddenly recalled the rabid faces of the miners when their carriage had driven through the village.

Arthur's warning shrilled in her ears: *This entire country is dynamite, waiting for the first spark.*

The spark has happened, Leena thought. *And everything is burning.*

In Golborne, they would've been able to disappear without a trace. But in a small town, there was nowhere to hide.

She reeled back suddenly, no longer thinking that it was safe to find refuge in the housekeeper's cottage where she had initially planned to take Bram.

Leena's thoughts darted wildly, and she remembered the posting inn they had stayed in on the night she'd met Lady Hargreaves.

She changed direction abruptly, to circle Lytham and go back in the direction of Weavingshaw and the forest, to the edge of the town where the inn was located.

39

The Posting Inn

Leena and Bram stood on the threshold of the inn directly under the glare of the bright lights, the stone steps slippery beneath their boots, icicles collecting on the eaves. Bram's arms encircled her tightly, his face deathly pale. He was lucid again; Leena thanked all the Saints to ever exist.

"We made it," Leena whispered, but really what she was saying was: *Is this the right choice?* "Come, let's go inside."

The sudden rush of warm air from within the inn was painful on her raw skin.

Waiting at the front desk was the ghost of a customer who was trying to hail her attention without success. Leena ignored him, ringing the silver bell instead.

The innkeeper's wife who had been present previously dashed out from the back door of the kitchen to answer. The robust woman took one look at their disheveled appearance and called for her husband. He came bustling out of the kitchen behind her, bringing forth smells of hearty stews that set Leena's stomach growling.

Leena remembered that he had not been present the last time

they were here. The innkeeper was a large man, so tall that he ducked his head under the doorframe to pass; the sound of his steps echoed like thunderclaps.

He smiled widely, his beefy hands spread in welcome, but his eyes were shrewd. "How can I be of service?"

"We need a room—"

"My apologies, madam, but we are full tonight."

Leena stared at him. It had never occurred to her that they could come all this way and still be flung back into the cold. "Please, sir, we were set upon by highwaymen—"

"We're a respectable establishment." He cut her off, an obvious glance at her bare ring finger.

Leena understood.

"*My husband* and I have had everything stolen from us—even my wedding ring—and they've wounded him terribly." She hoped that the innkeeper's wife didn't recognize them in their current state, so different from their first visit. "Our destination is Weavingshaw. We are guests of Mr. Martin and Lord Hargreaves."

She knew that it was a gamble using the names of these powerful gentlemen—especially when they were being hunted *by* those very men—but the innkeeper's hostility seemed to diminish slightly at the mention of her grand connections.

She tried not to sound desperate as she continued, "Of course, once we reach Weavingshaw, we will be speaking to the Magistrate to seek justice for our stolen belongings and my husband's attack." Leena was glad of the fact that Bram's coat was made of richly tailored material, effectively hiding the extent of his wound.

"My love," Bram interrupted, with such overdrawn affection that Leena tried not to show amusement in spite of their dire circumstances. "I always hide an emergency fund on my person." With some difficulty, he withdrew from his coat another drawstring bag bulging with coins. The innkeeper's gaze fastened on the pouch, devouring its contents. "I would like the best room with the warmest fire. And make haste; my wife's shivering."

The innkeeper bowed. "*Certainly,* sir. I see that I am mistaken; it seems we do have a vacancy after all."

"How fortunate," Bram drawled.

"Will you be wanting dinner?"

Leena agreed to this heartily, also requesting that a clean shirt for her husband, hot water, fresh gauze, and a glass of strong drink be brought up.

Away from the hearing of the innkeeper, Bram asked, "Strong drink? Are we celebrating our happy nuptials?"

"For your wound," Leena clarified with dignity.

"Ah, well," he sighed, taking the stairs slowly. "We have time to change your mind yet."

Bram kept his posture straight as the innkeeper led them both upstairs; his stagger was less pronounced, his laughter strong at the innkeeper's awful jokes, but the hand gripping the banister was white-knuckled. The moment they were left alone in the room, he slumped onto the bed without removing his shoes.

Like a beast that only licked its wounds in private.

Leena looked around the room. It was decent-sized, with a four-poster bed that had clean linen and a fire already blazing in the hearth. A small table stood at the side by the washstand.

Leena longed to collapse next to Bram. Her bones ached and her shoulder throbbed, but she knew that if she closed her eyes now, she'd sleep till morning and risk being possessed again. Not to mention that she needed to tend to Bram's wound.

"And how is my wife doing?" Bram propped himself up on his elbows, peering at her from beneath his lashes.

She flushed, telling herself that it was the fire that made her feel so warm.

"I had little choice. Even a fool would not believe that we are siblings traveling together, or even that I am your ward." She attempted to keep her voice brusque, but even *she* knew how her next words would open a floodgate of provocation. "Come, let's remove your clothes so that I can check your wound again."

Bram's laugh saturated the room. "Shall we start with yours?"

Leena stared back, caught half between shock and laughter herself. "You can barely stand on your own two feet. How is it that any chance you get, you are *still* speaking of my clothes?"

"They are a constant hindrance to me." The way Bram looked at her, so different from the way Lord Kilworth had looked at her only that morning, infused Leena with safety, with warmth, with . . . *something more.*

She took off her muddy, wet coat and laid it by the fire. "*There*—are you happy? Can we now please address your wound?"

"So eager for the wedding night." His voice was low. "I shall, most willingly, oblige."

Once more, she tried to hide the smile quivering on her lips as she undid his coat, and it was clear that fatigue had overtaken him again. She was worried by how quickly he became tired.

How quickly he drifted in and out of lucidity also worried Leena. She tried not to think about Mrs. Van's predictions or how little time they had to administer the cure.

With effort, Bram jerked up to a sitting position, one hand still grasping his left side.

Swiftly, Leena helped him shrug out of his wet coat before hanging it over the fire. As she was doing so, she felt the outlines of the red diary inside his coat pocket, and felt a sudden fierce anger at Theo for leading them to this point. For without him, they would never have sought the red diary to begin with.

Bram's fingers stumbled over the buttons of his ruined shirt until Leena took over for him. His skin was still burning through the layers of cloth.

She sucked in a gasp.

The bandages were soaked through. Somewhere on their journey, part of the wound must've reopened.

A knock sounded on the door. The innkeeper's wife stood on the threshold with two silver platters of food and a basket filled with the items Leena had requested.

The woman's eyes flashed to Bram's bandages before turning toward the stairs. Leena realized that she was listening for her husband's footsteps. The woman indicated a glass jar filled with a dark substance, dropping her voice to a whisper: "I've also packed you a poultice. Sterilize the wound first, then apply it. It will draw out any signs of infection."

"Thank you," Leena whispered back. Remembering the bag of coins, she gave generously from the stash.

The woman hid the coins in her sleeve then shut the door firmly, leaving Leena gripping the jar tightly.

She turned to look at Bram. He was bare from the waist up, only the bandages covering him, the firelight flickering across the hard planes and hollows of his chest, his dark head bowed. Leena's mind could not help contrasting him to the warlords of the past who had roamed these very northern moors—strong and agile, scarred, battle-worn, unconquerable.

Bramwell Avon *was* the north, in all its desolation—its hunger, its jagged edges and endless ferocity, a fortress against the changing seasons. Leena fought a pang of sadness at what his body had been made to withstand and was *still* withstanding.

"I've heard many confessions over the years from every manner of confessor," Bram said quietly. "Lords, ladies, beggars, cutthroats—I never cared who sat in the chair in front of me. Every one of them had their own purpose for revealing their secrets." He swallowed as if he tasted something bitter. "No one—and I mean *no one*—has ever told a secret for my sake. Not until you." He kept his head bowed. "Why did you do it?"

"Bram, we—" she started to respond, but caught herself at the last moment. He deserved more than the half lie she'd been preparing to give. "Because we are friends. Because I . . ."

She couldn't finish that last thought—she wasn't even sure what it was—but his eyes seemed to focus on her answer and the unsaid words behind it.

Oh, how I loathe *you.*

Leena was amazed that she had once thought that, when she now felt the very opposite. That she—

She turned away to gather both her materials and herself before kneeling in front of him. "I must change your bandages."

She reached around to untie the knotted fabric below his shoulder blade, and she was so absorbed by the task that she didn't notice how close her face was to his bare chest.

His hand formed a fist on the sheets.

She looked up at him, surprised to find his expression taut. "Have I hurt you?"

"*No.*" His voice was hoarse.

Then, to Leena's surprise, he leaned in even closer, dropping his forehead to rest on her shoulder. She halted, her hand hovering over his chest with the gauze caught between her thumb and forefinger. She wondered if he could feel the wild beat of the pulse in her neck, pounding against his cheek. "Continue," he said after a short while, his voice not losing its roughness.

Her hands now slightly shaking, Leena started unwinding the bandages again, partially impeded by their close proximity. But he did not shift, nor did Leena want him to.

"Lavender," he said suddenly. "You still smell of it."

Leena remembered how much the perfumed oil she'd worn had irritated him in the past. "I'm sorry—"

"No, don't be," he said, tilting his jaw so that his face was burrowed closer into her neck. "I had never before known that I could crave a smell."

Leena's eyes snapped away from the bandages and toward him.

The maddening part was that she knew *exactly* what he meant. His scent as he had carried her into the cave—sandalwood and fresh linen—had embedded itself into her waking hours, disturbed her rest. The wanting of him was ceaseless—a constant cacophony, impossible to silence.

Leena slowly pulled away once all the bandages were off and his torso was bare. The black spidery veins creeping from the wound site had lengthened. The cut was now clearly infected, the edges gaping and weepy, the skin angry and inflamed.

Wordlessly, she reached for the alcohol bottle.

"This will hurt," she warned, before spilling the entire contents onto the wound. He gasped, eyes widening briefly, before he slumped back, unconscious.

That was easier for Leena. She was inevitably going to hurt him as she cleaned the wound, scrubbing the infection from the edges, and she didn't want him to remember the pain of it in the way Rami remembered his amputation.

Once that horrid task was finished, she applied the black poultice the innkeeper's wife had brought, its vinegary smell stinging her nose, then wound the gauze around it. That proved to be difficult under the heavy weight of his body, but she managed to keep the wrappings as tight and as sterile as she could before dressing him in the new shirt the innkeeper's wife had provided.

As Bram slept, Leena reached into his coat to ensure that the red diary had not fallen out, sighing in relief when she felt the firm outline of the cover. Tugging it out quickly, wondering why this particular book had garnered so much dangerous attention, Leena flipped through the pages.

Bram had said that most of the pages were blank, but they were not.

Elegantly scrawled writing crowded every page, from margin to margin, the entries marked in the darkest of ink. Had Bram been so distracted by thoughts of the duel that he'd not properly investigated the contents of the diary? Surely one of these passages must be the reason why Hargreaves was hunting them.

Before Leena managed to delve further into this, Bram woke up again.

He had descended further into fever, incoherent questions tumbling from his mouth. He rose from the bed several times, restlessly grabbing for his pistol, forcing Leena to hide it within the pocket of her own skirt.

"Where's the Duke?" he demanded, looking at her without recognition.

"There is no Duke. It's just me," she said, trying to coax him back into bed.

He blinked at her. "They'll all die. I'll make sure of it."

"It's all right, Bram—"

He made a sound of frustration, as if she was being deliberately obtuse. "The Fray line will end with me, do you understand? *I will end their line.*"

His voice had risen in volume, and Leena glanced toward the door, afraid that the innkeeper might have heard the noise and come to investigate.

She tried to settle him, but she could see from his eyes that he was disoriented, his consciousness filtering through realities. He grasped for the pistol hidden in her pocket, and to calm him Leena placed a hand against his cheek, the short stubble scratching her skin.

Instantly, his entire body stilled, as if in both dread and anticipation.

Then, a deep shudder ran through him and he clasped his own hand around hers, tilting his jaw sideways to kiss the center of her palm.

The gesture was so uncharacteristically tender that it could only be the act of a delirious man—an insensible mind.

Leena could not deny that a growing part of her wished that it was deliberate, that this could be the flame that burned away all that stood between them—the contract, the title, the difference in their bloodlines.

It felt to Leena that everything up until this point had been an interlude—starting in the cave, igniting since then, catching fire now.

But she drew away shakily, trying to smile through the pangs of her own foolish heart so as not to distress him further. "You must rest—"

Bram's fingers tightened over her wrist, ignoring her. His brows furrowed. "*Damn* the demons and *damn* their visions of you. This time, I am going to finish it."

In one powerful movement, he pulled her toward him, crushing her body against his, taking her mouth with ferocity. He swallowed her gasp, and she could feel the rapid beats of his heart against her own chest.

It was a hard kiss, his lips bruising against hers, speaking to her of yearning, of *suffering.* Leena distantly felt his fingers intertwining themselves with her hair, then moving to command her face to turn just so, *to open to him.*

She clenched his shirt to anchor herself, her lungs incapable of drawing in enough air to keep her heart pumping in a steady rhythm. She could not form any coherent thoughts while his hands caressed her face, her hair, her neck.

But his next words almost undid her resolve.

"Not enough," he murmured against her jaw, his kiss suddenly turning gentle, trailing across her cheek to below her earlobe where her pulse thrummed, lingering there for a single incinerating moment, then back to the ache of her lips.

In that kiss, Leena could taste all the lingering looks he'd ever given her, all the rare smiles, all the frustration—*all for her.*

Against her better judgment, she felt herself meeting Bram with the same intensity—*it was always going to be this way.*

For a blazing moment, Leena could not think of the consequences as she threw her arms around his neck, balancing herself on her tiptoes, kissing him back unreservedly.

When he felt her response, whatever reserve he held over himself cracked. His embrace turned to iron, the kiss a searing possession.

She wanted to stay beside him . . . against him . . . with him . . .

She wanted—

No.

A spark of electricity coursed through her, and she gasped from the pain of it, jerking away. The motion was so powerful it almost caused her to fall back, and in a second the pain was gone. But it was enough to bring Leena back to her senses.

This was not the Bram in the cave, almost kissing her, then turning away. This was an insensate Bram, half intoxicated with fever and poison. Leena could never comprehend the number of choices that had been taken away from him throughout his life.

If he kissed her now, she wanted it to be something he had *chosen.*

She felt unsteady on her feet, as if the floorboards were shifting around her, and she grabbed the bedpost to keep upright.

Bram, too, looked stunned, a high color staining his cheeks. His breathing was ragged, and he dragged an unsteady hand through his hair. "The demons know the exact ways to drive a mind to insanity." His voice was hoarse as he reached out to trace her lips with his thumb, his eyes losing focus as he followed the movement. Leena's hand tightened on the post. "By far, you are the softest insanity—"

Then he staggered suddenly, his fist clenching against his wound, his face contorted in fresh waves of pain. Leena had never seen him like this, his shoulders trembling in agony.

"Bram," she cried, reaching for him, but the moment her fingers touched his brow, another jolt of electricity transferred from his skin to hers. She yelped, rearing back, and instinctively brought her throbbing fingers to her lips.

His gaze was withdrawn, as if he was being pulled inward by something that Leena could not see. Then he slumped sideways onto the bed, succumbing to unconsciousness.

When Leena touched his forehead, it was scorching.

The poison was eating him alive.

40

The Barricade

LEENA FELT LIKE it was mere moments before she was jerked awake by the door slamming open.

She hadn't meant to close her eyes, nor had she meant to fall asleep—especially as she hadn't even had the chance to line the bed with salt yet. Leena jolted into a sitting position, still feeling the burn of Bram's lips on her own. He lay beside her, his eyes still closed.

Leena sighed with relief when she realized it was not a phantom that had disturbed her but the innkeeper. His large frame bustled through the door, his forehead red and blotchy.

"Pack your belongings, m'dear. You both must leave now."

Leena's foggy mind could not adjust to the sudden change in events. She looked at the innkeeper without comprehension. "Leave? We've paid for the night."

The innkeeper scattered the coins on the floor, one rolling beneath the bed. "There—I've refunded you the full amount. Do not dawdle."

Leena rose from the bed sharply. "I don't understand."

The innkeeper waved a beefy hand. "Ain't your fault. The whole town's gone mad for revolution. No one has been down in the mines for a week. Tonight there's been talk that your friend Martin sent for the King's soldiers to capture those leading the protest."

Leena's blood froze, forcing her to be fully awake now. "What does that have to do with us?"

"The townspeople have gone bloodthirsty; they're even building a damned barricade against the soldiers," the innkeeper growled. "Once the townsmen hear of your relationship to Mr. Martin, they will tear apart my inn to get to you and your . . . *husband.*"

By initially claiming Martin's protection, she had successfully managed to procure shelter, but hours later this same protection had led to their eviction. She looked out the window, the glass laced with ice, the snow falling so fast that the night sky was a white haze.

"My husband is gravely injured." Leena drew herself up to her full height, staring at him with fierce eyes. "We've done nothing wrong. If we are forced out into this weather, he will not last the night."

The innkeeper shrugged, not bothering with false geniality anymore. "I'll not have trouble inside my inn."

He made as if to walk toward Bram, but Leena stood in his way.

"We will leave," Leena ground out, "but we will need a moment to prepare ourselves, and you will wait downstairs until then."

The innkeeper's eyes narrowed to slits, but he retreated, leaving the door open.

Leena knelt down and collected the coins off the floor, even stretching her aching shoulder to reach the one beneath the bed, trying to blink the tears from her eyes.

Dangerous as the town might be at the present, she had no choice now but to make her way to the old housekeeper's cottage, and who was to say that the old woman would even remember or welcome her? But that was the only refuge remotely open to them.

She was loath to shake Bram awake, not when he needed every moment of rest she could give him. His forehead still burned even beneath the cool cloth.

He blinked at her, trying to latch on to her words, but his mind was too hazy. Finally, he gained some understanding of the urgency of their situation and stumbled out of bed before shrugging on his coat. Leena patted his pocket again to ensure that the red diary had not slipped out—she dreaded losing it after they had sacrificed so much to acquire it—and was reassured by the feel of its firm outline.

It was jarring to see the dreaded Saint of Silence so vulnerable. Once, she'd gone to St. Silas for medication to save Rami's life. How everything had now shifted between them—power, hierarchy, even loyalty.

Leena took his hand, leading him down the stairs and into the lobby where the innkeeper watched them from behind the desk. She felt comforted by the heavy weight of Bram's pistol in her pocket; her own had been lost in the crypts.

Once more that night they were out in the bleak cold without shelter.

Leena stood on the steps, trying to remember the directions to the housekeeper's cottage.

That way was Weavingshaw, its lights visible through the white mist. To the left was the town, where even from here she could hear the steady hum of discordant chanting. To the right was the country road.

Leena struggled with herself for a moment before she led Bram toward the path that ran deeper into the maze of clustered houses. She huddled close to him to shield him from the bite of the wind, their boots struggling to grip the icy cobbled streets.

The shouting intensified. Once they reached the town square, Leena understood why.

It was complete chaos.

Townsfolk ran in all directions, collecting weapons to throw down by the steps of the church. Pickaxes, scythes, helmets, rusted swords, and farming equipment were all laid down in piles.

Chants could be heard like tidal waves, so it took Leena a moment to piece together what was being shouted: *Long live the people.*

Paint-splattered letters were written everywhere, on the fences, on the wooden posts, on the doors: *King Edmund will fall.*

Someone had attempted to form a barricade but had abandoned the project halfway, leaving a sad fence with a few wooden planks, a dozen chairs, and a wardrobe turned on its side. If the army was truly coming, then the entire town wouldn't last the week.

Leena recognized a handful of Martin's servants in the crowd, their faces lit by a steel-can flame. Leena kept her head low. She urged Bram onward, but he struggled under her grip.

Swerving, she saw a face in the crowd that she recognized instantly.

Mackenzie Crane, bruiser of the Black Coats. His right earlobe was completely missing, and his hand was heavily bandaged thanks to Bram's shot.

His head turned at that moment.

Leena's breath hitched. He had seen them, and was now cutting through the crowd in their direction.

She faltered, tugging Bram by the hand toward the first dark alleyway she encountered, quickening their strides.

But Mackenzie had followed them.

With a wild sort of fright, she heard hard footsteps clicking behind them on the cobblestones, steadily gaining pace.

Leena tore into the maze of streets, guiding them deeper into the township and the clustered houses. Still, no matter where she turned, Mackenzie's footsteps followed.

A flicker of shadow ahead of them.

Theodore Daye emerged, his eyes frantic, urging them forward.

There was no other way to go but onward. Leena briefly considered going back to face Mackenzie Crane rather than follow Theodore Daye, who had already betrayed them once, but that seemed like a deadlier option.

"Please," Leena sobbed, staggering to a stop. "Do not lead us astray again, Theo. *Please.*"

Theodore Daye halted at her words. His skin turned unearthly pale, and he averted his face. No longer did he beckon her forward. His entire body seemed to crumple in shame.

Leena heard the sounds of Mackenzie's approach growing steadily closer.

Bram's head came up. He tugged at her. "No . . . Leena . . . we cannot . . . Theo . . ."

"I know," she soothed, even though her own heart quaked.

But there was nowhere else to go.

Before Leena could decide whether to trust Theo and go forward, or turn around and face Mackenzie with Bram's pistol, the choice was no longer hers to make.

She hadn't seen the figure crouched in anticipation of their arrival until his strong hands had gripped her by the hair, dragging her away from Bram and into an open doorway at the side of the alley.

She scratched the attacker, hearing a grunt when she raked her nails down his arm, all the while trying to reach for Bram's pistol, but her assailant's grip didn't loosen.

"Enough, dearie."

She froze, recognizing that voice. "*You?*"

Only a single sconce burned in the house, and in that pool of light she could see the ugly face of Mr. Orley, demon leader of the Black Coats.

Bram staggered after her, lunging for the pistol that was hidden in Leena's pocket.

Orley, expecting this, jammed his fist into Bram's wound. Leena gasped as Bram let out a guttural moan before slumping onto the floor, unconscious. Blood bloomed through his shirt and stained the hardwood floor.

Orley wiped his hands delicately on a handkerchief. Theodore Daye stood by his elbow, refusing to meet Leena's eyes.

"Now that he is asleep, my love," Orley said pleasantly, "we can speak freely."

41

The Vessel

Leena tore into her pocket for her pistol, holding it aloft in trembling hands, but Orley barely spared it a glance.

"You're a traitor, Theo." The accusation came out choked from Leena's throat.

Theodore Daye flinched.

She could make out dim shapes of furniture in the weak light filtering from the sconce, and a hallway that extended farther into darkness. She could not see another door or window other than the one behind her.

She made swift calculations in her head. She could shoot Orley and drag Bram out, but she quickly dismissed the idea. She could not lift Bram. So she would have to shoot Orley and barricade herself with Bram in this house. She peered uneasily at the hallway behind Orley's shoulder, wondering if anyone else lingered in the shadows. She didn't know how many bullets she had.

As if sensing her thoughts, Orley let out a high-pitched giggle. "Ah, my friends have joined the party."

Mackenzie Crane stood blocking the entranceway, slamming the door shut and bolting it. He grinned at her, a smile crammed with the stolen teeth of others, waving his bandaged hand at her like a greeting. A young Burr stood beside him, leaning against the windowpane.

She kept the pistol aimed at Orley, standing in front of Bram like a shield, but she knew that her actions were the desperate ones of a captured animal.

Orley watched her in fascination.

"Theodore told me how you treated him like a friend. It's delightful. But Theo was mine all along, my dear." The blacks of his eyes widened, thin lips moving as if he tasted something in the air. "Ah, your distress is so sweet."

Leena's grip on the pistol tightened. "You're a demon."

He sounded pleased. "So our mutual friend, Mr. St. Silas, has not left you completely in the dark."

Leena's eyes hardened at Orley's gall to even utter Bram's name. "Can you see ghosts as well?" she grated out.

Once more, Orley's tongue poked out to lick his lips. A trace of color appeared on his cheeks, as if he were drunk on her fright.

"No, I was not blessed with that gift," he responded with an exaggerated sigh. "Mackenzie, have you ever heard of anyone possessing an ability quite like this lovely lady?"

Leena stilled as she waited for an answer. Her arm began to ache from holding the pistol aloft. She wished that Bram would stir, that he would give her any indication that he hadn't been more gravely injured, but she didn't dare turn her back to check on him.

Mackenzie's answer came slowly, as if awakened from deep thought. "No, I've never heard of such a thing."

A shiver ran down her spine and she thrust her pistol in the air. "You've lured us into a trap, Orley, using Theodore Daye. If you cannot see him, then how could you plan this?"

From behind Orley, Theodore's eyes were wild in his thin face, pleading for Leena's forgiveness. She turned away from him.

Orley held up a hand, the light glinting off the dozen rings he'd stuffed onto his elongated fingers. "I can speak to the dead. Their chattering is incessant, a gift that has always belonged to my family. We used to entertain at the courts of nobles." He sniffed. "We used to be *artists,* before I was so unjustly banished to this world."

There was so much new information striking Leena from every direction that she felt dull with it.

World?

Rather than allow herself to dwell on it, she released the safety on the pistol. From the side, she heard a similar click, and turned to see Burr holding a pistol of his own. This time his hands were steady, his gaunt boyish face splitting into a monstrous grin.

"For Adam," he whispered, and Leena remembered with a shudder the Algaraan boy they had buried.

"Now, now, hold fire," Orley cautioned. "We all can be of use to each other."

"Use?" Leena's laugh sounded shrill even to her own ears. "Are you not working for Hargreaves and the Wake?"

"I've worked for them in the past, yes," Orley replied. "It was I who told them about your abilities, and it was I who sent our ghost here to lead you on the hunt for the red diary."

It was further confirmation for Leena: Lord Avon was never going to come.

Everything we've been through, coming to Weavingshaw—it has all been for naught. Leena's chest was entirely hollow, as if her insides had been scooped out to fester outside her body.

"Do you want the red diary?" she asked dully.

All hopes of bargaining for their freedom were lost with the shake of Orley's head. "I do not care for the diary. It is the Wake who want it. *I* want *you.*"

Leena's own lips curled in disgust. "What do you want from me?"

"Hargreaves agreed to deliver you to me once his business had been concluded, but I began to believe that he would do no such thing. Yet you are endlessly valuable," Orley responded. "I needed you to be outside of the Saint's protection so that I might be able to act." At her expression, he laughed. "I needed you to be desperate, and I believed being hunted from all sides would make you *very* desperate."

"Aye, the King's army is approaching," Mackenzie said, rapping on the doorframe with one large fist. "They're not too far off. They will starve this town into submitting to the King's will." He flashed her another grin full of stolen gold. "It is truly your misfortune that the same day you leave Weavingshaw is the day for which the King's soldiers had planned their siege."

Leena stilled completely, her horrified eyes nearly too wide for her face.

"And I assume Lord Hargreaves is not far off," Orley continued, sensing her fear and taking pleasure from it. Leena wondered if whatever the Wake wanted with her was better than whatever these three had planned. Lord Hargreaves could be bribed with the red diary. Orley could not.

"Choose wisely, dearie. I am your best option." At her silence, Orley continued, his tone oily and persuasive. "All I want is to make a deal with you."

"Why should I trust you?"

Orley threw a pointed glance at Bram's collapsed form.

She stayed silent, her mind frantically debating the choices set in front of her.

"Can you believe it, Mackenzie?" Orley breathed, watching her with awe. "A vessel within a human. I never thought it possible."

"How can you be sure?" Mackenzie asked, tilting his head at her with significantly less amazement.

"I have never been *more* sure." Orley's fascinated gaze had still not left Leena.

Burr looked between the two of them. "What's a vessel?"

Leena jabbed her pistol in the air. "Answer him."

"Apologies." Orley bowed low. "But ever since Theodore told me that you could see past the veil of death, I haven't been able to stop thinking about you." He laughed when he saw repulsion twist her features. "Oh no, *not like that.* I'd never lower myself to a human. Lovely as you are."

"What is a vessel?" Leena asked now, through gritted teeth.

"I am a demon and I am far from home, trapped in this world littered with humans for centuries." Orley blinked, his eyes turning misty. Leena wanted to throttle him. "I want to return. But demons, unlike humans, cannot travel easily between worlds without a vessel."

"Like a key," Burr shouted, bouncing on his feet.

Orley snapped his fingers. "Exactly like a key. Your human Saints destroyed too many of them, and they are now hard to find, and exceedingly valuable. They take the form of objects. A pebble on a beach full of pebbles might be a vessel. A seed. A twig."

She felt suddenly lightheaded. "And what does that have to do with me?"

"A vessel has possessed you. I'm not yet sure how or when, but that is why you are connected to the spirit world." Orley smiled, showcasing surprisingly white and healthy teeth. "And it is why you will help me return to mine."

That was the reason her life had stagnated—because she was nothing more than a host for some sort of vessel?

The walls were closing in on her.

Every breath leaving her chest was a gasp.

"I will shoot everyone here," Leena yelled, but her threat was made from desperation. Bram was unconscious. Mackenzie Crane blocked the door. Burr held a pistol. An army approached. And the Wake was hunting them.

Then, a pounding at the door.

Burr parted the curtains to look out. "Soldiers," he called. "A few of them. They're preparing to break down the door."

Orley glanced at his timepiece. "Our time is up. You've got no choice, madam. You will take me back to my world."

"I want a deal," Leena demanded. If Bram had taught her anything, it was the importance of a deal.

The demon locked his jaw.

The pounding intensified, the wood of the door splitting.

"Quickly," he hissed.

Leena did not allow herself even a moment's pause to think. "I will not leave without St. Silas. You will take us to a safe place. And you will hand me the cure for Detritus Poison."

She wanted it in writing, but the hinges of the door began to rattle.

"Agreed, agreed," Orley said, then turned to Mackenzie Crane. "I relinquish all ownership of the Black Coats to you. Glad farewells, my friend."

Mackenzie raised a hand in parting.

Orley, oddly strong for a man his size, lifted Bram by the shoulders and dragged him down the dark hallway into the back of the house. There he led them into a chamber, empty save for a long mirror framed in gold and a few lit candles burned nearly to the stubs.

Leena looked down. The entirety of the wooden floor was covered with swirls drawn in salt, except for a path that led straight into the mirror. It was too dim to make out the shapes in the salt.

A scream curled in her sternum, an aching panic.

This room was *unnatural.*

No, it was the mirror that was wrong. Evil.

She felt the same shuddering fear looking at her reflection as she had staring into the dark waters of the Hall of the Lake. A feeling of anguish, deep within her bones, imprinted on her spirit—an ancient understanding that no human should go near that mirror. That it was not meant for them.

"Come," Orley urged, dragging Bram forward.

Leena took a step. Then another. A gallows walk.

Her reflection no longer resembled herself. The girl staring back possessed the same dark curls now loosened down her back, the same wild brown eyes, but her face was twisted and pained. Tear tracks ran down her cheeks. Terror was carving a new face out of the one she already had.

A voice inside her begged her to turn back, to claw her own eyes out before allowing herself to see what lay behind the mirror.

As if sensing her thoughts, Orley grabbed her hand in a fleshy grip.

"Now," he shouted. She could hear shouts from the other room—a shot being fired, a clash of steel. "Now! Take me *back*!"

She knew what would happen before she reached for the mirror.

At her fingertips, the solid glass dissolved like a curtain made of water.

She could taste sweetness on her tongue, like ripping the skin of a peach, as she stepped into the demon world.

42

The Timepiece

A fire burned Leena from the inside out, so potent it felt as if her spine was being ripped apart.

She collapsed to her knees, entirely blind to her surroundings, attempting to breathe through the pain. Blood dripped from her nose and eyes, splashing the hardwood floor like crimson teardrops. She began gagging, and it took her bleary mind a moment to realize she was also coughing up blood.

It took minutes for the agony to finally cease. Leena collapsed onto her side, blinking through the haze. The bleeding had stopped, and she wiped her face with the back of her sleeve.

Slowly, her senses returned.

They had entered a small room containing only a bed, a wooden chair, a washstand, and a fireplace stacked with wood.

Leena jolted up to a sitting position, searching for Bram.

He was on the mattress; Orley must've put him there. Leena staggered toward him, emitting a sigh of relief when she saw the ragged rise and fall of Bram's chest, although he was still unconscious.

A candle was already lit by the bedside, the candelabra caked with years of rust. A few art prints hung on the wall, but the glass in their frames was covered by a thick dust.

Orley stood by the window, and Leena was surprised to see tears dotting his eyes.

"I'm home," he choked out. "You do not know how long—" Another sob tore from him.

Leena peeked through the dirty window. Wherever she was, it was pitch-black outside and she could only see her own horrified expression reflected back, streaks of blood still running down her cheeks. It was dead quiet—no soldiers pounding at the door, no townspeople constructing a doomed barricade.

"We're in the demon world." The words felt foreign to Leena's ears.

"Yes, Bastmore. A safe place, as I promised." Orley bowed once more. "This is where I used to stay when I came to the island to entertain at the Duke's court. You are lucky that no traveling minstrel has taken up residence; they come and go as they please. You'll need to keep a candle lit by the window so that they know the room has been claimed—if that is indeed the way they still do it. It has been *years*."

Leena stared at him. "I meant a safe place in the human world."

Orley shrugged. "Then you ought to have specified."

"Take. Us. Back." Leena slammed a fist into her thigh with each word.

Orley wagged a finger at her. "That was not part of the agreement."

It took a long moment for Leena's tired mind to process this piece of unsettling news. It was another stab wound in a body that had already suffered a hundred.

"My theory was right." Orley clapped his hands in delight. His eyes roved her body as if she were a feast. There was nothing lecherous in his gaze, only fascination. "You *are* a vessel."

Her head felt heavy. "That means that the only reason I can see spirits is because I'm infected by a . . . a . . . parasite?"

"Not a parasite, a *vessel,*" he corrected, chiding her like a schoolteacher. "Who knows how one has got into you?" Orley paused, then looked at her in a faintly pitying manner. "Hmm. You hoped there was a reason for your ability to see the dead? No, my dear, there isn't. You are nothing—a happenstance, a host."

Leena swallowed.

The demon sniffed the air. "Is that shame I can taste? Yes. How delicious."

Leena reared back. "I'm not ashamed."

"Yes, you are. You are ashamed of your nothingness."

Leena rose up to her full height. She could not afford to dwell on this now. "Our deal still stands, demon. You'll fetch me the cure for the poison."

Orley's face tightened with distaste. He sighed, then headed for the door. "Once I fetch you the cure, we will be free of each other."

Leena watched him go, then she quickly turned to check on Bram.

The pulse in his neck pounded rapidly against her finger. His eyelids remained closed, his skin an unnaturally high color, and when she pressed a hand to his cheek he still felt warm.

Leena wanted to check his bandages, but didn't want Orley to come back and see the Saint of Silence in such a vulnerable position. Instead, she brushed a tendril of black hair away from his forehead and turned to investigate the room.

She went to the mirror first, attempting to stretch her fingers through it, but was met only with cool glass. Her reflection showed a wild version of herself, stained with blood. Leena wiped her cheeks until the skin was raw, just to return to a sense of self.

There was also a small room tucked away at the side that Leena hadn't previously noticed. It held a claw-foot tub with only a curtain to act as a door. The tap creaked when she turned it, then spewed forth rusty water.

Winter bit harder here, and she could see her own breath in the air. Beneath the bed, she found a musty blanket which she used to cover Bram.

Finally, just as she steeled herself to take another look through the window, Orley returned.

The demon held a brown package.

Seeing this, Leena started forward, desperate to get her hands on the antidote. Things would be better once Bram was healthy again. They would make a plan then.

"Ah, ah, ah," Orley admonished. "A deal is a deal."

He took out a glass vial filled with a red liquid from the package and gave it to her. "I am no longer in your debt. I have *handed* you the cure."

Leena gripped the glass vial, hope rising in her chest.

Orley lunged toward her, striking her cheek with such force that she staggered backward.

Pain burst behind her eyelids. Her ears rang. The world spun.

In her disorientation, Orley tore the vial from her hands. She scrambled forward, but it was too late. Orley unlatched the window, throwing the vial out.

She heard it shatter on the cobbles below.

For a moment she could only stare at her empty hands before lurching for her pistol, but her pocket was empty. To her terror, she looked up to see Orley holding the weapon, twirling it in his hands.

"The Saint will hunt me down for what I know about you," Orley said, turning the pistol toward Bram.

Leena flung herself at Orley, attempting to grapple for the gun, but he pushed her back. She slammed into the wall, shaking white dust from the ceiling.

"No," Leena begged. *"Please."*

He fired.

Once. Twice.

The chamber was empty.

In a rage, Orley flung the pistol to the side where it clattered against the mirror, shattering it to fragments.

Leena was too far away for any pieces to pierce her flesh, but she clawed on hands and knees to find a large shard. Gripping it so tightly that it drew a thin line of blood on her palm, she stepped between Orley and Bram.

Orley reared back, hands in the air. He licked his lips and grimaced at the taste.

Leena bitterly understood that Orley had fulfilled his end of the bargain—he'd *handed* her the vial—and she had nothing else to trade with him for the poison's antidote.

"Leave," Leena yelled. "Out. Now. Before I slit your sniveling throat."

Just before leaving, he turned back to her. "One day you will see, my dear, what happens to all the women who come into contact with the Avon men. You will soon understand that there is no limit to what they will sacrifice for Weavingshaw." There was a promise in his voice—someone who had seen calamity once and now saw it again in her. "One day you will remember me, and you will wish that I had killed him."

Leena spat at him.

The demon's face twisted as he wiped his chin with a flounce of his sleeve, then left without a departing glance. Leena bolted the door after him.

Light crept into the room, and she dared to peek outside to see Orley's huddled figure making his way up a long street.

Their safe place was in an attic, Leena realized, in a town.

It was snowing here too, but the snow looked like gray ash. The houses were built in rows, all made from black stone with towering spires and long thin roofs that stretched toward the sky. Walkways lined the canals, the water inky and fathomless.

A woman—*a demon?*—standing beside the canal held a naked baby by the ankles. Leena watched as she plunged the squirming babe into the dark waters, then held it for so long that Leena gasped before the screaming infant was wrenched out. The woman wrapped the baby in fur, but the infant's wails didn't diminish even as Leena withdrew from the window.

Forcing herself away, Leena turned to check Bram's bandages.

They'd bled through. She hung her head, weeping because she didn't have anything sterile to replace them with. She fell asleep like that, kneeling on the hard wooden floor, head resting against the mattress beside Bram.

When she finally stirred, it was dark outside again. No phantom had come to possess her body; perhaps the demon world was bereft of ghosts. The only light came from the low-burning candle. She would need to replace it soon.

Leena's breath hitched when she saw that Bram had also woken.

He was lucid.

She wondered briefly if he remembered their kiss—the way his fingers had laced through her hair or the way his lips had dragged across her skin.

There was no recognition of it when his eyes met hers, and she felt an odd squeezing in her chest.

Bram's forehead was cool to the touch, but she didn't know how long it would be before the fever ravaged him again. Perhaps it was better that way, she thought to herself—that Bram became too lost to hallucinations to notice death's long shadow darkening his doorway.

Somehow, he didn't seem as burdened by those grim thoughts as she was.

Instead, he looked at her oddly, as if she was something otherworldly and he'd been trapped in unholy reality his entire life.

"You stayed with me," he rasped, his voice almost reverent. One calloused finger moved to touch her, as if to confirm his own words—as if to dispel any fears of her being an apparition. He traced her cheek. "*Why* did you remain?"

She didn't have an answer for him. At least, nothing that would have sufficed.

His eyes caught sight of the bruise blooming on her jaw and he furrowed his brows, jolting to a sitting position. "Who—?"

"Orley," Leena clarified, a knot in her throat. "He's gone now."

Fury ignited in his eyes. "I swear, I will kill—"

He stopped suddenly, looking around the room, before stumbling upward. He clutched his left side as he staggered toward the window. He stared outside for a long moment, eyebrows knitted together, before turning to her swiftly.

His voice shook as he stared at her in bewilderment. "What have you done?"

She knelt with her back to the mattress, her voice hushed. "I had no choice."

He lowered himself slowly into the wooden chair beside the bed. He looked unnerved, clutching his timepiece, the gold chain swinging on a pendulum.

"Leena, I never wanted . . ." He swallowed. "I never wanted you to come here. I would never wish this place on you."

She reached for his shoulder and he inhaled sharply from the touch.

There was, Leena thought desperately, no room to play games with each other. She had landed them in the demon world as the only viable option for survival. Bram must now complete the last piece of the puzzle; otherwise their survival would hang on an even thinner thread than it did now.

It was time Leena received a confession from the Saint of Silence.

"Bram, I know your father had something to do with the demons, but Lady Hargreaves could not tell me more."

There was wreckage in his eyes—a past pain long buried but still felt.

Finally, his response came from a voice that was hoarse, as if dragged from him. "I was twelve years old when my father and Hargreaves took me here. They indentured me to the Duke of Fray, a powerful demon." Unevenly, he unclasped the timepiece he always wore from his chest, thrusting it toward her. "I still do not know what I was traded for, and so I have never been able to break the contract."

Leena took the timepiece, astonished to see that it was the same as both Margery's and Lord Avon's, all three indented with the same elegant scrawl: *Fray.*

Roughly hand-carved into the lid of the timepiece were five words:

Kill what you cannot survive.

"Open the timepiece."

She did so. The top number, where the twelve o'clock position should've been, was in this case marked as one hundred and twenty. The rest of the numbers seemed also to increase by a factor of ten. The one o'clock was written as ten, the two o'clock was twenty, and so on until one hundred and twenty at the top.

The single hand was halted just below the one hundred and ten mark.

"That doesn't tell time, Leena, it counts down the years."

One hundred and eight years.

Leena's eyes fell to his hands: green veins interlacing beneath the skin, strong fingers gripping the seat of the chair with too much force, the firm knuckles white and tense.

He continued, each word a jagged edge. "If I do not find a way to break the contract with the demons, I will be indentured past even the point of death."

Leena reeled back, jaw clenched so hard she tasted blood on her lips again.

Images of the first day she met him echoed through her mind—how he'd been shrouded in seclusion and cruelty. How little she had understood then of Bram's motivations . . .

The reaping of secrets . . .

The iron-clad contracts . . .

The misery he collected upon himself from the weight of his confessors . . .

The hunt for Lord Avon's ghost . . .

All in pursuit of breaking his own imprisonment.

Leena felt as if she could choke on these revelations—all that had tried to ruin him.

He was trapped, the timepiece he always wore an incessant reminder that even death was no freedom for him.

Her heart—*her entire being*—ached for him.

Helplessness concentrated in her throat, suffocating her.

Vessel . . .

Leena's mind shifted—the echo of remembrance building in her memory.

"Lord Kilworth spoke of a vessel before I . . ." She dropped the last words, not allowing her mind to linger on his death. "He called it the Limitless Vessel. He said Percival had hidden it. I wonder . . ."

At that moment, they both stared at each other in comprehension.

"Lord Hargreaves—"

"The red diary—"

Bram reached for the diary from his pocket, grasping it in his hand and staring down at it with a hard gaze.

"Do you think that is what they traded you for? The Limitless Vessel itself?" When Bram did not respond, still staring intently at the book in his hand, Leena asked another question before giving him a chance to answer the first. "What is the Limitless Vessel?"

It took him a moment to reply.

In that interim of silence, she wanted to steady the grip of his hand on the book, to draw him closer to her, to anchor them both within this unsettling life.

"It is common knowledge here, in Bastmore." There was a brief narrowing of his eyes, a return to the former Saint of Silence—one whose sharp mind was a blade, cutting and culling. "It's a powerful object, one that can open the gate between the human and the demon world indefinitely, ushering an uninhibited flow of demons aboveground. The person who controls this object would control that gate."

Leena nodded slowly. "It would make sense that Hargreaves is hunting for it." She paused. "Lady Hargreaves did try to warn me."

His glance fell to her. "Warn you?"

"Yes. Our time on the moor was very limited and I could not tell you more about Lady Hargreaves's memories." Leena brought a hand to her forehead, squeezing her eyes to remember every important detail. "It was in the last memory she left for me. It was after they had heartlessly sold you; your father and Hargreaves were bitterly fighting over an object. Lady Hargreaves did not know what that object was, but it was evident that Percival had hidden it and Hargreaves had killed him in a futile attempt to find it. That must be it. That hidden object . . . is the Limitless Vessel."

His grip on the diary did not loosen. "My father must've hidden its whereabouts, knowing such a secret would lead to his murder." He flicked through the diary once more, before slamming shut the cover with force. "I wonder if he left instructions on how to track this object within the Avon diary? It must be read more carefully."

"First we must find the antidote." Leena leaned forward, drawing in her brows with determination crossing her face. "Then, if the red diary indeed has the map that will lead us to the Limitless Vessel, we will follow this map and release you from the demons."

His gaze flashed to her at the word *we.* For a moment, looking at him—unable to look anywhere *but* at him—Leena began to understand the depth of his solitude. Of his loneliness. She remembered the way he had been back in Golborne, separated in his study, surrounded by those ledgers. All the while he'd been completely isolated, choked with his own secrets.

A hard realization shadowed his face.

"Leena—" He released a staggered breath at her name. "If this is all for the Limitless Vessel, that means that Hargreaves will send every man, every demon, every trader to hunt me for this diary." His eyes swallowed every line on her face, the curve of her cheekbones, the shape of her lips, as if desperate to imprint them to memory.

"You are not safe here. Should he get his hands on you, he will torture you, then kill you, to get to me."

Then he averted his gaze, his voice turned detached, but the hand gripping the diary was still harsh and unyielding. "That means you must leave me. You must leave me immediately." His throat moved.

"Leena Al-Sayer, I release you from your contract."

ACKNOWLEDGMENTS

This book would be nothing but forgotten scribbles without the tireless efforts of Chloe Seager, agent extraordinaire. Thank you for championing the book from its early stages to its last—I am constantly awestruck by how hard you work!

I am also indebted to my very talented editors, Anne Groell and Lara Stevenson, who have shaped my writing and pushed this book to its best possible version. Every editorial insight was right on the mark, and I'm so glad I had the chance to work with the two of you. The book would have been much worse off without you both as my editors.

I'm also incredibly grateful to the whole team at Madeleine Milburn Agency, including Maddy Belton, who was very kind to read the first drafts. As well as Valentina Paulmichl, who advocated for this book around the world—because of you I get to see my words in translation. And Hannah Kettles for being infinitely patient with all my queries about taxes.

The team at Penguin Random House has been nothing short of amazing. I am very beholden to copy editors Eleanore, Holly Reed, and Loren Noveck, who have saved me from public embarrassment by finding all my grammatical errors, as well as Madi Margolis for being a joy over email, Paul Gilbert, Erin Korenko, and Caroline Cunningham.

A huge thank-you to Micaela Alcaino, who remains my favorite artist. I knew my book was in the best possible hands the moment I heard you were designing the cover.

I'd also like to thank my tenth-grade geography teacher, Mrs. Sylvester, who gave me confidence that has carried me through my adulthood.

Thanks to my nieces, Zozo, Aya, and Mimi, who taught me not only how to work through all the noise, but also how much my heart can expand with love.

Of course, my adoration endlessly and endlessly to my husband, who makes me cups of tea without asking and buys me books just because.

And to my sister, Roua, who was the first person to teach me how to write. No one can tell a better story than you.

And lastly, but most of all, thank you to my Mama and Baba—who taught me how to read, who paid all my library overdue fees, and whose love I carry with me everywhere, especially in my words.

ABOUT THE AUTHOR

Heba Al-Wasity was inspired to write by her own experiences of being born an Iraqi refugee in Libya, growing up in Canada, and attending medical school in the UK. She has worked in emergency care and several psychiatric inpatient units, gaining firsthand insight into the ways that poverty and deprivation can lead to social inequalities. She is based in Greater Manchester, England.

Instagram: @alwasityhh

ABOUT THE TYPE

This book was set in Caslon, a typeface first designed in 1722 by William Caslon (1692–1766). Its widespread use by most English printers in the early eighteenth century soon supplanted the Dutch typefaces that had formerly prevailed. The roman is considered a "workhorse" typeface due to its pleasant, open appearance, while the italic is exceedingly decorative.